Comanche Blood

COMANCHE BLOOD

PROLOGUE

LATE 1878

The Comanche scrunched up into the protective rocks, as if trying to climb inside them. Dark, feral eyes peered out from below a mane of once-pitch-black hair that was gray now with the passage of years—hard years. His breathing was shallow and he grimaced as he tried to calm his pounding heart.

There was a small clink as a pebble trickled into another, and the man pushed even farther back into the rocks, trying to make his dark, reddish-brown skin become part of the stone.

His small, dark hand, strength diminished only a little by his age, clenched more tightly on the walnut grips of the almost-empty Remington Army .44 as he heard a soft shuffling on the rocks above.

His head jerked to the right when he heard: "Best be easy with that thing, *amigo*."

The Comanche grunted an oath when he saw the buckskin-jacketed white man standing less than ten feet away, the large bore of a .50-caliber Sharps buffalo gun casually pointed in his direction.

The Indian, tight as a coiled spring within the now-useless cover of the rocks, relaxed a little. As he did, he started to slowly raise the revolver, hoping the white man would not notice.

"Goddammit, Gray Wolf, don't do that," Zeke Tippett said. He sounded almost annoyed.

"I must," the Indian answered.

"Waugh," Tippett spat. "Don't be a bigger damn fool than you've already been," Tippett snapped. He would be damned if he would speak in Comanche just to placate the warrior.

Gray Wolf sat silent, unblinking in the bright, nearly heatless sun of the December afternoon. Then his shoulders slumped and he set the pistol down at his side. "You'll take me back?" he asked in Comanche. He felt defeated, but was defiant enough to insist on using his own language. He tried not to shiver as the cold soaked through his thin blanket and calico shirt to chill his bones.

"Got to, my friend. You know that well's me."

Gray Wolf threw his head back and straightened his spine, shrugging off the cold along with the defeat. "I won't go alive," he sneered. Then he began the slow, mournful, quiet chanting of his death song.

The white man sat down, cross-legged, placing the heavy rifle across his thighs. He was even older than the Comanche a few feet away. But he did not look anywhere near his almost sixty-five years. His hair, though fully white, was long, and thick, with fine waves. He was tall and his back rigid. His long arms and big, work-hardened hands had lost little of their strength. The wrinkles on his face, accentuating the watery blue eyes and thin, straight lips, came not so much from age as they did from nearly half a century of living on horseback in the open.

Tippett shoved the Stetson hat back, feeling the coolness of the high-country air on his forehead. After tugging off a glove, he pulled tobacco from a pouch hanging at his waist and cut off a hunk with his big Bowie knife. Slipping the wad into his cheek, he replaced his knife and sat with his back against a boulder. As he chewed slowly, spitting occasionally, he looked over the short, broad, dark Comanche chanting the hard-to-understand words with deadly earnest.

The Indian, who had not yet seen his sixtieth winter, looked far more worn and haggard than the Anglo. His thick gray hair hung lankily, and his face was creased with the years of battle and the almost constant hounding from the white soldiers he had faced. But his shoulders were square and strong; his face still determined; his eyes still filled with hate and the lust for battle. But there was more than that, too. The old Comanche, Gray Wolf, pined deep in his heart for the freedom he had known as a boy and young man, before the white people had covered his land like the dust blanketed the Llano Estacado.

Sitting there watching the Comanche, Tippett shook his head. They had come so far together, he and Gray Wolf. It had been more than forty years — hell, it'd be fifty before much longer, Tippett thought sourly, angry at what the passage of time had wrought since he had first met Gray Wolf.

He had been a young man then, brash and daring; and Gray Wolf just a boy.

BOOK 1

ZEKE TIPPETT, 1831

1

Zeke Tippett was only a few months past eighteen when he rode into the Comanche village near the Brazos River. Despite his youth, he had been in the mountains three years — and a full-fledged mountain man for two. It had been a hard winter and he and his four companions had not fared well in their search for beaver. They had been better off, he thought, with the brigade of the Rocky Mountain Fur Company trappers.

But he and his friends had left out in the dark of the night while the snow fell heavily after a row with hard-edged Milt Sublette, leader of that brigade. Being young and brash, they figured to do better on their own, but had not done so. In fact, if truth be told, they had barely made it through the winter alive and with their hair intact.

With spring coming, they prepared to leave their winter camp near South Park. But they could not decide where to go. So, they sat around the fire, night after night, after spending their days trapping, discussing their options.

"Damn it all, fellers, I say we go back with the Rocky Mountain boys," George Bender had said for perhaps the thousandth time. Or so it seemed to the others. "They'll take us back for damn sure."

Bender was a nervous sort, with a pinched face and frittery moves that were reflected in his voice. Tippett thought he sounded like a big cricket, what with the little chirpy words bubbling out of the narrow face like blood running from an open vein.

"What makes you say that?" Cass Calder grumbled. He was a huge, blocky young man, with a thick mane of red hair and a wild Viking-like beard and mustache.

"We still owe 'em for one thing," Bender twittered.

A third, Jim Bledsoe, said firmly, "Well, I ain't goin' back to them goddamn piss pots. I figger we ought to just go on to rendezvous and sign up with whoever we can. How about you, Zeke? What d'you think, hoss?"

Tippett was a quiet man, and when he spoke his voice usually was soft. He rubbed his sparse beard and said, "I reckon that goin' to rendezvous would be some foolish, Jim." Bledsoe wasn't the smartest man he had ever met, but he was a decent enough fellow, and a hard, earnest worker. Tippett hated calling attention to the scrawny young man's lack of mental abilities.

"Why?" Bledsoe asked, wiping a dirty palm across his runny nose, then cleaning his hand on his pants.

"Well," Tippett said slowly, "those Rocky Mountain boys are certain to be at those doin's. If you don't want to run into them hell-raisin' critters, I'd give that rendezvous a wide berth, was I you. It's what I aim to do."

He paused, then added, "So this ol' chil' aims to get me some more plews. Heaps of 'em. You boys want to do the same, you kin c'mon along."

"Where you gonna get more plews, boy?" the fifth man — Elmore Trent — asked with a snort.

"What I can't trap, I'll get from Injuns," Tippett said simply.

"What Injuns?" Trent sneered. Trent was quiet, too, but not from humility. Instead he considered his quiet a calm deadliness. And he had a badger's ill temper. He was also a hard worker, so the other men mostly put up with his surliness.

"Utes maybe. They ain't too far from here. Or Cheyennes."

"You're *loco,*" Bender said. "Them boys'll lift your hair certain."

"Shit. Utes is mostly peaceable, and nobody I know of has had much trouble with the Cheyennes. Besides," he added bluntly, "if any of them red devils aims to raise this chil's hair, I'll jist see to it I ain't the only one goes under that day."

"Feel purty sure of yourself, don't you, boy?" Trent said with a nasty twang to his high-pitched, nasal voice.

Tippett was of medium height and still gangly with youth. He was thin, but not gaunt, and the muscles lay in his arms, chest, shoulders, and back like strong, thick ropes. Those muscles contained a lot more power than they looked like they would, as some men — including Trent — had found out. Once, more than a year ago now, the scrawny young Trent had seen fit to take exception to the slow, methodical way Tippett worked taking beaver. When his words had little effect in speeding Tippett any, Trent took a swing at his partner, and a moment later found himself flat on his back, head ringing.

Later, Trent had tried again, rushing Tippett from behind. He managed to knock Tippett down, but the young mountain man sprang back up and proceeded to whale the tar out of Trent in the midst of a raucously cheering mob of mountain men. Since then, no one else had been foolish enough to test their mettle against Tippett. Except once. One of the men had filled himself with too much rancid rendezvous whiskey and felt his liquor-inflated muscles grow.

Trent looked at Tippett now, shaking his head a little, but knowing, too, that if anyone could pull off riding into an unknown Indian village in search of plews it was Zeke Tippett.

"Cain't say as I feel that way," Tippett said. "I just don't expect they'll try'n raise my hair when all I want to do is trade."

"Hell, you've dealt with Injins long enough to know you cain't trust a one of 'em," Bledsoe threw in anxiously.

"Didn't say I was gonna put my trust in 'em," Tippett said

evenly. He picked up a stray twig and tossed it into the fire, watching as it danced a moment in the heat and then sprang into flame.

"I still think you been hit in the head or something, Zeke. Maybe you been out in the cold too long and your brain pan's froze up, ol' hoss."

"You just go worryin' about your own topknot, Jim. I'll see to mine."

"What in hell you gonna trade with?" Calder asked.

"Still got a few sacks of beads and awls and knives and such I happened to find when we left rendezvous," he said to a low laugh from the others. "Reckon you boys found some, too."

"I believe I did," Calder chuckled.

"Suit yourself," Trent snarled. "But I ain't aimin' to take no part in such foolishness. How about the rest of you boys?"

The others agreed it was foolish, and sat arguing amongst themselves. They were still at it the next morning when Tippett saddled his horse and, towing his mule, rode out.

Several days later, Tippett found a band of Utes. It was true that he was mighty short in the way of trade goods, but he managed to connive a few plews out of the Indians as well as a worn horse to carry whatever plews he might find. Heading out of the mountains, he rode mostly south and a little east. He trapped a little, slowly building up a small pile of pelts, before he reached the plains, where summer was beginning to get a grip, so the furs he took were not prime.

He had no idea where he was going, but thought he might find some Cheyennes. He'd heard they were friendly enough, and he might be able to wrangle a few plews from them before having them direct him toward the Mexican lands. Many of the mountain men had talked of Taos or Santa Fe. They spoke with fondness of the hospitality of the people there, of the *señoritas* — pretty and willing — of the spicy and tasty food and the slow and easy pace of life. He thought he could do with some of that after a harsh winter spent cooped up in rickety, hastily cobbled together cabins in a small mountain valley.

The land was deceptively flat and mostly treeless. It seemed he could see forever, but the dips, rises, and washes kept coming up on him unexpectedly. He soon lost his bearings in the trackless emptiness and began to wonder if he would ever find anyone before he succumbed to thirst or starvation, or went stark raving mad in this immense, barren land. There was nothing here for him to fix on except the horizon, which kept its distance from him, moving ever farther away. There were no landmarks, nothing he could use to help him as a guide. Everywhere he looked, there was just the emptiness, like a yellowish-brown sea spreading out to foreign lands.

Eventually he entered an area of high, blocky mesas slashed with deep canyons. It was a land that could inspire fear. And it did. Tippett was hopelessly lost, knowing only that he had wandered far, far off whatever course he had hoped to follow once he had pulled south of the Arkansas in hopes of finding a Mexican town. He now prayed that he might find one, or even some friendly Indians soon. While this land was not the markerless expanse of the plains, it was every bit as inhospitable as the prairie, and possibly even more so.

He could not recall how long it had been since he had left his friends — a month, at least, perhaps two — when he finally saw thin plumes of smoke in the distance. Flocks of what he took to be ravens whirled around the smoke, indicating a village of some sort. He was glad — yet frightened. It explained the uneasy feeling he had had for two days. He was certain now that unseen warriors had been watching him for many miles. But he had no idea if the Indians out there were friendly.

Fear clawed at his belly. He rode on, the hot sun beating down unmercifully on him, making him drowsy despite the edge of uneasiness, which was the only thing that kept him from dozing in the saddle. Blearily he looked around. With a jolt from a new spasm of fear, he saw them coming. He counted a dozen of them.

They rode in fast and circled Tippett, whooping and reaching for the ropes to his mule and extra horse.

Tippett was too busy struggling with his mount and pack animals to pay much attention to his fright. "Git away from me, dammit," he yelled, wrestling with his reins and the rope to the pack animals. His rifle would have fallen had it not been slung through a loop on his jury-rigged excuse for a saddle.

The Indians stopped their circling, and the whirling kaleidoscope in front of Tippett's eyes spun to a halt. He finally got his animals stilled, and looked around. He was sitting smack inside the ring of Indians. Tippett had fought Indians before, but never alone. And he had never seen warriors like these. Their horsemanship was superb, better than any he had ever seen. Even while fighting with his animals, Tippett had taken note of that.

Three of the warriors wore buffalo-horn headdresses. The others were bareheaded, with but a few fluttering feathers. They were short, stubby men, whom Tippett thought would look awkward afoot. But mounted, each looked as if he were a part of his pony.

All were bare-chested and wore cloth or buckskin breechcloths and leggings over plain moccasins. Each had a bow and quiver of arrows. Four, including the one sitting ten feet in front of Tippett — a broad-chested man with a huge gold medal resting on his chest — carried lances whose flint or iron tips gleamed wickedly.

A cold, queasy feeling grew in Tippett's stomach, and the skin of his groin tightened. He was in deep trouble and there was no denying it. These were not Utes, and he was pretty sure they were not Cheyennes. Not if the stories he had heard around campfires in mountain camps were even half true. These dark warriors had to be Comanches, and the thought sent another sliver of fear cutting into his bowels. He tried hard, however, to ensure that no sign of fear crossed his boyish, handsome face.

The Indian with the medal on his chest said something in Comanche, but Tippett shrugged, not understanding.

This time the Indian used signs to ask, "What are you doing in the land of the Comanche?"

During his couple of years in the mountains, Tippett had picked up much of the hand language used by the Plains tribes, as did just about every other mountaineer if he expected to live long and trade with the Indians. So, he answered in kind: "I want to trade for furs."

"What do you have to trade?" the leader asked in signs.

"You'll see when I see your furs," Tippett answered in the same manner, not taking his eyes off the Indian's, letting the warrior know he was not to be intimidated.

The Comanche's face hardened, and Tippett suddenly thought he was going to be buzzard bait at any moment. The warrior moved closer and lowered the lance until it was parallel to the ground. He stopped and touched Tippett's breast with the lance's twelve-inch-long iron point.

Tippett's breath quickened, but he immediately brought himself under control. With a sneer, he threaded the reins around the fingers of his left hand, and then hooked the rope to the pack animals around his thumb. Still moving cautiously, so as not to impale himself on the lance, he rested his right hand on the butt of the flintlock pistol at his belt. His soft blue eyes stared into the Comanche's obsidian ones. Sweat trickled down his back and sides, but Tippett sat stock still. He could see lice crawling through the Indian's hair, but he ignored it.

The Comanche suddenly grinned and swung the lance up and away. With his hands he said, "I am Walking Bear. We will trade. Come."

Surrounded by dark, menacing warriors, Tippett rode the two miles to the Comanche village. It was much like any other Indian village he had been in — tipis spread along the creek, those of the chiefs and hardened war leaders amongst the stunted cottonwoods and mesquite, gaining what shade they could. The buffalo-hide sides of the tipis were rolled up several feet to air and cool the insides. In front of each was a rack with the man's war shield and some of his weapons. Inside the lodges, Tippett could see neatly placed parfleches, piles of buffalo robes used for sleeping, willow backrests, and horsehead altars.

Children, many of them naked, stopped their noisy games to stare at the strange sight of this bearded, pale-skinned creature. The women, some surprisingly lighter skinned and more handsome than Tippett would have thought, stopped at their work of cleaning skins or keeping the hordes of yapping dogs from the meat drying on rickety wood racks.

The women and children watched his entrance in wide-eyed silence. They had seen few men with white skin and hair that grew on their faces. These were *Kwerhar-rehnuhs* — whom the white-eyes would later call *Kwahadis,* and they were isolated in their Llano Estacado home. While the men raided far and wide, the women and children remained behind and thus were not so worldly.

Tippett was brought to a large lodge — far larger than he had imagined one would be — under the tallest cottonwood. It was used, Tippett would learn, for the band's large and important meetings. It was almost cool inside the dim interior, and he had to blink the brittle remains of sunshine out of his eyes as they grew accustomed to the dimness.

Walking Bear pointed and Tippett sat. Warily the visitor ate the bowl of stewed meat a woman had given him. He didn't want to think about what the meat was. From the stories he had heard told about the Comanches, it could be anything, from lizard to Mexican, and he had to fight back a shudder. A pipe was then passed around. Watching the man he figured was the civil chief, he saw that the Comanches went through the same basic ritual with the solemn smoke as did most of the other tribes he had dealt with. The smoke, which would carry their words to the heavens, was offered first to the four cardinal directions — east, west, north, and south — then to Mother Earth and Father Sky.

Tippett puffed in the proper way, all the while worried, not only for himself, but about his animals. He was loath to leave them outside, fearing they — and thus everything he owned in this world — might be stolen. He had no choice, though, so he tried not to think about it as he waited for the amenities to finish.

Finally, the main chief sitting across from him asked, through signs, to see what he had to trade. He held up a hand indicating the others should wait, and then warily stood. He breathed a sigh of relief when no one bothered him when he stepped outside. He released another when he saw his animals standing unmolested. A boy of about twelve was watching the animals, envy flickering in his black eyes. Tippett smiled and nodded his thanks to the youth, and pulled off the second horse two buckskin sacks holding his paltry store of trade goods, thankful he still had some left.

As he toted his few supplies into the lodge, he saw the boy — who had said his name was Little Hawk — start to curry the packhorse.

Considering the state of his supplies, the trading was pretty much an amusing hour for the Comanches as they spent most of their time laughing and insulting him, even though he did not know, of course, what they actually said. Tippett's dander rose now and again, but his nervousness kept a lid on it, even when someone offered a scrawny slice of jerky for the third of a bolt of red cloth that was all he had of the two bolts he had after trading with the Utes.

Finally, the Comanches tired of the game and called an end to it. The warriors gathered up their newfound booty acquired in trade and began drifting off, still chuckling. Tippett picked up the few scraps of detritus he had "won" and stowed them in a sack. He wondered why they hadn't just killed and scalped him. He never did find out, really.

Moments later, Walking Bear looked at Tippett and signed, "You will spend the night in my lodge?"

Tippett realized it was not really a question. He nodded, anxiety once more making a home in his midsection. He spent a fitful night in the war chief's lodge, sleeping poorly. The tipi was far too crowded for his liking, especially considering that he was lying here amongst people he had no reason to trust. He also worried that his animals and furs would be stolen. Worst of all, there was a lurking dread that the *Kwahadis* were saving him for some devilish sport.

Despite his powerful concerns, no one bothered him. He ate a morning meal with Walking Bear's family, feeling a bit more relaxed as no one looked even remotely threatening. After he had eaten, he looked at his host. "Will I be permitted to leave?" he asked in signs.

Walking Bear's great round face split with a warm and joyous smile. Then he nodded.

"Now?" Tippett asked.

Walking Bear nodded again. He rose and signed, "Come."

Tippett followed the warrior out of the lodge into the blindingly brilliant sun. They strolled through the village, but this time Tippett drew fewer stares and strange looks. He was a little surprised that the amusement of his arrival had worn off already.

Walking Bear suddenly stopped and called out in his own language. The youngster, Little Hawk, trotted over, and he and the war leader conversed in Comanche for a minute or so. Walking Bear turned to Tippett and signed, "Little Hawk will take you to your horses and furs."

Tippett held out his right hand, palm facing Walking Bear. Then he turned the palm downward, spreading his fingers a little — the sign for "Thank you."

Walking Bear grinned and ambled off.

Tippett followed Little Hawk, wondering about the youth. He figured the Comanche was nearly ready for the hunt if not quite the war trail, judging by what he knew of other Indians. Little Hawk still had a lot of boy left in him, but Tippett noticed that he had elements of a warrior showing in his face and posture — the ramrod straight back, the purposeful stride, the serious countenance.

Little Hawk led him to the fields outside the village where some horses were grazing. Not too many, though. The Comanches' main herd was off somewhere close but with enough room to forage without cropping all the grass near the lodges. A few hundred horses could devastate the grassland in a hurry.

Tippett saddled his riding horse and loaded his pack animals with Little Hawk's help. In thanks, Tippett gave the youth a knife. The boy beamed proudly before racing off. Tippett grinned. He wasn't sure, but he thought he had just made a friend. As he pulled himself into his patchwork leather and wood saddle, he thought, *Maybe these Injuns ain't as fearsome as the stories make them out to be.*

With directions he had earlier from Walking Bear, the mountain man headed west toward Taos.

2

Taos was something of a revelation for Zeke Tippett. From the tales he had heard from other mountain men, he half expected a bustling city like Saint Louis. But what he found a day after he rode down out of Palo Flechado Pass was a dirt brown town sitting in a small valley at the foot of pine-forested mountains.

The town seemed desolate, though enough people were around. He decided it wasn't so much desolate as forlorn. The people's clothing tended to blend into the dull brownness of the area and did nothing to brighten the place up. They also seemed too worn down to have much life left in them.

Dusty men led dusty burros along dusty streets, apparently going nowhere in particular. Farmers bent wearily over their crops in their fields outside ramshackle adobe houses. Things improved a little as he neared the plaza. The people appeared to be less defeated by their miserable lot.

Colors began to spring up, too, in the dress of the people, in the bright chili peppers that hung in *ristras* out front of homes and shops, in the colorful hues of varied vegetables for sale in stalls or from carts, and in the painted doors or window sashes that dotted some of the otherwise drab adobe buildings.

The rich aroma of food swept over him, brought by a warm, almost comforting breeze. He smelled nothing familiar, but each scent was enough to make his mouth water. He was hungry, but hadn't thought he was *this* ravenous. Regardless, the delicious aromas had his stomach voicing its displeasure at its emptiness. He wanted nothing more than to stop his horse and sample every kind of fare that was for sale, and then go back to his favorites for seconds.

He sighed. It didn't matter what he wanted or how much he wanted it, all of it was beyond his reach. He had no money and nothing to trade other than his plews. As soon as he traded those in, though, he would have cash money, and then he would indulge his stomach, and his soul and body.

He thought of the last — despite the newly realized hunger clamoring for his attention — when he started taking notice of the young women who sashayed, somewhat saucily in his view, around the plaza. To his American eyes, they were quite daring and risqué; completely unlike the young women he had known back in the States. Perhaps they weren't quite as uninhibited as many of the Indian women he had seen, but they were certainly a lot closer to those earthy women than were any of the white women he had known. They dressed in a fashion that would have been shockingly bold back in the settlements, with their ankles and sometimes even calves bared, as well as their shoulders and arms. Not all of them were clad in such brazen fashion, but a fair number were. And quite a few of them smiled warmly at him as he clip-clopped his way across the plaza.

He rapidly began to change his opinion of Taos, figuring that he had been mighty hasty in forming his initial impression. With what he took to be the inviting looks of some of the women, the aroma of rich food, and the comfortable earthiness of the Mexican village, he thought he might have found a place he could enjoy.

He pulled to a stop near an alley that led away from the plaza, suddenly realizing he had no idea which way to go. There were a couple of trading stores, but he didn't know who owned them. Now wary, he was quite unsure of himself. He realized, perhaps for the first time, that he was in a Mexican town. He knew no one and did not know the language.

Zeke sat there, undecided, wondering what he should do. A few soldiers were strolling about the plaza, which presented another possible problem. They might not be too fond of an American just riding into town. Of course, it had been Americans, mostly, who had told him about Taos, and the friendly people here. Still, he wasn't sure.

Suddenly a man appeared, grabbing his reins just above the bit. He was tall and considerably portly, but had a friendly face and seemed to pose no threat.

"You are new to Taos, eh, *monsieur*?" the man asked.

Tippett nodded, warily.

"I am Etienne Provost," the man said. His words were accented with an almost musical quality. "And I am a mountaineer, like you."

Tippett nodded. He was somewhat relieved, but remained cautious. He didn't know what Provost wanted. The corpulent mountain man might be nothing more than a bandit, despite his friendly look. After all, the way he was dressed, he certainly didn't *look* like a mountain man. A tall top hat was tightly pressed onto his big, round head, and a fancy, swallowtail coat stretched over a colorful vest. Looking down, Tippett could see that Provost had on a pair of fine, wool pants in the style he had seen many of the men here wearing. He was, however, wearing beaded moccasins, which lent at least a minimum of veracity to his words.

"Do you 'ave a license from ze Mexicans to trap or trade in zese parts?" Provost asked.

"Nope," Tippett responded with a shrug. "Am I supposed to have one?"

"*Mais bien sûr, monsieur*!" Provost answered "But of course!

Zese Mexicans officials, zey want t'ings zeir way all ze time. *Sacre bleu*!"

"Reckon that means I'm up shit's creek, don't it?" Tippett was more annoyed than angry. He felt it was just his luck to have such a thing happen. Here he had gone and walked right into a Comanche village — well, been captured, really, if he was to be truthful about it — traded with those fearsome Indians, if that's what it could be called, and then rode out again safe and sound, only to face losing his whole season's catch because some damn officials wanted a piece of paper he hadn't even known he needed.

"No, no, no," Provost said enthusiastically. Tippett's horse snorted and shook its head, a little unnerved by the voice. "I t'ink I can 'elp you, monsieur."

"And jist what is this help of yours going to cost me, ol' hoss?" Tippett asked skeptically.

"You wound me, *monsieur,*" Provost said, a hurt look condensing on his face.

Tippett shrugged. "Jist bein' practical," he said evenly.

"*Oui,* I can understand zat. You don' know me. Well, *mon ami,*" he added, face brightening again, "I will 'elp you for not'ing. What you t'ink of zat, eh?" He did not wait for an answer. "I will 'elp you because any time one of us mountaineers can pull ze wool over ze eyes of ze *emmerdant* — annoying — Mexican officials, we do all our *amis* a grand favor, *ne-c'est pas?*"

Tippett let slip a small grin. "I reckon I catch your drift, ol' hoss. So, what do we do?"

"You will come wit' me, *mon ami.* I will bring you to a man who will take your furs wit'out questions, eh, and 'e will give you a fair deal. Better zan you will get from anyone."

Tippett's senses suddenly sharpened. He had little in the way of book learning, but his instincts were strong, and usually accurate. He smelled trouble here, though not big trouble. He just felt as if he were about to be taken. His instincts told him that Provost was in the employ of one of the traders here, and that he got a portion of the trade for steering unknowing customers to the trader. He sighed. *What the hell,* he thought, *there's not much else I can do.* If there was any truth to what Provost had said about needing a license, he faced arrest, and possibly the confiscation of all his furs at any moment. As far as he could tell from rendezvous, all traders who supplied the mountaineers were thieves anyway. One was no better than the next.

"Let's go then," he said, giving no indication of his concerns.

"*Oui*. But first, what is your name, monsieur?"

"Zeke Tippett."

"I am glad to make your acquaintance, Monsieur Tippett. Now, *allons-y* — let's go."

They didn't have far to travel. Holding lightly onto the reins near the horse's neck, Provost went down the alley. He turned left at the end of it, took a few small streets, and another alley. Tippett began to think Provost might be leading him into a trap — an out of the way place where he would be attacked, with the robbers taking his plews, animals, and maybe even his life. He tensed and grew wary, resting a hand on one of his pistols.

They pulled into a yard fenced in with adobe walls. Tippett tensed even more, though he relaxed minutely when the several men who were working in the yard paid no attention to him. They stopped and Tippett dismounted. After tying his horse to a wooden post, he followed Provost inside. It was cool and dim in the trading post, and smelled of furs and buckskin, spices and cloth, meat and tallow. It was an agreeable place to Tippett.

A short, portly, barrel-chested man came into the front trading room like a king. He nodded at the two men. "*Bienvenue,* Etienne," he said, his voice deep and powerful.

"Monsieur Tippett," Provost said, "zis is Monsieur Ceran St. Vrain." As Tippett and St. Vrain shook hands, Provost added, "Like us, Ceran is a mountaineer. 'E 'as a big reputation in ze mountains."

"I've heard of you, Mister St. Vrain," Tippett said with a nod.

St. Vrain shrugged, as if it had no meaning to him. He was a short, burly man, with deep, agate eyes and a thick, short black beard. "What can I do for you, monsieur?" he asked.

"Well, Mister St. Vrain, I just pulled into Taos, and met up with Mister Provost here. I don't know nobody here, nor the way business is done. Mister Provost tells me the Mexicans expect you to have a trappin' and tradin' license. I assume that if you don't, they'll haul your ass over to the gaol soon's they find out." He looked quizzically at St. Vrain.

"Zat is ze way it is, monsieur," the trader acknowledged with another shrug.

"Well, Mister Provost dragged me over here, indicatin' that you might be of some help in this matter. That true?"

"*Oui*. We 'Americans' must stick together, *ça va?*"

"You're French, ain't you?" Tippett questioned.

"*Bien sûr, mon ami*. But I 'ave been here many years. Besides, to ze Mexicans, we are all Americans."

Tippett nodded. "Well, then, can you help me out?"

"I will buy your furs from you, monsieur. Right now. Before ze alcalde or 'is men find out zat you 'ave no license."

"Suits this chil'," Tippett said flatly. "Ye mind if I ask jist how much you're gonna pay Mister Provost here for bringing my business to you?"

Suddenly St. Vrain's dark-bearded face broke into crinkles of humor, and a throaty laugh burst forth. After some moments, he calmed down. "Ah, monsieur, I do not pay 'im or anyone else anyt'ing. 'E does not work for me. 'E just knows zat I am ze only American trader 'ere, and I am willing to 'elp other Americans."

Tippett remained skeptical. "How much are ye offerin' fer plews?" he asked.

"Four dollars a pound for prime plews," St. Vrain said without hesitation.

Tippett's eyes widened. He never thought he would ever see

such a price for beaver. He felt a rush of newfound wealth soar through him, but he quickly brought himself back to earth. There had to be another side to it. "How much are you chargin' for supplies?" he asked, thinking he had figured out that other side.

"No more zan any other man in zis business," St. Vrain said a little sharply.

Tippett shrugged. Again, he had little choice in the matter. "My apologies, Mister St. Vrain," he said quietly. "I ain't got much in the way of plews, and I'm a mite suspicious when a trader offers such a high price for them. I jist had to figure ye were gonna make your money elsewise, like with higher costs on your supplies."

St. Vrain nodded. "You're a reasonable man, monsieur. But truly, I'll give you a fair price on supplies. I will not lie to you, *mon ami,* I don' plan to give ze supplies away, but I am not a thief like some of ze ones you 'ave maybe met at rendezvous."

Tippett had enough beaver plews that, when traded in, made him think he had enough cash to be able to pay off the Rocky Mountain Fur Company leaders who had staked him a year earlier, before he and his friends had deserted the company. However, doing so would leave him virtually nothing to outfit himself for another season, let alone have any kind of spree here in Taos.

He left almost all his money with St. Vrain, having decided that he could trust the man. And he set about trying to have a good time, though his predicament ate at him. He felt bad about having run off from the fur company, and he was determined to pay back all he owed, trying to make his name — and his word — good again in the mountains. But that would mean being beholden to the company again — or trying to find somewhere else to outfit him against what he would earn the next season in the mountains.

He finally concluded that he had but one prospect. While he hated asking for help, he went back to the Bent-St. Vrain Company trading post, where he quietly explained his plight to Ceran St. Vrain's partner, Charles Bent.

"You expect me to believe such foolishness? Tradin' with the goddamn Comanche? Christ a'mighty, boy." If he had not been so stern-faced, he might have laughed. Bent looked a lot like his partner, being short but powerfully built. He was far fairer of face however, and did not have the thick black beard that St. Vrain sported.

"I don't take kindly to bein' called a liar, Mister Bent," Tippett said stiffly. He was aware that several men, rifles handy, were watching through the front door.

Bent shrugged burly shoulders. "Maybe you best come up with a better story."

"The truth, I've found," Tippett said with dignity, "is always best. And that's what I've jist told ye."

"You expect me to believe that you not only ran out on the Rocky Mountain boys, but that you also wound up trading for plews with Comanches?"

"Didn't say I traded for plews with the Comanches. Only that they had fun at my expense tradin' for what little goods I had for some scraps."

"And," Bent added, ignoring Tippett's rejoinder, skepticism still heavy in his voice, "that you plan to go back and try to pay off your contract with the company?"

There were some stifled chuckles from the onlookers.

"Yes, sir," Tippett said gazing steadily at Bent.

"Nobody trades with the Comanche, son." There was no easing of the harshness of his tone.

"You've done it, I hear," Tippett said calmly. "Less'n all them stories I've heard about you is lies."

Bent's lips twitched. "I don't much take to bein' called a liar, neither," Bent said darkly.

"I ain't called you a liar. Just said maybe all the talk I heard 'bout you is lies."

"A fine point, but one I reckon I'll grant you." Bent leaned back against the trade counter and lit a pipe. He puffed quietly for some moments.

It was growing warm in the close room, and Tippett was aware that more people had crowded into the doorway to watch. He paid them little heed as he continued to stare at Bent.

"I've traded with the Comanche," Bent finally said gruffly. "And the Kiowa. Of the two, the Kiowas're a little easier to deal with. I'd not get too caught up dealin' with the Comanches was I you, boy. They're mean bastards, most times, like as not. They don't have as much religion as the Kiowas or Cheyennes. And they ain't got no notion of pain, either, I sometimes think."

"They treated me well the one time I was there."

"Who you been dealin' with?"

"The only one I know, I reckon, is a feller named Walkin' Bear."

Bent almost looked impressed. "*Kwerhar-renuhs*. The worst of the Comanches." He puffed quietly a few more minutes. Then he asked, his dark eyes hard, "How the hell do I know I'll get paid back?"

"You got my word on it."

"Your word don't mean shit here, son," Bent said roughly. "Not after you cut ties with the Rocky Mountain boys."

That almost broke Tippett's resolve. He hung his head. "I'm powerful ashamed I did that, Mister Bent. And like I said, I got enough cash to outfit myself again for the next season. But then I couldn't pay my due with them. I reckon I could just stick down this way and trap; hope I make enough to cover this season and next, plus pay them back. That don't set none too well with this chil', though."

Bent stood and shuffled to the empty fireplace. He smacked the bowl of the pipe against his hand, and then tossed the used tobacco into the maw. He spun and clumped back, tails of his frock coat swinging. "You got a deal, Mister Tippett." He held out his hand.

Relief flooded through Tippett as he grasped the stocky man's callused hand. "You'll not regret it, Mister Bent," he said earnestly.

"I reckon I won't at that," Bent said with a grim smile. "I got me a heap of *amigos* in the mountains, boy. You cut and run on me like you did Bridger and the others, and someone here'll find you sure as hell."

"The only way I won't come back here to pay you off, Mister Bent," Tippett said with iron in his voice, "is if I've gone under."

3

Zeke Tippett worked northwest along the broad, purple spine of the Rocky Mountains, through Bayou Salado and North Park, and then the Snake River country beyond. He moved fast, stopping for a day or two every few days to trap and make meat. He was rather surprised, but thoroughly grateful, that he encountered no trouble. It was eerie, he thought more than once, but the few Indians he met on his journey — Utes and Shoshones mostly — had all been friendly. The weather had cooperated too, for the most part. Even better, the trapping was good, and his plews plush and bountiful.

Two months out from Taos, he wandered into a comfortable glade just beyond a copse of aspens and cottonwoods. Snow covered the ground, but it was a mere six inches deep. The trees were bare, their branches throwing spindly, grasping shadows on the sparkling white blanket.

Tippett entered the glade carefully. He had seen smoke a ways off across the meadow, and was not sure whether he was about to approach an Indian village, or a mountain man camp. But there was no other way to get from here to there — a tall, stark cliff rose to his right and an equally precipitous drop-off through a small stand of tangled brush and trees fell to the other side. So, he proceeded. He figured that even if it was an Indian camp, his luck had been good so far, and might hold.

Then he spotted two canvas tents to one side of the camp, snapping in the wintry breeze. He relaxed and grinned when he saw four men hunched around a fire. There could only be one man as big as the one he saw — Cass Calder.

The four heard his horse and mules picking their way along the snow, making small crunching sounds as they moved almost as one. Three reached for their rifles while spinning toward the approaching animals. The fourth slipped off toward the cavvy of horses and mules. Tippett grinned all the wider.

"Well, I'll be damned," George Bender muttered. "I think I'm seein' a ghost. Lookee here, boys, it's ol' Zeke Tippett."

Bender and the three others — the giant Calder, whiny Jim Bledsoe, and the ferret-like Elmore Trent — stood waiting as Tippett stopped and dismounted.

"We thought you'd gone under, amigo," Bledsoe said. "Ain't heard a thing about you since you rode off with that foolish idea of tradin' with the Injins."

"Weren't so foolish," Tippett said, smiling. He pulled a tin cup from the canvas sack hanging from his saddle. Squatting at the fire, he reached for the softly bubbling pot and filled his mug with coffee. "I made me enough to pay off the RMF boys. Sent the specie on to them through one of Charlie Bent's men headin' toward Blackfoot country. Paid 'em in full, by God."

"You ain't tellin' true," Trent snapped.

"You callin' me a liar?" Tippett demanded, his face suddenly glaring red.

"Well, I wouldn't say that, 'zactly," Trent said hastily. "It just don't seem possible is all."

Tippett's face stayed hard, but he said quietly, "Then how'n hell d'you think I got me these mules and all these here supplies, boy?"

"Figgered you threw in with Bridger or Sublette again, or maybe Hudson's Bay Britishers."

"And you figure those boys'd let me traipse all over alone after I run out on the RMF? My name'd be shit all over the goddamn mountains."

"Reckon not." Trent experimented with a grin and found it rather uncomfortable. "Maybe you stole 'em, though," he added in surly tones.

Tippett's sternness cracked some. "Well, that might've been the way of it," he agreed, though his voice was flat. "But it weren't."

"Come on, Zeke," Calder said easily. "We got us fresh buffler hump and ribs a roastin' there as you can see. It's time you tasted some. And fill your cup again, too." He grinned. "I might jist find some awardenty in the packs somewhere, too."

Tippett smiled at the other man. Calder was even bigger than Tippett had remembered, and it took him a minute to realize why. Calder had lost the remaining vestiges of the slackness of youth over the summer. Still, he had retained his quietness. He was a hard man to rile. But with his size and strength, especially now that he had filled out, he was a fellow that few men would want to anger anyway.

"Thankee, Cass," Tippett said. "That'd suit this ol' chil'." He refilled his cup, and tried to settle himself a little more comfortably, though it was almost impossible, given the slushy, muddy condition of the ground around the fire. "So, how've you boys been gettin' on?" he asked.

"Just fine," Jim Bledsoe said, his Adam's apple bobbing.

"That's a heap of buffalo shit, and you full well know it," Bender said. He smiled ruefully at Tippett. "We was some late when we got to where rendezvous was supposed to be," he explained. "Hell, it was into August already. We figured there weren't gonna be too many of the boys left, but we was hopin' we'd see some stragglers and they might help us set things to right with the Rocky Mountain bunch, difficult as that might be. We'd talked it over for a spell before we all decided it was somethin' needed to be done." He grinned.

"But there weren't nobody there. We heard later that Bill Sublette never made it. We headed east and finally come on Tom Fitzpatrick on the North Platte, down around Willow Valley. He come up from Taos with supplies, led by Kit Carson. Had mayhap forty boys with him, but other than Fitzpatrick, the only Rocky Mountain chil' there was ol' Fraeb, who'd come lookin' for Fitzpatrick. Well, shit, Fraeb got 'em all worked up, and them ol' beavers was about half-froze to raise hair on us, or anyone else they could lay hands to."

Tippett laughed, and was joined by all the others — except Trent, who scowled. "So, what'd you do?" Tippett asked with a chuckle.

"Well, we damn well paid 'em back," Bender said, still smiling. "But it were some touchy for a spell. Ol' Fraeb set the boys on us. A bunch got a-holt of me, Jim and Elmore right off. Weren't much we could do about it, though we put up what fuss we could. But it was plumb funny when they tried takin' ol' Cass there."

The laughter bubbled out of him and he paused to let it run its course. Finally, he said, after swiping tears of joyful remembrance from his eyes, "Well, seein' that all them other boys wasn't havin' no success in such doin's, ol' Kit set his mind on bein' the one to count coup on Cass ..." He broke off, laughing once again.

The picture set Tippett and the others off. "Christ," Tippett gasped between guffaws, "little ol' Kit, not much more'n five-foot nothin', settin' hisself against ol' Cass?" He roared with laughter at the thought. But he knew it was true. Carson was that type. One with no give-up in him, and he would as often as not hold his own against larger opponents. Still, the picture it conjured up for these men was rather ridiculous.

"Sure did," Bender said, wiping tears away. "But that ol' scut learned in a sprightly hurry that mayhap he'd made himself a mistake in the undertakin' of such a task. Cass backhanded him once, and sent him flyin' ass over teacup ten, mayhap twenty feet. He was out when he landed."

Tippett glanced at Calder. The big young man sat looking at the ground, a touch of pink coloring his face and neck where the beard and long hair did not cover the skin. "What'd you do then, Cass?" he asked.

"Nothin'," Calder mumbled.

"That true, George?" Tippett asked.

"Mostly. Everybody just stood 'round for a spell lookin' at Kit layin' there. A couple of the boys tried rousin' him, without much success. Then a few of them ol' coons made to go against Cass again. So Cass says to 'em, 'Any of you walleyed scuts sets a hand to me, I'll break your goddamn neck.' That stopped 'em. 'Least for a minute.

"It was enough to let Cass to speak his piece. He just stood straight and tall and said to them coons — mostly Fraeb — 'I know we run out on your amigos, Henry. I'm plumb ashamed of such doin's. And I know we're in your debt. But you got no call to come against us like this. We've come all this way to make good's best we can. You're welcome to whatever we got so's you can be paid back. Anything left over — if there is anything — we can use for our stake for the next season.'"

Bender paused in the silence to pull a sizzling chunk of buffalo from where it hung on a green stick over the fire. He cut off a piece and passed the rest on. Tippett removed his fur mittens, took the proffered food, and did the same.

Taking a bite gingerly, Bender chewed slowly and then continued, "Well, everybody looked at Fraeb and Fitzpatrick, them bein' the Rocky Mountain boys. They talked between themselves for a spell, whilst the others kept a wary eye on us. Finally, Fraeb said he'd let us be. He took all the plews we had, though, dammit. Once they was traded in, there weren't shit for us left." He shrugged.

"Looks like you did all right, though, seein' as to what possibles you got," Tippett said around a mouthful of greasy hump meat.

"Hell, weren't even enough left fer a good drunk fer one of us," Trent said, half in self-pity, half in anger.

"How'd you get all them possibles, then?"

"Begged some, borrowed more," Bender said. "Behind Fraeb's back, Fitzpatrick advanced us a fair amount of plunder. I reckon he figured that since we come back to pay 'em off, we'd be good for it. Since there was close to fifty of us there — and a passel of Snakes — we had us a wee rendezvous. We was some lucky at shootin' and racin' and wrasslin' contests, too. We wagered what we could, and it paid off handsome." He paused to chew some more of the dripping hump meat. "How about you, Zeke?" he finally asked. "You really trade with the Utes?"

"Some." He spit into the fire, thankful for the flames' warmth. "More with the Comanches, though," he added quietly.

"You're lyin' through your teeth," Trent snarled.

Tippett surged up, tossed away the hunk of meat and flung himself across the fire. He slammed into Trent's chest, knocking the gaunt young man on his back. But the inertia carried him off Trent, and he slid on his side in the snow.

By the time he scrambled to his feet, Trent was up, butcher knife in hand, and charging. Tippett tried to leap to the side, but his feet slipped on the slush, and he fell. Trent rushed by, managing to nick Tippett's arm. But now Trent lost his footing as he tried to stop and turn. He kept his feet, but was slow in pivoting.

Tippett shoved himself up. He took one step with his left foot and then kicked out with his right. The hard-soled moccasin caught Trent's knife hand, and the blade spiraled away into the darkness.

As his foot came back to earth, Tippett pushed his weight onto it and launched his right fist. His knuckles made a satisfying splat when they connected with Trent's cheekbone, opening a large split in the flesh over it.

Trent staggered, knees suddenly wobbly, but he remained standing. He could offer little defense, though, and Tippett whaled the tar out of him, each fist bringing a grunt or moan. Trent finally fell hard.

Tippett moved in to finish Trent off, but felt himself enveloped in large steel bands.

"That's enough, hoss," Calder said quietly in his ear.

"But, Cass . . ."

"Just ease off, amigo."

After a minute, Tippett drew in a deep, ragged breath, then relaxed. "All right," he muttered.

Calder freed Tippett from the powerful bear hug he'd had from behind his friend's back. But he was wary lest Tippett was fooling.

Tippett stopped and picked up his fox-fur hat and set it on his dark brown hair. Then he retook his seat at the fire. He grabbed a sizzling rib, burning his fingers a bit. He gasped, but angrily refused to put the meat down.

Calder and Bender also sat. Bledsoe checked on Trent, who slapped Bledsoe's hand away and managed to sit upright. Bledsoe had a hurt look in his eyes as he joined the three other men at the fire.

"Tell us about them Comanches, Zeke," Bender said, trying to ease the tension. "I've heard they're the meanest critters south of the Blackfeet."

Snow began to fall as Tippett sat staring into the flames. Then he sighed. "Well, they can be, I expect. But they treated me well." He described his journey.

"Sounds like you done all right, considerin'," Bender said.

"Sure does," Bledsoe added.

Tippett felt Calder staring at him, and he glanced at the big man. But Calder's face was blank.

"Where you aimin' to trap, Zeke?" Bender asked.

"Ain't sure. Up on the Snake, I reckon. Blackfoot country, maybe."

"You're loco," Bender said with a grin.

Tippett smiled, his anger gone. "I ain't *that* loco. I ain't thought much on it, though. Might try Flathead country, or maybe over by the Nez Percé."

"How about throwin' in with us?" Bender asked.

"What do the rest of you boys think?" Tippett questioned.

"I'd like that," Bledsoe said shyly, as if afraid to speak.

"That shines with this coon," Calder rumbled.

"Elmore?" Bender asked, his hands fluttering like they usually did when he was nervous — which was nearly all the time.

Trent scowled. He stood shakily, stalked to a tent and stomped in.

"Reckon he don't mind," Calder said with a chuckle.

Tippett nodded. "Reckon throwin' in with you boys wouldn't put me out none."

4

The five found a comfortable valley northwest of Pierre's Hole and wintered near a small band of Flatheads. In doing so, they enjoyed the amenities of the village — like the company of the young women, who were happy to offer their favors to these lusty young men in exchange for certain considerations.

Tippett almost immediately took to a woman named Pine Leaf. The daughter of a prominent war leader, Pine Leaf was barely fifteen. She was plump in a way that was highly pleasing to him, and had a wide, round face with prominent cheekbones. She was industrious as well as caring, and she made a fine home for Tippett in the small buffalo-skin lodge.

He was also happy to be back with his friends — except for Trent. But Trent gave him no trouble through the winter. He often cast surly, hate-filled glances at Tippett, but never bothered him.

The weather here wasn't too bad; they had made plenty of meat and a fair amount of forage for the animals. With regular visits to the Flathead village, the caring comforts of the women, and enough work to keep them busy, Tippett was content to while away the winter in such a place and in such company.

But even all that began to pale as the seemingly endless winter dragged on. Taking its own sweet time, spring eventually edged into the high, snow-covered valley. It was, at first, just an occasional breath of warm air; then came a day or two when the temperature rose above freezing. Shoots of grass appeared as the thick carpet of snow ever so slowly disappeared.

As soon as they could, the men began wading into the frigid streams to trap, and as spring really began making its presence known, the five made plans to leave.

"You fixin' to come to rendezvous with us, Zeke?" Bender asked one morning. They were sitting around a small fire in Tippett's lodge. Outside, mist hung low over the valley, masking the nearby peaks.

Pine Leaf and the other Flathead women who had spent the winter in their camp were back with their people. They might return while the men were still here, or they might not. The men would miss them, if they didn't return before they left, but not too much. It was a new season, and new things beckoned.

"Reckon not, George," Tippett said. "I expect I'll head down to Taos. Trade my plews in and pay off Bent and St. Vrain. I ain't ever aimin' to do nothin' like we did to the RMF boys again."

"Shit, Taos is full of goddamn greasers from what I heard," Bender sneered.

Tippett looked at him with distaste. But he said calmly, "They treated me well. Ol' Kit likes it, as do a heap of other mountaineers. Besides," he grinned widely, "them *señoritas* plumb shine, hoss. Plumb shine!" He howled.

"They can't be better'n Flathead women," Bender said firmly, with a lecherous smile. "And especially not better'n a Shoshone. Goddamn, Zeke, you 'member that time down to rendezvous back in '29?"

"Hell, I'll be buried ten years afore I forget them doin's," Tippett said with a big laugh.

It had been the first rendezvous for all of them, and a wild time it had been. A two-week debauch of women — the first of those, too, for all the five but Calder — harsh whiskey, dancing, drumming, singing, more whiskey, hell raising, and more women. Then there was gambling, fighting, more women, more whiskey, tale telling, and, finally, more women.

"Waugh, them Shoshone women do shine," Calder growled with a grin.

Even petulant Elmore Trent smiled.

"They purely do," Bender nodded cheerfully. "Hell, Zeke, you should've been with us this last rendezvous. I met me this one Shoshone squaw. Raven Wing she was called. Purtiest woman I ever seen."

"Probably looked like the ass end of a buffler," Tippett said with a snort.

The others chuckled, but Bender ignored it. "I convinced her I had no foofaraw to give her, but I still wanted her some bad. Talked that harlot right into my robes, by Christ."

Calder burst into laughter. "And you're lucky you got out of her lodge with your stones still attached," he said with a roar. "Goddamn fool promised her heaps of all kinds of foofaraw, he did. Christ, I think he even promised to shoot down the moon for her, was she desirous of havin' it."

Bender was laughing hard now, too. "Well, hell, I *had* to have that woman. Lord, Zeke, you should've seen her. Face like an angel, breasts as soft and full as..."

He was drowned out by Calder's gales of laughter, and by his own gasping guffaws. It took several minutes before Calder could talk again, and when he did, his belly still wriggled with suppressed laughter. "Shit, once she found out he didn't have enough foofaraw to pay for a roll in the robes with a hunnert-year-old grandma, she pulled out her carving knife, and set out to geld him." He had to break off to laugh again.

"Well, what in hell happened, boy?" Tippett asked, when he was able.

"He come runnin' through the camp — his goddamn britches in

hand — with this goddamn squaw chasin' his scrawny bare ass, wavin' her knife in the air, shouting in that goddamn fractured language of hers how she was gonna cut his nuts off. All the while, he's screamin' for help, his pecker and his shirttails flappin' in the wind."

Calder had to stop to let the laughter roll again. "He managed to hide behind me, and I got her calmed down enough so's we could discuss things. I finally give George a bolt of cloth and some hawk bells so's he could give 'em to her," Calder wiped his watering eyes with a meaty hand.

"Yeah, and we lit out first thing next mornin'," Bledsoe added. "We weren't very trustin' of that squaw and her people no more."

"And you want me to go to a rendezvous with you boys?" Tippett asked with a chuckle. "Lord, you went to that last one, nearly got the shit beat out of you by the Rocky Mountain boys, then you try to set the whole Snake tribe against you? You're plumb *loco*. I'd be better off with the Comanches."

"Like hell," Bender said, wheezing from laughter. "It'll shine. Plumb shine. Jist like in '29."

"Sorry, boys, but I ain't aimin' to meet up with some of those folks, 'specially if they remember you. And, like I said, I got to go pay Bent and St. Vrain back anyway."

"I understand," Bender said, unconcerned.

"Mind if I ride along with you, hoss?" Calder asked.

"Not a'tall," Tippett said, somewhat surprised. "Any of you others care to join us?"

None did.

They went about their business that day, checking their trap lines, pressing tanned furs into packs, and packing what supplies they had. Tippett, wanting an early start, turned in soon after dark. He was up before dawn, and found that Calder had already stoked the fire, set coffee on, and had meat roasting. Calder was loading the packs of plews and their supplies onto mules, so Tippett joined him.

THEIR JOURNEY WAS UNEVENTFUL AND NOT MUCH FOR THEM TO talk about in their later years: They weathered an attack by Crows; talked their way out of another with Utes; traded out of a third with Arapahos. They fought two spring snowstorms, one of which left them stranded without wood or fresh meat for five days. They were reduced to eating a few of their precious beaver pelts and were considering starting on their moccasins before an old buffalo bull wandered into their gunsights. They killed the large old beast, and gladly ate the tough, stringy meat as if it was the best they had ever tasted.

They lost two horses to exhaustion but bought replacements from a band of Shoshones. And they nearly drowned several times trying to cross turbulent rivers swollen with snowmelt.

The two were trail weary and covered with dust, grease, and blood when they rode into Taos just after dark so as not to be seen and went straight to the Bent-St. Vrain trading post. Tippett wanted to get rid of the plews as quickly as possible, lest the Mexican authorities accost him for not having a license and confiscate his furs.

Charles Bent greeted them. He was wearing an expensive frock coat and a top hat of fine beaver fur. He grinned.

"Told you I'd be back, Charlie. Your man get my specie up to the Rocky Mountain boys?"

"Yep. The Thunderbolt said you paid too much, but he'd keep the extra just for the inconvenience."

"Ol' Milt ain't subtle, is he?"

"Nope." He pointed at Calder. "Who's your friend?"

Tippett made the introductions. Then Bent aimed a finger at the pack mules outside. "Looks like you boys done well."

"Reckon. Ready to settle up?"

"If you are."

Tippett and Calder pulled in more than a thousand dollars each for their haul. Tippett settled with Bent, and then paid for supplies for the next season. "I can trust you to hold these things here, can't I?" he asked with a grin.

Bent laughed. He had trusted Tippett, and been rewarded; now it was time for the reverse.

Tippett bought a few packloads of inexpensive trade goods — cloth, knives, awls, two trade rifles, powder and ball, sheet iron for arrowheads, pots, blankets, beads, and hawk bells.

"What'n hell you buyin' all that plunder for?" Calder asked.

"The Comanches."

"You're sure you want to do that?" Calder asked dubiously.

"Yep."

"Reckon you know best then." He said nothing more about it.

Tippett found as he and Calder set out the next morning that he was — under the mild hangover he was suffering — eager to see the Comanches again. He was surprised Calder had decided to come along, though. He had thought he would do Calder a favor — and be able to get the Comanches some gifts — by going to Taos before visiting the Indians. He figured that Calder would want to stay in Taos.

Not knowing how — or even if — he would be accepted by other bands of Comanches, Tippett made sure they avoided any other Indian camps until he was sure he had found Walking Bear's village. That took some doing, but he finally managed it.

With his loaded pack animals, Tippett was welcomed warmly into the camp. Even Calder was greeted with friendliness and hospitality — though it was somewhat reserved. The Comanches, the vast majority of them short of stature, were awed, Tippett thought, by Calder's massive size.

But the big mountain man's warmth and humor, evident even if he and the Indians did not speak a common language other than signs, won them over. Especially the children. The young ones, hiding behind their mothers at first, soon drifted out. And before long, they were climbing all over Calder as if he were just a big, friendly horse. Calder seemed to be enjoying himself just as much.

Tippett grinned as he watched his friend and the dark-skinned little boys and girls.

After the amenities were taken care of, the pipe smoked and more, Tippett, with all the eyes of the village on him, began to pass out the trade goods. He did so with a free hand, not expecting anything in return. But the Comanches, not to be outdone, grandly provided him with beaver, wolf, and buffalo pelts in return. But not too many, since he was more extravagant in giving than accepting. He wished to thank the Comanches for their friendliness the year before; and they knew that, though neither side said anything.

The action helped to cement Tippett's place — and Calder's — in the hearts of the people of the village.

Tippett went to sleep that night — in a lodge loaned to him and Calder — feeling good. He was pleased with himself, and with his life.

TIPPETT WOKE THE INSTANT CALDER'S HAND TOUCHED HIS shoulder, reaching for his knife, until he realized who it was. Not that he could have done anything, considering that Calder had the advantage of wakefulness, size, and strength.

"There's bad doin's here, amigo," Calder whispered.

Tippett sensed urgency in Calder's voice, though no one else would have. He pushed aside his sleeping robe and sat up. A screeching howl suddenly rent the quiet night. "What the hell . . ." Tippett muttered as he and Calder jumped up, grabbing their rifles. They bolted outside into the predawn blackness — and stopped.

The camp was a milling mass of confusion. Comanche men boiled out of their lodges, grabbing weapons from racks outside their tipis. Most headed toward the horses; others toward an unseen enemy. Another ululating war cry tore through the night, followed by a chorus of others.

Little Hawk ran by and Tippett grabbed him. "What's goin' on?" he asked.

The boy shrugged and tried to get away.

"Hold him, Cass," Tippett said. Calder grabbed the boy, freeing Tippett's hands. Zeke asked the same question in sign language. His hands waved frantically, as horsemen loomed out of the dark.

"Cheyennes!" Little Hawk signed frantically.

"Shit," Calder mumbled. He let Little Hawk go and the boy ran off.

Tippett spun and ran toward the horse herd. Within moments, Calder was racing alongside his friend.

A mounted Cheyenne bolted between them, knocking them both sprawling.

"Son of a bitch," Calder muttered as he scrambled up into a kneeling position. He brought his rifle up and fired.

The ball smashed into the Cheyenne's back, knocking the Indian forward over the head of his pony, where he was trampled despite the pony's efforts not to step on its former rider.

Tippett spun to face his lodge as he heard another horse coming at him and Calder. Cass was almost done reloading when Tippett fired.

The Cheyenne was blown backward off the horse. If the gunshot hadn't killed him, the snapping of his neck when he landed certainly did. But the horse did not slow, and was heading right for Calder. Tippett shoved his friend as hard as he could with his left hand, while dropping to his own right. Calder fell out of the way as the pony thundered past where he had been kneeling a moment before.

A pinkish hue was tingeing the eastern horizon, throwing a little light on the village, as Tippett jammed a ball down into his rifle. Then he and Calder were running for the horse herd where their animals mingled with those of the Comanches.

They leaped on the first ponies they found. Calder looked faintly foolish on the small mustang. They charged after the Cheyennes, who were racing northeastward, pushing a substantial portion of the Comanche horse herd in front of them.

The two whites were not alone in their pursuit of the thieving Cheyennes. Many of the Comanche warriors also were whipping their horses after the Cheyennes. Some remained behind to defend the village should the horse-stealing foray be a ruse.

Tippett smacked the pony's flank with his rifle barrel, urging more speed from the panting animal. He was rewarded with a burst that brought him alongside a Cheyenne. The enemy warrior wore a wolf-skin headdress, the fur trailing halfway down his back. He rode with the ease of a man born on a horse's back.

Tippett, holding his rifle near the middle, raised it over his right shoulder so the muzzle was pointing behind him. As he caught up to the Cheyenne, he jerked it forward. The curved butt of the rifle thudded against the Indian's head. Tippett was not sure if the Cheyenne made any sound; the pounding of several hundred hooves deafened him. But the warrior fell, and Tippett lost sight of him.

Tippett grabbed the rope rein of the Cheyenne pony and charged recklessly ahead, controlling his own racing mount with knee power. He reveled in exhilaration as the dust-filled wind whipped at his face. He spotted another Cheyenne and managed to catch that one, too. Tippett saw that this one was nearly as big as Calder, and wore a headdress that trailed down onto the pony's rump.

As Tippett pulled alongside the Indian, the Cheyenne glared at him. There was no fear in those dark, cold eyes, and the Cheyenne lashed out violently with his quirt. Tippett sucked in a mouthful of choking dust as the pain from the blow burned across his forehead. Anger burned in his chest as hotly as the Indian's lash.

"Bastard!" he yelled and then hit the Indian the way he had the other. The blow stunned the Cheyenne but did not knock him from his horse. Tippett hit him again and again. The Cheyenne tried twice more to strike Tippett with his quirt, but the mountain man kept just out of reach.

The Indian's horse swerved toward Tippett's pony, trying to ram it. But the Comanche pony was too swift and surefooted, and it darted out of the way. Tippett lashed out at arm's length with his rifle. The barrel scraped across the Cheyenne's temple, opening a bloody crease.

"Fall, goddamn you!" Tippett roared. He swung the rifle again as hard as he could. He almost lost the weapon when it cracked into the back of the Indian's neck. The Cheyenne crashed off the right side of his pony, lost amid the dust and thundering hooves.

Tippett pulled to the other side of the racing Cheyenne pony, and managed to grab its lead rope with the same hand that was holding the other Cheyenne horse's rope. He slowed gradually, easing the blowing horses to a stop.

The Comanches had regained control of their herd, and in the still growing light Tippett could see Cheyennes racing away.

Tippett looked for Calder. It took several minutes for the dust to settle enough for him to see his friend, who was maybe a hundred yards to the right heading toward the Comanche camp. He held the ropes to a Cheyenne pony and two scalps were clutched in the hand that held the mane of his own horse. He spotted Tippett and grinned, holding up his trophies. Then he whooped.

Tippett grinned back and raised the rifle in his fist as a victory salute. He decided he, too, should take scalps. He had done so before, but had never really cottoned to it. He took the one from the Cheyenne he had just killed.

The women and children — who had raced off for the safety of the trees and ravines when the attacked started — were returning to the village when Tippett arrived.

Tippett found the body of the first Cheyenne he had killed in the village, and took that scalp, too.

The camp was a swirl of activity. Men and boys were circulating among the horses, trying to calm the animals after the racing chase across the prairie. Several women were wailing in grief at the deaths of four warriors. Some men were crowing their victory.

"Them was some doin's, eh, Zeke?" Calder asked with a grin as he walked up. There was almost nothing that could frazzle his giant friend, Tippett thought. He was happy-go-lucky nearabout all the time.

"Hell, yes. What're you aimin' to do with the ponies you took?"

Calder shrugged. "Maybe give 'em away. I reckon the Comanches ain't so different from other Injuns in takin' a shine to a generous ol' chil'. Maybe I'll keep 'em, though. Ya never know, they might come in handy."

"Well," Tippett said with a wide grin, "you can be so foolish, but not this chil'. I aim to see about gettin' me a woman." He winked.

"Why, you ruttin' ol' buffler bull," Calder said with a laugh.

Tippett laughed, too. It was almost funny, he thought. Not more than a few minutes ago he was scared to his teeth, in the midst of a battle. Yet he had been calm. Scared, but calm. Now he was relaxed and joking. He found himself to be that way always.

"Well," Tippett said, chuckling, "maybe you ain't got no interest in women no more. Your balls all dried up? Or just shrunk up from fear after this fight?"

For just an instant, Tippett thought he might have gone too far. But he knew in a blink that Calder was not a man to take such things seriously, especially when said by a friend, and obviously in jest.

"Shit," Calder drawled. "I'm so pent up, I could hump this goddamn pony."

"I reckon we can find a Comanche squaw here dumb enough to want to mate up with an overgrowed ox like you."

Calder's laughter rumbled up and out, an odd sound it seemed in this out-of-the-way Comanche camp in the *Llano Estacado*. "Hell, I ain't so sure of that, *amigo*."

Tippett was laughing, too, while still keeping one eye on the chaos around him. "Well," he chortled, "you always got them stolen ponies. Just keep away from my horses, though, dammit."

"Hell, that thinkin' don't shine at all," Calder sputtered with laughter. "Just cuz this ol' coon's got hisself so big a pizzle," he grabbed himself by the crotch, "it scares off most women, don't mean there ain't *some* who like a real man."

"Shit, you'd have trouble pleasin' a flea with that little thing," Tippett laughed.

Calder snorted. He and Tippett fell silent as they watched two Cheyenne prisoners being dragged into the camp. "I reckon them boys is ass deep in trouble," Calder said quietly. Then he grinned again. "You got your eye on any of these squaws in partic'lar?" he asked.

"I reckon I might," Tippett said noncommittally, but he grinned.

5

There were no real formalities to the marriage. After the camp had returned somewhat to normal (though the victory dances and raucous celebrating made that difficult to judge), Tippett went to Walking Bear. Through signs, he let the Comanche know what — and who — he wanted.

The Comanche, who because of his exploits in war was an influential man despite being hardly older than Tippett, nodded. And he went to make arrangements. That afternoon, as the camp fully swung into their victory celebration, Walking Bear returned and, through a combination of signs, Comanche, Spanish, and dribs and drabs of English, explained what must be done.

"You think you could find someone for me, too?" Calder, who had accompanied Tippett and sat alongside him, asked.

Walking Bear nodded without hesitation. "Yellow Bird," he said. "She was married, but her husband was killed by Navajos. Several men are courting her. But . . ." He left the hand sentence hanging.

Calder nodded. "That shines," he allowed.

Soon after Walking Bear left, Tippett strolled outside. He got his two captured Cheyenne ponies and brought them to the lodge to which he had been directed, and tied them. He stepped back to wait.

It took an hour, but then the young woman he admired stepped outside. She took the reins to the two horses and led them to where her father's animals were kept with the rest of the Comanche herd.

Tippett grinned. She was his. He went back to his lodge where he sat eating jerky alone. Calder was gone, but he returned soon after, a grin plastered from ear to ear. Tippett chuckled and tossed his friend a strip of the hardened buffalo meat.

After eating, they went outside to watch the celebrations. Both even allowed themselves to be convinced, after much persuading, to try their luck at the heavy footsteps of the dances. The drums resounded, pounding into their blood, getting the white men into the spirit of it all.

Finally, the Cheyenne prisoners were brought out, and the Comanche warriors began their sport. Tippett and Calder watched with stony faces, letting their hosts know they were not afraid. But they did not enjoy it; found it sickening even, and as soon as seemed reasonable, they returned to their lodge.

They spent the rest of the afternoon seeing to their equipment. Rifles had to be cleaned, greased, and reloaded; knives and tomahawks had to have an edge. Their new furs had to be bundled. They worked almost furiously, not because they were anxious to get everything done, but to try to shut out the hooting at the sport with the unfortunate Cheyennes.

Late that afternoon, Walking Bear called for entrance to the white men's lodge. When bidden, he entered. Following him were two young women who stood shyly behind the straight-backed warrior.

"Is good?" Walking Bear asked in English.

"*Sí*," Tippett and Calder answered in unison.

"*Bueno*." Walking Bear left without another word. There was nothing more to be said. He had done his job — acted as intermediary to arrange these marriages. Now it was up to the two white men. The Comanche grinned a little at that thought. It would be an interesting thing to watch, he mused. But he would not do that. Still, he might just keep his ears open later, hoping to hear some of what the two young women would say to their friends about the white men.

TIPPETT TRIED NOT TO LOOK AT CALDER. HE JUST STOOD LIKE A dope, not knowing how to proceed. He knew what to do, but he was plumb embarrassed to make any moves with Cass and Yellow Bird just on the other side of the lodge. He stared at Painted Wing, his mouth dry.

Painted Wing was a short, not-too-dark girl of fifteen. Because of her skin tone, Tippett figured that she was half — maybe quarter — Mexican, the daughter or granddaughter of a captive. She was not broad, as were so many Comanche women, but Tippett figured she would get that way eventually. She had a wide, pleasing face with generous lips, a strong, bluntly flat nose, prominent cheekbones, and a toothy smile.

Since Painted Wing had been taking part in the celebration — and because it was her wedding night — she wore her finest beaded and quilled buckskin dress, the fringed bottom of which reached to just below her knees. Small silver cones attached to that fringe tinkled softly when she moved. Tippett figured she had bought the smoky tan dress — or traded for it — since the Comanches did not seem very adept at making such finery. Because of the heat, she wore no leggings. Her moccasins matched the dress in color and design.

She set down the parfleche she was carrying. "You are hungry?" she asked slowly in Comanche.

"Yes," he answered in the same tongue. He wasn't sure he had understood her words, or had just guessed what she had said by her actions.

She knelt and opened the parfleche. She took out her only pot, a blackened iron one. She began to rise, still not looking at Tippett.

"I'm not hungry for food," Tippett croaked in English. He was oblivious to Calder and the plump, seventeen-year-old Yellow Bird — and what they were doing. His throat was constricted and it was hard to breathe in the dark, smoky tipi.

Painted Wing finally looked at him. She smiled a bit shyly, understanding. Despite her age and limited experience, she was wise in such things. She knew what Tippett wanted. Besides, it should be fun if he was any good. If not, she would teach him.

Unblushing, she tugged the dress up over her shoulders and head, folded it nicely and set it down. She moved toward Tippett.

He stood, mouth agape, watching Painted Wing move the few feet separating him. He could not focus. Instead all he saw were flashes of images: full, rounded breasts, dusky and capped by darker coral areolae that peaked in short, blunt nipples; grease-shiny hair hanging loosely over smooth, square shoulders; the slight smooth swell of belly, with the deep-set navel; eyes flashing with lust; bright teeth smiling in joy; short, well-formed legs topped by the darkly moist tangle of pitch black hair; flaring, silky hips built for bearing children — or for passion.

She moved close and began unbuckling his wide leather belt.

"Damn fool," he muttered. He pushed her hands lightly away and took over the task. Before long he was as naked as Painted Wing. He was glad it was dim in the room so that she could not see his embarrassment.

Suddenly she was pressing her front against him, and he felt himself responding. Fear and indecision fled as he wrapped strong arms around Painted Wing's satiny shoulders and stroked the long, soft planes of her back. She ground herself against him.

She was so small. He could rest his chin on her head even when she was standing. And he could easily envelop her in his arms.

As her arms went around the small of his back, Tippett's hands moved lower and lower, rubbing light circles on her flesh, until reaching her baby-smooth buttocks.

She tried to melt into him, almost hypnotized by his hands.

His hands slid upward, moving toward the front. He forced them in between their bodies, until he could grip her firm breasts. His thumbs ran over the small nipples. Painted Wing shuddered. Then she reluctantly pushed away from him.

Tippett looked surprised, and kept his hands attached to her bosom. Painted Wing grinned at him, and took his hands in her own. She spun, towing Tippett around so that his back was to the tipi flap, and hers toward the buffalo robe. With a lusty smile, Painted Wing dropped his hands and stepped backward until her heels touched the sleeping robe. Keeping her eyes on him, she sat and pulled off her moccasins. Tossing them aside, she stretched out on her back, inviting him.

"Lord a'mighty," he mumbled. Almost shaking with desire, Tippett knelt between Painted Wing's legs. Bracing himself on his arms, he kissed her, surprising her a little. But he didn't care. And she responded. He finally broke off the kiss, and then planted smaller ones over her face, her neck, then her breasts, savoring the strong womanly taste of her flesh.

Painted Wing groaned and raised her hips, her womanhood seeking his manhood. He obliged. She locked her feet around the small of his back.

Tippett was vaguely aware of Calder's grunting and Yellow Bird's squealing as he exploded. A second later, Painted Wing screeched as her passions erupted.

With a great sigh, Tippett slumped down onto Painted Wing's heaving breasts. Both sucked for air, and the woman suddenly found it much harder to breathe with the mountain man resting his weight on her.

He finally realized that, and rolled onto his back, still holding her, so that she was on top. "Good?" he gasped in Comanche, using one of the few words in that language that he knew.

"Yes," Painted Wing answered, panting.

It was not long before they regained their breath. They laughed when they heard Calder's bellowed climax, followed almost immediately by Yellow Bird's shrieks of ecstasy.

With a lecherous grin, Painted Wing looked at Tippett and began grinding her pelvis into his.

"Yes?" he asked, not really surprised.

"Yes." She grinned and nipped him on the nose.

"Hey," he said in mock severity. And he returned the compliment. Then he slid his lips onto hers. His tongue forced her lips apart and sought out her tongue.

Painted Wing accepted it. Warmth flowed from his probing tongue through hers, down her throat and into her womanhood.

Tippett cupped Painted Wing's buttock globes and kneaded them gently, as she squirmed and wiggled. Her body warmed and strengthened his loins. Still having not broken off the kiss, the Comanche woman hiked her hips and slid her shins up alongside Tippett's hips. Then she plunged down onto him. She moaned low in her throat, lips still locked onto her man's. A groan from Tippett escaped past their lips.

The two bucked and wriggled, the excitement building to a crescendo. Painted Wing felt it build inside of her like a flash flood sweeping down a wash. There was no stopping it, as she felt an explosion that spread outward from her pelvis. She pulled her lips free and screamed in her passion.

Tippett snorted through flared nostrils as he erupted with a snuffling moan. He arched his back, raising Painted Wing's body on his hips. He shuddered before his hips sank. Painted Wing mumbled something in Comanche. Tippett nodded. He did not understand the words, but he understood the feeling.

Tippett relaxed, listening to the sounds of revelry coming from outside. Yet in here he was insulated from all that.

"Are you hungry for food now?" Painted Wing asked in sign language before resting her head on one hand overlapping the other on his chest.

Tippett folded his arms behind his head. He grinned and said, "*Haa*"— "Yes."

BOOK 2

LITTLE HAWK, 1832

6

Little Hawk had never felt such excitement. Not even when the Cheyennes had attacked the village two moons ago and the white men had joined in the battle.

The moon was not quite full, but it would be in a few days. By then he would be on the war trail. They would leave tonight, and soon they would attack the Mexican people he so hated.

He fairly shook as he tried to suppress the eagerness raging in his body and soul. This would be his first time on the war trail — his chance to become a warrior. It was something he had trained for since he could stand, something that every Comanche boy worked towards. It was their main reason for living. Now, at almost fourteen summers, he was ready.

Little Hawk was short and ungainly when afoot. But when he was astride a horse, he was all grace and power. He could ride as well as any *Nermernuh* — the dark-skinned people that the Mexicans and the white-eyes called Comanches. It was as if he and the pony were one, a flowing, nimble mingling of manflesh and horseflesh.

The youth also was an expert with the short bow of sinew-backed Osage orangewood favored by his people. He was even better with his flint-tipped lance. At least in practice. He had not, of course, used either against an enemy yet.

He had learned well under the tutelage of his uncle, Calls From Afar, and from Walking Bear, to whom the boy had attached himself. He had learned how to follow sign; and how to find his way in the trackless *Llano Estacado*; how to find water in the wide, barren spaces of the Comanche homeland; how to get every last ounce of strength and endurance from a pony; how to survive in his harsh, violent world.

Now it was time for Little Hawk to use those skills for real. The day had come for him to become a warrior, to win honors against an enemy that would establish his presence in the small band.

Walking Bear had gone around the village several days earlier, calling for warriors to follow him on the war trail. There were few real chiefs among the *Nermernuh*; war chiefs held sway only as long as the people believed in them, and only while leading a raid. If the warrior was brave enough and sage enough, people might be willing to listen to him more than some others.

Walking Bear was one such warrior. His honors were many, and with his huge herd of horses, he was among the richest of Comanches. He had proved himself fearless in battle, and thoughtful in his counsel. The men were eager to join him whenever he felt like a raid on the scattered white settlements. Or to listen to him when he spoke around the council fire.

When Walking Bear had stepped from his lodge that afternoon, he wore his buffalo-horn war bonnet, his favored blue blanket breechcloth, and bone-pipe breastplate. He was painted — from upper lip to the middle of his chest in black, the upper left side of his face was red and the upper right side yellow. He sat at a small fire in front of his lodge and pounded a drum. Moments later, he began to sing.

As the afternoon wore on, warriors who had agreed to follow Walking Bear came to his lodge, sat, and joined in the singing or drumming.

Little Hawk stepped out of his small tipi behind his father's. He had been living there almost two years, since reaching puberty.

"You're almost a man," his father, Kills Twice, had said. "You must have your own lodge to keep you from the women. It's no good for a young man to be tempted by his sisters."

Little Hawk had nodded, well-versed in the deeply held Comanche taboo — that brothers and sisters of marriageable age were forbidden to touch, or even sit near each other.

"And," Kills Twice had continued, "you will not be able to gain your spirit power in my lodge." His words drifted off. He did not have to explain to his son that Little Hawk would have difficulty realizing his spirit power because of the presence of his mother and sisters. Women were not conducive to a warrior gathering his spirit power.

Kills Twice was a short, barrel-chested man with a wide moon face that often was split by a smile. He was one of the most respected warriors within this band. He often called the war parties and seldom was it that any man turned him down. He had of late let some of the younger warriors, like Walking Bear, take more of a lead in such things, as befitted his added years. But he knew — as did all the others — that he could ride and fight with any of them.

"And so, you will have your own lodge," Kills Twice had said solemnly, an unusual expression for him.

Little Hawk had nodded gravely. He went to his father now and said quietly, almost as if ashamed, "Father, I'm almost a man, yet I haven't tasted battle. You had gone to war against the Cheyennes and the Spanish by the time you had seen as many summers as I have."

"This is true," Kills Twice said. "And you wish to go to battle?"

"I wish to become a man. A *Nermernuh*!"

"You won't be afraid because you're a boy?" Kills Twice said with the hint of a derisive smile. "You'll be able to endure like a *Nermernuh*?"

"Yes!" Little Hawk hissed. "Yes, to all those things!" His face burned with embarrassment mingled with fervor.

"So, you want me to take you on the warpath with Walking Bear?"

"Yes." Little Hawk paused, then said, "I've gone with Walking Bear and Calls From Afar — and you — to hunt buffalo for two summers. Now it's time for me to taste the blood of the *Nermernuh*'s enemies."

Kills Twice sat for a time, sucking on his long pipe. Then he asked gravely, "You have made your medicine?"

Little Hawk nodded. "Yes." He had told no one, but when Walking Bear had called for the war party, Little Hawk had gone off by himself to a spot he considered his own. There was a spring there, and a few trees below a small yellowish mesa. For two days he had fasted and prayed — until his spirit helper came to him. The powerful gray wolf that streaked across the *Llano Estacado* in Little Hawk's vision was the ruler of his domain. Fierce, regal, with nothing to fear. His enemies feared him and cowered whenever he was near. The wolf had pounced on a brown rabbit, tearing the hare into morsels, which he gobbled down, paying no attention to the coyotes that gathered, or the vultures that circled in the dense blue of the sky.

"It shall be so," Kills Twice finally said.

Little Hawk's eyes were hot with excitement, all embarrassment gone. He leaped up.

"Wait," Kills Twice commanded.

With a touch of worry, Little Hawk sat back down. He found it difficult to sit still.

"I'm not ready to go," the older warrior said. "I must prepare myself. You will not go to Walking Bear until I am ready."

"Yes." Little Hawk sat, waiting, outwardly patient. Inside he was raging with a frenzied eagerness. It seemed forever, but it was only a short time before Kills Twice was painted — the left side of his face black, the right half white — and dressed for battle. They left.

Little Hawk sat quietly amid the singing, drumming warriors. His eyes flashed as the music resounded in his blood and the chanted words bored into his brain. *Next time, I will join in the singing!* he thought, for that was the province of warriors.

He was not sure when darkness fell. He just became aware that it was no longer light. Soon after, a blazing fire was built. Warriors who had been saved from death by a comrade mounted their war ponies and rode through the village four times. The women chanted and cheered, urging their husbands or fathers or would-be lovers to great deeds. Then it was time for the war dance. Only the leader and his several lieutenants actually danced. But everyone else sat in a circle around the fire singing and drumming.

Little Hawk was proud when Kills Twice — a subleader on this foray — danced. He was a fine dancer, with strong, sure movements.

Occasionally, one of the old men stopped the dancing to regale the listeners with stories of his days as a warrior in his prime.

It was still dark when the war party mounted and rode southeastward. They made a fearsome sight under the bright yellowish light of the clear, bloated moon.

AFTER TWO DAYS IN THE SADDLE, SOME OF LITTLE HAWK'S enthusiasm ebbed. Not too much, but enough to allow him to think. Mostly he reflected on the impending battle — and all the honors he would gain.

Soon, he thought, soon he would be able to strut before his people, no longer a boy, but a man, and one respected by his people. He would show the Mexicans. He would kill as many as he could, taking their scalps. With them he could impress the white man when Tippett returned to the village. And he would steal horses, plenty of horses. He would be rich, and a great warrior.

He chafed at the length of time it took to get anywhere. And he fretted at having to care for the other warriors' horses and do all the menial tasks about the camp each night. He was not a warrior — yet — and so had to suffer these many indignities. But soon . . .

A WEEK OUT FROM THE VILLAGE, WALKING BEAR CALLED A HALT. He had seen something. With silent hand gestures, he directed his men.

Little Hawk sat on one of his father's trained war ponies feeling like he had to urinate. It infuriated him, but he finally convinced himself it was not fear, but excitement. He looked over the rancho, down the slight ridge. The biggest building was the small church. There were two adobe houses on each side of the church. Little Hawk counted twenty horses in the square adobe corral next to a stable. The stable had two short side walls and a long back wall of adobe. The roof was made of cactus skeletons and thin logs covered over with what grasses had been handy. Logs were nonexistent here, and like all the settlers in this vast land, the residents had used the materials available.

It was late afternoon, the day cloudless and stifling hot. Insects swarmed around the Comanches but were ignored. The sun was dipping, but Walking Bear held his men, waiting for just the right moment.

Six men worked in a field to the Comanches' right; another went into one of the houses. A woman filled a bucket from the well before going back inside. Three children ran around the garden near the largest house.

Little Hawk watched as the sun headed toward the Guadalupe Mountains far, far to the west. It was almost time. He tested the tautness of his bow string, and made sure his knife was in its sheath. He checked behind him, finding reassurance in the feathered ends of his dozen arrows. His lance felt balanced in his hand.

He took a deep breath to settle his excitement and his embarrassment at being the only one not painted. Since he was not yet a warrior, he did not deserve that honor. But after today, he would no longer go into battle unpainted. Of that he was sure.

He watched Walking Bear. The war leader nodded, raised his lance, and then brought it forward.

Little Hawk swallowed once, his mouth now as dry as a *Llano river* in August. He edged his pony over the rim of the sage-covered ridge. The animal picked up speed along with the others as the Comanches raced silently down the gentle slope.

7

Exhilaration flowed through Little Hawk's body as he thundered down the hill on the back of one of his father's war ponies. The wind tore through his hair and swept across his high, broad cheekbones.

The Comanches were silent, not wanting to alert the Mexicans. Little Hawk watched as another man came out of a house. The man glanced up the ridge — and saw the Comanches. He yelled and pointed toward the slope. Then he disappeared back into the house.

One of the men working in the corn field looked up, startled. He dropped his hoe, yelled, and ran toward the buildings. The other five did not stop to see what had set their friend off; they just dropped their baskets of corn and raced after him.

Walking Bear howled a war cry, shattering the silence. The others joined him, until their cacophony almost drowned the drumming hooves.

Three Comanches, led by Walking Bear, headed for the corral; the others angled to head off the men running for the buildings. A shot rang out from a house, then another. The Comanches did not slow.

Kills Twice cut the path of one Mexican. The farmer stopped, puffing, as Kills Twice swung his horse around. The Comanche warrior smacked the Mexican hard on the top of the head with his lance. Then he raced toward another of the six men.

Another warrior — Coyote — shoved ahead of Little Hawk and thundered past the same Mexican, also striking him with a lance, counting the second coup.

Little Hawk was angry at that. He had been planning to count coup on the Mexican right after his father. Now that Coyote had done so, it would be useless for him to count coup on the man; the Comanche code allowed only two coups on one enemy. Angrily he raced up to the man and impaled the staggering farmer on his lance.

He released the weapon, leaving it stuck in the rapidly dying Mexican, and kicked his pony harder. He edged ahead of Coyote and two other warriors to count second coup — with his hand — on another farmer, just after Kills Twice had done so.

Several Comanches had blocked the last of the four Mexicans from reaching any of the buildings. One farmer turned and ran back toward the field, hoping to lose himself in the tall corn.

Little Hawk easily caught the man. As he raced by, he grabbed the man by the hair. He hauled the farmer onto the pony with him, proud of himself. All his training and practice had not gone to waste. From the time he was barely nine, he and the other boys practiced such a thing so that now, though he was only thirteen, he had the strength to haul a full-grown man up from the ground. It was a move all the Comanche males trained for, since they often used it to grab up a fallen comrade while on the run.

He hurried back to the others. The last three farmers were circled by a swirling phalanx of warriors, herding the men away from the dangerous area in front of the houses. Rifle shots still erupted from the houses periodically. Only White Antelope had been hit, but not seriously. Several Comanches were racing back and forth in front of the houses, taunting the people inside.

Little Hawk saw Walking Bear and the two other warriors racing up the ridge, pushing the stolen horses. Little Hawk heard screams and turned to see the three Mexican farmers fall, riddled with arrows.

The Mexican across Little Hawk's pony's neck struggled. As warriors rushed the two houses, pounding at the doors and shuttered windows, Little Hawk dumped the man on the ground. Before the Mexican could rise, Little Hawk slid off his pony. Grinning wickedly, he grabbed the Mexican's grease-slick black hair. He yanked the man's head back, exposing the throat and throbbing carotid arteries. Blood spurted as a gash appeared in the throat. Little Hawk dropped the bloody thing, its life flickering out as it hit the dirt.

He glanced around. His comrades had burst into one house through a sagging door. By the time Little Hawk had peeled the scalp from the body at his feet, the warriors had broken into the second house. Screams and shouts erupted from within.

Seconds later the warriors emerged herding three young women before them. The women — two hardly more than girls — were pale with fright. They cried and sobbed; one beseeched God to rescue her, and she repeatedly made the sign of the cross on her prominent chest.

A warrior named Bear's Paw laughed as he came out of the house, an infant impaled on his lance. He jiggled the babe on the weapon, causing much amusement among his friends. His laughter stopped as his head exploded in a flying mass of blood and skull. A moment later the others heard the report of the rifle that had killed him.

Angry as a disturbed nest of hornets, most of the warriors rushed toward the house from which they thought the shot had come. Little Hawk and Kills Twice stayed to watch over the captive women.

A gunshot, followed swiftly by a bloodcurdling yell, came from inside the house. There were more screams, few yells, and then laughter. Comanche warriors strolled out of the house, shoving another woman ahead of them. Coyote carried the head of a

Mexican man by the hair. He tossed it down and danced briefly around it, his exaggerated steps and arm motions eliciting bursts of laughter from the others.

"Check the last house," Kills Twice ordered curtly.

"Why?" one asked, as Coyote stumbled to a halt.

"There might be others."

"So? These lowly things can't hurt us," Coyote said sharply.

"Tell that to Bear's Paw's women who will have no man to keep them. There might be others in that house, waiting to shoot us when we turn away. Now check that house! Unless you're afraid," he sneered.

Coyote was furious. "I'm afraid of no one!" he screamed. He stalked to the last house. Using his stone war club, he attacked the wood door with a raging intensity. Several others joined him. Within minutes the door fell, and the warriors swarmed inside. There was a screech, and what sounded like a hasty prayer, before silence. Then the warriors returned, all but Coyote looking sheepish.

"Well?" Kills Twice asked sharply.

"A brown skin was in there. And a child," White Antelope said.

Kills Twice grunted, not surprised he had been proved right. "Coyote, carry Bear's Paw. We'll see he's buried as befitting a brave *Nermernuh* warrior."

Coyote knew better than to argue.

"Take one of the women, White Antelope. And Big Thumb take one. Little Hawk and I will take the last." He leaped onto his pony, then grabbed a plump Mexican girl by the hair with one hand and the back of her dress just below the shoulders with the other. He yanked the screaming woman across the horse in front of him.

Little Hawk hurried to get his lance. While he was at it, he quickly skinned off the Mexican's scalp. He stuffed the two scalps into the buckskin string that served as a belt. Jumping onto his pony, he grabbed the last woman — the youngest and fattest — and hauled her, screeching, onto his pony.

Two warriors entered the house, then came out with burning sticks. Flames were already licking at the inside of the house. They quickly set fire to the other buildings including the church.

With howls of victory, the Comanches rode up the ridge. Within an hour they were camped in a break with a spring and a few small trees. Their horses were picketed, as was the stolen herd taken by Walking Bear, Eagle Wing, and Blood Drips Down. Several fires were going and fresh antelope was cooking.

The newcomers turned their horses out to graze and tied up the captives. The presence of Bear's Paw's body dimmed their high spirits only a little. They ate, regaling each other with their exploits.

Soon Walking Bear stood. He grabbed his crotch, and said with a grin, "I have a need." He strode the few feet to where the women were tethered to a small cottonwood. Their dark eyes glistened with fear.

Walking Bear picked out a trim young woman, pretty despite the fright etched on her face. He cut her loose and indicated she should stand. She refused. Walking Bear chuckled and grabbed her by her long, dark hair, and yanked her up. Holding her by the hair with one hand, he pulled his steel knife and brandished it before her face.

Her eyes got even bigger. Walking Bear touched the tip of the blade to the small depression at the base of her throat. He slid the knife into the neckline of her wool dress and slowly sliced downward. The material parted reluctantly. Being poor, the woman wore only a cotton shift as an undergarment. That also peeled away under the relentless blade, exposing her chubby breasts, then her belly.

The other Comanches chuckled and laughed. They hooted approval as the material split further, revealing the dark thatch of curly hair.

The woman stood rigid, her muscles as hard as adobe. Her breath came in short, frightened gasps that jerked her chest in and out. Her eyes were large and luminescent, radiating the fear lurking in them.

Walking Bear slipped the knife into his plain, hardened buckskin sheath, then jerked the garments away. The woman screamed and blubbered as Walking Bear flung her to the ground. With a flourish, he whipped off his breechclout. He paraded for several moments before his friends — and the women, who gagged with horror.

Then Walking Bear fell on the woman, plunging himself savagely to the hilt in her. She screamed in pain, and choked as the bile rose in her throat. She whimpered as Walking Bear thrust and pounded on her until he was through. He arose to the approbation of his friends.

Little Hawk watched with wide, interested eyes. There was more to being a warrior than battle, he had known. Now he had proof of it.

Kills Twice took another woman; then White Antelope took one, and Blood Drips Down the fourth, while Eagle Wing took the first. Until all but Little Hawk — and Coyote, who was preparing Bear's Paw for burial — had taken his turn.

"Well, son?" Kills Twice asked.

Little Hawk stood with a grin. He pulled off his breechcloth, and showed he had little to be ashamed of in the company of the men. He took the one he had carried here. He threw himself on her and relieved himself roughly, quickly, inside her. While the others were still grinning their approval, he felt himself roused once again, and took the one Walking Bear had taken first. The warriors roared.

8

Coyote had prepared Bear's Paw's body well, washing it, shutting the eyes with red clay, and then painting the face with vermilion. Coyote pulled Bear's Paw's hands in and knees up before wrapping the body in a blanket and binding it with rawhide. The others had paid Coyote little heed, but in the morning, Walking Bear said, "We'll go home. Bear's Paw deserves a proper *Nermernuh* burial."

The two oldest captive women were slain after the Comanches decided they had no more use. Pushing the stolen horses ahead of them, the warriors raced for their village, taking the straightest route, not sleeping. One of the remaining captives rode in front of Walking Bear; the other in front of Kills Twice. Coyote held the rope to a horse on which the bundled body of his friend rode in a hastily made travois.

As the Comanches pounded across the flat countryside cut with washes and breaks, Little Hawk thought about the Mexicans. They had not been very brave. They were weak and puny, seemed afraid of battle, and had done poorly in protecting their women and children.

He wondered if all white men — and the Mexicans were white-eyes, despite their dark skin — were alike. Were they all so impotent? Could they all be? But that could not be, he thought. Take the white man who had come into his village a summer ago, alone and unafraid. He was not like these frightened Mexicans.

Zeke Tippett was the first white man Little Hawk had seen, and he had been awed and somewhat frightened. Never before had he seen a man with skin so pale, or one with so much hair on his face. He had almost grown used to that thought when Tippett had returned with the other of his kind. The awe-inspiring Cass Calder, who was so huge he dwarfed even the great war leaders of the village.

But Little Hawk had found there was nothing to fear from these men. That was evident when the Cheyennes had attacked the camp. He had learned then that those white men lived as the Comanches did, by the knife, the tomahawk — and the gun.

Little Hawk was fascinated by those guns. He had seen them before. Indeed, some of the warriors had them. But still, to him they remained magical sticks that spit fire and killed without the person seeing what had killed him. That was the most frightening thing he had ever known. He knew they would be effective in war — not as effective as his stout, sinew-backed bow and his buckskin quiver of iron-tipped arrows — but a good thing to have.

And Tippett was a good man. Not a *Nermernuh*, of course, but like the guns, a good thing nonetheless. Little Hawk remembered that he had seen no fear in the *tahbay-boh's* eyes the first time Tippett rode into the Comanche camp. Had he shown fear when Walking Bear and his warriors encountered him, Tippett would have been seized. In the camp, the Comanche warriors would have truly tested the *tahbay-boh*. And when the warriors were done with the bleeding, whimpering thing, the women — the even-more cruel women — would have had their time with him. But Tippett had shown no fear, impressing Little Hawk.

The Comanches stopped on a ridge covered by brown grass overlooking the village. Dawn was breaking behind them. A good time to re-enter the village. "You will tell the People we have returned, Little Hawk," Walking Bear said.

As the youngest of the war band, Little Hawk expected it. He was tired and sore from the long, punishing ride, but there would be a celebration tonight. And he would take part, for he was a warrior!

He raced down the hill, his pony kicking up clods of earth. He slowed as he entered the village and spread the word that the victorious war party was returning.

Cuts Through, the elderly mother of Kills Twice, began the singing and shouting. She grabbed a lance and, singing a victory song, led a procession of Comanches out to greet the returning warriors. Walking Bear proudly hooked the scalp he had taken over the lance. Kills Twice did the same moments later, and then his son did likewise. Cuts Through led the way joyfully back to the village.

As they wound into the camp, each man stopped at his own lodge. Little Hawk, who had no woman to tend him, stopped at his father's lodge and gave his horse to his mother, Burning Grass.

The two captives also were remanded to the women of the village. They were hollow-cheeked and shocked. Each would be given to a warrior as a wife. They would, in time — if they lived — become used to their captivity, and their brutal treatment. They might even learn to like their lives here. If not, they would lead a miserable existence for as long as they stayed alive. Once married, they would be accepted by all the band and be accorded whatever rights and privileges any other woman in the village had. Their children would be considered full Comanche by the *Nermernuh*, with no stigma being attached to having a mother who was a Mexican captive.

Burning Grass, aided by her two daughters, led the animals away to care for them. The two warriors entered the lodge, filled horn bowls from the stew pot, ate, and then rested. With the darkening shadows of the late afternoon creeping over the camp, Kills Twice and Little Hawk cleansed themselves. They painted their faces and dressed in their war clothes. The music and singing were already beginning, and the two men stepped out of the lodge to see the scalp pole set up, surrounded by brown grass. They joined the others streaming that way.

Kills Twice sat next to Coyote, with Little Hawk on his other side. "All went well, Coyote?" he asked.

"Yes," Coyote nodded. During the afternoon, he and Bear's Paw's two wives saw to the slain warrior's burial nearby in a cave cut into an arroyo. They had made sure Bear's Paw was well-supplied for the afterlife. The ten finest horses in Bear's Paw's herd had been killed to provide him with a safe ride. And his weapons were laid out, along with food, clothes, and other such things Coyote thought his friend might need to dwell comfortably with the Great Spirit.

"Tomorrow will be the giveaway?"

"Yes."

"It is good." Kills Twice nodded at Bear's Paw's two widows as they made their way toward the celebration that was about to begin. Though filled with grief, they would join in the festivities, accepted by all since Bear's Paw had died in battle after counting coup.

When all the warriors had assembled — and all those who had taken scalps in the latest raid had placed them on the scalp pole, the grass was fired. Drumming started, followed by singing.

"Come, son," Kills Twice said, standing. He and the other warriors who had gone on the raid began dancing around the blazing pole.

Little Hawk needed no encouragement. He had been watching these rituals since he was old enough to stand, and had dreamed of taking part for almost as long.

The line of men — each clad in red — weaved and churned around the burning post as the drumming and singing became more insistent. Finally, the women and other warriors joined in, dancing in a larger circle around the men of the war party.

Little Hawk felt the mantle of tiredness fall off him as he stutter-stepped around the fire. The music throbbed deep into his heart, veins, and loins. He ignored the sweat streaking through his paint and trickling down his sides. He was a man at last! A *Nermernuh* warrior! That joyful knowledge flooded through him, carried on the rhythm of the drums and ululating voices that drifted into the night sky.

He felt himself drifting on wings above the camp, looking down at his small figure swirling and stomping to the music. He was one with himself, and one with the guardian spirits that watched over him. Indeed, he was almost one with the Great Spirit himself, floating as he was so high above the Earth Mother.

From his perch aloft, he saw something moving toward his body below. It was a large, silent gray wolf, fearsome and unfearing. The firelight glowed blood red in the animal's eyes as it looked up at him, and light flickered off its long canine teeth.

BOOK 3

ZEKE TIPPETT, 1834

9

"Ride, goddammit!" Zeke Tippett bellowed, smacking the rump of the dark prairie mustang. He watched a few moments as Painted Wing's pony raced off across the plain. He smiled grimly at his son, White Buffalo, flapping wildly and screaming in his cradleboard hanging from his mother's high, big-knobbed saddle horn. Painted Wing was too busy to try to calm the boy who was just over a year old.

Tippett turned back. The seven Cheyenne warriors were half a mile away. Tippett knew he could not outrun them so he stopped to make a stand, sending Painted Wing and the baby on their way. Tippett figured the Cheyennes would come at him first, aiming to kill him, scalp him, and steal his animals and possibles before going for the woman. He aimed to make sure they did not get past him.

Outwardly calm, Tippett tied the horse and four mules in a circle, with himself inside, protected by animal flesh. He pulled out his trade rifle and new .54-caliber Hawken. Priming both flintlocks, he slid the trade gun through a loop on a pack of beaver plews.

The Cheyenne were maybe two hundred yards away when Tippett slid the Hawken up over the pack of plews and fired. There was a flash of smoke, a slam against his shoulder, and a roar. A second later, Tippett grinned in satisfaction, for there was one riderless horse coming at him.

He set the Hawken down, grabbed the trade rifle, yanked the hammer back, and sighted. There was another roar, and a second Cheyenne fell. With practiced speed, Tippett poured an estimated dose of powder down the barrel of the trade rifle. Around his neck he wore his bullet block — a small chunk of wood with a dozen holes drilled in it. In each hole sat a patched ball. All he had to do was set one of the balls over the muzzle and punch it down a bit with the short starter. It saved a heap of time. He grabbed the ramrod and slammed the ball home. Pouring a little priming powder into the pan, he snapped the frizzen shut and did the same with the Hawken.

When he looked up, the Cheyennes were only fifty yards away and coming fast. Half a dozen arrows thudded into packs of beaver plews. Two mules brayed in annoyance, and his big bay horse whinnied in fright behind him. Tippett jammed the Hawken's wiping stick into the ground at his side and slid the rifle over the packs again. He fired and saw another Cheyenne sail off his pony.

Several more arrows thumped into packs as the three remaining Cheyennes swirled around him. Tippett yanked out his belt pistol. Like the two rifles, it was a .54 caliber and devastating at close range.

"Come on, ye shit-lappin' sons a bitches," Tippett roared.

Tippett fired as a Cheyenne rode swiftly in front of him. The pistol ball splattered the side of the Indian's head, knocking the warrior sideways off his horse. The others raced northeast, leaving the last warrior where he lay. Each scooped up one of the other dead.

By then, Tippett had dropped the pistol and hurriedly reloaded the Hawken. He sighted again as the Indians raced for safety. It was a long shot, but he tried it anyway. A Cheyenne carrying a dead comrade snapped straight up, as if hit. He dropped his friend, but, hunched over his pony's neck, kept going with the other two warriors.

"Waugh, that's makin' 'em come now, Zeke," Tippett shouted. He was almost delirious with his victory. Hastily he reloaded all his weapons. Hanging his pistol on his belt with the metal bracket riveted to the stock, the trade rifle went into a buckskin saddle scabbard. He kept the Hawken in hand as he untied the animals and then scalped the Cheyenne lying near him.

A quick check of the animals showed one mule to be wounded. Not too bad, but it wouldn't help matters. He softly worked the shaft back and forth, loosening it. It had not sunk in very deep, and it was but a few moments more before he had the arrow out. He held a piece of buckskin over the gash to halt the bleeding. The flow slowed to a trickle, then stopped. Tippett tossed the bloody rag away. The mule had brayed and bucked a few times during its ordeal, but mostly it stayed calm.

While he had worked on the big gray beast, Tippett kept a worried eye on the north, praying the Cheyennes would not return with reinforcements. Tippett pulled off his beaver-felt hat with the wide brim and low, round crown and swiped the sweat off his forehead with the sleeve of his dirty, red calico shirt. Setting the hat back on, he pulled himself up onto the big bay. Settling his scrawny backside into the hard saddle, he headed slowly southward.

Painted Wing met him a mile farther on. She had pulled into a wash with grass and a trickle of water left from yesterday's short, violent thunderstorm. Her pony grazed, while she sat placidly breast-feeding White Buffalo. She smiled as Tippett rode in.

"Ain't ye afraid?" he asked as he dismounted.

"Of what?"

"That I might've been killed by them damned Cheyennes."

"I knew it was you." In the three years they had been together, Painted Wing had learned Tippett's language quite well — much better than Tippett had learned hers. Her accent was heavy but she was understandable. They conversed mostly in English since

Tippett had trouble with Comanche pronunciation, though he could speak it tolerably well enough when he had to, and could understand it fully.

"How'd ye know that?" he asked, kissing her cheek. His son was busily sucking at Painted Wing's full right breast. Tippett touched the boy's head lightly. It was still a miracle to him.

"I knew you'd kill them damn Cheyennes," she said with conviction.

He nodded and realized how tired he was. It had been a long, though profitable winter. And the trek down toward Bent's Fort had not been an easy one. Plus, a battle almost always made him tired. It seemed that when the fighting was going on, he was pumped full of energy; and when it was over, he was drained. The sun was hot and comforting, making him sleepier.

"Rest a little," Painted Wing whispered, stroking his hair where it lay over his shoulders under the hat.

"We got to get on the way," Tippett muttered.

"We got time, dammit." She had picked up much of Tippett's penchant for oaths.

"Reckon ye're right." Tippett stretched out with his Hawken at his side. He shoved his hat down over his eyes. Suddenly he sat up. "Ye got anything to poultice a mule?" he asked.

"I reckon I might be able to find somethin'."

"All right," Tippett said wearily. He lay back down again. "Jist don't go wanderin' too far. And keep your eyes and ears open."

Her answer was fuzzy as the peace of sleep overcame him.

TIPPETT AWOKE AND SHOVED HIS HAT BACK. HE BLINKED A FEW times and knew by the angle of the sun that he had been asleep about an hour, but Painted Wing had a simple camp set up. A small fire fueled by dried buffalo dung was snapping. Meat was cooking and a coffee pot sat on a rock near the blaze. Their sleeping robes rested under the stunted cottonwood that was the only tree he had seen for miles. The mules had been unloaded, the heavy packs of plews and trade goods stacked to one side, the injured mule poultice, the horses unsaddled, and the hobbled animals were grazing. A sleeping White Buffalo hung in his cradleboard from the cottonwood.

"What're ye doin'?" he asked, mildly irritated. He hated to give in to sleep that way. It cost them valuable time. "We ain't stayin'."

"Yes, we are," Painted Wing said firmly.

"But we got a far piece to travel yet."

"There's no better place to stay between here and Bent's."

Before he could retort, he caught himself, still irritated. He tried to calm himself knowing she was right. And, unless there were more Cheyennes lurking about, they would be safe enough. "I expect we can make it to Bent's with a long day tomorrow."

"Yep. Hungry?"

"I expect," he said slowly. He rubbed his stubbled jaw — since he had been with Painted Wing, he tried to keep shaven except for a mustache, since she did not like beards. Then he grinned. "But feedin' can wait, I reckon."

"What you got in mind?" she asked in mock coyness.

"I reckon this ol' ruttin' bull can use a woman's care. Ye ain't of a mood, mayhap I can find me one in some Cheyenne camp nearby."

"Hoo, listen to this booshwa," Painted Wing said with a chuckle. "Them Cheyenne squaws'll cut off your ..."

"Well," he threw in hastily, "I don't *want* to avail myself of them, ye understand. ..."

"What gives you the notion I ain't interested?"

Tippett shrugged, but he grinned.

Painted Wing set down the moccasins she was making and wiped her hands on a cloth. She stood, eyes smoldering with lust, as she walked towards him. Stopping before him, she shed her dress and moccasins. Naked, she crawled atop him and kissed him hard.

"We can't do much with me all covered up like I am," he muttered into her mouth.

"Reckon not," she said, kissing him several more times before reluctantly sliding backward and up a little until she was resting on her shins, one to each side of him, her bottom perched lightly on his crotch.

She jerked and pulled his shirt off over his head as he arched. She spun, until her backside was facing him. He grinned and stroked her back and buttocks while Painted Wing undid the four horn buttons of Tippett's buckskin trousers and peeled the pants off. She had to stretch quite a bit to do so, exposing her womanhood to him. Tippett's hands slithered to it, stroking its wetness.

Painted Wing shuddered with pleasure and brought her hips down onto him for a few moments. He arched his back as the pleasure raced through him like a lightning bolt. He groaned as she spun to face him. Joyfully, she kissed him even while lifting her hips. She sank back down, gasping as he entered her. She bounced up and down with abandon, moaning as the ecstasy built within her loins and surged throughout her body until a blinding flash of warmth and goodness burst inside her. She shook, glistening with sweat.

He moaned and gasped seconds later, shuddering as the relief of his rapture flood through him and then out.

Painted Wing fell onto Tippett with a huge sigh, her breasts ballooning on his hard chest. "Damn, that was good," she panted.

He could not speak so he just nodded enthusiastically.

When their breathing had returned to normal, he reached behind him and grabbed his hat and set it on her head. They both grinned. Then Painted Wing said, "I'm a bad wife. Damn, ought to be put under."

"What for?" Tippett asked, surprised.

"You need food. You have fought enemies today and pleasured your woman. What have I done? Nothin'. I ..."

"Buffler shit," he said, trying not to be angry. It was her way to feel guilty about not taking good enough care of him. A *Nermernuh* woman should take better care of her man. It didn't matter to her that he was not a Comanche and that she did fine by him. "Ye done more'n enough today. Don't let me hear ye say elsewise."

She nodded solemnly, stood, and picked up her dress.

"Leave it off," Tippett said, his voice choked with lingering lust.

Grinning, she dropped the dress and got Tippett a bowl of food.

10

The adobe fort on the plains along the Arkansas River was a beehive of activity as was the area within a mile of it. Tippett rode through the wide, iron-studded wood doors into the placita, knowing that for the past half-mile his progress had been monitored by someone using the telescope in the small watchtower over the gateway. Trappers, Indians, tradesmen, traders, and laborers bustled about, or lounged, as was their wont late on this warm afternoon.

Tippett was hot and tired, and thus irritable, but he smiled as he rode in. There was something about this place — opened only the year before — that comforted him. Across the small plaza-like courtyard from Tippett was a wide entryway into the corrals at back. Horses, mules, cattle, or occasionally a buffalo calf, were kept there at night. The corral's adobe walls were covered with long, spindly cactus to discourage potential horse thieves. During the day, Mexicans drove the animals out onto the plain to graze.

To the left of the passageway were the carpenter's and blacksmith's workrooms, and then William Bent's sleeping room. Above the opening was a room with a billiards table from St. Louis and a bar. On the northwest side, a walkway led to one of the two round bastions. Ceran St. Vrain's quarters were on the southwest side.

On the lower floor to Tippett's right were storerooms, the wash house, well room, and at the rear, the cistern and powder magazine. Above those rooms were trappers' quarters and the clerk's quarters. Immediately to his right, on the fronting wall, were laborers' quarters. In the same position on his left was the Indian trading room. It was small, so not too many Indians could crowd in at one time and overwhelm the trader. Against the left side were the main trade room, the council room, and dining room, with the kitchen and pantry off in the back of the dining room.

The fort was compact, well laid out and comfortable, but sitting in the middle of nowhere created problems. There was not enough well water to supply the place, so supplies were kept up daily by a crazy old French-Canadian who lost several toes to frostbite in his dim past. He would cart a wagonload of barrels to the river, fill them, and haul them back. Then he would load the wagon with refuse and some of the plentiful manure so faithfully deposited by the many horses and mules. He carted it off to God only knew where and dumped it, keeping the fort relatively clean.

Two bare-chested men worked the big fur press in the center of the plaza; red chili *ristras* hung from the *vigas*, brightening the sandy brown fort. The aroma of roasting buffalo meat and the smell of cottonwood logs burning in the fireplaces drifted on the breeze.

Tippett stopped in front of the trade room. Bent and the chief trader stepped into the stifling afternoon. "Welcome, Mister Tippett," Bent said. "I see you've come through another season with your hair and your health."

"I expect I did."

"You had no troubles then?"

"Not much to speak of." There was no need to mention the bitter, brutally cold winter, the raging snowstorms, the occasional starving times, or the other such troublesome things that made up the life of a mountain man. "Had a run-in with the Cheyennes a day or so back," he said tightly, concerned about Bent's reaction. Bent was close to the Cheyennes.

"That could be worrisome. You all right?"

"Yep. But at least one Cheyenne ain't goin' to the Spirit Land."

"That's more worrisome. It could hurt business, but more important, it could send the Cheyennes on the prod against any white man."

"Then they shouldn't've come agin a white man in the first place."

The short, stocky Bent nodded, then stood thoughtful for a moment before shrugging. "Well," he commented quietly, "there's nothing can be done about that. I reckon I can talk to Walkin' Thunder and see if I can convince him to smooth things over."

"That'd shine. I weren't aimin' to cause you and the other boys any grief, but I wasn't about to let those devils raise my hair just because they might be friends of yours."

"Reckon I'd do the same. Will you be staying with us to celebrate our nation's Independence Day?"

"When's that?" Tippett asked as he and Painted Wing dismounted.

"Tomorrow," Bent said, not surprised that Tippett did not know the date. "We'll get things a-goin' with a *fandango* tonight."

"This chil' ain't had a *fandango* in a coon's age. Ye got a place for me and Painted Wing to put our possibles?"

Bent pointed to a small room at the northeast corner of the fort. "You can have that if you ain't plannin' on stayin' overly long."

"Thankee, Bill." Painted Wing led the pack mule with the supplies across the plaza, toward it.

A man with a dark black beard strolled up. He was short, though a couple of inches taller than Bent. "Mister Tippett," Bent said, waving a hand graciously toward him, "my partner, Ceran St. Vrain."

Tippett held out his hand. "I've heard of ye, of course, Mister St. Vrain. Pleased to meet ye."

"Ze plezair, he is mine, *monsieur*." St. Vrain shook Tippett's hand.

"*Gracias*. Ye here for the *fandango*?

"*Oui*." The stern visage cracked a little.

"And to check up on me at my brother Charlie's request," Bent laughed.

"Zat is not true," St. Vrain said severely, but he grinned.

"I know that as well as you do, Ceran," Bent said, still smiling. "Care to join us while we take in Mister Tippett's peltries, Ceran?"

"*Non*." He wandered off, black frock coat flapping in the breeze.

"He really here to check on ye?" Tippett asked.

"Ain't likely. Charlie trusts me. And the three of us have been dealin' together long enough to be able to put our trust in each other. I think he just likes it here but don't want to admit it."

Tippett chuckled as he undid the ropes holding the bales of beaver plews on the mules. Bent waved his hand and a young Mexican wearing a straw sombrero, muslin shirt, cotton pants, and *juaraches* hurried over.

"Help Mister Tippett, Popé," Bent said.

"*Gracias*," Tippett said as he pulled a pack of pelts onto each shoulder. Without seeming to strain, he strolled into the trade room and dropped the ninety-pound bundles. Popé followed with two more. With the two men working, it was but minutes before all the bundles were stacked on the trade room floor.

The chief trader, Sean Murray, looked at the packs. "Looks like ye done well, Mister Tippett," he said in his heavy Irish accent.

"I expect. There's six, mayhap seven hundred pounds of prime plews there. I'd say ye folks owe me right on thirty-six hundred dollars. Minus what I owe for next year's supplies, Bill. That about right?"

Both men looked rather embarrassed. "I'm afraid not," Bent finally said. "The price of plews has fallen some since last year."

"How much?" Tippett's face was tight.

"Not too much. Down to five dollars a pound."

"Ain't too bad, I expect," Tippett grumbled. "That's only a dollar." He squinted at Bent. "And I reckon ye'll charge me this year's price for supplies?"

"Have to," Bent said with a shrug.

"No, ye don't," Tippett said with resignation. "But I ain't one to begrudge a feller earnin' his keep. Ye got to make a livin' same's everybody else, I expect."

"Kind of you," Bent said. Tippett was not sure whether Little White Man, as the Cheyennes called him, was being sarcastic. "Tell you what. I'll pay five and a quarter a pound. I'll take a little beatin' that way, but I'll make it back on next season's supplies."

"I expect," Tippett said dryly.

"Just don't go flappin' your gums about what a kind-hearted soul I am."

"I'd as soon hump a buffalo bull," Tippett said with a chuckle.

They concluded their business quickly. Tippett paid off what he owed and bought a few things for himself. He left his cash — just over two thousand dollars — with Bent for safekeeping, sticking only a few *pesos* and gold coins in the possibles bag at his belt.

Tippett greeted some friends outside before going to his room. The sun was low, and the celebrating would start soon. He, Painted Wing, and White Buffalo went to the wide, sluggish river where they washed off months' worth of dust, blood, and sweat.

In their room, the two adults dressed in their finery. Tippett was proud of Painted Wing. She looked plumb fine in her creamy buckskin dress. It was intricately beaded across the bosom with a sun design. The colorful beads were highlighted by dyed porcupine quills. Little tin cones on the ragged sleeves and fringed hem clattered. She had gotten the dress, matching moccasins, and leggings from some Crows they had come across up along the Yellowstone. They had cost a good horse, two buffalo robes, and a mirror but Tippett felt it was worth it. Painted Wing's hair was freshly greased and the part painted with vermilion. Her pitch hair hung loose down her back, framing her wide face. She wore large loop earrings of Spanish silver.

Tippett wore golden-tanned elkskin pants with long, heavy fringes down the outside of each leg, and a calico shirt with a dark green striping on white. Red suspenders set off the shirt. A wide belt of hard leather, studded with brass tacks in a design of Painted Wing's imagination, circled his waist. Clipped to it were his two .54-caliber flintlock pistols. On the left side was a hard leather sheath with a large butcher knife. An iron-headed tomahawk rested through the belt at the small of Tippett's back. A bone-pipe choker with a grizzly bear claw in the center circled his neck, as did a heart-shaped, buckskin pipe carrier. Under the shirt, against Tippett's heart, was a small pouch filled with his "medicine." But he was most proud of his tall top hat of the finest beaver felt. A red bandanna formed a hatband and held three eagle feathers on the left side. Tippett was freshly shaved, his hair slicked down with a coating of bear grease.

Tippett and Painted Wing stepped into the placita, which was crowded with trappers, laborers, tradesmen, and Indians — all of them in the fanciest get-ups they had.

As Tippett moved into the placita, a young Cheyenne with a fierce countenance looked at him. His eyes got very large and shouted something Tippett could not understand.

11

Silence descended like a shroud over the fort as the Indian moved towards Tippett, his eyes fierce and piercing.

Tippett shoved Painted Wing, who was holding White Buffalo, back into the room. But he never took his eyes off the Cheyenne who seemed familiar. Other Cheyennes marched behind the young man. Mountain men, traders, and laborers crowded up behind the Indians. White men on the upper level walkway brought their rifles to full cock and waited. From the corner of his eye, Tippett could see Bent wave a hand. A second later, three mountain men shoved several Cheyennes near the gates outside and then slammed and barred the huge double doors.

The young warrior yanked out his knife, still advancing on Tippett. The mountain man spit a stream of tobacco juice at the ground. It landed sloppily in the dust, splattering the Indian's beaded moccasins who then pulled his own knife and waited.

Suddenly Bent and St. Vrain stood between the red and white men. "What's this all about, Yellow Blanket?" Bent demanded in Cheyenne.

Yellow Blanket stopped inches from Bent. "This man," Yellow Blanket snarled, waving his knife in Tippett's direction only inches from Bent's face, "killed some of the People. I will cut out his heart and dance on it." His face was a copper etching of rage.

"You'll do no such thing," Bent said in English, forcing the Cheyenne to listen. "Leastways not in my place."

"Is he afraid?" Yellow Blanket sneered. "Does he need Little White Man to protect him?"

Tippett could not see it, but Bent grinned. "I let this son of a bitch go at you, boy, and you'll be dead and missin' your hair before you could get your war cry out."

Tippett recognized the warrior. Yellow Blanket was one of the ones who had gotten away in the fracas the day before.

"Just tell me what you're all fired up about, Yellow Blanket," Bent said calmly.

"This white-eyes killed four good warriors. White-Faced Buffalo, Yellow Grass, Snow Lodge, and Turned-In Knee lost their lives to the fire sticks of this white-eye. And the spirit of Turned-In Knee will not be free since this piece of buffalo dung has his scalp."

Tippett understood only a few words since Yellow Blanket had spoken in Cheyenne. But he got the gist of it and grew angry. "Why, ye lyin' son of a bitch," Tippett started.

Bent held up a hand, bringing Tippett to a stop. "You're full of buffalo shit, Yellow Blanket," Bent said. "Now, I reckon you and your *amigos* set on Zeke, fixin' to raise his hair and steal his pelts. Then he kicked your ass good and put four boys under. Now you want to kill him before he could tell everybody what a piss-poor warrior you are." Bent paused. He had been speaking English and wanted to give all the Cheyennes enough time to understand the words.

There was a stunned silence that rolled over the fort. Then someone coughed, and another cut wind, eliciting a few sniggers. Yellow Blanket's dark, coppery face was mottled with rage and his black eyes bulged. Sweat trailed down from his greasy hair through the dust on his face.

"Now, if you can't control yourself, Yellow Blanket, you best get out. I don't want you causin' trouble in here. That goes for the rest of the People!" Bent added with a roar. "You can't keep to your best behavior, go on back to your camp."

Yellow Blanket spun and stomped away toward the gates, tiny bells on the heels of his moccasins tinkling dully in the silence. He jammed the knife into its sheath. Suddenly he stopped and spun. He marched back, slamming his shoulder into Bent's as he stormed past.

Bent started to rebuke the Cheyenne, but decided at the last moment to hold his tongue.

Yellow Blanket stopped two feet in front of Tippett. With a sneer coloring his handsome face, the Cheyenne snapped in English, "I'll have your hair, white-eye bastard."

"Any time ye think ye're ready, asshole," Tippett snarled. And he spit a juicy wet stream of tobacco juice at Yellow Blanket, splashing it all over the front of the Indian's creamy beige war shirt. Tippett almost laughed at the rage on Yellow Blanket's face as the Indian yanked out his knife and raised it to slash Tippett. The white man smashed a fist into the Indian's face, knocking him down.

Yellow Blanket leapt up, set to finish off this impudent white man. But the cocking of hammers too numerous to count stopped him.

"Don't cut my trail again, Yellow Blanket," Tippett growled. "Or I'll have your hair — and your balls — hanging from my lodgepole."

Yellow Blanket, face colored by rage and humiliation scrambled up and raced toward the gates. The mountain men there barely had time to get the gates open before Yellow Blanket rushed through.

There was some laughter, but not much, since this could still turn serious. There were maybe two hundred Cheyennes outside the fort, not counting the forty or so inside.

"Black Kettle," Bent called. A warrior of perhaps thirty years old stepped up. "I gonna have any more trouble with your people?"

"No."

"*Bueno*."

The Cheyenne turned and spoke to his people. Two warriors hurried out through the still open gate.

"I hope those two ain't goin' out there to raise up a war party," Tippett said.

"Nope. Black Kettle told 'em to tell the People to stay calm. I expect White Thunder will keep 'em under control." He paused, then said, "All right, boys, let's get some music a playin'."

The band — two fiddles, a concertina, a guitar, and a jaw harp — struck up a jaunty number. Most of the whites uncocked their rifles and pistols. As many as could grabbed the few Cheyenne women in the fort and started swinging them around the plaza in spirited reels. The others clapped hands or danced with each other.

Bent strolled toward the gates and whispered something to the several men there. They nodded and shut the gates but did not bar them. And they stood watch. Bent ambled toward Tippett, who stood, feeling the relief wash over him. That confrontation had been too close. The whites would have easily won the battle inside the fort and most likely driven off the Cheyennes outside without much trouble. Still, a number on both sides would have died. And all for one buck's need for revenge.

"He won't let this drop, Zeke," Bent said.

"Ye want me to leave?" Tippett asked, his eyes and jaw hard.

"Yep. But tomorrow's soon enough."

"I'll be gone early. 'Less I get to wrasslin' too much with some liquid lightnin' tonight." The last was said with a grin.

Bent was not amused. "Your woman's a Comanche. You plan on headin' to her village?"

"Yep."

"You got a heap of Cheyenne country to cover before you get out there."

"Reckon that's true. I'll cross the river soon's practical. Far as I know, the Cheyenne don't go south of the river too often."

"Often enough."

Tippett shrugged.

"I think it best, too, if you were to reprovision elsewhere." When Tippett looked at him in surprise, Bent said, "I want no one's blood on my hands. Not yours, not Yellow Blanket's. I know these Cheyennes far better than you do, Zeke. They're good people. But they've got their own ways. I want no part of getting in the middle of a feud. Get your supplies at the store in Taos. You've paid already. I'll message Charles and tell him what's happened."

"I'd be obliged if ye was to send the rest of my specie with him. If you trust that feller?"

"I do."

"I expect Yellow Blanket will be comin' after me ..."

Bent nodded in agreement.

"... and should I go under, ye can have Charles send it on to my family back East. I'll write ye a paper sayin' such."

"A wise thing. I'd not be comin' past here on your way up to the mountains again in the fall either. Head through the San Juans out of Taos. Miss Cheyenne country altogether."

Tippett thought for a few moments. He rested his arm across Painted Wing's shoulders and spit the last of his tobacco out.

"Makes sense. What about next year, though? Ye want me to avoid the fort here and jist head on to Taos?"

"Reckon not," Bent said with the first hint of a grin. "If Yellow Blanket puts you under, you got no more problem. If you put him under, things'll be mostly forgot by next year."

Tippett nodded as someone staggered by and thrust a bottle into his hand. Tippett grinned and tilted the bottle in a mock salute to Bent. Then he drank deeply, eyes watering more than a little as the harsh whiskey blazed a burning trail down his esophagus.

Tippett and Painted Wing took part in the festivities, with Tippett resisting the urge to get roaring drunk. If he was to be on the trail early, he'd need his wits about him.

He and Painted Wing danced a little, and he even lent Painted Wing out from time to time to other men for dancing. When he did, he stood there holding his son uncomfortably while Painted

Wing whirled around. At midnight, the men fired their guns into the air and a Mexican set off firecrackers. It was a fine July Fourth celebration.

The fort was mostly asleep in the morning as Tippett loaded his supplies on one mule. He spotted Bent coming out of his quarters and nodded at him. Bent and Ceran St. Vrain were, along with Tippett, quite possibly the only men in the fort not hungover. Bent nodded back.

An hour later, after a large breakfast, he rode out of the fort.

Painted Wing followed, White Buffalo hanging in his cradleboard from the saddle horn. Painted Wing held the rope to the pack mule.

They made their way silently past the sleeping Cheyenne camp, Tippett hoping that Yellow Blanket would not challenge him here. Then they were across the Arkansas and riding east.

Two days later, Painted Wing called him. The urgency in her voice made him spin sharply in his saddle. The woman pointed. Less than a mile off three warriors were racing towards them.

"Shit," he muttered.

12

Tippett stopped his big bay horse and watched the three warriors. Painted Wing sat on her pony, unafraid. She might be foolish, but she had the utmost faith in her man.

Tippett looked at his woman and started to tell her to ride off, the way she had last time. But before he could say anything, she shook her head. He grinned. "All right, woman," he said.

He dismounted and stepped a few feet away from his horse. Setting the curved, brass-covered butt of his Hawken on the dirt, he leaned on the muzzle and waited. As the Indians neared, he saw Yellow Blanket leading them. He did not know the names of the other two, but they were the ones who had gotten away with Yellow Blanket.

When the Cheyennes were but one hundred yards away, Tippett straightened and brought the Hawken up. He squeezed the trigger, resulting in a flash of smoke and a roar. A Cheyenne fell from his horse, the blood from his throat getting lost in the red of his painted chest.

"Get down there behind that mule, Painted Wing," Tippett warned as he unhurriedly reloaded the rifle. She did as she was told.

Several arrows flew in his direction, but Tippett ignored them.

The Cheyenne would want to count coup first, and then perhaps torture him just a bit before killing him. He was outwardly calm, but he raged inside. How dare these warriors come after him like this!

Tippett raised the heavy rifle once again and blasted another Cheyenne into eternity, leaving only Yellow Blanket to come charging at him. Tippett spit. Yellow Blanket thundered up and took a vicious swipe at Tippett's head with his war club — a buckskin-wrapped wood handle capped by a buffalo jaw with two iron knife blades through it.

Tippett ducked as Yellow Blanket roared past. "Hell," he roared, "ye can do better'n that."

Yellow Blanket pulled his horse up and slid off the pony.

"That's better, ye fractious son of a bitch," Tippett snarled. "I've had about enough of your nonsense." He set his Hawken down and slid out his iron tomahawk.

"I'll have your balls," Yellow Blanket snarled in Cheyenne. Tippett did not understand the words, but he caught the meaning. Up close, Yellow Blanket presented a horrifying picture. His face was painted almost entirely in black, with only wide white rings around his bloodshot eyes. His bare chest was painted in red and yellow stripes. He smelled of grease, sweat, and blood. His muscles looked flabby, but Tippett was not deceived by that. This young man most likely was as strong as a buffalo bull, and as ill-tempered.

"Ye talk more'n most ol' women, Yellow Blanket," Tippett snapped.

Yellow Blanket spit at Tippett, the mucus landing thickly on the mountain man's shirt. He hefted his war club, swinging it easily back and forth in front of him.

"Bastard," Tippett said, calming down, as was usual for him when danger arose close to hand. He held his tomahawk in his right hand, and his eyes watched those of the Cheyenne as the Indian circled to his left. After one circle, Tippett said in annoyance, "Hell,

Yellow Blanket, if I knowed ye was aimin' to dance, I'd've brung a drum."

Yellow Blanket rushed at Tippett, war club raised to strike. With a forceful expulsion of breath, Tippett spit a glob of tobacco and juice. He ducked as the brown liquid splattered the Indian's eyes.

The Indian screamed a Cheyenne oath and swung the war club blindly. But it cut only air, since Tippett was gone. He stumbled to a stop, scrabbling at his face with his free hand to clear his eyes.

"Dumb bastard," Tippett muttered as he swung the tomahawk. The blade cleft Yellow Blanket's neck where it joined the shoulder. Blood fountained up, but the Cheyenne did not fall. He stood for a moment as Tippett yanked the tomahawk out. Yellow Blanket wavered, body dead but brain unaware. Then he fell, toppling like wheat cut by a scythe.

There was no sense of victory for Tippett, only a simmering resentment. He scanned the prairie as he swabbed down his rifle with a piece of greased cloth, then reloaded the weapon. When he turned to check on Painted Wing, he saw that his horse had an arrow in the meat at the top of one foreleg. He had never heard the animal squeal.

"Goddamn," he snapped, stepping up to the horse. The wound wasn't bad, but the grass around the bay was bespotted with blood. "Easy now, horse," he whispered, trying to calm the animal. He cursed softly, knowing he had to get the deeply imbedded arrow out. He took a deep breath and then suddenly yanked at the feathered shaft of the arrow.

The horse squealed and reared, front hooves carving the air. Tippett stepped out of the way, bloody arrow in hand, as the animal came back down to earth. The steed started to bolt, but Tippett managed to grab the reins and jerk himself up into the saddle. The horse raced off, but Tippett controlled him after a short spurt. Then he spent a time calming the animal as he brought it back to where Painted Wing waited with her pony and the mule.

While Tippett worked on the bay, Painted Wing peeled the hair from the three Cheyennes. Tippett grinned viciously when she showed him.

"Ye think a poultice like ye fixed up for that mule would work on this horse, Painted Wing?" Tippett asked, concerned.

"Might," she shrugged. "But I ain't got no more root to make it up from. And I don't expect to find none 'round here."

"Dammit. Well, I'll have to go easy on him," Tippett said, not happy with this turn of events.

They rode off, Tippett worried about his horse, which favored its left foreleg. The wound opened up periodically as they rode, and Tippett would stop and hold a piece of buckskin against the injury until the bleeding stopped. A tense week later, they arrived at Painted Wing's village. Tippett was walking, as he had the past two days, the long-legged bay in tow.

Little Hawk was one of the first to greet him and Tippett grinned. There was something different about the boy, a radiating aura. "Ye been to war, ain't ye, Little Hawk?" Tippett asked.

The young man, who had a hard look to him, grinned and nodded. "Yes," he said in Comanche. "Against the Mexicans. Two summers ago, after you left. Last summer, too. And we just returned. But soon we'll go again." His eyes glimmered with expectation.

"Ye get many horses, Little Hawk?"

"*Si*." He paused. "My warrior name is Gray Wolf." He held himself proudly. "What's wrong with your horse?"

"Took a Cheyenne arrow. But," he added grimly, waving a hand at the still-fresh scalps hanging by rawhide loops from his saddle horn, "there's several less of them ill-natured varmints left."

Gray Wolf and the other warriors who had gathered around whooped war cries. It was always a good thing when a Cheyenne died, and even better when the spirit would not be freed because the scalp was taken. It was unfortunate, Gray Wolf thought, that the white-eyes were so squeamish that they would not hack off a fallen enemy's arm or foot or testicles — anything to prevent that enemy from being whole in the afterworld. But talking scalps would do.

"I reckon this old hoss ain't gonna make it," Tippett said sadly. "He's hurt purty bad."

Gray Wolf left some of his newfound warrior's dignity behind as he hurried to examine the wound. Then he said, "I can make him better."

"Ye certain?"

"*Si*. But he needs strong medicine. Medicine only I can make," he boasted. "And rest. You cannot ride him for many moons."

"I need me a good horse."

"I'll trade. You give me this horse, I'll give you one of mine. I have many horses. Good ones." He was lying only a little.

Tippett laughed. "I reckon ye do, boy. But this hoss ain't jist any old hoss. He's mighty special to this chil'. I ain't aimin' to trade him off for no sack of buzzard bait."

"I'll give you two ponies. The best ones. You can pick them."

Tippett looked thoughtful, but the decision was not hard to make. Tippett needed a horse, and the one he had would not be fit to ride for months, if ever. He hesitated only because the horse had carried him through many dangers. They were used to each other.

But he knew, too, that the bay would be well cared for here. The Comanches were complete horse people and would never knowingly, or maliciously, mistreat a horse. They might take a horse that was next to dead and ride it another hundred miles, killing it in the process, if they needed to. But to just mistreat a horse was not their way.

"All right, Little Hawk. I mean Gray Wolf. Ye got him. But," he added with a wink, knowing it was not really necessary to say it, "Don't ye go mistreatin' him, or ye'll be answerin' to me." His jaw hardened, "And make no mistake, boy, I'll take him back and see if someone else can tend him if ye ain't got no ponies worth takin'."

"I have many good horses," Gray Wolf answered haughtily. He grabbed the horse's reins and led the animal away.

It was true that he had many horses, most stolen from the Mexicans. But none was as fine as this beautiful bay. The Mexican horses were larger than the prairie mustangs, but not as big as this long-legged, big-chested bay. Gray Wolf was proud to have it. With training, he thought, the bay would make a magnificent war horse.

Gray Wolf decided he would try to cultivate the friendship of this *tahbay-boh*. The white-eyed warrior was strong medicine, Gray Wolf thought, and he would make sure their friendship developed.

13

Gray Wolf made it a point to spend as much time as he could with Tippett while the mountain man was in the village. Though Gray Wolf was now a warrior — proud, vicious, and dangerous — he was barely sixteen and retained a little of the enthusiasm, excitement, and playfulness of youth.

But he was wise enough already to know that he must learn as much as he could about these *tahbay-boh*. He could not see that the future would bring mighty clashes with these pale-skinned people. His people, the *Nermernuh* — and especially the Antelopes, the *Llano Estacado*-dwelling *Kwahadis* — were the lords of their domain. Still, Gray Wolf knew he must learn of these people. Someday the knowledge would serve him well. He was not sure why, only that it was true.

So, he hung around Tippett, risking becoming a pest, spending much time in the mountain man's lodge, talking. And, while he asked many questions, he also taught Tippett much about the ways of the Comanche. He and Tippett spent hours together, friendship blossoming. They hunted and talked across the great expanse of the *Llano Estacado*.

Tippett rode one of the ponies he had taken in trade for the bay.

It was a dark chestnut-colored mare, fleet of foot and stout of heart. Tippett was pleased with her. A week after arriving — time enough for Tippett to determine that Gray Wolf wanted nothing from him but information — Tippett called on Gray Wolf and they rode out together.

"Would ye like to learn to shoot, Wolf?" Tippett asked.

"Yes," Gray Wolf said, his sparkling eyes the only sign of the excitement that stormed inside him.

"*Bueno*. Find us a herd of buffler."

As they rode, Gray Wolf asked shyly, "Where's your big *amigo?*"

"Stayed on at rendezvous," Tippett said.

"Rendezvous?" Gray Wolf asked, struggling with the strange word.

"A grand tradin' fair. Mountaineers come from all over the mountains to trade their plews. Suppliers come from back in the settlements with goods they trade to the men for plews. Indians come, there, too. Some to trade, some to sell their women. It's one hell of a doin's. Goddamn, shinin' times for all. Drinkin' like ye never seen. Plenty of women, whiskey, and food. There's games, racin', fightin', and all such kind of carryin's on."

Gray Wolf's eyes were excited once again. "Will you take me?" he asked, almost breathless with the fear of rejection.

"Reckon not, Gray Wolf." Seeing the Comanche's downcast face, he said, "It ain't that I wouldn't want ye to go, ye understand, but I expect ye'd not be very welcome there."

"But you said there are other...Indians," he said, the word known to him, but unfamiliar in his own use.

"The Indians who show up at rendezvous ain't *Nermernuh*. Mostly Snakes, Flatheads, Bannocks, and Nez Perce."

"But you take Painted Wing and your friend has taken Yellow Bird."

"They're women, not warriors."

Gray Wolf nodded, understanding but unhappy. Less than half

an hour later he found a small herd of buffalo, no more than a dozen animals. Most were grazing on the already-browning summer grass. A few were wallowing, sending up great showers of prairie dust. Three calves cavorted under the not-so-watchful eyes of the rest of the herd.

Tippett and Gray Wolf dismounted and tied their horses to a wind-twisted mesquite. Tippett had the Hawken in hand and he grabbed the trade rifle from the buckskin scabbard. He and Gray Wolf hunched over and scurried toward the herd, coming up from the downwind side so the shedding beasts would not catch their scent. At about a hundred yards from the herd, Tippett halted. He sat quietly, making no sudden moves. Gray Wolf sat alongside him.

"This here's primin' powder," Tippett said, showing Gray Wolf the small powder horn attached by two short thongs to the other powder horn. "Ye sprinkle a bit here in the pan, and then snap this thing — it's called a frizzen — shut." He went through the motions on the Hawken as he spoke, then handed Gray Wolf a trade rifle.

The fires of excitement burned in the Comanche's eyes as he almost reverently took it. He stretched out and aimed. There was a flash of smoke and thunderous noise. Gray Wolf yelped in surprise as the rifle slammed hard back against his shoulder. When the smoke cleared, Gray Wolf looked. All the buffalo were still standing.

"This damn fire stick's no good," Gray Wolf said in a huff.

"Like hell," Tippett said with a grin. He took the rifle back, reloaded it, and then dropped a buffalo. He handed it back to Gray Wolf. "Works jist fine. It takes time to learn how to use it."

Throughout the rest of the morning, he patiently helped Gray Wolf learn to shoot. Finally, Gray Wolf hit a buffalo. He did not kill the animal, only broke one of its legs. The beast went down, kicking and bellowing. Frightened, the rest of the herd ran off, their hooves rumbling on the plains.

"I'll stick with my goddamn bow," Gray Wolf said firmly in

English, a language being taught to him with all the glory of its profanity and patois by Tippett.

Tippett laughed. "Ye'll get the hang of it after a spell."

"The bow's better," Gray Wolf said firmly. "Gun takes too long to reload. I can shoot six arrows, maybe more, by the time you get that damn gun loaded."

"Maybe so," Tippett said, chuckling. "But ye ain't gonna drop no goddamn buffler from two hunnert yards with an arrow." He reloaded the Hawken as he talked and then started cleaning the trade rifle.

"Shootin' buffler while hidin' in the grass ain't a warrior's way," Gray Wolf said stiffly. "Better to ride a good buffler pony and kill with your bow. Or better, with a lance. Anyone can sit with a gun and shoot down bufflers all day with a gun."

"Ye cain't," Tippett laughed again. "Besides, this here's a hell of a lot better way to put meat in the pot than your way. Though," he said with fondness, stopping the wiping motion with the ramrod, "runnin' buffler's purely the best thing a man can do. Next to takin' a woman, of course. Ye had a woman yet, Gray Wolf?"

"Yes." Gray Wolf straightened his back. "Many times."

"Ye're full of shit," Tippett laughed. He replaced the wiping stick and poured a measured dose of powder down the trade gun's barrel.

"I have," Gray Wolf hissed insistently. "Mexicans. Many times."

"Captives?" Tippett asked, the joy gone from face and voice.

"*Si,*" Gray Wolf said with a proud grin.

"That ain't havin' a woman, goddammit. Just pokin' your lance into some dumb captive ain't no fun. I reckon," he said, a smile tugging the corners of his mouth, "it's better'n doin' yourself. But, to really have a woman, ye got to take your time, build up to things, get her to help. It's a heap more fun that way, boy, I'll tell ye.

"Hell," he added after a moment's thought, "doin' what ye do to them captives, ye might's well keep a buffler cow tied behind your lodge for such purposes."

Gray Wolf wasn't sure whether to be angry or laugh, but anger began to win out a little. "A warrior would not be so goddamn unmanly as to treat a woman soft," he sputtered.

"It takes a strong man to be tender to a woman."

"It ain't our way," Gray Wolf said simply. "Hell, a young warrior ain't even supposed to make advances on a woman. It's all right for a woman to sneak into my lodge, but it ain't right that I go to hers."

"Goddamn good Christ!" Tippett exploded. "Ain't ye learned yet what ye do in private has nothin' to do with what ye do in public?"

"What?" Gray Wolf asked, startled.

"Ye can be proper as all hell when there's pryin' eyes about. But goddamn, when ye're in your lodge..." He paused. "Ye ever had one of the girls come crawlin' into your lodge?"

"Yes." He tried to grin, but did not succeed.

"And ye treated her just like the goddamn captives, didn't ye?" When Gray Wolf nodded in shame, Tippett shook his head and said disgustedly, "Ye're as dumb as a goddamn tree. Ye get a willin' woman in your robes and all ye can think to do is jump on and jump off."

Gray Wolf's face burned with shame. "But..." He stopped, then said, "Do not all *tahbay-boh* treat women that way?"

"Hell, no," Tippett said, laughing again. "Just like I reckon all your warriors don't treat women so poorly as ye do."

"Will you teach me how...?" Gray Wolf stopped in embarrassment.

"No goddamn way, Gray Wolf," Tippett said with a snort of laughter. "But I'll *tell* ye. Next time it happens, take your time, and let her do some things. Ask what she likes, and what she wants."

"But she'll think I'm weak," Gray Wolf said, fear of the thought lancing deep into his insides.

"Like hell. Jist like with my people, she ain't gonna say nothin' outside that lodge. She does, it'll make her look worse'n ye. This way ye can both have your fun, and nobody'll be the wiser."

"You think so?" Gray Wolf asked hopefully. He might be a strong, vicious cutthroat, but in some matters, he was still a boy.

"Damn right," Tippett said as he finished reloading his trade rifle, "Why, I reckon more'n half the men in your village treat their women better in the robes than they let on." He rubbed his chin and realized he had not shaved in several days.

"Do you treat Painted Wing so?" Gray Wolf asked slyly.

"Hell, yes." Tippett said, still scratching absently at his stubbled face. "Keeps her plumb happy. She shines in the robes, boy. Goddamn. But I'll cut out your heart ye ever tell anyone I said so."

BOOK 4

GRAY WOLF, 1836

14

Gray Wolf needed horses. For months he had been watching the daughter of war chief Runs-At-The-Enemy. It could not be said that he loved Red Moon. But he had noticed that she was a good worker, adept at the many things required of the wife of a great warrior.

And, after speaking to Tippett, Gray Wolf had begun applying some of the things the white man had "taught" him. The first woman to approach his lodge after that informative session was Red Moon.

The attractive daughter of Runs-At-The-Enemy had done this before, and not only with Gray Wolf. She liked Gray Wolf best, though he was a poor lover. But she came to him again, hoping he might learn the secrets of treating a woman. As she crawled into Gray Wolf's sleeping robe, he awoke and moved to cover her, acting instinctively. But he caught himself and pulled back. She was shocked, thinking he was rejecting her. She started to leave, but he croaked, "Wait."

Red Moon stopped and settled back down, frightened and wondering. Gray Wolf was breathing heavily, trying to get his raging hormones under control. With difficulty, he managed.

"What would you like me to do for you?" he asked, voice cracking with nervousness and shame. It was so new to him to talk to a woman in such a way.

Red Moon was shocked and so said nothing for some moments.

Gray Wolf cursed silently, thinking himself a fool to have listened to the damned *tahbay-boh*. Now this woman, whom he wanted more than any other, thought him unmanly and would not want to share his robes this night, let alone become his wife.

"You really want to know?" she asked, voice quavering. Red Moon was fifteen, with small, firm breasts and well-rounded hips.

"Yes," he whispered.

Tentatively, she took one of his hands in her own. She placed it on her left breast and released it. Gray Wolf, not sure what to really do, rubbed his palm in small circles, feeling a surge of warmth in his crotch as Red Moon's nipple bloomed at his touch.

"Good," Red Moon whispered.

Gray Wolf rolled more toward his side and moved his hand to the other soft breast. Red Moon began to writhe mildly. With a little trepidation, Red Moon pulled on Gray Wolf's slightly resisting head until his lips were brushing her left nipple. The warrior caught on quickly. He tongued the ripening tip. He began to feel more at ease. *This was not such a bad thing*, he thought, as he switched hands and mouth on Red Moon's succulent breasts. After some minutes, he was rampant, and started to climb atop her. "Wait. Not yet," Red Moon whispered, afraid again that she would go beyond the limits.

Startled, he rolled back off her and onto his side again. "And so?" he asked, nervous and angry both.

"There is more we can do before..."

"But I am ready." He felt like he would burst.

"I'm not," Red Moon said almost firmly.

"Then what can I...?"

Once more she took his hand, but this time placed it lightly on her damp vagina. Under her direction, he began stroked the cleft and she helped him find the small pleasure button. Red Moon moaned and wriggled her hips as Gray Wolf stroked and rubbed her. He was quite pleased at the reaction. *I'm glad I listened to that* tahbay-boh *after all,* he thought as he increased the speed of his hand. Gasping, Red Moon pulled his head down to her breasts again. Gray Wolf grinned into the dark before touching his lips to the perked nipples, never slowing his hand.

Suddenly Red Moon screeched. Her back arched and her pelvis ground against Gray Wolf's hand. The warrior was taken aback, but he continued to stroke her, re-stoking the passions that rose in her as quickly as a small wash filling with water in a rainstorm.

Gray Wolf could wait no longer. He thought he would explode outside her. The pleasure when he sank his shaft in her was almost indescribable and within moments had built to a crescendo. He moaned, and Red Moon shrieked again, bucking and rocking under Gray Wolf.

Much later, when he could breathe again, Gray Wolf asked, "Will you become my wife, Red Moon?"

"Yes," the woman answered without hesitation. "But it must be done the right way."

"Yes."

So Gray Wolf needed horses. He had taken some, but not nearly enough to set himself up and still give Runs-At-The-Enemy some for his daughter. And he needed more war honors. He made his medicine and then called for warriors to follow him. But he was young and unproved as a leader, so there were few takers — mostly other young men seeking glory and riches in order to build up their standing or to get a bride.

Six of them set out, a small string of extra ponies trailing them. They rode southward in majesty, painted, unafraid, across the land until they came to an isolated Mexican ranch.

As dawn broke, the residents appeared outside to begin their chores. The Comanche warriors swooped down, shrieking fierce war cries. Three headed for the small horse herd, the other three for the hapless men and women. The Mexicans bolted, racing for the house. But they were not quick enough. Small, sturdy mustangs bore their riders down on them. The three warriors, resplendent in their streaks of paint, brandishing deadly lances and bows, surged around them.

Two of the three Mexican men and one of the two women went down immediately, the men pin-cushioned with arrows, the woman impaled to the ground by one of the feathered lances. A shot came from inside the house and then two more. But the warriors were unafraid. Gray Wolf had made powerful medicine for all of them, and they had made their own. Each had made sure he did not break any of the taboos that would negate that medicine so they would be safe from enemy bullets.

They swooped around the small adobe house, moving fast and continuously, not allowing anyone inside to have a clear shot. And they were joined by two of the other warriors who had left the stolen horses in the care of the sixth Comanche. Finally, the Comanches pulled back and set the deep grass on fire. They watched it race, fanned by the winds, toward the house. As the flames licked at the edges of the mud house, smoke seeped inside.

Two men burst from the house, frantically trying to beat the flames out. The Comanches raced in under the smoky cover. The two men were soon riddled with arrows, though one yet lived. In glee, the warriors swarmed off their horses and onto the two men. Both were scalped, the one still alive screaming with the pain. Whooping with their pleasure, the warriors, in full view of those remaining in the house, stripped the men naked and mutilated them horribly, the one man's screams of agony slowly fading away.

The Comanches danced, oblivious to the scattered shots from the house. They taunted those left in the house and remounted, waiting as the prairie fire surrounded the house and baked it.

Finally, the ranchers could stand it no more. The door popped open and they fled outside, screaming with fear: one man, four women, and six children, one a babe in arms.

The Comanches charged down on them. The man died at the point of a lance, as did two women. The other two women were grabbed by the hair and dragged onto Comanche ponies. Three children — two girls and a boy, all about seven or eight years old — also were taken, as was the infant. The others were slain.

Once again, the Comanches triumphantly crowed over their victims, living and dead. They chuckled with glee as they watched the first woman they had lanced squirm feebly against the lance that pinned her to the dusty, grass-covered ground. Laughing, two warriors tore the lance from her flesh and then ripped her clothes off. While the others cheered, they violated her brutally and cut off her scalp. Shouting, they rode off, leaving her to die in the hot sun.

They rode eastward hard and fast, pushing the horses ahead of them. Covering more than a hundred miles before they stopped, they felt they were far beyond pursuit — should anyone attempt any.

The captives were abused terribly, the two women ravished time and again. Gray Wolf gleefully took part. While making love to a woman he cared for might be fun, so was the brutal penetration of a petrified, vulnerable captive. There was something quite exhilarating in scaring the piss, literally, out of a blubbering prisoner.

The captive children — all except the baby — were beaten frequently. It was, the Comanches figured, a good way to teach them who their new masters were. Unless they caused too much trouble on the trail, all would be adopted and, if they proved themselves, could even become full members of the band, as could the women, if they did not go crazy from their treatment.

All the captives were still alive when Gray Wolf led his victorious war party back into their village. The eight adult scalps they had taken fluttered from their war lances and the young men rode with straight backs and proud faces.

Gray Wolf's honors were many. Since he had led the war party, he was credited with its success. In addition to the scalps and prisoners taken, each man had counted coup several times, and they had brought home much plunder and twenty-two ponies. As the leader, Gray Wolf was entitled to keep the lion's share of the loot, but he magnanimously gave away most of the plunder, keeping only the horses.

That night several women snuck into his lodge, but he rejected them all — except for Red Moon.

Gray Wolf made two more raids that summer, one against the Apaches, and the second against another isolated Mexican ranch, far to the southeast, not far from the big town the Mexicans called San Antonio. In each he was successful, bringing back between the two raids several dozen scalps, a number of captives, and plenty of booty. But more important, he returned with more than two hundred horses.

After the third raid, he had sixty horses. He picked out a dozen of the best and took them to Runs-At-The-Enemy's lodge. He tied them to a pole and stepped back to wait.

Red Moon hesitated only long enough to make it look proper before she stepped out of the lodge, untied the horses, and led them to graze with the rest of her father's herd.

15

It was still brutally hot on the *Llano Estacado,* but the Comanches felt the coming fall in the air. Preparations for the buffalo hunt to make meat for the winter would be made within the next moon. Still, Gray Wolf figured there was time for one last raid before the hunt, and then winter. When he called for warriors this time, he sent word to some of the other bands of *Kwahadis*.

Warriors began drifting toward Gray Wolf's village, ready to ride behind this brash young man with the powerful medicine.

On a brightly moonlit night, Gray Wolf rode out leading almost one hundred warriors, all painted and armed for war. They rode boldly through the desolate countryside. Not long ago there had been several ranches here in western *Comancheria,* but there were fewer now. The Mexicans had pulled back more and more under the frightening raids of the Comanches. Other white-eyes had not dared to venture in. The Comanches virtually had this country to themselves once again.

Little did the Comanches know that off to the east, only a few months ago, a new breed of white man, far different than the Mexicans, had fought and died to win their independence from Mexico. Before too many more years passed, those reckless, fearless men who had won their freedom at San Jacinto would be pouring into most of *Comancheria*, except perhaps the *Llano*. But that was yet to come. So Gray Wolf rode proudly, his paint, buffalo horn headdress, and hard face giving him a ferocious look. His warriors rode arrogantly behind him. Then came the women and children who chatted excitedly.

They splashed fearlessly across the wide, shallow Rio Grande. Two days later, they began attacking farms and ranches, striking fast and hard. While some would drive off whatever horses were to be found, others would count coup, killing anyone they did not think would make a good captive; they destroyed crops and burned houses. As they did, their women and children would sit on a convenient ridge or even on the plain to watch and cheer at the carnage wrought by their men.

Then they would be off, heading for the next victims, leaving in their wake a trail of ravished women, mutilated men, and dead children. Before any alarm could be raised from one place, they would be in another. For nearly a month they kept the countryside in terror. Sated, they finally rode northward to their homes. Hundreds of captured horses fanned out to all sides, shaking the ground with their hooves, driven by boys almost ready to go on the hunt.

The victory celebrations lasted almost as long as the campaign into Mexico. And only one warrior had been killed, and one wounded.

Gray Wolf found himself considered among the greatest war leaders the *Kwahadi* — indeed, the *Nermernuh* — had ever had. His medicine was very strong, seemingly unbreakable. Adding to his mystique was the birth of his son, Horse Tail, to Red Moon on the journey home.

Soon after their return, with the days chilly and the nights downright cold, the men of Gray Wolf's band sat in council to determine the fall hunt.

"It is late," Walking Bear said. "The buffalo are fat, and we shouldn't delay. Soon snow will cover the plains. We must hunt now."

There was no disagreement. "Who shall we send to find the site for our hunting camp?" Gray Wolf asked.

"You have someone in mind?" Walking Bear asked.

"My brother, Hits-With-A-Fist. And perhaps Buffalo Droppings."

Several evenings later, the Hunting Dance was held. And the next morning, all those who were able left, taking only the tools needed for hunting and butchering, and many horses to transport the meat and robes. Only the old, infirm, and small children remained in the village.

As the procession reached the spot chosen by Hits-With-A-Fist and Buffalo Droppings, the warriors nodded in satisfaction. A stream ran nearby, providing water. Small cottonwoods lined the stream's banks and mesquite trees were scattered across the prairie. There would be enough wood for their needs and grass was plentiful. And, though they could not see the herd, they could hear the snuffling of buffalo.

"You did well, brother," Gray Wolf told Hits-With-A-Fist. "A good choice. And you did well in making racks to dry our meat."

Hits-With-A-Fist's dark eyes gleamed with pleasure and excitement. "Can I join the hunt this year, brother?" he asked, trepidation clouding his voice.

"I will think on it," Gray Wolf said solemnly.

The women hurriedly set up their lodges and started fires. A cold wind in the air and thick clouds had darkened the afternoon skies. That evening, as rain drummed on Walking Bear's hide tipi and thunder boomed, Gray Wolf said to his chief, "Hits-With-A-Fist asks to join the hunt. I'd like him to."

"How many summers is he?" Walking Bear asked, digging a piece of antelope meat from the bowl of stew.

"Fourteen."

Walking Bear grinned lopsidedly. "A little older than I was. And you, too, eh? I think it will be good. He has chosen well here." He shrugged. "I see no trouble."

It rained for two more days, and frost tinged the grass in the mornings. The evening of the second day, the clouds fled. The warriors decided the hunt would take place the next morning.

The men were ready before dawn. All were stripped to breechcloth and moccasins. They sat astride well-trained buffalo ponies, lances or bows in hand. Excitement ran through the camp like the aftereffects of a lightning bolt. They moved out silently. Even the most rambunctious and rowdy warriors were soundless, mindful of the importance of the work ahead. The hunters came up on the downwind side of the buffalo, spreading out until they made an arc around the herd, leaving only the windward side open.

Walking Bear, the most respected warrior in the village, gave the signal. The warriors, almost all riding bareback, burst toward the herd, shouting. The buffalo stood blankly for a few moments before lumbering forward. But each way they went, there were screaming, yelling demons. Soon the buffalo were running in a circle, bulls on the outside, cows and calves in the center.

Gray Wolf angled toward a huge old bull whose neck hide would make a fine shield. Gray Wolf raced in, he and his pony like one. When his left knee was only inches from the bull's thick coat, Gray Wolf brought his lance up in both hands and thrust it forward. He might have fallen off the horse had his knees not been hooked into a rope coiled around the pony's body just behind the forelegs.

The spear plunged through muscle and fat, glancing off a bone as it ripped toward the buffalo's kidneys. The animal bellowed and put on a surge of speed. With a shake of his monstrous head, the bull tried to gore Gray Wolf's horse. But the pony skipped out of the way as Gray Wolf used the lance almost as a lever to shove the buffalo away. The bull, feeling the piercing pain of the lance point in his innards, snapped his head forward and ran on, yanking the lance out of Gray Wolf's hand. In a few seconds, the bull collapsed.

Gray Wolf whooped. He urged the horse toward a fat cow. As the horse closed in on the buffalo, Gray Wolf snatched his bow from across his shoulders and grabbed half a dozen arrows.

The horse pounded alongside the cow and Gray Wolf shot an arrow. The shaft sank into the buffalo's side until it disappeared. At the sound of the bow's twang, Gray Wolf's pony swerved out of the way, and angled at full speed toward another buffalo. Gray Wolf glanced behind and saw the cow stumble, and he nodded.

The killing was over in less than an hour, leaving carcasses all over. The women and children hustled out and attacked the buffalo with knives and tomahawks. The men, still flushed with excitement, joined the butchering. Meat, hides, bones, hooves — everything was usable and so was taken.

16

Winter spread over the *Llano Estacado* like an ill-fitting, soggy set of buckskins — uncomfortable, damp, cold, and rough. But the Comanches had plenty of dried buffalo meat made into jerky and fat-rich pemmican. And they knew where fuel for their fires could be found in the mostly treeless *Llano*.

Gray Wolf and Red Moon settled into their comfortable buffalo-hide lodge to set about raising Horse Tail. When outside the lodge, Gray Wolf would have little to do with Horse Tail, leaving the baby in Red Moon's care. But inside, he was an attentive and loving father, a far cry from the vicious, humorless, bloodthirsty warrior. He enjoyed having Horse Tail around the lodge and would play with the infant for hours, sometimes to Red Moon's annoyance, since Gray Wolf and the baby got underfoot, making her work harder.

Beyond raising the child, Gray Wolf's life during the winter months was a time of leisure. Only rarely did someone call for a war party, so the warriors had much time to themselves. Gray Wolf, like most of the other warriors, used the days to make arrows, repair weapons, or recuperate from wounds. Much of the day was spent sleeping and eating. And warriors would visit, regaling each other with stories of their prowess and swapping tales. There were the evenings of dancing and singing. Such things were held for social reasons mostly, allowing the women, as well as the men, to visit friends.

Both sexes also took part in gambling, often betting wildly. The Comanche, like most other Indians, loved to gamble and would carry on such pursuits for hours, sometimes days at a time.

One day, when the winter had eased its icy bite briefly, another band of Comanches camped nearby. Several men and their wives came into the village for sport and talk. Gray Wolf waited before joining in since he held little respect for some of the other band's warriors.

Finally, though, he and Red Moon went to Walking Bear's lodge where a game of hand was ending. A warrior from the visiting band — Black Cloud — had won nearly every game amassing a large pile of winnings. He was still of a mood to play but could find no one willing.

"How about you?" Black Cloud demanded of Gray Wolf with a sneer. "Will you test Black Cloud's medicine?"

Gray Wolf gazed levelly at the warrior for some moments before offering a grunted, "Yes." He sat across from Black Cloud as Red Moon went to gamble with other women playing their own game — one involving half a dozen plum stones used like dice, and a small basket.

A dozen or so men from both bands crowded around, eyes glittering with excitement. Gray Wolf, stony faced, lay down his first wager: a necklace made of grizzly bear teeth. Black Cloud nodded and wagered a beaver sleeping robe. Black Cloud took the pebble in hand. He made fists of both hands and moved them behind his back. Seconds later he brought both out in front, fists closed tightly.

Gray Wolf stared at Black Cloud's eyes for some moments before turning his hard gaze to the tightly clenched fists. "There," Gray Wolf grunted, pointing to Black Cloud's left fist.

With a grimace, Black Cloud opened his left fist revealing the pebble in the fleshy folds of skin. He handed over the sleeping robe, then asked. "Again?"

"Yes," Gray Wolf said, humor improving slightly. He tossed the robe behind him, leaving the necklace as his wager. Black Cloud brought forth a knife taken from a *tahbay-boh* caught in *Comancheria.*

Gray Wolf won that game and each after that. He lost only once as the night progressed. His attitude improved with each victory as Black Cloud's soured. But Black Cloud played on, hoping his medicine would return. The crowd cheered Gray Wolf since Black Cloud had gloated when he had won from them. Now it was their turn to rub it in.

Finally, Black Cloud had lost everything — his lodge, robes, all his seventy-five horses, his stores of jerky and pemmican — all but the clothing he wore, a blanket, his bow, quiver of arrows, and lance.

"Once more," Black Cloud pleaded, desperation in eyes and voice.

"You have nothing more to wager," Gray Wolf said in disgust. He was appalled at Black Cloud's lack of control.

"I will bet Running Deer, my wife," Black Cloud said in a strangled voice.

There was a murmur of excitement from the others. And for the first time, Gray Wolf realized there were many more people in the lodge than there had been some hours earlier.

"No," Gray Wolf said flatly.

"Are you afraid?" Black Cloud sneered, regaining some haughtiness.

"Bah, you have lost everything," Gray Wolf spit. "Keep your wife. Maybe she will keep you warm since you have no lodge or food."

"She won't want me when I have nothing," Black Cloud snapped, anger flashing in his eyes. "She'll be a good wife. You're young and," he added with a touch of condescension, "a mighty warrior, I've heard. You should have a second wife."

"I'll choose my own second wife," Gray Wolf said, his voice as cold as the cloudless winter night outside.

"She is a good wife," he said. "Running Deer," Black Cloud commanded.

A young woman stepped forward from the rear of the lodge. She was, Gray Wolf noted with appreciation, quite beautiful. She looked sturdy and strong. She was angry, too, Gray Wolf saw, probably at her husband's foolishness. But she smiled sweetly at Gray Wolf.

Gray Wolf glanced at Red Moon who kept her face averted. The warrior knew his wife was not pleased with these events, but also understood that if Gray Wolf could afford a second wife, which he could, he would have one. And it would make her own life a little easier to have someone with whom to split the many tasks — preparing jerky and pemmican, making clothes, butchering, making utensils, and tanning hides.

A fragile, barely recognizable grin flickered across Gray Wolf's lips. "I'll take your wager, Black Cloud," he said good-naturedly.

Black Cloud scowled. "Then play," he snapped.

Gray Wolf, who had had the pebble for several rounds now, enclosed the small object in a calloused fist. He went through the ritual of switching the pebble from hand to hand behind his back before bringing the closed fists out in front.

Black Cloud licked his lips as his hooded eyes flickered from Gray Wolf's eyes to his hands and back. Finally, he reached out a finger and lightly touched the middle knuckle on Gray Wolf's clenched right hand. With a bored look, never taking his eyes from Black Cloud's face, Gray Wolf turned the fist upward and opened it to reveal an empty palm.

Black Cloud muttered darkly and stood, sweeping in a rage past the jeering onlookers and out into the cold, star-speckled night.

Gray Wolf stoically accepted the congratulations of the others before walking out with Red Moon who had Horse Tail in the cradleboard on her back. Running Deer followed, filled with fear and worry. She had nothing but the garments she wore. Still, tomorrow they would go to get her lodge and belongings.

Black Cloud was nowhere to be found the next day when Gray Wolf, two younger brothers, and Running Deer went to the other camp to take his winnings. Running Deer pointed at a lodge, embarrassed.

"You are a poor wife to keep such a lodge," Gray Wolf sneered.

Running Deer hung her head, whispering, "Black Cloud is a poor hunter. He never took enough buffalo to keep the lodge in good repair."

"I should have known," Gray Wolf grumbled.

They stopped in front of the shabby tipi. "Leave it," Gray Wolf ordered, "unless you need the skins for a travois."

"I'll do without," Running Deer said, hope blooming.

Gray Wolf nodded. "Get what you want. I'll see to my new horses." He grinned. In one sitting he had nearly tripled the size of his horse herd. He was one of the richest men in his village.

With his two younger brothers, he went to find his new ponies. Cutting out two, he told a boy to bring them to Running Deer to be used for travois. By the time he was finished culling out the other horses that had belonged to Black Cloud, Running Deer was finished. She had two travois laden with robes, blankets, parfleches of jerky and pemmican, cooking utensils, and some personal items.

BOOK 5

ZEKE TIPPETT, 1837

17

Zeke Tippett rode into the Comanche village followed by Painted Wing, four-year-old White Buffalo, and two pack mules. Tippett was in an ornery mood, for when he had stopped at Bent's Fort to trade in his plews, he had found that the price of furs had dropped even more. All he could get this year was a little better than three dollars a pound from Bill Bent and his new chief trader, Alexander Barclay.

"It ain't hardly worth my time and trouble, Bill," Tippett groused.

"Not much I can do, *amigo*."

"What do ye see for the price of plews next year, Bill?" Tippett asked unhappily, downing the mug of beer Bent had given him.

"Droppin' more," Bent said, more than a little ruefully. He had been in this business a long time and hated to see it fall apart. The fort was doing well, but the emphasis in trading had shifted to buffalo hides rather than beaver pelts. Bent, and his partners would make out. But men like Tippett would be hurt if they did not change. Bent liked Tippett, despite the mountain man's closeness to the Comanches, and would be sad if his friend was hurt. But he had his own business to look out for and could not feel much sympathy for others.

"I'd advise you to find yourself a new line of work, Zeke," Bent added. "I can always use men here — traders, hunters, whatever. I could find somethin' worthwhile for you to do."

"I'll think on it," Tippett said sourly. "I ain't much given to settin' in one spot for too long a spell." He took his two thousand dollars, minus the eleven hundred to outfit himself for the next season and stuck the remainder in his possible bag.

"You gonna hang around for the celebrations?" Bent asked.

"Reckon not, Bill. I want to get on down to the village." He smiled ruefully to try to ease some of the anger. "Painted Wing's been hankerin' to see her people again."

Tippett did not even want to spend the night. He was angry — not at Bent, really, just at life. How could such a thing happen? Three years ago, beaver pulled in six dollars a pound, sometimes a bit more. Now it was down to three, and he knew it would not go up again. It was worrisome and he wanted to be off on his own to mull it over.

So, he mounted the big black gelding he had gotten the summer before in Taos. Painted Wing stepped up onto her pinto after settling her fiery toddler on his own pony. They rode out, Tippett silent and worried.

Tippett was in better humor the day after arriving at the village when a welcoming feast started. Food flowed, drums pounded, and singing resounded. He swapped tales that evening in a large lodge with the other warriors. It was stifling in the tipi despite having the sides rolled up to bring in the almost nonexistent breeze.

Gray Wolf, who sat arrogantly Tippett thought, told of winning everything from Black Cloud, including Running Deer.

Tippett sat back and took a long sip of whiskey letting the talk work around the circle of warriors. He shook his head, thinking of how little he knew and understood of the Comanches' ways and customs. There was so much he did not know yet, despite having been visiting them — and living with Painted Wing — for more than five years. He shrugged it off. Perhaps he would never understand.

He spit out the last of his tobacco as Blue Star — Gray Wolf's thirteen-year-old sister — came along with a bowl of hot, savory stew, made of pemmican and fresh antelope Tippett had brought in yesterday. He nodded thanks and began spooning in the meal using the carved horn spoon he carried in his possible sack.

Blue Star moved on, filling another bowl to give to Runs-At-The-Enemy who sat next to Walking Bear, who sat next to Tippett. As she straightened from giving Runs-At-The-Enemy his bowl, she lost her balance. To catch herself, Blue Star thrust out a hand. It landed on Gray Wolf's left shoulder. The hand slid off the shoulder and skidded down the chest before landing on Gray Wolf's upper thigh.

Silence came immediately and Tippett saw the look of terror on Blue Star's face as she managed to right herself. Gray Wolf looked from one warrior to the next. All sat with looks of frozen disgust, their eyes hard and jaws tight.

Tippett started to ask what was wrong but snapped his mouth shut before any words came. He had been in this camp too many times to ask foolish questions that would do nothing more than to anger his hosts further. He would find out in due time what the problem was.

The girl stood just behind Gray Wolf, terror stark in her eyes. Suddenly Gray Wolf was on his feet with the quickness of a cat, his knife flashing momentarily in the glimmer of the fire. It was over before Tippett could move. The metal blade buried itself three times in Blue Star's breast.

She whimpered only a little, the fear in her eyes fading into sorrow and then into the blankness of death. She fell weakly onto Walking Bear. But the hard, young warrior sat stonily, his face a mask of anger, loathing, and sadness, as the girl slumped to the ground.

Without a word, Gray Wolf dropped the knife and stalked out of the tipi into the chill wind, his head held high.

Tippett breathed deeply trying to settle himself. It took several minutes. When he did, he relaxed, taking his hand off the horn-handled Bowie knife at the small of his back. The ache to charge after Gray Wolf and kill him was strong. But he knew he would die in the trying. He did not know why the Comanche had turned on his sister like a rabid animal and he could not bring himself to ask. Not now.

Already he could hear the mourning wail of Burning Grass, the woman who had borne both Gray Wolf and Blue Star. It was an agonizing ululation of grief, stark in its loneliness.

He spit the sour taste from his mouth and watched the spittle ooze, sizzling, down a crackling piece of wood. He shoved himself up, knowing the others watched him with curiosity. Angrily he strode to his lodge. Storming inside, he said sharply to Painted Wing, "Get our things together. We're leavin' out."

She started to question him but was stopped by his fury. Tippett's fists clenched and unclenched as he fought his boiling rage. Finally, he hissed, "Jist have our things ready by the time I get back with the horses or I'll leave ye here with these savages."

He stomped out and headed for his horses. He was back in fifteen minutes. Painted Wing was not ready, but he had to saddle three horses. By the time he had done so, Painted Wing was ready. Tippett did not know then nor did he ever find out — why she had not just thrown his things outside the lodge, divorcing him. But she hadn't.

Without a word, she helped him pack their two mules. She tossed White Buffalo into his saddle, making sure he was bundled up well in a blanket against the cold. Then she mounted and rode out behind her man, following him as she had done since they were married.

18

"You know what happened to Blue Star?" Tippett asked quietly.

He had not spoken to Painted Wing for two days except to issue infrequent, terse orders. Mostly he would just stop and dismount in the afternoon and she would know that this was where they would camp. Most other orders he could give would be useless and so were avoided.

On the third night out, he could hold back no longer. He had finished eating and was puffing on his pipe when he asked the question.

Painted Wing nodded, still a little afraid to speak.

"Then why'd he do it, dammit? Why would Gray Wolf go and put under a young girl like that? His sister, no less!"

"Because he had to," Painted Wing answered quietly in Comanche.

"What the hell do ye mean, had to?" Tippett demanded in English. "She weren't hurtin' no one. She was a little girl, for chris sakes." The more he thought of it, the angrier he became.

"Because she touched him."

"What?" Tippett exploded in rage. "All she did was try'n break her fall." The words came out in staccato bursts of rage.

"She was his sister, goddammit."

"What the hell's that got to do with it? So, his sister went and touched him. It ain't nothin' to want to raise hair over."

Trying to get the idea across in Comanche to a white man with a far from perfect grasp of her language was difficult. Her command of English was good, but not developed enough to explain something like this easily. But Painted Wing tried time and again, using parts of English, Comanche, Spanish, and even signs.

Tippett grew exasperated, overriding the anger some. He fought, and managed, to control his temper. He kept questioning and prying, guessing, and wondering. Slowly it began to grow on him what Painted Wing was saying. Finally, he asked, "You mean brothers and sisters ain't ever supposed to touch each other?"

"It is our way," Painted Wing said in Comanche, relieved at having finally gotten Tippett to understand. "Once boys reach the time of becoming men," she added without embarrassment, "or the girls are ready to become women, they cannot be near each other. It is why the young men who are almost ready for the war trail get their own lodges. It keeps them from their sisters in their parents' lodge."

"That's one of the dumbest goddamn things I ever heard," Tippett snorted, thinking again that these people must be *loco*.

"Then the *tahbay-boh* let brothers and sisters do that which married men and women do?" Painted Wing asked in Comanche.

"'Course not. It ain't right. Goes against God's ways, and such."

"And so it is with the *Nermernuh*."

"But to kill her just for touchin' him? Christ, woman! That ain't right. She jist lost her step is all and reached out for support."

Painted Wing tried to make him understand that since their band, and all Comanche bands were so small, and that people usually married within the band, that not even the slightest hint of incest was to be tolerated. To do so could sentence the entire band to death. The Comanche roamed too far and wide from each other to allow much intermingling between various factions of the same larger band, and even less between the different larger bands. It was their survival.

But Tippett still could not understand it, and he withdrew into scowling silence. It would take time before he would be able to see that Gray Wolf was not a heartless savage who relished killing so much that he thought nothing of slaughtering his younger sister. Tippett would learn, eventually, that Gray Wolf was duty-bound, custom-bound, to do what he did. So it had been for a thousand years, and so it would be for the next thousand as far as the Comanches could see.

Still, at the moment, Zeke Tippett was at odds with any and all Comanches, including Painted Wing. Making it worse were the tales he had listened to in the village. Tippett had heard the litany of death and destruction with a deep-seated loathing. He had seen it all before with other tribes. But somehow this was different. He had no great love for Mexicans, but neither did he hate them. They had been kind enough to him in Taos and he had ridden with several of them in the mountains and got along well.

He knew in his head, if not his heart, that to the Comanche male, war was life. It was all the Comanche warrior lived for. They had done so since time began. The Comanches had always fought anyone who was an outsider. They seemed to get along only with the Kiowas. Despite this knowledge, the gory recital sickened him. Tippett had killed his share of men. But it had always been a necessity. He had taken scalps, too, as did most of the other white frontiersmen. But rape and mutilation, as well as war for war's sake were beyond him.

He tried to put the thoughts from his mind, but they continued to plague him. They even ruined his stay in Taos. He rode out with his wife and son in tow after only a week, heading back to the *Llano*. At the village, he was received coldly, but he ignored it.

The following morning, as he ate slowly, not really tasting the food, he said to Painted Wing, "I aim to head back to Taos."

"When?"

"Soon's I finish this," he said, holding up the meat.

"I'll be ready."

There was a sour feeling deep in his belly. The sight of Blue Star's fading life, the thought of falling plew prices, all the bloody talk he had endured had gotten to him. He could not stand being in this village another minute. But he was even more loath to do this.

"Ye ain't goin'."

Fear planted itself on Painted Wing's face.

"Don't go lookin' at me that way," Tippett said, angry at himself for acting this way. "I'll be back for ye. I jist got to get away from here a spell is all. Ye got plenty of meat, and your visit last time was short. Ye jist enjoy your visit and showin' off White Buffalo."

"You'll be back?" Painted Wing asked with a fright-drenched voice. She would have no trouble getting another husband, but she did not want one. She wanted this tall, strong, blue-eyed, *tahbay-boh.*

"Soon's I can," Tippett said. The words came out easily, despite the lack of conviction behind them. An hour later he was riding westward across the broken, deadly *Llano Estacado*. He liked Taos and looked forward to going back again. The dirty, brown, raucous town, with its full, hearty life usually was good for him.

CHARLES BENT GREETED HIM WARMLY, AS DID THE OTHER MOUNTAIN men lounging around town. None questioned his short stay there just a few weeks ago or his arrival again. For that, Tippett was thankful.

He found a room and gussied himself up in cream-colored buckskins decorated with bits of silver and plenty of beads. He slicked his hair back with bear grease and scraped the stubble off his face with his Bowie. Then he went prowling. He spent time in several *cantinas,* imbibing the locally distilled Taos Lightning, letting the sights, sounds, and sensations wash over him. The tensions ebbed. In the plaza, he struck up a conversation with a beautiful, young, cigarillo-smoking *señorita.* As they parted, she promised him at least one dance at the *baille* that night. For the first time in several weeks, Tippett smiled.

19

Tippett rode through the heavy double doors of Bent's Fort. He had spent a week in Taos before the urge to move on had gripped him. Much of his time there was spent with Maria Santiago y Gonzalez, but that had quickly paled. Her father owned a large hacienda outside town with plenty of cattle. He would want someone of higher breeding, or at least standing, than Tippett, and the mountain man wanted no truck with such foolishness anyway.

So, he rode out, pack mule in tow, heading northeast up the mountain through a great forest of pines, cottonwoods, and aspens, past Wheeler Peak and down through Cimarron Canyon. He turned north and worked through Raton Pass. Then he turned northeast again, picking up the Puragtoire River, and then winding through *Piñon* Canyon. Not far beyond that, he headed almost due north, across the flat, grassy plain leading to the Arkansas. Bent's Fort was across the wide river.

As he rode in past the high adobe walls, Cass Calder greeted him. Tippett's spirits lifted considerably. He whooped at his friend as he dismounted and tied off his horse.

"Whar's that Comanch' you usually drag about? Ye give her up?"

Tippett grew serious. "Not yet. But I've thought hard on it."

"Well, shit, let's have us a snort. I'll even buy. I got a few *pesos* left. Ye can talk about it, if ye're of a mind to. Or not, as ye'd like."

"Thankee, Cass. I reckon I could use somethin' to cut the dry in my throat. Don't know, though, as I feel much like jawin'."

Calder unloaded Tippett's pack mule while Tippett unsaddled his horse. While they worked, Bent strolled up. "How do, Zeke," he said pleasantly. He looked around, surprised. "Where's Painted Wing?"

"At the village," Tippett said sourly.

Bent nodded, knowing better than to pry. He drifted off. He would learn about it sooner or later anyway.

Tippett and Calder led the animals to the corral. They headed up to the billiards room/bar. After his eyes adjusted to the dimness, Tippett said harshly, "You never said Trent was here."

"No reason to."

"Hell, ye know goddamn well I don't take a shine to that Injin-baitin' son of a bitch."

Calder shrugged and paid for two jugs at the bar. Then he and Tippett headed outside. Plopping down near a small fire in the courtyard, they each uncorked a jug, saluted each other, and poured some of the badly distilled, flavored-with-God-knows-what liquor down their throats.

Setting the jug down in the dust at his feet with a great sigh, Calder asked, "Now jist what'n hell's got so stuck in your craw, boy?"

Tippett ignored him, staring across the compound.

"Suit yourself," Calder said without rancor. They sat silently, sipping, enjoying the afternoon sunshine and its warmth. Tippett finally lighted his small pipe and Calder soon followed suit.

In fits and starts, Tippett told Calder about Gray Wolf and Blue Star, the first he had spoken of it since Painted Wing explained it.

When Tippett finished, Calder said in exasperation, "What's the big deal in such doin's, boy? It's done. Hell, ye cain't go around your whole life carryin' such plunder around with ye."

"That ain't easy, Cass."

"Well, goddammit, I know that. But ..." Calder paused, then asked, "Gray Wolf ever tell ye why he done it?"

"Ain't seen him since. But Painted Wing explained it. From what she says, even an innocent touch like that is bad medicine. The worst."

"Mebbe they ain't so wrong," Calder said softly.

Tippett's look was venomous and he fought to keep his temper in check. "I expect not," he said, letting some anger surface. "But that ain't the whole of it neither." He explained his misgivings at listening to the atrocities the Comanches described in such detail.

"Hell, Zeke," Calder roared, "what do ye expect of Injins? War's their way."

"But this weren't the same somehow."

"Shit," Calder snorted. "It's all right for Comanches to kill other Injins, but it ain't right for 'em to go killin' Greasers? That how ye figger it?" His voice was hard, though his face was not. He was not really angry at his friend, just wanted to shock Tippett into coming to his senses.

"Maybe, Cass," Tippett said, his voice sounding far off.

"Mebbe, hell. You've seen what them goddamn Greasers do to an Injin village when they get the chance," Calder said, ignoring the Mexican laborers around them. He paused for another sip from the jug before plunging on. "'Sides, who was it put a bounty on Injin scalps in the first place? It was the Spanish, as ye well know. And whilst them Mexicans might say they ain't the same as the Spaniards, we know different. You've seen those bean-eaters sellin' Injin hair down in Taos. And ye know goddamn well the Greasers don't give a good goddamn if it's a scalp off'n buck, a squaw, or a squallin' brat. Long's it's Injin — or pass for Injin — hair, they'll pay good *pesos* for it."

"It still don't seem right somehow, Cass."

"What don't?" William Bent asked. Both mountain men turned to see Bent standing just behind them. "Mind if I join you?" he asked. When Tippett said nothing, Bent stepped around and just to the side of the fire in front of Tippett and Calder. He squatted, not wanting to wreck his fancy coat and trousers. He grabbed Calder's jug and took a swig. He set the jug in the dust and asked, "What don't seem right, Zeke?"

Tippett still sat tight-lipped, so Calder explained it fast.

"Well, now," Bent said slowly. Over Tippett's shoulder he could see Elmore Trent sitting on the wood walkway, his back against an adobe wall. "Maybe it don't seem right. Then, again, you ain't an Injun. Still, you got an Indian wife and a child. And you been with the Comanches long enough to know some of their ways."

"I've never seen 'em in such lights before, Bill," Tippett said, finally breaking his silence.

"All Indians make war, Zeke, you know that. Hell, up north, where it's colder'n Satan's ass half the time, they make war plenty. You've gone against the Blackfoot, the Rees, and others. They ain't no worse, or better, than the Comanches. Even the Cheyennes, as close as I am to 'em, can be savages when on the war path."

"Still don't make none of it right," Tippett groused.

"By whose lights? Yours? Or theirs? Look, a Comanche, more than any other Indian maybe, lives for war. It's his whole life. A young buck can't have no say in councils, can't get a wife, can't do shit less'n he's been blooded on the war trail. Look at the way they treat their old folks. Give 'em no respect at all. They ain't like the Cheyennes or the Kiowas who give their old warriors a place of honor. To them, an old warrior's useless. If he can't take the war trail, they got no use for him. It's why they all aim to die young."

"Bunch of savages is all they are," Tippett said acidly, pouring a good dose of whiskey down his gullet.

"They might be," Bent said after another sip. "But the Comanches hold sway over a heap of land. They control damn near everything from the Rio Grande to the Arkansas, from Taos to the

Gulf water. They got more horses than the Cheyenne, Arapaho, and Kiowa together."

"Well, I reckon for this once Zeke's right," Trent spat. Tippett and Calder spun to look at him. "Ain't any Injuns worth shit. The warriors're all afraid to fight less'n they got five to every one of the enemy. Even then they ain't likely to stand. And their women're nothin' but goddamn trollops who'll spread their legs for anyone's got one of these," he slid up the wall grabbing at his crotch.

Tippett was on him like a flash, the blade of his Bowie glinting in the dying sunlight. He cuffed Trent twice with his free hand, then grabbed a shank of shirt in his fist. The knife hovered a hair's breadth from Trent's throat.

"Ye've set yourself agin me before, ye shit-stinkin' bastard, and I warned ye not to do it agin. But out of the kindness of my heart, I'll give ye one more chance. I don't ever want to see ye again. First time I see ye — it don't matter where it is — I'll have your hair stretched and danglin' from my Hawken." Tippett slid the knife away and grabbed Trent with both hands. He pulled him forward, then slammed him back against the adobe wall. "Now get out of my sight."

Trent scuttled toward the corral and rounded up his animals. With haste born of fear, he took his miserly belongings from his rooms above and loaded them. In less than half an hour, he trotted out.

"He'll not let it rest, Zeke," Calder said softly.

"Shit, am I supposed to tremble over that pissant festerin' sore?"

"Nope," Calder said cheerily. "Jist watch your back."

Tippett took a drink, watching the sun setting through the entryway to the corral. He sighed and rubbed a hand over his face. "I been an ass, ain't I?" he said.

"Sure have," Calder answered agreeably.

Bent said nothing.

"I expect you're both right," Tippett said quietly. "But, hell, it jist don't set well with this chil' at all. But I aim to try'n see that all this buffalo shit don't stick in my craw no more."

"Ye goin' back after Painted Wing?" Calder asked, grinning.

"I expect." Tippett tried to sound hard, but the smile gave him away. "Damn, I miss her somethin' awful," he allowed.

They both laughed in the gathering dusk.

20

It was the worst season Tippett ever had. The plews were few and their quality poor. They would bring in little even if prices were high. Tippett despaired of even making back his stake this season.

Calder grumbled and complained in their winter camp with a band of Shoshonis near the Wind River. Calder had been living with a Flathead woman for two years and he had hoped to winter with those Indians, but he and Tippett had gotten off to a late start.

After their talk at Bent's Fort, Tippett had headed out the next morning in a big hurry for the Comanche village. He had gotten Painted Wing who was much relieved to see him, though she did not let on until that night when they were in their robes.

They packed and moved out hurriedly, young White Buffalo stoic, and made good time back to Bent's. The next morning, they rode out: Calder first, followed by his son, Charger, and his woman, Shining Beads, with four pack mules clumping behind her. Calder had never taken the Comanche woman, Yellow Bird, out of her village that time he had "married" her when he and Tippett visited. Then came White Buffalo, Painted Wing, with Tippett's four pack mules strung out behind her, and finally, Tippett.

They trapped through the San Juans and into Bayou Salado and the two other "parks." But those well-frequented spots had been trapped out years before. Both men knew that but had hoped others had left it alone long enough for it to become repopulated.

But it was not so. Tippett and Calder found only two dozen beaver in their traps. So, they pushed ever northward and westward, through Pierre's Hole and along the Snake. But winter caught up with them.

Within two days, they found a band of Shoshonis. The chief, Walking Knife, consented to let the mountain men and their families winter nearby. Hastily, Tippett and Calder, with the help of their women and several Shoshonis, made camp. Then they settled in, spending some time with the Shoshonis, but mostly keeping to their own small camp. They trapped the streams and brooks as long as they could, finding their catches little improved. It preyed on Tippett's mind.

"These here plews is plumb awful, Cass," he said one night as the two men sat puffing their pipes in Tippett's lodge.

"That's a fact," Calder understated. "I've made beaver come with the best. And this ol' chil' ain't never seen such poor doin's."

"I ain't sure of what to do, neither," Tippett said sadly. "Bent offered me work, but I ain't certain I want to take it. I'd hate like hell to be cooped up in that goddamn adobe prison all the time."

"That don't shine with this hoss, neither," Calder said. "But, hell, there's other jobs down there to keep ye in the high lonesome. Tradin' with the Injins, and such..."

"I can jist see me tradin' with the Cheyennes and Arapahos after I raised hair on more'n one of 'em."

"Shit, trade with the Comanch'. Bent's done it, and I reckon he'd be pleased as a pig in a yard of shit to have someone tradin' with 'em reg'lar. Thar's other things, too. Ye could take to leadin' freight trains for Bent 'twixt his fort and the settlements. Or hunt, keepin' those hungry bastards supplied with buffler and such."

"I expect I could. But none of 'em shines, dammit. I've been my own boss too long to set traps in another man's waters."

"I feel the same. But sure as God made these here Stony Mountains, the beaver trade's dyin'. I reckon we ought to get out while we still got our hair."

Tippett nodded sadly. He knew it was true, but that didn't make it any easier to swallow.

"The Bear is right," Painted Wing said to Tippett that night as they snuggled in their robes. She had been calling Calder the Bear for some time now, mainly because of his size and the amount of hair on his chest and back. "The beaver are no more."

"I know," he said, irritated. He was angry at the looming loss of a career he held dear. And he was angry at himself for not having foreseen it and made other plans. It ate at his insides like maggots on a buffalo carcass. "But that don't make me like it none."

"You'll find somethin' else to do," she said. Painted Wing had utmost confidence in him. "Come to me," she whispered, pulling at him.

He was reluctant and held back. With a smile Tippett could not see in the lodge lit only by the flickering embers of the fire, Painted Wing climbed atop him.

"Quit it," Tippett said without much conviction.

"No," Painted Wing said softly, but firmly. "You got to get these thoughts outta your mind, Zeke."

"Soon's I get my mind set on what I'll do," he grumbled.

"That'll come. You'll see. Now help me here, dammit."

A flash of anger snaked through him, but fled rapidly. He grinned and placed his arms around her, comforted by her heat, the exciting sensation of her naked genitals against his, the smooth thighs pressed on his legs, and the soft skin of her back under his hands.

"Ye got somethin' in mind?" he asked impishly.

"Perhaps," she mumbled as she lowered her lips to meet his.

Much later, Painted Wing collapsed onto Tippett's chest,

breasts mashed flat. When her breathing had returned somewhat to normal, Painted Wing said, "Soon White Buffalo will have a brother — or sister."

"Ye're pregnant again?" he asked excitedly, eyes popping open.

"*Si*. I reckon this one's another boy."

"That shines," Tippett said with a grin.

But despite Calder's ambivalence and Painted Wing's soothing ways, Tippett could not rid himself of the vexatious problem of what to do. He would not mind hunting or trading for Bent, save it meant that he would have to knuckle under to Bent's control. Such was not his way. He knew he also could join the robe trade, taking buffalo for hides instead of beaver. But for some reason he could not really fathom, the thought was not appealing. There was something wrong, he decided, in slaughtering buffalo by the score from a stand. He hunted buffalo that way for food and saw nothing wrong with it. But he had run buffalo. There was something almost spiritual about such a thing and it seemed sacrilegious to hunt the magnificent beast from a stand.

The budding of spring temporarily halted his troublesome thoughts. With a sense of anticipation and urgency, he and Calder began setting their traps again. But their poor results soon put Tippett back into his ill-humored mood.

The Shoshonis left to hunt buffalo, and Tippett and Calder broke camp. Painted Wing was not showing much sign of her pregnancy, and even if she had been, she would not have let it limit her working. As they rode through the snow-covered valley, Tippett, at the rear as usual, looked back with sadness. He thought this might be the last time he saw the glistening snow-capped Wind River Mountains.

The lightly sifting snow changed to a steady, chilling rain, and Tippett shook his head and grinned lopsidedly at the same time thinking of how fitting such a thing was for his mood.

Their luck improved some in Round Valley and the two mountain men pulled in more than a hundred beaver. The plews were not prime, but they were better than anything else they had gotten this season.

Just after that, Calder decided he would head on to rendezvous. "Might be the last goddamn one," he grumbled, his voice its normal avalanche rumble. "I can understand the fur trade's gone to hell and back and ain't worth Ute shit no more, but I'll be goddamned fried and ate up by wolves if I was to miss the last big doin's."

"I understand," Tippett said with a nod, pleased, as he nearly always was, with Calder's blunt good humor. "Hell, I'd go on there myself, but my loyalties lay with Bent and the Comanches."

Calder nodded. "Ye watch your hair, ye understand?" he growled.

"Ye do the same, but why any Injun would want that scraggly thatch of yours hangin' from his lodgepole is beyond my ken," Tippett said with a laugh to mask his sadness.

Calder chuckled, the sound like large rocks being shaken inside an empty keg. With a pregnant Shining Beads and their son Charger following, Calder rode northwest across the mountain valley. Tippett watched, the heaviness in his heart growing. In his sadness, he worried that he might never see his friend again.

He shrugged. He had more momentous things to think about. With barely two pack of plews, none prime, he would have to hustle to make enough to stake himself for another year...if there would even be another year for him in the mountains.

He spit, half in anger, half in disgust. These were some poor doings, he thought, when a man works his ass off half his life and winds up with hardly nothing to show for it but a case of rheumatism, a sour stomach at the thought of all the rotgut consumed, and the memories of shinin' times in the hard expanses of the Rocky Mountains.

Well, Tippett thought, the sadness clinging to him like a shrunken war shirt, *ain't nobody can take them thoughts away from me. No, by Christ, they're mine for all times.*

A month later, with Painted Wing seemingly ready to drop the baby at any time, they rode into Bent's Fort again.

"Looks like you had poor pickin's this year," Bent said as Tippett dismounted in the courtyard.

"Piss poor," Tippett said heatedly.

"It's going to get worse, Zeke," Bent said softly.

"I know." There was an almost haunted look in Tippett's eyes.

"Offer of a job's still open."

"I'm obliged, Bill. But I expect I'll pass. It don't mean nothin' against ye, but I been on my own hook too long."

"I understand," Bent said. "But you keep to mind that it's open as long as I got anything to do with this fort. Looks like Painted Wing's near ready to foal. Ye aimin' to stay till it's done?"

"I expect."

"Take the corner room again."

Tippett nodded. "Ye aimin' to buy my plews?" His eyes were hard.

"Reckon so," Bent said calmly. "But the price ain't worth shit. I can't pay more'n a buck and a half. Maybe two, if they're prime."

"Jesus Christ." Tippett muttered glumly.

21

When he arrived in Taos, Tippett was still not sure what he would do with himself. He did know, though, that he would not be trapping beaver any more. That was clear enough when he had taken the measly stack of dollars Bent's chief factor handed to him.

"You want me to take out next year's stake from that, Mister Tippett?" Alexander Barclay had asked in his still-thick Scottish burr.

"Shit," Tippett snorted, stuffing the money in his possibles bag. He shuffled outside into the heat. Clouds were building to the north and the west and Tippett knew there would be rain soon.

It came several hours later and lasted nearly seventy-two hours. That was bad enough, keeping most of the men cooped up. But even worse were the tornadoes that spun wildly across the prairie. One touched down so close to the fort that anything not tied down was flung about. Tippett and Painted Wing sat it out in the stark comfort of their room. And it was then that Painted Wing decided it was time to give birth.

Worried, Tippett muttered, "Hang on, woman." He headed into

the shrieking, roaring wind. It battered him, smashing him against the wall. The dust was so thick he could barely see two feet in front of him. Garbage and God knew what else were tossed around. Tippett slitted his eyes and gritted his teeth, yet still felt dust and sand burrow past his teeth into his mouth. He pulled himself up to a post holding up the second story of the fort. Then he shoved himself forward, straining every muscle until he reached the next one. He repeated the move over and over, working his way along the north wall of the fort, and then the west wall. The worst spot was the entryway to the corral. The corral walls blocked little of the wind that roared like the steamboats Tippett had seen fighting up the Missouri River.

In that vulnerable spot, the wind smacked Tippett down twice before he could make the relative safety of the carpenter's shop. He stopped, holding onto a cottonwood post, breathing heavily from the exertion, and hoping he was not sucking too much dirt into his lungs. With another supreme effort, he shoved off again. But the rest of the way was easy compared with the first part. He finally shoved into the dining room. Several men looked up to see who was foolish enough to be out in such a storm. A few grinned, others scowled as wind whistled in before Tippett closed the door. Tippett leaned against the door, panting for a moment. Then he hurried across the dining room to the small kitchen that opened off it toward the rear.

"What you want in heah?" Charlotte Green asked as Tippett entered her sanctum. Charlotte was the wife of Dick Green, and they were Charles Bent's slaves. Dick Green was a huge, well-muscled man with pitch black skin. His wife was shorter, and very plump, with a wide, fleshy, expressive face, and coal-colored eyes surrounded by great circles of white. She was dressed in a simple, clean muslin dress, with a starched white apron across her vast middle.

"Painted Wing's time's come. I ain't used to such doin's and ..."

"Whyn't you jist say so," Charlotte said, yanking off her apron. "Dick!" she roared. "Git yo'self out heah. Bring mah bag. Mistah Tippett's wife's time has come."

"Yes'm," Green said, shuffling into the kitchen from their rooms in back. He showed much deference to Charlotte when other people were around since she was well thought of by everyone in the fort, seeing as how she was the only woman around regularly.

The black woman grabbed a buckskin sack from her husband. "Well?" she demanded of Tippett, "Is you gonna wait the whole day?"

"No, ma'am."

The twister had blown off, and the wind, which normally would have seemed to be blowing in gales appeared almost calm after the tornado. The rain still fell in solid sheets making a morass of the courtyard. Tippett and Charlotte took the long way, staying under the cover of the roof and out of as much mud as possible.

In the small room, Painted Wing was squatting in the middle of the floor and grunting. "Lo'dy," Charlotte muttered, hurrying to her.

"What can I do?" Tippett asked, licking his lips. This was no place for a man. The last time Painted Wing gave birth, the women of the Shoshoni band with whom they had been staying had brought Painted Wing to a special lodge. Tippett gulped.

"Git," Charlotte ordered, already busy.

He spun and raced out, back to the dining room. He sat at a table, nervously sipping at a tin cup of coffee sweetened with molasses. The other men left him alone.

Bent entered. He got coffee before sitting across the plank table from Tippett. He had deduced that Painted Wing was in labor. "It'll be all right," he said soothingly. "Painted Wing's strong. And Charlotte's good at such doin's."

"I expect," Tippett mumbled into his coffee cup. "I ain't worried."

"Like hell." Bent grinned but let the subject drop. He sipped steaming coffee for a short while before saying, "Alexander tells me you didn't pay for a stake for next season. Givin' up the trade?"

"I expect." Tippett sat back and stuffed a piece of tobacco from his twist into his pipe. He lit it from a candle on the table. "Hell, I knew ye was tellin' true last year when ye said the price of plews'd drop more. But I never expected things to get so bad so fast."

He looked stunned. "Well, it don't make no never mind. Beaver don't shine no more and I expect it never will again. I got to turn my sights to somethin' else."

"You given it any thought?" Bent asked, peering over the rim of his mug, the steam curling around his broad face.

"I ain't done much of nothin' else. I got some ideas, but I reckon the one I like most will take a heap of specie." He grinned. "Us ol' mountain boys ain't known for our frugal ways, Bill, as ye goddamn well know. I reckon I pissed away most of my future on hand games and monte and euchre, and buying foofaraw for Painted Wing, and liquor and shit. Much as I'd hate it, I might have to start workin' for someone. But, damn, I'd like to try some of my other ideas first."

"Mind tellin' me what they are?" Bent set his empty mug down.

"I expect not."

"I understand, Zeke. But let me tell you something before you go makin' any decisions. You might not be so bad off as you think."

"What's that mean?"

"Well, you've always left your money with me after payin' for your stake. Did you think I was just sitting here on it? Hell, no."

"What'd ye do with it?" Tippett asked through a cloud of smoke.

"Invested it. Put some in the bank, and used some to buy trade goods or land in Missouri. I don't have the figures, though I can get them easy enough. But I'd say you were worth several thousand dollars."

"What?" Tippett burst out, coughing from sucking in too large a lungful of smoke.

"I'll get you the latest figures from my books before you leave, Zeke. Let you know exactly where you stand," Bent said with a grin.

"Thankee," was all Tippett could say. He was humbled and awed.

"Think nothin' of it." Bent walked out, leaving his mug.

Charlotte burst in and flounced to where Tippett was sitting. He knew it was good news by Charlotte's broad, gap-toothed smile. "You got yo'self another son, Mistah Tippett," she announced.

"By Christ, boys, I'm a papa again!" Tippett shouted. "I'm buyin', if any of ye is man enough to brave the storm for the bar."

There was a stampede toward the door. Tippett followed more slowly, quite happy.

He and Painted Wing stayed at the fort a week before setting out for the Comanche village with White Buffalo, and the new baby — whom Tippett called Cass, after his friend, and whom Painted Wing called Born-In-The-Storm. They lingered in the village, Painted Wing proudly showing off her new child, before preparing to leave for Taos.

"I'd like to leave White Buffalo here," Painted Wing said to Tippett the night before they were supposed to leave.

"No," he said flatly.

"He needs training."

"I'll train him in what he needs to know."

"You don't know the proper ways," she muttered.

"I'll see he gets schoolin'. He don't need to learn to use a lance. He's half *tahbay-boh*, and, by Christ, I want him raised right."

"He'll come back to the *Nermernuh* one day. You know that. You've seen it with half-breeds. The *tahbay-boh* won't accept 'em, so they always come back to their tribe where they'll be accepted."

Tippett knew she was right, though he was loathe to admit it. Maybe he could civilize the boy later, he thought with a grin. As if he was so civilized himself!

"Ye made arrangements?" he asked softly.

"White Buffalo'll stay with Blood Drips Down and Yellow Grass."

"Your sister and her husband going to be able to teach him?"

"Yes."

"The idea don't shine with this chil'." But he had no choice.

BOOK 6

GRAY WOLF, 1840

22

There were always things to occupy Gray Wolf's mind. But what he mostly thought about was war. There was always the war trail for a vital war chief. Raids took more time since the warriors often had to ride far from the *Llano Estacado*. The Mexicans were retreating and the Utes and Apaches seldom braved this country any more.

Still, those enemies could be found after much riding across the tracklessness of the bleak *Llano*. The Mexicans still had many fine horses to be stolen, and there were captives that could be taken, captives who could be ransomed. Gray Wolf often chuckled to himself whenever he thought of it. The Mexicans were stupid. They would eagerly try to buy peace at every opportunity. And pay dearly, offering many goods for each returned captive.

He laughed when he thought back a year and how his warriors had raided far to the south near the poor excuse for a river the Mexicans called the Rio Grande. The Comanches had taken seventeen captives. A few died on the arduous trip back to the *Llano* and a few were given to families that had lost sons or brothers. Until only three were left — a girl and two boys. No one wanted them.

The council of warriors agreed they would be taken to New

Mexico to be ransomed. Gray Wolf rode along, quiet but observant. He could not understand why his companions abused the youngsters. He held no pity for them in his heart but was curious that the prisoners were treated poorly when they were going to be sold back to their people.

In Taos, the fearsome, arrogant Comanches made it known they had prisoners to ransom. Gray Wolf listened intently as a Sergeant Valencia offered twenty-five dollars in goods for each prisoner.

"No," Walking Bear said flatly. "It is not enough."

Walking Bear waved his hands and the oldest captive — a boy of perhaps ten — was brought up.

The Mexican authorities were incensed at the sight of the bedraggled, abused waif. "Fifty dollars in goods," Valencia said, trying to contain his temper. It would not do, he thought, to anger a war party of twenty hard Comanches.

"Not enough," Walking Bear said in Spanish, suppressing a grin.

The Mexicans were anxious to have the captives back. They always thought they were helping the hostages by offering more and more for them. They did not realize they were playing into the Comanches' hands. The Comanches were not as stupid. They had realized long ago that the more abused a captive, the more money would be paid for him.

Watching the dickering, Gray Wolf soon became aware of this and his already low opinion of these white men sank further. It was a lesson well learned, he thought, as the captives were handed over for one hundred dollars in goods each.

The Comanches rode out with kegs of powder and bars of lead, iron for arrowheads, flour, bolts of cloth, cooking pots, and more.

On the journey home, Gray Wolf thought about the differences in men. The Mexicans looked somewhat like Comanches. Both generally were short and dark. But their thinking was so different. Mexican ways were not good. The men were afraid. Men who bought abused captives rather than taking them back by force were not much men at all to Gray Wolf.

The strange ways of the *tahbay-boh* made no sense to Gray Wolf. They always seemed willing to forgive and forget, to ask for peace, to offer a few presents to calm the *Nermernuh*. Gray Wolf scratched absentmindedly at the lice crawling across his body. It made no sense to the Comanche warrior.

But new white men were moving into the vast lands of the Comanche. The *Tejanos* — Texicans, as they called themselves — were a different breed from the Mexicans. More like the Comanche in some ways. They took what they wanted and never backed down. When attacked, they might run, but they would always come back in strength and force.

Gray Wolf had seen few of these truly pale-faced people. Zeke Tippett was the only real white-eyes man he had known. And he wondered if these people had any women. Most he had seen or knew about took to Comanche women eagerly. Perhaps there were no pale-face women.

Or so Gray Wolf had always thought, until four summers ago. A *Nawkohnee* band from northeast of the *Kwahadis* had raided a small settlement near the Navosota River. They killed several men, ravished and killed five women, and took several captives. Of the captives, three were female — two women, and one girl. Gray Wolf had seen them when he spent a few days in the band's villages on his way to a hunt. He was highly curious of the females. They were not much to look at, nowhere near as bosomy and well-rounded as a good Comanche woman. He wondered if their skin was indeed as white as billowing clouds of snow.

"Their skin is white all over?" he asked the warrior who had kept one of the women as a slave. Gray Wolf's curiosity was highly aroused.

"Yes," the warrior grunted, pleased that he had something few other Comanches had. "Would you like to see?"

"Yes," Gray Wolf nodded, eyes glittering with interest.

The woman — Rachel Plummer, captured in the raid on Parker's "Fort" — stood stock still. She had been a captive more than two months, and sorely abused, humiliated, and tortured much of that time. But she had learned quickly that to resist this bull-faced warrior, or any Comanche male, was to invite more pain.

So, when she was motioned closer, she moved. She kept her head down and said nothing when Black Buffalo Head slit off her shabby buckskin dress saved from the trash heap. Nor did she speak when Gray Wolf came close to her, looking her over as if she was a horse. After her early debasement, she was used to such treatment.

Gray Wolf was more curious than aroused. He went behind the woman and touched her hair and the pale skin of her upper back. She did not jump at the touch, but she bit her lower lip to keep from screaming.

Gray Wolf ran his hand down her back and across Rachel's ghostly buttocks. Then he looked at his hand to see if the paleness had come off. With a look of wonder, he rubbed harder and harder to see if the milkiness would transfer to his dark hand. Rachel bit her lip until it bled. Her breath came in short, bitter rasps.

Gray Wolf muttered as he stepped around to Rachel's front. He squeezed a breast and ran a finger roughly over the nipple. When Rachel did not react, he squeezed harder, pinching the rosy end. Rachel winced but kept quiet. She did the same when Gray Wolf grabbed the other breast and squeezed hard.

"She will provide milk for many baby warriors with these," Gray Wolf said, bouncing Rachel's breasts in his hands. He laughed.

Black Buffalo Head also laughed. "Older ones, too."

Still grinning, Gray Wolf knelt and stared at Rachel's privates. Then he took his right hand and shoved it between the woman's legs, forcing her thighs apart. He plunged a thick middle finger into her. Rachel clamped her lips tightly shut and showed nothing on her face.

Gray Wolf stared up at her, amused. Then he stood, pulling his hand free. His breechcloth was tented at front. He stared at it a moment, grinning. "Better than Mexican?" he asked.

"Yes," Black Buffalo Head said with a lecherous smile. "But not so good as *Nermernuh*. She's a pleasant change." Black Buffalo Head laughed in good humor, pointing to where Gray Wolf's breechcloth stuck out. "Try her," he said joyfully.

Gray Wolf nodded. He stepped up to Plummer and not-so-gently shoved her toward a pile of buffalo robes. Rachel had been so abused and degraded early on that she knew she could do nothing, so she sank back and lay utterly still. Gray Wolf shoved aside his breechcloth. Forcing Rachel's legs apart with his knees, he plunged into her. Rachel grimaced in pain and disgust as Gray Wolf grunted a few moments as he pounded inside her. With a muffled groan, he jerked stiffly and then sank onto the women. A moment later he was up and adjusting his garment, grinning widely.

"Not as good as *Nermernuh*," Gray Wolf said agreeably, "but better than a buffalo cow." He and Black Buffalo Head laughed.

THE *TEJANOS*, GRAY WOLF REALIZED ON HIS JOURNEY BACK FROM Taos, would not be so easily frightened or fooled as the Mexicans. And they would need watching. He had not seen many yet since they had not come close to *Llano*. But he knew from the more eastern bands, like Black Buffalo Head's, that more and more of them were coming into the country, taking land from the Comanches.

He put it from his mind as he neared his village. There was no need to worry. The *Tejanos* could not defeat the Comanches and there was little chance they would get to this land so far from all else.

To others, the *Llano Estacado* might be a stark, foreboding land inhabited by nothing more than Comanches and rattlesnakes. But Gray Wolf saw it in grander, but still more personal terms. To him it was a land both familiar and filled with wonder. It was his Mother Earth and held more beauty and versatility than any *tahbay-boh* could ever see.

The harshness of his land could not keep the *Tejanos* away. They kept coming, probing the indistinct outer fringes of *Comancheria*, penetrating a little deeper with each passing year.

Then one late winter day came word to all the Comanches that three *Pehnahterkuh* chiefs had sought a parley with these *Tejanos*. A big meeting was to be held in San Antonio. The *Pehnahturkuhs* were to go; any other Comanche who wished to go was invited.

The men of Gray Wolf's band argued long and fervently over whether anyone should go, and when that was decided, over who would go. Gray Wolf's father and uncle, Kills Twice and Calls From Afar, were chosen. Walking Bear, Gray Wolf, and his brother, Hits-With-A-Fist, decided to escort them. In early March, as the *tahbay-boh* reckoned that month of miserable weather, the small band of Comanches set out.

23

Gray Wolf sat bolt upright in his lodge, dropping the horn bowl and splattering the contents in the dirt. He raced outside. From afar, in the city, he heard gunfire, screams, and piercing war cries.

"Red Moon!" he yelled. "My horse." He took the two steps to the rack where his weapons were kept. He swept up his bow and quiver and slung them across his back. Then he grabbed his lance.

Red Moon hurried up with Gray Wolf's favorite war pony. Gray Wolf leaped on, grabbing the horsehair rope rein tied to the horse's lower jaw.

Suddenly Walking Bear loomed in front of the horse. "No!" he commanded sharply.

"There is trouble in the *tahbay-boh* town. I must help."

"There's nothing you can do. Your father and his brother wouldn't want your help. The rest are *Pehnahterkuh*," Walking Bear almost spit. "They are hardly worthy of being called *Nermernuh*!" Walking Bear grabbed the rein of Gray Wolf's horse. He waved his hand in the general direction of the town. He did not have to be there to know what had happened. "Hear? It is all over."

"Then I will die in seeking revenge!" Gray Wolf hissed.

"We have lost too many of the People already," Walking Bear said calmly, though he seethed inside. He, too, wanted to don his war clothes, paint his face, and ride out to strike at the *Tejanos*. "We cannot afford to lose more. You will stay!"

He had no authority to order Gray Wolf about in such a manner. But he was hoping that in so doing, the younger warrior would see that it was the wisest thing.

"So, you say that we should sit here and wait for the *Tejanos* to come for us?" Gray Wolf snapped. His blood roared in his veins and thumped in his temples. His nerves crackled and snapped.

"We'll strike camp," Walking Bear said, "and move there." He pointed to a ridge several miles northwest. "When night comes, you, me, and Hits-With-A-Fist will go into the white-eyes' town quietly. And we'll find out if any of our people live."

"And I will cut out the heart of any *tahbay-boh* I see," Gray Wolf said through bloodless lips.

"No! We will help all the People we can. Then we will ride back to the *Llano*. Once our families are safe, we can prepare properly for war. Then we will have the heads of as many of these *Tejanos* as we can find." He spit, showing his anger and the finality of his statement.

Rage coursed through Gray Wolf like a spring flood. He understood the wisdom of Walking Bear's words. But he wanted only to kill *Tejanos*.

"Red Moon. Running Deer. The lodge," Gray Wolf ordered. "Quickly." He looked down at Walking Bear. "I will watch."

Walking Bear nodded and released the horse. With much dignity, Gray Wolf moved his horse away and stopped, dark eyes scanning the flat below the grassy ridge, searching for signs of *Tejanos*. Behind him, his two women and Walking Bear's three hurriedly pulled down the lodges and packed. Hits-With-A-Fist rounded up their extra horses.

Within hours they had found a new site for their camp. But the lodges would not be put up here, nor would fires be made. Gray

Wolf, Walking Bear, and Hits-With-A-Fist painted themselves. The women and children crept quietly about, not wanting to disturb the men.

When the sun dipped below the horizon and the sky sank from wispy blue through indigo, purple, and into black, the three warriors mounted their ponies and rode away from their small camp.

Before they had reached the town, Gray Wolf, who was leading, stopped and slid off his horse while hissing for silence. He pressed a hand over the pony's nose to keep it quiet. Walking Bear and Hits-With-A-Fist waited patiently, listening.

Suddenly Gray Wolf slipped into the night. He took half a dozen steps and bent. In the dim light of the half moon and stars, Walking Bear saw Gray Wolf straighten with a youth in his grasp.

"It's Crooked Arm," Gray Wolf called over his shoulder.

The boy struggled a moment before he realized he was with friends.

"Do the *Tejanos* follow?" Gray Wolf asked urgently. He nearly shook with anticipation of a battle.

"No."

Gray Wolf was disappointed, but it did not last. He put aside his thirst for revenge. He tossed the boy onto his pony and jumped up after him. They galloped back to camp.

"Hits-With-A-Fist, keep watch," Gray Wolf ordered as they arrived. "Red Moon, you will make a fire and cook."

Before long, Gray Wolf, Walking Bear, and the boy were sitting around a small fire eating a stew of buffalo meat and prairie turnips. "Did you see what happened?" Gray Wolf asked Crooked Arm.

"Yes." The ten-year-old was frightened but trying not to show it.

"Tell us," Walking Bear said softly.

Crooked Arm set down the horn bowl, still half full. "This morning, the great chief Mook-war-ruh gave the *Tejanos* two captives. The *tahbay-boh* said we must give up all our *tahbay-boh* captives before the parley. But Mook-war-ruh was too smart and gave up only two. Later, the *tahbay-boh* chief invited the war chiefs into a small stone lodge. Mook-war-ruh and the other twelve war chiefs were dressed and painted in their best," Crooked Arm said proudly.

"They was all who were allowed in the stone lodge by the *tahbay-boh* chief. But I snuck in before they shut the doors." He grinned at the momentary remembrance of his mischievousness.

"All the others sat outside on the plaza. The *Tejanos* asked where the other captives were. Mook-war-ruh told the *tahbay-boh* chief that they were with other bands over whom he had no control. But, he told the *Tejano* chief, he was sure they could be ransomed."

Gray Wolf and Walking Bear nodded at this tactic. It had been the way of doing business with the Mexicans for many, many years. But the look on Crooked Arm's face stopped the nodding.

The boy looked stricken. He wanted to cry, but that was not a warrior's way. And, though he was still a boy, he would be a warrior soon and so he struggled to keep calm.

"Eat," Walking Bear said, pointing to the bowl at the boy's feet.

Crooked Arm picked up the bowl and with his horn spoon shoveled some of the now cold stew into his mouth. After several spoonfuls, he put the bowl back down on the ground.

"When Mook-war-ruh said this, the *tahbay-boh* chief got very angry. Long-knives came into the room, but we weren't afraid. Then the interpreter — a *tahbay-boh* who had been a captive of the *Nermernuh* — looked sick as the white-eyes chief talked to him. He argued with the soldier chief, but finally told us what had been said."

"And what was that?" Gray Wolf asked harshly.

"He said the war chiefs were to be held until all the *tahbay-boh* captives were returned."

Gray Wolf's eyes burned with hatred, but neither he nor Walking Bear said anything.

"Then," Crooked Arm gasped, "the war chiefs leaped up, weapons ready. With my small bow, I shot a long-knife before I was knocked down trying to give the alarm to those outside. There was much noise from the long-knives' guns, and shouting. The stone lodge smelled of blood and smoke from the guns. I finally ran outside."

Crooked Arm sat trying to sort out the horrors he had seen and heard. The blood, and shiny knives slicing flesh. The dull thump of a war club as it cracked a skull. The frightened, angry screams of the Comanches outside. The sharply muttered curses of *tahbay-boh* soldiers.

"All the war chiefs were killed in the stone lodge," Crooked Arm finally said, fighting back tears. "Many of the People outside tried to run, some into lodges, most toward the river. Long-knives hunted for us. Several warriors died trying to protect the women and children as they fled. I think all the People were killed or captured. I managed to hide in a barrel near the river. When night came, I slipped out, and down to the river. And then..." He stopped.

Gray Wolf and Walking Bear said nothing, each wrestling with his grief and rage. Gray Wolf's father and uncle had died in the council house; Walking Bear's brother and his family were among those who waited outside, wearing their finery, thinking this a fine celebration.

"The *tahbay-boh* will suffer for what they have done," Gray Wolf said fiercely, his fury untempered.

Walking Bear nodded, but stayed silent. His stone-hard face gave testimony to his anger and determination.

"There is nothing we can do tonight," Gray Wolf said, surprising himself. "We will sleep. In the morning we will decide what to do."

Walking Bear expelled mucus from his nose into the small fire. Without a word, he stood and went to his sleeping robes.

Crooked Arm curled up where he was and fell asleep. Gray Wolf checked on Hits-With-A-Fist. Assured that his brother was awake and would stay that way throughout the night, Gray Wolf went to sleep.

The group was ready to leave in the morning, having decided to return home to raise a war party, when they spotted a lone rider coming toward them from San Antonio. They watched until it became clear the rider was a Comanche woman. She stopped at their small camp.

"The *tahbay-boh* chief has freed me to spread the word to all the camps of the People," she said fearfully.

"And what words are those?" Gray Wolf asked, his voice sharp.

"All who lived through the fight at the stone lodge will die unless all the *tahbay-boh* captives held by the *Nermernuh* are freed."

A chill ran the length of Gray Wolf's spine. He was not afraid, just unbelieving at the treachery of the *tahbay-boh*. "And how long do the People have to turn in these captives?"

"Twelve suns."

"We have no such captives," Walking Bear said. "But we will pass the *tahbay-boh* chief's message to any of the People we see." He paused. "Now, you must ride hard, to alert other bands."

The woman, a *Pehnahturkuh* none of the *Kwahadis* knew, nodded. With fear etching deep, permanent lines in her face, she galloped off.

"The *tahbay-boh* will pay," Gray Wolf whispered. Walking Bear and Hits-With-A-Fist nodded in furious agreement. They mounted their ponies and rode hard, heading for the *Llano Estacado*.

24

Zeke Tippett rode unsuspectingly into the seething cauldron of Gray Wolf's village. He was seized and dragged off his horse.

Painted Wing screamed and tried to force her pony through the swirling mob of angry, screeching Comanches. But she could not. She was pulled from her saddle, Born-In-The-Storm's cradleboard still tied to her back. The women — her friends, even relatives — clutched at her as the enraged men hauled Tippett toward a post in a clearing.

Tippett fought hard. But it was belated and inadequate. So surprised was he that he was nearly at the post before he lashed out with foot and fist. He felt a brief flush of glee when hard knuckles or moccasined toes connected with bone and flesh. "What'n hell's goin' on, Wolf?" he bellowed after he was tied to the stake.

Gray Wolf and the other warriors stood jeering at him. "The *tahbay-boh* will die," Gray Wolf shouted, rage shaping the words.

"What'n hell are ye talkin' about, Wolf?"

Gray Wolf did not answer. He just stood back and watched as Tippett's clothes were sliced off. Then he stared with a cruel grin as the other warriors, led by Hits-With-A-Fist, turned their slow, deliberate attentions to Tippett with knife and fire.

As knives flicked off bits of Tippett's flesh and flaming brands seared white skin, Gray Wolf explained in a hollow, dead voice what had happened. "And so," he finished, standing close to Tippett, "all white-eyes must die." He stared deep into Tippett's eyes as Buffalo Droppings peeled a strip of flesh off Tippett's arm.

Tippett spit tobacco juice at Gray Wolf. The filthy brown liquid hit the Comanche's dark chest and trickled downward. "I ain't no goddamn *Tejano,* Wolf," he growled. The anger kept the pain subdued.

"So, you are afraid," Gray Wolf shouted over the din.

Tippett spit again. The tobacco juice landed in the center of Gray Wolf's forehead. "Bullshit," Tippett snarled. The other warriors backed off, watching intently. "I can take whatever ye can dish out. I jist didn't know ye'd turned into a gelding." He laughed derisively. "Shit, such a great warrior. Needs me trussed up to a pole so's he can roast and cut me. Afraid to face me." Tippett spit a third time.

Gray Wolf's face condensed in fury. It was a hideous face, cut with thick lines of anger and the ropes of pulsing veins. He stood squarely in front of Tippett. The white man stared back, unafraid.

Then Gray Wolf brought his fury under control. "You are brave," he said in Comanche. "Braver than any *tahbay-boh* I have seen. Still, you are *tahbay-boh.*" The words dripped with hatred. "Like the *Tejanos.*"

Tippett spit out the brown glob of tobacco, just missing Gray Wolf's right moccasin. "Shit, I ain't like most others. Ye know that. Texians ain't like Mexicans. And they ain't like the French who come through here times a while back. Ye know men're different, though they might look some the same. Hell, your people look just like Apaches or Utes to most white-eyes. But ye are different from them, ain't ye?"

Gray Wolf nodded grudgingly.

Tippett was sweating, and he was in pain. It was a hot enough day, and the flames still held by some of the Comanche warriors were close. He was talking earnestly because he believed in what he was saying. But he was also talking eagerly and sincerely because as long as he talked and Gray Wolf listened, the torture would not continue.

"Me'n ye have had our differences, Wolf. But we've always respected the other and what he was. Ye can't let that fall by the side 'cause ye've got a black heart toward them shit-eatin' *Tejanos*."

"You were angry at my people," Gray Wolf said slowly. "I have not seen you in two winters. But the last time we spoke, you had a black heart toward the *Nermernuh*."

"No," Tippett said seriously, "I had a black heart toward *ye*. For what ye did to Blue Star."

"See," Gray Wolf said, anger flushing his face again, "you are like the *Tejanos*. Your pale skin is the same. And your hairy face. You don't understand *Nermernuh* ways."

"There's a heap of your ways I don't know beans about," Tippett admitted. "Some of 'em don't make sense to me. That don't make 'em wrong. I'm over what happened. It's your way. I don't understand it, but I reckon I'll never understand everything about your people. Jist like ye'll never understand all the ways of the *tahbay-boh*. People're different. We all got our own ways as peoples."

Gray Wolf stared into Tippett's eyes for some moments. "Yes," he finally commented. "The outside of men might be the same, but the insides are different."

Gray Wolf turned to face his people. The warriors, still in a howling fury, waited anxiously to get back to their bloody sport. But Gray Wolf stood, firm as the cliffs that backed up the *Llano Estacado* to the northwest and west. Gradually the warriors quieted, though they still held their flaming torches and blood-stained knives.

"My people," Gray Wolf finally said, "this *tahbay-boh* is not a *Tejano*. He is like one of us, though his skin is white. He has eaten in our lodges, fought our enemies. He has honored our medicine, and has hunted the buffalo with us. He has married into our band. And he has showed his bravery. I would have this...friend...free."

The warriors began to debate, the argument at times growing heated. The warriors took their time, each with something to say and being allowed to say it. None was more important in what he had to say than any other. And none would interrupt when another was speaking.

Tippett sweated as he waited, blocking out the pain. Gray Wolf stood silently, arms crossed across his chest, face impassive. Tippett would still be in deep trouble if the angry warriors chose to ignore Gray Wolf. And there'd be nothing his friend could do about it.

Finally, as was the Comanche way, the warriors came to a consensus. They would accede to Gray Wolf's wishes.

Tippett fought back some anger as Gray Wolf cut him loose. Tippett could have been bitter, but Gray Wolf's words about the treacherous attack in San Antonio served to keep him angrier at the Texans than at the Comanches.

As Gray Wolf led Tippett toward his fire, Painted Wing broke free and raced for her man. She clutched his arm as if she would never let go. The baby, still on his mother's back, gurgled happily.

Inside Gray Wolf's lodge, Tippett let Painted Wing poultice his wounds. He was in pain and would have scars for the remainder of his days to remind him of his ordeal. But he would not let the suffering show in front of the Comanches.

When Painted Wing was done, Tippett suffered Coyote Tail's ministrations. The medicine man danced around Tippett, waving his eagle feather fan in one hand and a gourd rattle in the other.

"You're here early, my friend," Gray Wolf said after Coyote Tail left. The two men, with Walking Bear and Hits-With-A-Fist, sat at Gray Wolf's fire eating dripping, half-raw buffalo meat.

"*Si.*" He spit out a piece of gristle that even his strong jaws and teeth could not handle. "I wanted to make my peace with ye, Wolf. I've had a bad heart toward ye, and I wanted to set it to rights. Reckon I come at a bad time, though, eh?" He managed a grin.

Gray Wolf did not return it. He was no longer angry at Tippett, but he still seethed underneath at the destruction the Texans had wrought on his people. "These are bad times for the *Nermernuh,*" Gray Wolf said solemnly. "The *Tejanos* have bad hearts. And bad medicine."

"We all got to adjust our thinkin', Wolf. Hell, even me." He grinned sourly. "The beaver trade's dead. I stuck with it long's I could, but I give it up last summer."

Gray Wolf looked surprised. "And what do you do with your life now?" he asked. A vague uneasiness filled him. For so many years things had been the same. Now changes were coming too fast.

"Opened me a store in Taos."

Gray Wolf forgot his own troubles in his sudden gust of laughter. "You?" he said in English. "Tendin' store? Damn!"

Tippett felt a flash of anger, but he cooled quickly. "Yep, I'm a storekeeper. I don't spend no more time there than I got to, though." he said with a rueful grin. "Hired someone to run things for me."

Gray Wolf laughed some more, and Tippett reluctantly joined him.

Talk turned to general things, but always kept coming back to the Comanches' problem of the Texans.

Though the warriors talked bravely about annihilating the Texans, Tippett knew there was an undercurrent of fear in the Indians. Not fear of battle, or of dying in battle. It was not a physical fear. Instead, it was a fear of the future, of seeing their lifeways disappear, blazing out like grama grass in a prairie fire. They had seen, even if they would not admit it, what had happened to other tribes east of them. Though the Caddos and Tonkawas and dozens of other small tribes had been their enemies since time immemorial, the Comanches were aware that those people had been destroyed by the steady stream of *tahbay-boh*. More and more were coming. It seemed an invincible tide...one that would roll on and on across Texas, and then perhaps the *Llano Estacado*, until it had taken over everything.

"When do ye aim to take to the war path against the *Tejanos*?"

"Soon," Walking Bear said quietly. Since Kills Twice and Calls From Afar had died, Walking Bear had found more weight on his shoulders. Much of the burden of running the village, of protecting the people, had fallen to him when those two valued warriors died.

"After the spring hunt," Gray Wolf said. "Will you join us?"

"Yep," Tippett said, managing a grin. Running buffalo was one of the immense pleasures of life. There was nothing quite like it.

"And when that's over," Gray Wolf said, unsmilingly, "will you take to the war trail against the *Tejanos* with us?"

Tippett worked over a back molar with his tongue for a few moments. "I can't do that, Wolf," he finally said softly. He dipped his hand into the pot, wincing at the hot liquid. He grabbed a small piece of meat and popped it into his mouth. "It ain't my doin's. They ain't done nothin' against me, and I'd jist as soon leave it at that."

The Comanches nodded, accepting it.

25

Gray Wolf sent out word that he was organizing a war party to go against the Texans. Then a messenger came from a *Pehnahterkuh* band.

"Buffalo Hump, the great war chief of the *Pehnahterkuh,* calls on all the *Nermernuh* warriors to join him," the messenger said.

"I am taking the war trail against these *tahbay-boh,*" Gray Wolf snarled. "I will ride for no one."

"The *Pehnahterkuh* have suffered most at the hands of the *Tejanos* and so should be at the head of any group going to war with them," the messenger said with simple logic.

There was much wisdom in that and Gray Wolf finally agreed, though still with some reluctance, to join Buffalo Hump.

The different bands of Comanches gathered on the northern edges of the Edwards Plateau, a flat, rugged escarpment dotted with sage and short grass. The Plateau's eastern side was cut with treacherous arroyos and draws.

More than two hundred warriors had amassed under Buffalo Hump's call. But only that venerable warrior was better known than a twenty-two-year-old *Kwahadi* named Gray Wolf. Not only had the others heard of Gray Wolf's prowess in war, they had also heard of the powerful medicine he always brought on the war trail.

After arriving at the Plateau, and having Red Moon and Running Deer make his small camp with others of his band, Gray Wolf set out alone to make his medicine. He found a small, rocky cliff overlooking a steep-walled arroyo. There he gathered branches from scrub pine and made a small fire at the rim of the cliff. Sitting behind the fire, looking east, Gray Wolf fasted and prayed to his spirits for two full days. On the third, he fell into a trance, and his vision came.

He went back to the camp and rested and feasted until the next afternoon. When he stepped out of his lodge then, he was prepared for war. He wore only a breechcloth, moccasins, and a buffalo-horn headdress. His face was streaked with black paint — the color of death — and there were ribbons of the paint streaming down his chest.

The drums had begun as had the dancing. Gray Wolf strolled arrogantly toward the growing circle of dancers around the central fire. The drums muted and the dancers slowed, waiting for him. There was a tingling in the air like that after a lightning storm.

"My brothers," Gray Wolf said boldly, "many of you have lost fathers or sons at the hands of the *Tejanos*. It is the way of the *Nermernuh* to avenge these wrongs. We must make the *Tejanos* pay for what they've done. My medicine will make it so."

There was a grumbling of anger. Gray Wolf let it simmer a few moments before he roared, "My medicine is strong!"

A howling rose, splitting the hot afternoon sky with its primitive urgency and unyielding fierceness.

"The *Nermernuh* will be victorious," Gray Wolf roared over the cacophony. "The *Tejanos* will be helpless!" Then Gray Wolf let out a piercing shriek that seemed to echo off distant buttes and mesas. As the sound faded, the drums picked up anew, throbbing deep into the warriors' hearts, forcing their legs into action.

Buffalo Hump sat nearby, feeling the pulsing of the drums work its way down into his very being.

"You'll have to watch that one," his son, Eagle Catcher, said quietly. Hate and anger burned in the younger man's eyes. He was jealous of the energetic, charismatic Gray Wolf.

"Why?" Buffalo Hump asked, almost amused.

"Given time, he'll take the place that's rightfully yours as the leading warrior of the *Nermernuh*," Eagle Catcher insisted.

"So be it," Buffalo Hump said easily. "The People need all the good warriors we can find. He's a true *Nermernuh*. He is brave, fearless. He'll never give up. You should learn from him, son." Buffalo Hump joined the dancers. His son stalked to his lodge.

The women made a larger circle, ringing the men, cheering them on, boasting of their men's prowess and bravery, exhorting them to an even greater lust for blood.

Having worked themselves into a bloodthirsty frenzy, the men leaped on their ponies and rode out. A full, heavy moon shimmered down, lighting their path. It was a Comanche Moon to the whites, many of whom had learned already to fear the nights on which such a golden orb found life. The women and children followed the warriors out of camp. They rode only a little that night. The dancing had tired them, but it was the Comanche way to leave at night.

Under Buffalo Hump's direction and Gray Wolf's ferocity, the Comanches made a sweeping loop from the Cimarron River, southeastward past San Antonio, and to the eastern coast of Texas. They raided and plundered almost at will, driving off hundreds of horses, stealing, raping, and slaughtering. Gray Wolf's blood lust knew no bounds and many warriors took to his lead. By sheer force of will, he and Buffalo Hump, in whom the embers of hatred burned deep and unyielding, kept the band on the move, laying waste wherever they rode.

At the Gulf Coast, they swung north, pushing thousands of stolen horses. Many animals were laden with tons of stolen goods.

The procession kicked up huge clouds of dust, marking their trail. They moved faster, not allowing the women and children any rest. They knew the Texans would be organizing against them. So, they were not surprised when a band of Texas Rangers came up on their rear. Gray Wolf and several other warriors swung about and raced toward them. The others pushed the long column of people and animals even harder.

Gray Wolf and his men, including Hits-With-A-Fist and Walking Bear, engaged the Rangers, killing two and driving the other off. Hits-With-A-Fist was slightly wounded in his right arm.

As they rode back toward the others, they noted that many of their stolen goods had been dumped. Gray Wolf scowled at the waste but said nothing when he caught up to the column. Several days later, Gray Wolf and his *Kwahadis* split off from the *Pehnahterkuhs*, taking some of the loot and several hundred horses. The few captives went with the *Pehnahterkuh*.

When the *Kwahadis* had reached the safety of the *Llano Estacado*, Gray Wolf's band celebrated wildly for many days. But soon after, a desperate, exhausted *Pehnahterkuh* stumbled into Gray Wolf's village and collapsed. Walking Bear was nearest, and hurried to the man. Walking Bear's eldest wife rushed over with a buffalo bladder canteen and poured stagnant water into the warrior's parched mouth. The man revived, looking at Walking Bear with haunted eyes.

"What have you to tell us?" Walking Bear asked urgently.

"After we divided," the warriors said, choking, "the *Tejanos* found us at Plum Creek." His eyes closed, and he seemed to have fallen asleep. Walking Bear jerked his head, and his wife splattered a little water on the *Pehnahterkuh's* face. The man snapped his head from side to side. His eyes glazed with internal pain, and the *Kwahadis* noticed for the first time that the blood on the man's war shirt was still wet.

Walking Bear lifted the man's shirt. A gaping hole under the last of the ribs on the left side oozed blood. The wound was covered with squirming maggots and it smelled of festering. Gray Wolf shook his head, knowing the man had little time left. "Tell us more," he urged.

"They rode in just after dawn, shooting," the man gargled. His breath came in rasping gulps and exhalations. "There was screaming and horses bolting into the new day. Confusion. I was shot. I..." He groaned and clutched his wound. His breath rattled against his ribs. His eyes opened again, but they saw little. "I lay as dead. The *Tejanos* took many scalps, but soon tired of that. They took much of the things we had won. Eighty People died there."

Gray Wolf's gasp was drowned out by those of the others. Eighty of the *Nermernuh*! It was unthinkable.

"Was Buffalo Hump among those...?" Gray Wolf asked.

"No," the man said, his voice cracking with the pain and impending death. The warrior shuddered and fell back, dead.

The men debated long into the night. Too many warriors had died of late. And with Buffalo Hump, Gray Wolf, and Walking Bear the only great Comanche war leaders left, things looked grim.

BOOK 7

ZEKE TIPPETT, 1843

26

Zeke Tippett was searching for meat when he spotted three men riding toward him. He stopped and stood in the stirrups to see better. Shading his eyes, he stared. The three walked their horses, unaware of Tippett, then disappeared into a fold of the brown earth.

Tippett settled into the saddle and patted his horse. Then he rested his left hand lightly on the rifle lying sideways in front of him, behind the pommel, and moved his horse into the shelter of the thick brush along the river bank, towing the four pack mules with him. For the past year, Tippett had been leading freight trains along the Santa Fe Trail. He was not entirely happy with such work, but it kept him out of the confinement of the store. As he had on the other trips, he left the store in the hands of a trusted manager. He also left Painted Wing, Born-In-The-Storm, and their newest child, a girl he named Libby and who Painted Wing called Light Calf, in Taos.

He heard the three men before they came into view. As they passed, he looked them over carefully. They were of varied size and build, but they were uniformly dirty and tired. All wore homespun pants and shirts, worn boots, and floppy felt hats. Each carried a brace of pistols — new repeating Colt pistols, Tippett noted — and each had a percussion rifle in a saddle scabbard.

Leaving the mules behind, Tippett stepped the horse out of the thicket. "Howdy, boys," he said quietly.

Startled, the three jerked to a stop and turned their heads. Hands snapped toward pistols at the same time. They saw him and relaxed. As Tippett approached, one asked, "Who're you?"

"Name's Zeke Tippett. Ye?"

Instead of answering, the man asked, "What're ye doin' out heah?"

"Huntin'." Tippett stared at the man silently a moment before adding softly, "I'm guidin' a freight train down to Santa Fe. Right now, I'm makin' meat." His face hardened. "What're ye doin' out here?"

"We're lookin' for Injins," the same one spoke, his tone surly. "Comanches. To bring them in for a peace talk."

Tippett laughed, disconcerting the three. "Ye'd get further tryin' to pluck fly shit out of sand," Tippett said, still laughing.

The three looked angry. "What's that mean?" the one asked, fidgeting. He was uneasy, as anyone would be sitting so near a madman.

"Shit, the Comanches ain't gonna be too charmed at the idea of a parley with any *Tejanos*."

"Why not?" the man asked, seemingly truly at a loss.

"What's your name, boy?" Tippett asked, not unpleasantly.

"Josiah Branch," the man said, uncomfortable again. "This is Sam LeBeouf and Dave McGreely." Each doffed his hat nervously when named.

"Well, Mister Branch," Tippett said almost patiently, "the last time the Comanches agreed to a parley with ye *Tejanos*, ye got 'em together, half of 'em in a room, under a white flag. Then slaughtered 'em all — men, women, and young'in's." Tippett's face was grim.

Branch gulped, afraid under this hard-looking *hombre's* stare.

The man's mouth flapped like a fish on a riverbank. "They're still upset over that?" he asked, trying to sound calm and reasoned. "That was years ago."

"Of course they're still angry over that, boy. Goddamn!"

"Well, things're different now," Branch finally squawked.

"Different how?" Tippett exploded, venting some steaming anger.

"We...I..." He hung his head, ashamed — or trying to make Tippett think he was. "There's new leaders in Texas now," he said.

"That don't mean shit to me — nor the Comanches."

"But they want to be fair to the Comanches — all Injins. They want peace so the people of Texas can live without fearin' for their lives every minute. They want a parley to let the Comanches know there'll be land set aside where they can live in peace, too."

Tippett boiled, uncertain whether to laugh at the Texans, or kill them. Finally, he settled. "What band ye lookin' for?" he asked.

"Comanches. I told y'all that." Branch was sure Tippett was mad.

"I asked ye what band," Tippett said, wonder in his voice.

"There's different kinds?" Branch's face betrayed astonishment.

Tippett shook his head in amazement, surprised the Texans had lived to get this far. "Well, ye got the *Kwahadis, Pehnahterkuhs, Nawkohnees, Yampareekahs, Kotsotekas*. Those are jist the main bands. Each has dozens of smaller bands."

"I never knew," Branch said, surprised. "I just always thought Comanches was Comanches."

"They are, more or less. They all got most of the same ways, but they don't have a hell of a lot to do with each other usually." Tippett shrugged, knowing he was not explaining it very well.

"Well," Branch said with determination, "I reckon we're lookin' mainly for the ones who raid down toward San Antone most often."

"I expect that'd be the *Pehnahterkuh*. They're closest. And," Tippett added pointedly, "they suffered most from the treachery in that parley three year ago."

"It wasn't no treachery," Branch said rigidly. "Those Injins were told — several times — to bring in *all* their white captives. They were holdin' a heap of 'em. But they only brung in a couple, one a goddamn Greaser. The woman they brung in was abused terrible." He was in a high dander, and it overrode his fear. "Only animals or savages'd do such a thing to a woman," Branch continued, gaining steam. "Jesus, she was degraded beyond belief. Beaten, burned, raped..."

"Still don't give ye the right to massacre a passel of Injuns whilst ye're supposed to be talkin' peace."

"Like hell. Those goddamn savages tried to extort all kinds of trade goods from us in exchange for the captives, which they were supposed to turn over to us in good faith."

Tippett scratched absentmindedly at the scraggly growth of hair on his neck. He almost grinned. "It always worked with the Mexicans."

"Goddamn!" Branch exclaimed. "Y'all comparin' us to some goddamn Greasers?" His own eyes were hard, and his hands tickled the walnut grip of the .36-caliber Colt.

"Didn't say no such thing," Tippett retorted. "It's just that the Comanches did it with the Mexicans. Figured it ought to work with the *Tejanos*, too." He shrugged. "They were wrong."

"Goddamn right, they were wrong."

"Still ain't right to go killin' women and kids."

"Those bitches fought harder'n the men, dammit," McGreely said harshly. His hand rested on the butt of his Colt.

"Hell," Tippett said with a rasping chuckle, "any woman'll fight like a grizzly sow when someone's threatenin' her young'uns. But," he added, dropping any pretense at humor, "that don't mean they should be shot down."

"What the hell do y'all know about it?" LeBeouf asked snidely.

Tippett turned burning eyes toward the man, but he spoke calmly. "I know what's right and what's wrong. And I know you goddamn treacherous Texans massacred a heap of Comanches for no good reason."

LeBeouf started to retort, but he was cut off by Branch who said, "You seem to know a heap about them Comanches, Mister Tippett."

"I been dealin' with 'em more'n ten years." He ignored the hard looks thrown his way, but he took note of the fact that McGreely and LeBeouf were easing out their pistols. Tippett thumbed back the hammer of his Hawken. Several years back, he had it converted from flintlock to percussion. "Don't," he warned. When the two men had slid their hands away from their revolvers, Tippett looked at Branch. He sighed. "If ye're lookin' for *Pehnahterkuhs*, you're a far piece off."

"Where could we find 'em?" Branch asked, relieved. He was not afraid of a fight, but he had sense enough to prefer talking.

"'Tween the Brazos and the Colorado maybe. Or along the San Saba, or maybe over on the Trinity."

"And where are we now, exactly?"

Tippett pointed northward. "Few miles from the Santa Fe Trail, up past the North Canadian."

"Damn. We traveled all this way for nothin'. And we been all through that country you spoke of. Damn." Frustration was written across his wide, sunburned face.

"How long you boys been out?" Tippett asked.

"More'n a year. Up and down the Brazos, around the Red and the Sabine. Hell, I don't know where to look no more. Now you tell us there ain't no Comanches to be found around here."

"Didn't say there was no Comanches around here."

Branch looked surprised. "You think you could help us find them?" he asked hopefully.

"I got me a job, *amigo*."

Branch sat in thought, then nodded to himself. "Look, we been out here so goddamn long a little more time ain't gonna make a difference. How about if we ride along with your wagons? Me and the others'll stay out of your way. Y'all find any Comanches along the way, y'all can introduce us. Y'all don't, we'll just tag along till

Santa Fe, then hire you to take us to whatever Comanches y'all can find."

Tippett ran his fingers through his long, greasy hair. Then he nodded slowly. "Reckon that won't put no one out. Jist don't go pesterin' me. I got enough to do without ye makin' trouble."

"You'll never know we're along, Mister Tippett," Branch said happily, holding his hand out.

Tippett shook it and then said, "Well, I've got meat to make." With a twinge of concern, Tippett rode into the thicket. A moment later, he was back with the mules. He soon killed a buffalo and two antelope. As the Texans helped with the butchering, Tippett asked, "Why'd they send ye boys, 'stead of Rangers, Mister Branch?"

"The Rangers were disbanded more than a year ago, Mister Tippett," Branch said with some bitterness.

Tippett was surprised but said nothing. He just worked his knife through the bloody muscle flesh of the buffalo.

27

Four days later, Tippett suddenly called a halt. He turned to Joe Savoy, captain of the freight wagon train, and said, "There's Comanches yonder. Get the wagons brought up and have the men stand ready."

"I thought you was friends with the Comanches," Savoy joked.

"I don't know *all* of 'em in the world," Tippett grinned tightly.

Savoy grunted an acknowledgement and hurried off to prepare.

As Tippett moved away, Branch pulled his horse up alongside. "You expectin' trouble, Mister Tippett?" he asked.

"Jist bein' cautious."

"They Comanches?"

"Yep."

"If'n they're of a mind to be peaceable, I'd be obliged if'n you was to let us meet with 'em. Give 'em our proposal."

"Depends on their hearts, *amigo*." Tippett was starting to like the three Texans, especially Branch. They were hard men who took no guff. Such was Tippett's way, too. "If'n they got good hearts, ye might be able to parley. If not, the only way ye'll want to meet 'em is from behind a wagon over a gun sight."

Tippett trotted away alone, angling southwest across the

scrubby prairie, hoping to come up over a short ridge that drifted to a flat on the other side. He was less than halfway to the ridge when the Comanches topped it and roared down the slope. Tippett stood his ground. There was little he could do about it anyway. The Comanches would cut him in half before he got anywhere near the wagon train. And, he decided, if his time had come to go under, he would prefer to do so facing his enemy. He cocked the Hawken and made sure the percussion cap was seated on the nipple properly. He checked his two big pistols, and then he waited. The warriors seemed to be coming at him in slow motion, and he could see everything clearly. He could pick out the greasy paints of red and blue and yellow and black that decorated man and animal. But an unreal quality hung over the charge.

Then he started, peering urgently at the colorful, swarming mass of warriors. "By Christ, it is him," he breathed. He stood in the stirrups so he could be seen. With all his lung power, he bellowed in Comanche: "Gray Wolf! It's me, Zeke Tippett!"

There was no slowing of the Indian ponies, and Tippett yelled again, more urgently. He saw Gray Wolf look up. Tippett hoped the young Comanche was leading this war band. If he was, Tippett and the wagon train might have a chance. Sweat was trickling over his ribs and seeping out from under his broad-brimmed beaver-felt hat. He could tell that Gray Wolf was studying him as closely as possible from the back of a racing war pony. With a huge sigh of relief, Tippett could hear Gray Wolf yelling to his warriors, aborting the raid.

The warriors, hard-pressed to stop their speeding mounts, swirled around the white man like a slow wave. As they passed Tippett, they curled around, circling him until they were stopped, surrounding him.

Tippett was outwardly calm. He was still nervous, vividly remembering the last time he had seen these men. But he nodded at Gray Wolf and grinned. "Howdy, Gray Wolf," he said evenly. "It's been a time since I seen ye last."

"Yes. Why don't you come to our village no more?"

"I been back. Ye've been on the war trail most times, though."

Gray Wolf shrugged. Then he asked, "Is Painted Wing still with you?" He had heard of white men who tired of their red-skinned women and traded them to another. He didn't like that but didn't know why.

"Sure," Tippett said with a large grin. "I leave her in Taos when I'm on the trail, though. Set her up in a house there."

Gray Wolf shook his head at the way he could see his world changing. More and more white men were using the Santa Fe Trail, which was one reason he was here now. He had taken to raiding those wagon trains when he could. It bothered him that his old friend was leading those wagons from one white man's city to another and that a Comanche woman was living in a closed-in mud box the *tahbay-boh* favored. It angered him. This was not the way a *Nermernuh* was supposed to live. Then he shrugged mentally. Painted Wing's life was not his concern.

"We got us another young'un, too," Tippett said with a grin. "A girl. We called her Light Calf." Tippett had named the baby Libby after his mother. But he and Painted Wing always called the girl by her Comanche name, Light Calf.

"*Bueno*," Gray Wolf said, pleasure lighting his face. Then he grew more serious. "Are there any *Tejanos* with the wagons?"

"*Si.*" Tippett watched Gray Wolf's face go hard, and he quickly added, grinning some, "They told me they come lookin' for *Nermernuh*."

Gray Wolf's face was like a carving in the rock walls bordering the *Llano*. "And I am looking for *Tejanos*," he hissed in Comanche.

Tippett's expression matched Gray Wolf's. "Don't go gettin' your bowels in an uproar, Wolf," he snapped. "They ain't lookin' for a fight. They're lookin' to meet with the People to make peace with 'em."

"Like they did three winters ago?" Gray Wolf spit in fury. "No, I will kill them! The *Tejanos* cannot be trusted."

"Ye got reason to hate *Tejanos*, Wolf. But these three were sent out to arrange a parley to make peace with the People."

"I will not talk with them," the Comanche hissed. "I will kill them. My medicine is strong against them."

"No one's doubtin' your medicine. But if that's your thinkin', ye'll have to kill me and a heap of other *tahbay-boh* first."

"I will take them!" Gray Wolf snarled, his face a mask of hate.

Without seeming to move, Tippett shifted the Hawken a trifle, enough to make sure that Gray Wolf had seen it. "Don't be an asshole, Wolf," Tippett said calmly, though he was nervous. "Them boys is under my protection, and I ain't gonna let ye take 'em. That wouldn't shine with this chil' at all."

Gray Wolf's eyes glittered like coals. He reached out the wicked-looking lance and touched the iron tip to Tippett's chest. "I have sworn to kill all *Tejanos* I find," he spat. He prodded Tippett lightly with the lance. "No one will stand in my way."

"Ye'd best move that goddamn lance, Gray Wolf," Tippett said evenly. "'Less'n ye fix to test your medicine again my Hawken."

They glared at each other, neither wavering. Finally, the Comanche pulled the lance back.

"There's no call for ye and me to go settin' against each other," Tippett said. "We been friends too long." He wisely did not mention some of their past differences.

Some of the fury melted from Gray Wolf's face. "You're right, my brother," he said slowly. "My heart is black toward the *Tejanos*, and it has clouded my sight, much as firewater does. We'll let you pass."

"And the *Tejanos*?"

"We will not harm the *Tejanos* now."

"Much obliged," Tippett said dryly. "Them *Tejanos* wanted me to ask ye if'n ye'd let 'em set to a parley with ye. But I don't expect ye're the ones they ought to be talkin' to."

Gray Wolf grinned ever so slightly. "I'll never sit with *Tejanos*," he said softly, but the words were coated with iron.

Tippett sighed. He was still tense, but he sensed Gray Wolf would not cause trouble, and that was a relief. Tippett uncocked the Hawken and rested it across the front of his saddle. He pulled his horse up so he was next to the Comanche. He placed a hand on one of the Indian's shoulders. "Ye're a mighty warrior, Gray Wolf," he said earnestly. "But don't let your heart rule your head. It'll ruin your medicine ye do it too often. Your people need ye, and I'd hate to see ye go under 'cause ye weren't usin' your head 'stead of your heart."

Gray Wolf nodded solemnly. "Those are good words, my friend. I will listen to them." He nodded once again. Then he wheeled his horse. At the head of his warriors, he raced off in a hanging cloud of dust.

Tippett took a few seconds to let the butterflies that had invaded his stomach settle down. Then he rode back to the wagons. "Ye can set the wagons movin' again, Joe," he said to Savoy.

As Savoy hurried off to get the freight wagons rolling, Branch approached Tippett. "Is there any chance we can speak to 'em, Mister Tippett?" he asked, certain he knew the answer.

"Nope."

"Because of one unfortunate incident." Branch sounded bitter.

"Comanches're people who live by their words. They don't make promises they don't fix to keep. It sets 'em apart from most whites."

"How can y'all say that?" Branch demanded. It seemed as if he could defeat the truth with anger and loudness. "The Comanches've broken every peace made with them. Every treaty, too. They no sooner agree to a peace and they're off raidin' again."

"Ye jist don't understand Comanches, Mister Branch. Ye folks single out one man from a band and make him the big chief of the whole goddamn nation. Christ, no Injuns work that way. Ye want to parley with 'em and make a lastin' peace, ye got to understand that."

"But they have chiefs . . ."

"Sure they got chiefs. That don't mean shit to most Comanches. A war chief's got power only as long as he's leadin' a war party. Once that's over, he's got no more authority than anyone else."

"They have civil chiefs, don't they?" Branch asked, exasperated. *I've got him now,* Branch thought. He mounted his horse, and alongside Tippett, he rode off.

"They ain't nothin' more'n advisers. They give counsel and advice when asked. In the council they get no more say than any other warrior — less'n they're a real good speaker. They might be listened to a bit more 'cause they got wisdom, but nobody has to obey 'em."

"But they've signed treaties, made peace. And then broke 'em."

"Only by your lights, Mister Branch." He pulled two strips of jerky from the possible bag dangling from his saddlehorn. He held one piece out to Branch, who accepted it with a nod.

"First off," Tippett said after he had gnawed off a piece of jerky, "the only way the Comanches, or most other Injins, will be held accountable is if'n all the warriors agree to it. If a warrior ain't signed the treaty, he ain't breakin' it. Another thing ye need to know is that each band is separate. It ain't often each band has anything to do with another. They even marry inside their own band most times. Only at rare times do they get together in large groups."

"Like for the Sun Dance?" Branch asked, interested, and trying to show he had some knowledge.

"Comanches don't hold a Sun Dance, Mister Branch," Tippett said, successfully keeping the derisiveness out of his voice. "Their allies, the Kiowas, do. Comanches might sit in on that once in a while. But they don't participate."

"Oh," Branch said, feeling foolish.

"Anyway," Tippett said, starting on another piece of jerky, "if one band makes peace with ye, it's only bindin' on that band. It don't have any effect on the other bands. Plus, they see the white man in the same terms. They figure that since each band is separate, then any band — or town — of whites is separate, too. They got no concept of a great chief directin' all things from some far-off place."

"That's the dumbest goddamn thing I ever heard."

"Maybe so to us. But it makes sense to a Comanche. And that's a good thing to keep to mind if ye do get to parley with any."

As the wagons caught up, they rode alongside on the left flank. Branch's brow furrowed as he thought about what he had just heard. All of it went against everything he had been taught since he was a youngster. Yet it seemed to make a great deal of sense, and, if thought out long enough, would explain many of the problems between the Comanches and the Texans.

"I'll try to do so," Branch finally said. "But I reckon it'll be harder'n hell."

"Why?"

"Well," he said, still feeling the flush of knowledge, "I been taught all my life that Injins are nothin' more'n goddamn bloodthirsty savages. They must be ignorant, or so I was taught, since they have no concept of government or even of religion."

"They got a fine religion, Mister Branch."

Branch held up his hand, nodding vigorously. "I'm sure they do, Mister Tippett. But I was *taught* they do not. I ain't sure I still believe it, but I spent a lot of years learnin' such things. They can't be forgotten or shoved aside after a few minutes talk. Even if I did, things change, Mister Tippett. The Comanches'll have to learn new ways. They can't go on raidin' like they been."

Tippett grinned. "They've been doin' so for a long spell. I reckon your treaties ain't gonna slow 'em down much."

"But they must. The Injins back East had to learn."

"Taught 'em well, didn't ye?" Tippett asked bitterly. "Butchered off a heap of 'em and shipped the rest out here. This land was to be theirs for all time, they was told. Now ye want that, too."

"Civilization moves on, Mister Tippett. It always has. The Injuns got to learn that. We are tryin' to save 'em by makin' 'em see the error of their ways. Gettin' them to agree to a peace, we will've taken the first step toward bringin' 'em into society."

"Ye set yourself a hell of job, Mister Branch," Tippett said sourly. He finished the last of the jerky strip. "And I doubt much if ye'll be able to finish it. No Injins out here're gonna give up their ways so easily. They're all gonna fight like hell."

"They can't slow civilization. They must take to our ways...or perish."

"I expect most of 'em'll go under then. There's no way on God's earth ye can make farmers out of Comanche warriors. Nor most others."

"We'll see, Mister Tippett, we'll see."

Tippett was afraid Branch might be right. But if he was, there'd be one hell of a lot of dead Comanches.

28

The men rode in silence, feeling the staggering heat on their hats and backs. Tippett kept his eyes moving, searching the ground, watching the sun-drenched blue sky, seeking any sign of enemies.

Branch raised himself from a warmth-induced stupor and asked, "Y'all think we'll find any more Comanches before Taos, Zeke?"

"Reckon not, but ye can never be sure. Comanches might be found anywhere. They'll think nothin' of ridin' a thousand miles for a raid."

"You sound proud to be a friend to 'em."

"I am. They're good folks. Best horsemen and fighters I ever saw."

"They ought to be good fighters with all the warriors they got."

Tippett laughed in bemusement. "Where'd ye ever get such an idea? Hell, there ain't more'n a couple thousand warriors in all the bands together. And they ain't ever fought all together."

"But there've been many reports of hundreds of warriors attackin' places all over only days apart."

"One small bunch most likely," Tippett chuckled. "I've known some that raided five, six places over several hundred miles in a week."

"But that can't be true," Branch said incredulously.

"It is," Tippett said. "Hell, they'll ride a hundred miles without stoppin' after a raid."

"Why?" Branch interjected, interested.

"In case someone thinks to chase 'em. They don't have the white man's failin' of settin' around to face overwhelmin' numbers and get rubbed out for it. They hit fast and hard, then skedaddle. Before anyone thinks of chasin' 'em, they'll be a hundred miles away."

Tippett pulled a tobacco twist from his waist-belt possibles bag and cut off a chunk. He shoved it into his mouth and talked around the wad. "And if they need to, they can do it on horses the white man's give up on. Hell, I once heard someone say a white man could ride a horse till it was ready to fall and then leave it. A Cheyenne'd come along and ride it another fifty miles and leave it for dead. A Comanche's come along and ride it another hundred miles, then kill the damn thing and sup on it." He chuckled a little.

"I don't know as if that's true, but I've seen Comanches do some things ye'd not believe. If'n more folks took time to get to know the Comanches, there'd be a lot less trouble."

"It's hard to do that, Mister Tippett," Branch said solemnly, "when your family's been wiped out by those bloody savages. I've seen what they do to people, especially women, in their raids. And I've seen the results of their treatment of white women."

"Ain't purty, is it?"

"Hell, no," Branch commented indignantly.

"Shit," Tippett swore, drawing the word out. "I've seen Comanche camps after the Greasers've been there. It ain't no purtier. And I know goddamn well the Texans're as bad, given the chance."

"We only pay back in kind, Mister Tippett," Branch said softly.

"The Comanches're fightin' for their land, their families, and their ways. It's more'n ye can say."

"Like hell," Branch snarled. "No offense," he added hastily.

"It's true, though. This ain't your land. It's Comanche land. It might help if'n ye folks saw that."

"I doubt that'll be possible as long as the Comanches raid."

Tippett was angry. He tugged on the reins and moved away from the Texan. He left the Texans alone as they plodded along the parched north plains of what would someday become northeast New Mexico, heading for the cooler mountains to the west. The land rose steadily, though mostly imperceptibly, reaching for the jagged peaks.

As the plodding, creaking train of freight wagons reached Rock Crossing on the Canadian River, Tippett decided it was time to leave the wagons. He did not want to see Taos, nor Painted Wing. He often felt this way as he made his way on the last leg of the long journey but usually fought off the feeling. This time he gave in to it. So, he told Savoy, the wagon leader, "I don't expect ye'll need me no more this trip, Joe. Ye got plenty of meat, and ye're close enough to Santa Fe, so I expect I'll be moseyin' on."

"Where to?"

"Toward the San Saba. I'll help them damned *Tejanos* go and find some Comanches. Not that I expect it'll do any good. But I give 'em my word, and I'll see it through."

Savoy nodded, wiping sweat off his face on one soiled calico sleeve. "Goddamn, it's hot," he muttered. "You need anything?"

"Just some flour, jerky, beans, and such."

Savoy scratched the stubble on his chin. "Take what all you need, Zeke. I don't want you gettin' caught short." He tossed the dregs of his coffee into the fire and stood. Savoy stared through the new dawn. "Damn, if it's this hot without light up yet, Christ, what's it gonna be like come noon?" he complained.

"Hot enough to fry your scrawny ass ye don't keep it in some shade," Tippett chuckled.

"Shit," Savoy scratched his belly under the filthy shirt. "Well, I reckon I'd best get my boys movin' or we'll never get anywhere. You got any messages for home?" He cocked an eyebrow at Tippett.

"Ye get a chance, stop by the store and tell Carter I'm well. Same with Painted Wing, if'n ye can swing by the house."

"Done." Savoy held out his hand. Tippett stood and shook it firmly. Savoy left, shouting loud and profane orders at his men. Tippett grinned and headed to where the three Texans huddled miserably around their small cook fire. They were sipping coffee and chewing on chunks of half-seared antelope.

"Ye boys want to go find some Comanches," Tippett said in mock ferocity, "ye'd best get off your asses and saddle up."

The three stared at him in surprise. Then Branch said, "I thought you said we'd not find any out this way."

Tippett squatted. "But there's plenty out east a ways. Ye boys saddle up. I'll fetch some possibles and we'll be off." Tippett stood and left. He was back in less than fifteen minutes. "Ready?" he asked.

The three nodded and mounted. "Here," Tippett said, draping the rope to a pack mule across LeBeouf's saddle. "Ye can lead him." Tippett turned his horse, not interested in LeBoef's objections.

They rode hard, stopping only when they had to or when the horses needed rest. Tippett was not pushed by any sense of urgency as much as he was by a desire to be shed of the Texans. Still, it was more than two weeks before Tippett spotted a sure sign of a camp. He stopped and pointed, "There's a village ahead, Mister Branch."

"How can you tell?" Branch asked, squinting into the bright sun.

"Buzzards. They always follow an Indian camp. Plenty of old carcasses, garbage, and such for 'em to feed on."

"Comanches?" Branch asked, nodding in accepting the information.

"Most likely. Only other Injuns that might camp in these parts are Kiowas or maybe Cheyennes. Both're friendly with the Comanches, though not so long ago the Comanches and Cheyennes was bitterest of enemies." He scowled, thinking of his run-in with

Yellow Blanket. "Most anyone else is too scared of the Comanches to come here."

"What band?" Branch asked, proud that he had remembered.

Tippett smiled briefly. "This far north, most likely *Pehnahturkahs* or *Yampareekahs*. But I can't be certain till we get up close."

They rode on slowly. Soon they could see the drifting smoke of cook fires and faintly hear sounds wafting up from the camp. Shortly after, Tippett spotted warriors riding toward them.

Tippett pointed. "Welcomin' committee," He said. "Now ye boys jist keep your traps closed and do whatever I tell ye."

Tippett faced forward and kept riding. He called over his shoulder, "They're *Pehnahterkuhs*." He wondered if the Comanches would kill them. Of all the Comanches, the *Pehnahterkuhs* had the most reason to hate the Texans, since they had taken the brunt of the devastation three years ago in San Antonio. He hoped they would at least listen to him. He was not sure this band would know him or accept him if they did. Tippett stopped, with the three others behind him. He held up his right hand, palm outward in a gesture of friendship. The warriors advanced suspiciously. They stopped within ten feet of the white men.

"I am White Horse," Tippett said in Comanche, "a great friend of the *Nermernuh*. I have lived in the camps of the *Kwahadis* for many winters. I am the brother to He-Who-Is-The-Gray Wolf, a warrior whose deeds are known by all the *Nermernuh*."

"We have heard of you, White Horse," a warrior said in Comanche. He snarled fiercely. "Why are you here?"

"I bring these others," he said, again in Comanche, struggling with the very different tongue. Tippett took a deep breath and plunged ahead. "They are *Tejanos*, and they ..." He stopped when he heard the angry rumbling of the warriors. He shifted the Hawken across his saddle. He figured he would be fighting for his life at any moment. "Hear me out," he snapped, voice overriding those of the warriors. When the Comanches quieted, he said, "They come from the great chief of the *tahbay-boh* to seek peace with the *Nermernuh*."

"The *Tejanos* do not speak true words," the warrior snarled. "They take our land from us and kill our women and children. They talk of peace and then kill our great leaders. We will kill them now."

At a loss for the words he needed in Comanche, Tippett fell back on his own fractured language, figuring the Comanches would understand enough of it. "All they want to do is talk, There ain't but three of 'em. Ye can kill 'em easy enough later. But I thought the People were great warriors, unafraid. I expect I was wrong, though, if'n ye eight are needed to kill three goddamn *Tejanos*."

"We are afraid of no one," the warrior said in his own language, choking back his fury. "Come, we'll show you."

29

Tippett felt the same twinge of fear as he rode into the *Pehnahterkuh* village as he had the first time he had entered a Comanche camp. But he kept his head high and showed no fear. He knew the Texans were so scared they might wet their pants, but they had wanted to find Comanches to talk to and Tippett had found them some.

The Comanches were lined up, watching in hard, hateful silence as the four white men plodded into their midst. The whites turned their horses over to the Comanches and sat in a clearing in which a fire was burning. They looked mighty lonely facing several dozen Comanche warriors and the women and children in a semicircle behind their men.

Several women, none young or attractive, served food. Tippett ate hungrily, the three Texans with some trepidation, as if they feared they would be poisoned or like they did not know what they were eating and were afraid to ask.

When the food was done and a pipe passed around from warrior to warrior, white to white, one old chief commanded, "Speak."

Tippett translated as Branch stood and spoke. "My Comanche

brothers," he started, cursing himself silently because his voice was wavering from fright, "I know there has been bad blood and bad hearts between your people and mine."

Branch settled himself and pushed on: "But the time's come for us to live in peace." He paced a bit as he talked and used his arms to emphasize the earnestness of what he was saying. "I know y'all were done wrong down in San Antone and there's nothin' I can do to change that. But we can't keep on killin' each other neither."

He paused to marshal his thoughts and sip water. Tippett thought the Texan was doing well. He might be spouting a pack of lies, but he seemed to be making believers of at least a few Comanches.

"It's a bad thing," Branch continued, with Tippett giving out the words a moment later as best he could in Comanche, "that you lost so many of your great war chiefs and so many others of your people in San Antone. But continued fightin' will only lead to more misery for both our peoples. My people have suffered, too, from Comanche attacks. We've lost many people in your raids."

Tippett was rather amazed at Branch's sudden eloquence, even more so at *what* the Texan was saying. It showed that Branch had been listening to Tippett when he had talked of Comanche ways and customs and of how the Comanches viewed the massacre in San Antonio.

"Both sides," Branch said, having relaxed completely, "have seen many horrible deeds done by the other. That ain't right in nobody's sights. We want to live in peace with the Comanches, we think the Comanches want to live in peace with us. Like you, we have people who call for war for no reason. And men who've done unspeakable things.

"We ain't blameless, but neither are you. The Comanches have men who don't care for those of another race. But there's many good men among our peoples. Men who want to live in peace. All the chiefs of my people want to parley with your chiefs at your convenience. We need to talk out this bad blood between us so we can forge a strong, lastin' peace between the white man and his red brothers."

Tippett was impressed. He had not thought Branch capable of speaking so well. But the Comanches were not quite so impressed. When Branch sat, drinking gratefully from a deer bladder canteen, the Comanches took their turn. Tippett translated for the Texans.

One after another the warriors stood and angrily mentioned bits and pieces of what had happened in San Antonio three years before, and the treachery of the Texans. And almost to a man they called for the death of the three Texans who sat before them, as well as for the death of the *tahbay-boh* who had brought the Texans.

Tippett's face grew grimmer as the words rolled out in the harsh tongue of the *Nermernuh*. And the Texans grew more frightened. LeBeouf looked ready to bolt, while McGreely seemed set to pull his revolving pistol and start shooting. Either action would be disastrous.

Branch whispered to both men as another warrior stood and less than eloquently called for the deaths of the four whites. Branch tried to calm his two companions. Tippett, still translating, though he knew the three Texans were no longer really listening to him, felt some solemn satisfaction in seeing the way Branch conducted himself.

"How many more are gonna speak?" Branch asked Tippett as a fat, grease-coated warrior with a scarred face rose.

"All of 'em's got a right to, and might do so," Tippett said. He grinned grimly. "Besides, the longer they talk, the longer we stay alive. Ye might take the time to try'n think of a way to talk them out of puttin' us to the torch rather than worryin' if they'll do it."

"Can I talk again, Mister Tippett?" Branch asked quietly.

"Yep. Jist wait till one of 'em's done, and then stand."

When the warrior finished, Branch rose. He was worried, but he could not sit and do nothing. "My friends," he said, feeling bad about using such a phrase, "I have said I know there are differences between us. But you must realize that if you kill us, there'll only be more bloodshed. For if you kill us, my people will send others. Those others won't come to talk. They'll come to kill Comanches."

"And we will kill them," a warrior shouted.

"Maybe you will," Branch said calmly. "But some of you will die, maybe many. And others'll follow them." He adopted a harsher tone, hoping he would not antagonize the Indians any more. "You can't kill all the white men. We are too many."

Tippett grimly appreciated the Texan's speech. Branch was a feisty man, short, wiry, and tough as nails. Tippett suspected that Branch was much like him in some ways. Like now. Tippett felt a bit better because there was less gloom over him and the others.

"I expect ye might've done some good," Tippett said, leaning over. "Standin' up for yourself like that'll make the Comanches take notice. They got no tolerance for men who can't control their fear."

"Controlling their fear?"

"Sure. Ye don't think I ain't scared, do ye?" He grinned. "Shit, I'm as scared as ye or your two *compañeros*."

"But you don't look..."

"Hell, neither do ye. Ye been actin' fine. I know ye're so scared ye're about ready to shit your britches. But ye're controllin' it. They don't know how scared ye are. All they know is that ye look like ye ain't scared of 'em at all. That's what counts."

Branch flushed with pride, but said nothing.

The noise from the warriors had dwindled and an old man rose. "I am Paha-yuca," he said softly, the simple words sounding grand.

"Who's he?" Branch whispered.

"Civil chief of this band. I expect they're one of the bands of Wasps. He commands a heap of respect amongst these bands."

"This *tahbay-boh* speaks true," Paha-yuca said softly. "The *Nermernuh* cannot win against the *tahbay-boh*. The *tahbay-boh* are as many as the buffalo, as many as the blades of grass. My heart is black toward the *Tejanos*. I'll never change that. But the *tahbay-boh* have powerful medicine. More powerful even than the *Nermernuh's*." He waited as if he had nothing else to do, until the grumbling stopped. "I've seen their great numbers," Paha-yuca said firmly. "San Antonio is a small village of the *tahbay-boh*. Others are much larger.

"And I've seen the new weapons of the *tahbay-boh*. The weapons that spit fire many times without reloading. It would not do to kill these three *Tejanos* — nor White Horse, the great friend of the *Nermernuh*. That would bring many *tahbay-boh* against us. We've already lost many great war leaders. There are few great ones left to lead us into war. Few with medicine powerful enough to battle the *tahbay-boh*. It is better to see what the *tahbay-boh* chiefs have to say of peace. If there're many presents for the *Nermernuh*."

"There will be many presents for the Comanches," Branch vowed.

Paha-yuca sat and the argument continued, but with less vehemence. Finally, he rose again and spoke: "We should give the *tahbay-boh* a chance to live in peace if the *Tejanos* will leave us alone. It is the only way the *Nermernuh* will survive."

Tippett hoped the old chief's wise counsel would be accepted. Tippett could see the end of the Comanches if they continued their war with the whites. Perhaps if they made peace now — as they had made peace with the Cheyennes three years ago — they would survive.

To Branch's relief, the warriors began to swing to Paha-yuca's side, eventually agreeing that they would meet later in the year.

Branch beamed, but Tippett said, "Don't think ye done *too* good."

"Why?" Branch asked, dismayed.

"I told ye before, Mister Branch, that most bands don't have much to do with the others. Paha-yuca only holds sway — and that's only because his counsel's respected — over a few small bands. It's too late in the year for him to try to talk a bunch of far-flung bands into comin' to a peace parley. He'll bring in the few bands he has some say over, but that's about all."

"Then we'll have to make do with them, Mister Tippett."

BOOK 8

GRAY WOLF, 1843-46

30

Gray Wolf was troubled. For days he remained angry at his old friend Tippett for trying to help the three *Tejanos*. His hatred for the Texans burned through him like a river of lava and threatened to spill over onto Tippett himself.

But he found no solace in the village so he finally approached Lame Bear, a civil chief noted for his wisdom. He gave the old man a gift of a horse and some meat. Then he said, "Father, I am troubled."

The old Comanche nodded. "This I have known," he said, his voice soft and rustling like leaves in a light wind.

"The *tahbay-boh* grow closer to the land of the *Kwerhar-renuh* with each moon. They have no respect for the land, but want to own it."

"A man can no more own the land than he can the air we breathe or the sun which gives us warmth."

"So I've always thought. But the *tahbay-boh* think otherwise. His ways are bad. The land grows foul where they live and the animals flee. Their ways are strange. How they live in one place, in lodges of stone or mud or wood. It's not right that men should live so."

"That may be so," the old man murmured. "We must ask the spirits for help."

"I've done so. But still my heart is black toward the *tahbay-boh*. They are so many and we are so few. It may be hard to cleanse these spirits from our land. They don't live in the right way. How can a man be a man when his whole life is spent digging in the Earth Mother with sticks and things made of iron?"

"There are white-eyes whose ways are much like those of the People," Lame Bear said. He felt the infirmities of his many winters heavy on his shoulders, making his body sag like an old woman's breasts. He had seen much glory in his youth. He had captured many horses and killed many enemies. He had kept his land free of the Spaniards. But now he was bent with the years and nearly toothless. He was accepted now only because of his wisdom. It angered him that he had not died in battle. That would have been a glorious death.

Such was not his fate, however. And so, he sat each day, staring at his fire, dreaming of days past. At times he could feel the wind rushing in his face as he raced along on his pony, and see the blood welling up from where his arrow had dug into a buffalo's insides; he could smell the pungency of a buffalo wallow or the acrid smoke of a burning farm. He was shamed to have to rely on younger men for his meat, which his almost toothless gums had difficulty in chewing.

Lame Bear knew he had little time left and it pleased him when young men came to him for advice. But he could see the changes coming. The old ways of the *Nermernuh* were shifting a little each day. There was nothing he could do except try to make it a little easier for the young men to see those changes and accept them. He would be gone soon, but these others had many years to face. They would not have an easy time of it. But they must carry on the ways of the People.

He brought his mind back to the problem at hand as he heard Gray Wolf say, "Yes, there are *tahbay-boh* like that. Like White Horse."

"Yes," Lame Bear said, wanting to be left alone with his dreams.

"But he has changed, Father," Gray Wolf said vehemently. "He no longer lives like a *Nermernuh*. He has taken our sister, Painted Wing, to the white man's town and put her in a stone lodge to live."

"Has she said she wants to come home?" Lame Bear's last wife, Moccasin Tracks, hobbled over and handed him a dish of stew made with meat Gray Wolf had brought. She was twenty years younger than he but looked ten years older, such was the hard life of a Comanche woman.

"No," Gray Wolf said, almost bitterly. He did not know why he was bitter; Painted Wing was nothing to him.

"Then it must be what she wishes. She's welcome here. She knows this."

"You speak the truth, Father," Gray Wolf said. He accepted the bowl of stew Moccasin Tracks handed him and rooted around in it for a piece of meat. "But there's more. White Horse no longer comes to our village. Instead he spends his time bringing more people to our land."

"They don't stay in our land," Lame Bear said simply. "They pass through, like the wind, and then are gone, toward the setting sun."

"But the wind doesn't kill our buffalo. The *tahbay-boh* kills more than he needs, leaving the meat to feed the buzzards and coyotes."

"They, too, must eat." Lame Bear winced as he struggled to gnaw a piece of meat, pain stabbing from an exposed nerve beneath a tooth.

"Their wagons cut deep grooves in the Earth Mother and their animals eat the grass our horses need." He chewed a piece of meat until it was quite pulpy. Surreptitiously he slipped it out of his mouth and slid it into Lame Bear's horn bowl.

The old man noticed and nodded, barely perceptibly. "There is plenty of grass for all," he said.

"But soon there will not be. Already we must move our village more often to find grass for the horses and meat to fill our bellies."

Lame Bear smiled as he found the chewed piece of meat and popped it into his mouth. That was better, he thought. "Yet there is plenty," he said, almost content. Gray Wolf slid another piece of masticated buffalo meat into Lame Bear's bowl. "No one has starved; we've lost no horses. The Great Spirit has made enough for all, if their medicine is good. The People must make good medicine and follow it."

"How can I be sure our medicine is powerful enough to destroy the evil spirits that come among us?"

"You may never know."

"Then I must keep fighting," Gray Wolf said firmly.

"If that is where your medicine lies, you will do well. But don't let your heart rule your head. To do so would remove you power."

"White Horse used those same words to me, but my head is confused and my heart tells me to kill all the *tahbay-boh* I can."

"Including White Horse?"

"The spirits will decide," he said. He sat a while longer, chewing meat until it was soft and then dropping it in Lame Bear's bowl, making the old man happy.

Gray Wolf, on the other hand, was not. He had come to Lame Bear seeking answers and had gotten none. His heart still burned with a searing hatred of all white men. It would not let him be still.

The problem continued to plague him, driving him. Even joy with his family did not help. He had a third wife now, Blue Eyes, a Mexican captive Gray Wolf had bought. His son Horse Tail had died in infancy, but Black Arrow had been born to him and Red Moon, nearly four years ago. He had a daughter, too, almost a year old. Yellow Star was the issue of Running Deer.

Finally, he could stand it no longer. A week after talking with Lame Bear, Gray Wolf set out alone. He carried his iron-tipped lance, a shield of hardened bull hide, a bow slung in a case across his back with a quiver holding twenty arrows, a knife, a tomahawk in his rawhide belt, and a pistol taken from a dead Mexican with powder horn and a small pouch of lead shot. His face was streaked with black war paint and the five horses he brought also were painted. His buffalo-horn headdress, a breechcloth, and moccasins were his only garments, though a buffalo sleeping robe and a blanket were tied to one of the horses along with a small supply of meat.

He rode north, eyes searching for signs of a white man's freight wagons. He would test his power against the white men with the loaded wagons. He would show them the strength and powerful medicine of the Comanche. By himself he would drive the white men back. The Cimarron Cutoff of the Santa Fe Trail, like the rest of the trail, was well-marked with deep ruts cut sometimes six abreast in the earth.

More than a week passed, but Gray Wolf did not give up. Hour after slow hour he rode along the trail, watching, waiting. His patience was finally rewarded. He could hear the cursing mule skinners and braying, snorting mules that struggled against their harnesses. The creaking of heavy wheels not properly greased rode up out of the undulating, sere land. And Gray Wolf could see the great hanging clouds of dust kicked up by the hundreds of hooves.

He rode up a ridge and hobbled his extra horses. Remounted, he waited, wanting to savor the moment the whites discovered him.

31

The screeching procession of wagons rolled into sight, but it was another hour before they were close enough for Gray Wolf to attack. He waited, painted face frozen, eyes narrowed. He grinned grimly when he saw he had been noticed. Knowing his lance would be useless, Gray Wolf stabbed it into the ground. He grinned humorlessly again when he watched the effect his action had on the white men.

The freighters were hurriedly trying to bring their wagons up and form a protective circle or box. Fear was stark on most of their faces at the prospect of facing a Comanche war party. Most had been along on this trail often enough to know that they seldom saw the Comanches before being attacked. So, they figured that if there was one sitting up on the grassy ridge, there must be a heap of others nearby.

Gray Wolf slipped the bow out and strung it. Then he grabbed a handful of arrows out of the puma-skin quiver. With a piercing shriek, he heeled the small, wiry pony into a run. He raced down the slope, watching the freighters frantically trying to control their mules, oxen, and horses while creating a fortification.

One man suddenly shouted, “Hell, there ain’t but one of ‘em.”

The others looked around wildly, checking, then back at Gray Wolf. They were dumbstruck by the sight of a single warrior racing toward them, screaming his head off. Their looks changed to glee as they realized they were not facing a war party. Most of the men came out from behind the wagons, watching, no longer afraid.

Gray Wolf was within fifty yards of the wagons when the same man who spoke before yelled, “I want first crack at ‘im.” The man raised his rifle and aimed. But he was too slow. As he looked down the sights, an arrow ripped into his belly. He grunted and headed down, ready to land on his seat. But a second arrow tore into his throat, knocking his upper torso backward until he fell flat on his back.

“Get to cover!” one of the other men shouted.

The mule skinners dived for the cover of the wagons as Gray Wolf slid down to hang off the side of the horse so they could not see him. He circled the wagons. From behind the protection of the heavy wagons and bulky cargo, the men shot hastily. Still the pony darted around and around. Gray Wolf fired arrows from under the horse’s neck.

One freighter fell, two arrows piercing his heart. Another freighter screamed as an arrow lodged in his leg.

Gray Wolf swung up onto the pony’s back and raised his bow over his head in victory. He slid over the side again as he heard someone bellow, “Shoot his horse, goddammit. Put the bastard afoot.”

Guns roared from behind the wagons and Gray Wolf could feel bullets slamming into his pony. The animal screamed in pain but kept running, bringing his rider to the bottom of the ridge. A bullet found the horse’s heart and the pony went down in a tangle of legs. Gray Wolf was ready and landed on his feet, running. He spun and ran toward the wagons. He fired two more arrows, wounding another mule skinner before a bullet punched him to the ground. Blood welled from the right side of his chest. As he struggled to get up, he could feel more bullets whizzing past and see the puffs of dust they kicked up.

He tried to nock another arrow but found that his fingers would not work. Then he realized it was quiet. Through blurred vision, he saw the freighters ambling toward him. Gray Wolf straightened his shoulders, steeling his face. With a deep breath, he pulled his war club and waited for his end, hoping to sell himself dearly.

The mule skinners stopped briefly when Gray Wolf began his death chant. It came low from his throat, building as it soared past his lips. It was an eerie sound, drifting slowly away across the prairie:

The buffalo have died
so will I now
My spirit will be
with the eagles; I die

The freighters were wary. They were not men easily scared, but this sound was inhuman and frightened them with its haunting quality.

Blood splashed from the gaping hole in Gray Wolf's chest, splattering on his moccasins and the grass at his feet.

The whites gained courage when they saw Gray Wolf's wound. "Well, lookee here, boys," one said, an evil grin spreading across his dark, weather-beaten face. A white scar cut across one dusky cheek.

"What're we gonna do with 'im?" another questioned. He was nondescript in dress and looks except for the magnificently large nose that roared out of the center of his face like a mountain ridge.

"I reckon," Scar Face said slowly, nastily, "that we ought to skin him alive. Peel the hide right off him."

"Sounds about right," a third retorted. No one would have noticed him in a crowd. He was medium height and weight, perhaps a little older than the others. He wore a bright green shirt of linsey-woolsey.

"Shut up that goddamned noise, goddammit," Scar Face said. "Goddamn, sounds like a cat some 'un stuck into goddamn boilin' water."

"Worse," still another said. "I say we kill 'im now and git it over with. Just to stop that damned howlin'. Christ, he's worse'n any coyote I ever heard." He was short and stocky and his left hand had suffered some trauma sometime, leaving it twisted.

Scar Face pulled out his knife slowly, letting Gray Wolf get a good look at the large, heavy blade. He advanced in measured steps. "I reckon I'll just start off with somethin' goddamn small and useless."

"You gonna take his stones?" Big Nose asked with glee.

"Goddamn right," Scar Face said, hate, and more than a little fear, coursing through his voice.

Gray Wolf did not even blink as the white men guffawed at their companion. Their laughter stopped suddenly when Scar Face straightened up as if slammed by a mighty fist, and then fell over on his back.

The crack of a gun echoed across the land and the mule skinners saw the spreading stain of blood on their friend's shirt front. Startled, they looked around, fear leaping into their eyes.

"Where are they?" Twisted Hand asked, voice quavering.

Then Green Shirt pointed. "There's one."

They all looked up to see a solitary figure riding rapidly toward them, hooves kicking up clouds of dust.

"Git ready to fire," Big Nose said. "We'll take care of this one and worry about the others later."

"That ain't no Injun," Twisted Hand said.

"I don't give a damn," Big Nose retorted. "I aim to kill him before he kills me!"

But it was too late. Zeke Tippett thundered up, his horse breathing hard. "Get back to your wagons and head out," he snapped.

"The hell we will," Big Nose snarled. "This here sumbitch kilt two boys." His eyes grew hard. "And you just kilt another."

Tippett leveled a Paterson Colt at him. The Colt was not big, only .36 caliber, but it could be fired five times, though Tippett had filled only four of the chambers, and it would kill just fine this close. "I'm tellin' ye, Sam, that if any of your boys moves, I'll gut shoot ye and then him."

Sam Flinch stared hard at Tippett for a few moments, but then dropped his gaze. "All right, boys," he said, trying to save at least some face, "I reckon we can let him git away with this just this one time." He looked back at Tippett and said, "But I aim to git you for this, Tippett, you Injun-lovin' son of a bitch. And I'll git..."

Tippett had had enough of the man's jabbering, so he reached out and smashed him in the face with the pistol barrel. It broke Flinch's jaw. "Mind your manners, Sam," Tippett said calmly.

"Look here, Zeke," Twisted Hand Tim Marshall said. "This damned Injin attacked us. We was mindin' our own business, moseyin' down the trail nice as you please. Then all to a sudden he comes up like all the devils in hell was bitin' his ass, shootin' arrows every which way. All we did was to defend ourselves once he commenced it all."

Tippett shrugged, unconcerned. "He's got a bullet in him deep, Marshall. I reckon he'll go under before much longer. There ain't no call for ye to go cuttin' his balls off like ye was plannin'."

"He would've done the same to us," Marshall said.

"Don't mean I'd allow it was I around. Now, I'm tired of you flappin' your gums. Ye boys lift up this sack of shit" — he gestured with the revolver toward Slade — "and haul him back to the wagons. See to the dead and wounded and then move out."

"You'll be leadin' no more freight trains on this trail, Tippett," Marshall said harshly. "I'll see to that."

"Waugh. I'd not hire on with the likes of ye anyway. And there's plenty of others who'll value my services."

"We'll just see about that."

"Suit yourself. But don't threaten me again." Tippett spoke softly, but there was no denying the danger in the words. "Now get."

The men grumbled, but Marshall said, "Come on, boys, let's go. Ain't gonna git us nowhere standin' here jawin'." He had dealt with Tippett before and sort of liked him. He was real pals with the dead men back at the wagons, but not enough to want to go to war with Tippett — or the Comanches. Still, this did not set well with him.

Slowly the men began heading toward the wagons. Two lifted Slade's body; another helped Flinch who was holding his jaw.

Tippett watched until the men were a little distance away. Then he stuffed the Colt into his holster — a soft leather pouch that had, through use, molded itself to the pistol. He reached out his hand. Gray Wolf, who had been standing silently, weaving a little, took it. Tippett pulled, and Gray Wolf, using the last of his strength, leaped. Tippett kicked the animal into a trot. Gray Wolf sucked in gulps of air to ease the pain. He leaned his head on Tippett's back a moment before jerking upright, shamed at his weakness.

32

Tippett and Gray Wolf rode until night nearly covered them. When they stopped in a grove of stunted mesquite, and one large cottonwood, on the banks of a trickling creek, Tippett was a little shocked at Gray Wolf's condition. The Comanche sat in tight-lipped silence, but the agony could be seen in his dark eyes. He clung to his pony's mane with a fierce determination and Tippett had to pry the Indian's hands loose. Gray Wolf turned glassy eyes on the old mountain man and then slumped unconscious, held up only by Tippett's grip.

Tippett lay Gray Wolf gently on the ground and then hurriedly started a fire. In a small old tin pot, he boiled up bark and yarrow root. When it was the consistency he wanted, he pulled it off the fire and set it aside to cool. He knelt at Gray Wolf's side and bent over him. The Comanche looked ghastly. His face was as pasty as his dark features could get, and Tippett knew his friend had lost a considerable amount of blood. Pulling his knife, he quickly sliced into Gray Wolf's chest. The Comanche moaned, but did not regain consciousness. With knife, finger, and then knife again, Tippett rooted around. Finally, he felt the partially flattened lead ball and managed to work it out. Working hastily, Tippett used the small sewing kit — long, sharp needle and buffalo sinew — from his belt possibles bag and sewed up the incision he had made in Gray Wolf's chest.

Wiping the sweat from his forehead on a sleeve, he slathered the wound with the concoction he had made. Tippett bandaged the wound as best he could after cutting up a cotton shirt.

Tippett used the wiping stick from his Hawken rifle and hung two strips of fresh buffalo meat over the fire. He ate and then spread out his buffalo robe. After checking Gray Wolf one last time, he turned in.

Tippett was only a little surprised when he awoke to find Gray Wolf still alive. The Comanche was even awake. He still looked in bad shape and his face was hard-set, reflecting the deep pain he felt. "Ye up to eatin' some?" he asked.

"Yes." It was a whisper.

"Well, I'll have something for ye before long. Don't go nowhere." He grinned, trying to comfort Gray Wolf. The Comanche stayed implacable. Tippett moved off and made water. He dunked his head in the stream to help him wake up. Then he rekindled the fire and set more meat up to roast. He filled his small coffee pot with water, then tossed in bite-size chunks of buffalo meat. He put it on a flat rock in the fire, moving it when it began to boil too rapidly.

He ate the half-raw meat he cooked for himself. Then, he pulled out his old horn spoon from his possible sack and sat next to Gray Wolf. He braced the Comanche's back up against his saddle.

Gray Wolf looked at the thin soup distastefully, and Tippett laughed. But he said sternly, "Don't go givin' me no guff, Wolf. Ye'll be a heap better off with some of this in your belly."

"I want meat," Gray Wolf tried to snarl, but it was more like a kitten's growl than a puma's roar.

"Ye ain't got the strength to eat meat, boy, and ye goddamn well know it. Now jist open that big mouth of yours and take some of this. I got some small hunks of meat in there ye can sink your teeth into."

Without much enthusiasm, Gray Wolf sipped the watery brew and ate the few pieces of boiled-tender meat. When he had finished the meager meal, Tippett said, "Now get some sleep, *amigo*."

Gray Wolf nodded. His strength was disappearing fast and he had no will to argue. He was asleep before his eyes were fully closed.

For nearly a week Gray Wolf lay, passing from delirium to fever and back again. He had only moments of lucidness, and Tippett made sure there was stew ready all the time for whenever Gray Wolf awoke. Tippett tended his friend as best he could, changing the poultice as frequently as he dared, and trying to keep Gray Wolf from the worst of the hot afternoon sun and heat. At night he bundled Gray Wolf into his own heavy buffalo robe to keep the chill off him.

One day Gray Wolf said, weakly but firmly, "I want meat."

Tippett cooked thin strips of buffalo and gave them to Gray Wolf who complained loudly at the tiny pieces. Tippett ignored him.

When he had eaten all the meat Tippett had cooked, Gray Wolf fell asleep again, a smile of some contentment lingering on his face. When he awoke again, the sky was deepening in color as night fell.

"Hungry?" Tippett asked.

"*Si*."

"I was about to fill my meatbag. I expect there's enough for two."

Tippett shared the meat — seared on the outside, raw inside — cutting off bits for Gray Wolf. He smiled as the Comanche bolted them down. After finishing, Gray Wolf looked a little better. His dark, round face was not so sickly. As he sat leaning against Tippett's saddle, he asked, "How'd you come to be here, my friend?"

Tippett shrugged. "I was tendin' business back in the States. On the way back, I started lookin' along the trail for some wagons. Thought maybe I could hook up with some boys and earn a few *pesos*. Reckon I found some." He smiled softly. "And just in time, too."

Gray Wolf tried hard not to smile. His hatred of the wagon men was now as deep as it was for the Texans. But he could not stop himself and the smile broke through. It was not often that a Comanche warrior would thank someone, but he thought this was a time such a thing would be appropriate. "I'm glad, my friend," he said in Comanche.

"I expect ye would've done the same were things the other way."

Gray Wolf grew serious. Pain crossed his eyes. It was not a pain caused by the wound, but rather the agony of shame. "I don't know," he said softly in Comanche. "My hatred for all the *tahbay-boh* turned my heart black against you."

"Why?" Tippett asked, though he was not particularly surprised.

"You lead the wagons that cut the face of our land," Gray Wolf said sadly. "Their wheels dig deep into the earth. The *tahbay-boh* with them kill our buffalo. Their mules foul our water. They have no respect for the proper ways of life."

"But they're jist movin' through, Wolf."

"One day they'll come to stay. The Spanish came and stayed until they were driven out. But the *Americanos* are different from the Spanish. They're much like the *Tejanos*." His words dripped with hatred. "They'll dig their feet into land they've taken from my people. They'll fight like a cornered bear. And more'll come with each moon. Soon there'll be more *Tejanos* in my land than *Nermernuh*."

"They're gonna keep comin' whether ye fight 'em or not."

"You say we shouldn't fight?" Gray Wolf asked, growing angry. "You should've let those men take my manhood. It'd be the same. Are the *Nermernuh* really to learn to become like the *tahbay-boh*? Should we be content with digging little holes in the ground to plant things that can't even be eaten?"

"Hell, Gray Wolf, I don't know what I'm sayin'. I jist know ye can't win. There's jist too many white-eyes."

"If I took your horse, what would you do?" Gray Wolf asked vehemently.

"I'd find ye and put ye under," Tippett said simply.

"And if I took your traps and your food and everything else of yours?"

"Same thing. I ain't likely to let anyone take my plunder."

"But you say such a thing is right when the *Tejanos* or *Americanos* take what is the People's?"

"It ain't the same," Tippett said without conviction.

"No? The *Tejanos* take the *Nermernuh*'s land, the land where we've lived and rode and made war and raised our children and hunted the buffalo. Is that right? Is it right that the *tahbay-boh* kill our buffalo? They take food from our children. Their animals foul our water so that we can't drink. Would you not fight for these things?"

"Yes, but..."

"They talk with a snake's tongue. They say one thing now, another later. They tell one band this and another something else. They say there's room for all. But as they say that, more *tahbay-boh* take our land and kill us."

"What they're doin' ain't right, Gray Wolf," Tippett said. It was his turn to feel the searing pain of shame. "I know that as well's ye. But there ain't shit ye can do to stop 'em. Maybe ye *should* become like the white-eyes, learn farmin' and such."

"As long as the sun has risen, we've gone to war," Gray Wolf said. He had a faraway look in his eyes. "We fought the Utes and the Apaches long before the *tahbay-boh* came to this land. Then we fought the Spanish and the *Mexicanos*. Now the *Tejanos*. It is our way. The Utes, Apaches, and the others know this. It is their way.

"But the *tahbay-boh* doesn't know this way. He talks of peace while he sends others to steal our land. He talks of peace while others attack our villages, take our horses, kill our people. Yet if we do these things, they call us names and send men to kill more of us. To them, what we do is murder; what they do is punishment."

Tippett sat silently, numbed by the shame of knowing his people would do such things. He could not defend the actions of the encroaching Texans and Americans. But he knew the Comanches could not win a war against them. The People would be annihilated like so many other tribes before them. He could not reconcile it, either for himself or for Gray Wolf. He shook his head, disgusted and depressed. "Ye aim to keep fightin', then?"

Gray Wolf also knew the Comanches could not win a war with the whites. But his heart would not let his head rule. "Yes," he said, a touch of pride coming through the weakness brought by his wound. "It's the only way."

"And ye'll put me under?" Tippett asked, sad but unafraid.

"I have thought of it many times, my friend."

"Jist for bringin' some freight wagons across your land?"

"For that, yes. But more for helping those *Tejanos* two summers ago." He spit, as if the word left a sour, foul taste in his mouth.

"Ye're gettin' to be as bad as the damned *Tejanos*, Gray Wolf. Those three I helped never did nothin' to ye."

"They're *Tejanos*. My heart is black when my ears hear that name."

"That's what I mean, Wolf. The *Tejanos* get attacked by Comanches, and they'll go find any Injins that're convenient and kill 'em. Don't matter if they're peaceable. They see Injins and start killin'. Ye were half froze to kill those *Tejanos* jist 'cause they were *Tejanos*. Didn't make ye no never mind they hadn't done nothin' to ye."

"All the *Tejanos* have stolen our land."

"And all Comanches have killed *Tejanos*."

"We didn't ask them to come here."

"But they're here, and ye know goddamn well they're gonna stay."

"I think you speak the truth, my friend," Gray Wolf admitted.

"Ye still fixin' to put me under?"

Without hesitation, Gray Wolf said, "No. You saved my life. But more than that, you saved my spirit."

Tippett, sitting cross-legged, grabbed his crotch. Grinning, he said, "I saved somethin' else near to ye, too, eh?" He laughed.

Gray Wolf sat solemnly for some moments before smiling, and then laughing. "I've been in so much pain here," he said, tapping his chest, "that I haven't checked that." He grabbed his crotch. "Yes," he smiled, "all is well."

Gray Wolf felt well enough in the morning to walk a few steps and make water the way he should instead of in his breechcloth, which was heavily fouled after so long. As he limped to the fire, Tippett tossed him something, saying, "Here."

Gray Wolf was still too weak and sore to make much of a reaction so the piece of cloth hit him in the chest and fell at his feet. He stood staring down at it for some moments. It would be, he thought, interesting to bend over and pick it up. He did not think he would make it, but he had to give it a try.

First, he crouched, squatting, back straight. He reached out a hand to retrieve the cloth, but could not quite make it. So, he had to bend at the waist. Though it felt to him as if there were a burning stick under the skin of his chest, he showed nothing on his face. He grabbed the cloth and leaned backward until he was straight again. Sweat curled down from his greasy black hair and meandered across the dark forehead to get lost in the thin eyebrows. Squatting, he stared ahead. Tippett grinned at his discomfit.

With a straight face despite the effort it took, Gray Wolf rose straight up. He stood, weaving. Black circles spun before his eyes, and the horizon wavered. He snapped his eyelids shut, blocking out the swaying land. After some minutes, he bravely reopened his eyes. The land had settled and his stomach no longer felt like it would leap up his throat and out his mouth.

"What's this?" he asked, holding out the section of blanket.

"New breechcloth for ye," Tippett said, amused. "That one ye're wearin's so fouled, it'll scare off the buffalo before long."

Gray Wolf winced, partly from the pain, partly from Tippett's statement. He nodded. Carefully, so as not to fall, he stripped off the old one and tossed it as far as he could. He was about to put the blanket loincloth on when he suddenly stopped.

Gray Wolf looked over at Tippett and grinned. Wearing only moccasins, he strolled to the water, and plopped into a pool, letting the water run across legs, behind, and crotch. He stayed only a few minutes, got out, and let the sun dry him. He put on the new garment.

"Took ye long enough, boy," Tippett said in good humor. "Hell, it ain't ye I'd like to see prancin' 'round buck-ass naked."

"No?" Gray Wolf asked in mock innocence.

"Hell, no," Tippett laughed. "Ye don't shine with this chil' a'tall. Even if ye was ten year younger and female, ye'd still be too goddamn ugly to get excited over."

Gray Wolf laughed, too. "You envy what I have," he said.

"Shit," Tippett chuckled. "It'd take two of yours to make mine."

Gray Wolf sat, relieved. The strain of moving around was hard.

"While ye were primpin' like some squaw with a lodgeful of foofaraw, I was roastin' meat," Tippett said, grinning. "Can ye eat?"

Gray Wolf just grunted an affirmative. He felt hungry enough to eat a whole buffalo by himself.

Gray Wolf grew stronger with each passing sun. Then one morning he pushed himself up. Tippett, who was off making water, watched the Comanche who headed toward the horses. "What'n hell do ye think ye're doin'?" Tippett asked loudly as he buttoned his trousers.

"I'm well," Gray Wolf said defensively.

"Like hell. Plunk your ass down before ye set that wound to bleedin' agin."

"I'm not an old woman who needs help," Gray Wolf said proudly. "I'm..." He did not finish the sentence as he crumpled.

Tippett ran over and knelt at Gray Wolf's side. "Ye all right?"

"Yes," the Comanche whispered.

"Damn fool. Serves ye right." He carefully lifted the small, broad Comanche warrior and carried him back to the north side of the cottonwood, where Gray Wolf would have shade. The sun was fierce and the heat oppressive. Tippett had thought the rain they had had the afternoon before last might have cleared some of the humidity out of the air, but it had only made it muggier. Tippett was annoyed.

He hoped Gray Wolf would recover soon. Partly because the Comanche was his friend. But he also wanted to get back to Painted Wing. He missed her terribly after so long on the trail. He wanted her with him in the robes. He could feel her plump flesh under his hand, the weight of her breasts, her silken thighs, her...

"Damn," he growled to himself. "Best get your mind off'n such thoughts."

Less than a week later, the Comanche was fit to ride. Tippett said, "We'll pull out come mornin'."

33

Gray Wolf set out to seek a vision for the medicine it would give him and the *Nermernuh*. In the two years since he had been wounded by the freighters, he had been plagued by doubts and worries. It was time to set those things right.

He went to his favorite spot for these things — an isolated copse near a tiny, sweet spring tucked into a crevasse of the earth at the foot of a long, low mesa. He sang and danced, chanting prayers to the spirits. He had nothing to eat or drink.

After three days he was still chanting hoarsely when he saw it. The same gray wolf he always saw. It was his namesake, his power. He saw the wolf's snarling muzzle, the slow, patient stalking, and the rushing attack. Then the throat of the victim — a *tahbay-boh* — was torn out by the wolf's hungry, glimmering fangs.

Gray Wolf snapped to consciousness. He offered a few bits of tobacco and meat to the spirits in thankfulness that his medicine was still strong. Then he ate heartily and rode back to his village.

He called for warriors to join him in his quest against the settlers. After hearing of his vision, many heeded his call. Among them was a fourteen-year-old ready for his first war party. His name was White Buffalo. The blue-eyed youth was taller than most of the Comanches already and his skin was lighter. His hair was not as dark as that of his companions and he spoke English uncommonly well for a *Nermernuh*.

White Buffalo joyfully became a willing participant in the carnage. If his white father, Zeke Tippett, had left any seed of civilization in the boy, the youth had subjugated it. He had no compunction at slaying whites. He eagerly took his part in raping the helpless women and in mutilating the men, some still living. After four raids, he carried five white scalps on his lance.

Gray Wolf was glad to see it. He had thought that perhaps too much of Tippett would be in White Buffalo and the youth might be unwilling to attack any *tahbay-boh* since he was, at least in part, one of them. He smiled grimly, though, watching the boy during his first attack. The youth had dashed the brains from a child with his war club and then threw a woman down and forced his young manhood into her as she screamed and the battle raged around him. White Buffalo pumped only briefly before his release. He leaped up, crowing in victory, before tearing off the woman's scalp of fine, sandy hair. Then he rejoined the melee as another warrior ripped aside his loincloth to fall upon the bleeding, moaning woman.

The Texas pioneers seemed nearly helpless before the onslaught. Surviving families and groups of stone-faced Rangers — companies of which had been reformed recently — gathered to follow the Comanches. Soldiers, who had flooded into Texas to fight the Mexicans resisting the American takeover, battled Comanches when the chance arose. But usually to no avail. Even the Rangers had trouble keeping up.

Eventually, small groups of warriors drifted off from the main band to go home. After two months, their bloodlust was sated and they wanted to see their families. Finally, only about twenty warriors, including Gray Wolf, White Buffalo, and Walking Bear, were left. They had stopped with perhaps two hundred stolen horses in a grove of cottonwoods along Horse Creek.

"We have them on the run now," Hits-With-A-Fist said firmly. He had a wild look in his eyes. It meant death to the *Tejanos*.

"We are tired," Runs-At-The-Enemy argued. "And our families will need food. Winter will come in another moon. We must make meat." Runs-At-The-Enemy was older and no longer as eager for battle as were the younger, lustier warriors like Hits-With-A-Fist.

The argument continued into the night, with a warrior leaving the fray occasionally to thrust himself into one of the two captives from the last raid, and then rejoin the talk around the fire.

Finally, they all went to sleep, the problem unresolved. White Buffalo was up just before dawn cracked the eastern sky. He stood next to a cottonwood, urinating loudly and with much pleasure. As he did, he took careless note of the stolen horses milling about, mixed in with the Comanches' other ponies. Something did not seem right to him, but he could not place what it was. He finally shrugged, putting it down to his newness on the war trail.

He stuffed his dingus back into his breechcloth. He was heading back to his blankets when he thought of the women. At his age, his hormones were always boiling, and his dingus often hard. It would be difficult to get back to sleep this way, he figured, so he veered off to where the two naked captives were tied to a tree trunk.

They stirred when they heard his approach and one awoke. She was tall and had a thick waist and broad rear end. She had a face that reminded him of a horse, with long teeth and prominent nose. Her skin, except for her face and hands, had been ghostly white when she had been captured and stripped, having never seen the sun. Now much of her skin was fiery red from the exposure of most of a full day naked on horseback. Her breasts were small for a woman of her otherwise large dimensions. But White Buffalo cared not a whit about that.

She cringed and whimpered as White Buffalo neared. And she tried to crawl behind the other woman. White Buffalo grinned at her terror. He stood there in full view of the woman, and shoved his breechcloth aside. He was firm and hard. He broke wind loudly, pleased with himself. He noted again that something did not seem right to him. He stood, dingus in hand, trying to ignore his raging hormones and trying to pay more attention to his surroundings. It was quiet. No birds were chirping; there were few signs of an awakening world.

White Buffalo moved his head very slowly, trying to catch a scent, a movement, a sound, anything, however slight, that might indicate what bothered him. He finally spotted a branch of a bush swaying for a few moments before stopping. The breeze was blowing west to east, yet the branch moved northeast to southwest. No bird had taken flight, leaving the branch to sway. It must be...

He opened his mouth to scream an alarm.

He neither heard the gunshots, nor saw the four round balls that slammed into his head and chest, spiraling him around until he fell into the dirt, dead.

The warriors leaped from their robes and blankets into the cool, fresh light of the just-born dawn as a fusillade raked the camp. A few headed for the horses, others covered their companions with return fire. A warrior fell, then another. The small camp had, in the thirty seconds since White Buffalo died, become a raging storm of confusion — running men, neighing, snorting horses, choking clouds of dust, gunfire, screams, grunts, shouted curses, and whining bullets.

The Comanches were far outgunned since the soldiers and Rangers were armed with repeating pistols. The Indians slipped behind trees or slunk along the ground under the cover of the dust and clouds of bluish powder smoke, looking for the enemy.

The Dragoons, who had been led by a few hardened Texas Rangers, charged into the camp. Fierce hand-to-hand fighting broke out near the Indians' horse herd. The Rangers tried to drive the horses away, leaving the Comanches afoot and so effectively trapping them. The Rangers had succeeded in scattering perhaps half the horses while the soldiers engaged the Indians. But the

Comanches fought like demons and were able to keep the rest of the horses.

With desperate cries, the outnumbered, outarmed Comanches fought the Dragoons and Rangers while trying to get mounted. One by one they managed. Screaming in fury, Gray Wolf and three other warriors pushed the horses into the midst of the encampment, blocking their friends from most of the soldiers' guns.

"Where's White Buffalo?" Gray Wolf screamed over the cacophony.

Walking Bear shrugged his big shoulders. He liked the half-breed who had proven himself a brave and resourceful warrior already. But at the moment, he had more important things to worry about.

The other Comanches mounted quickly. They killed a soldier and wounded three others in the swirling chaos. Gray Wolf shouted for his men to retreat. He headed for the two captives. He would make sure neither would be rescued. As he slid off his horse, he could see more clearly beneath the hanging cloud of dust and gunsmoke. Then he spotted White Buffalo. He groaned at the loss.

In a rage, Gray Wolf pulled his steel knife and stuck one screaming woman with it in the nether region. He ripped upward, until he hit bone. He yanked the knife out and plunged it in several inches higher and split her from belly button to breastbone. He whirled like a cat and performed the same bloody deed on the other. He roared, the sound cutting through even the thunderous noise of the Comanche's departure with their horses. In a blink he was at White Buffalo's side. He grabbed the body and threw it across his own horse and then leaped onto the pony. He quirted the pony into a run.

Soon, he thundered alongside another Comanche pony — he did not trust the stolen horses — and threw himself onto it. Controlling the animal with his knees, he kept a hand on White Buffalo, trying to keep the flopping body from falling off the galloping horse.

The vigilantes followed the racing Comanches. But the Comanches killed another soldier and a Ranger, and wounded two soldiers in the running battle. The Indians lost one more warrior. Soon the Dragoons gave up the chase, to the disgust of the three Rangers left.

"We ain't used to givin' up so easy, Cap'n," the Ranger leader, Captain Wallace McNelly, growled.

"Our mounts are tired," Army Captain Horace Montgomery said, nonplussed.

"This ain't the way to fight Comanches, you chicken-hearted son of a bitch," another Ranger snapped angrily.

Montgomery stiffened. "You speak to me in such manner again, *Mister* Trent, and I'll have you shot!" He meant it, and both Trent and McNelly knew it. McNelly waved a hand, silencing any further outburst from Elmore Trent.

"My men have been on the trail for two months," Montgomery said coolly. "We are no match for those bastards out in the open like this. It's best to leave it be."

McNelly wasn't happy with it, but he knew better than to argue. Besides, Montgomery had a point — tired soldiers would be no match for Comanches in the open. McNelly was used to leading his hard, tough Rangers who had learned to fight the Comanches their own way.

McNelly and his three men had been following the Comanches after the latest raid, and had come upon Montgomery's troops. It hadn't taken much to convince the soldiers to join the chase. Montgomery had thought at the time that it would be a lark, something to give his men a little taste of battle against these ill-equipped heathens.

Now McNelly had lost one of his men and was angry. "You'll see that Wigglesworth gets a decent burial along with your men, won't you, Cap'n?" he said harshly.

"Yes, Mister McNelly."

McNelly nodded. "Time to ride, boys," he said to his men.

THE COMANCHES RODE HARD FOR MORE THAN FIFTY MILES BEFORE finding a camp of *Yampahrehkahs*. They left their dead, including White Buffalo, and the wounded there. Gray Wolf refused the *Yampahrehkahs'* invitation to stay in the village to recover. Bolstered by half a dozen *Yampahrehkah* warriors, Gray Wolf rode out again after stopping barely long enough to gobble down a meal of hot, fresh buffalo hump.

Gray Wolf's small new band returned to raiding with a renewed vengeance. But even the warriors who had been with Gray Wolf since leaving their *Llano Estacado* village began to wonder about him. All but Gray Wolf had their fill of war and wanted to return to the comforts of their lodges. Gray Wolf would hear none of it.

"Any who don't wish to follow me can leave," he said harshly as the twelve men sat around the fire several weeks after leaving the *Yampahrehkah* village. "I will not stop you."

"You cannot kill all the *Tejanos*," a *Yampahrehkah* said.

"I will," Gray Wolf boasted. His eyes were red-rimmed and wild. His breath came in short bursts and spittle slithered from the corner of his mouth. He seemed almost crazed.

"They are too many," Walking Bear said quietly. There was a mild rebuke in his voice and some condescension. "Even for the mighty Gray Wolf. We need to rest. And we must make meat so our families will live. So, our women might bear more *Nermernuh* to fight the *tahbay-boh*."

Gray Wolf was still not convinced. "Go, my friend, if that is what you wish. "No one will think the less of you." The cast of his countenance belied the statement.

Gray Wolf did not want to think of going back to his village. There was a chance he might encounter Tippett there and he would have to tell the old mountain man how he, Gray Wolf, great warrior of the *Nermernuh*, had let his friend's son be shot down like a dog by a ragged band of soldiers. How his medicine had failed the youth.

Walking Bear, Hits-With-A-Fist, and most of the others stayed on. But the next morning, two of the *Yampahrehkahs,* with two score extra horses, started for home. Two days later the Comanches swept down on an isolated farm. It was barely past dawn but a man was working outside. Gray Wolf thought it almost funny, and sad, that a man had to spend his whole life bent over digging in the earth.

The farmer looked up at the first sound of thundering hooves. Anxiously he turned and yelled, "Beth! Grab Jesse and get to the root cellar. Injuns!" He spun back to face the rushing horde. He was armed only with an old single-shot musket.

An arrow thudded into the man's left thigh and he grunted with the pain. But he stood his ground. It had been a lucky shot, he figured, since the Comanches were still some distance away. He tore the arrow out, thankful it had not sunk very deep in his muscle. Hurriedly he fired. The shot grazed a Comanche's arm.

In haste he tried to reload the old rifle. He knew he was dead; he just prayed he would be able to stall the Indians long enough to allow his wife and their one youngster time to get into the root cellar behind brush at the back of the sod house. God willing, they might survive and make their way to safety. An arrow ripped into his right shoulder. He dropped the rifle. "Christ," he moaned.

The Indians were nearing, but the farmer wasn't ready to give up. He scooped up the rifle, gritting his teeth against the pain. It was difficult to aim the rifle, with the arrow sticking out of his shoulder. He fired. But his aim was off, and he hit nothing but air.

The door of the house flew open and a woman rushed out, another old musket in her hand. As she reached the man's side, he snapped, "Git back in the house, dammit. Jesse needs lookin' after."

"The hell you say, Samuel Jenkins," Beth Jenkins said, heedless of her language. "If you're goin' under, so're me'n Jesse."

"Dammit, woman, you know what these savages do to a white woman when they catch one." He shuddered.

"They ain't gonna get me alive, Sam." She tapped a knife at her waist. There was no fear to be seen in the woman, though her husband knew it lurked inside.

It was too late for argument. The Comanches circled tightly, almost brushing the farmer and his wife. One grabbed the woman's dark brown hair and tugged.

Beth whirled in fury, yanking free. She smacked the warrior's hand away. "Don't touch me, you bloodthirsty, depredatin' heathen."

The Indian's face darkened with rage and he yanked out a large, stone-headed war club. He raised it, ready to crush the woman's head, but a sharp command from Gray Wolf stopped him.

As leader of the war party, Gray Wolf had absolute control over the warriors. His orders were to be obeyed or the warrior in question could leave. With a scowl of hate, tempered by surprise, the warrior slipped the club away. He looked fiercely at the two whites.

Walking Bear called to Gray Wolf and pointed to the house. A boy of five had appeared in the open doorway and was standing there holding a hatchet in his small hand. He was too young to be afraid, though he knew something was very wrong.

"You leave my little boy alone, you hear me," the woman said angrily. "What right've you got to come here like this, tryin' to kill us and steal what little we got? It ain't right."

Gray Wolf grinned a little at the woman's outburst. She was, like all the other white women he had seen, rather ugly. She had no breasts, compared with a good Comanche woman who had given birth. She was tall, and her skin pasty beneath the dirt. Her nose was too long and her eyes too round.

He glanced at the boy a moment before turning his attention back to the two adults. Then he said to the man, in English, "You got a goddamn brave woman and little boy. We won't hurt you."

Sam and Beth Jenkins stood, clutching their pitiful weapons, looks of disbelief on their faces.

Gray Wolf raced off. His warriors followed, confused. None was as perplexed as Gray Wolf himself. After all, they were only *Tejanos*. Why should he care about them? Like all Comanches, he was impressed by conspicuous displays of bravery. His warrior ethos respected the bravery they had shown. They had been willing to die for what was theirs. *But this is my land!* Gray Wolf thought angrily.

Still, the Texans thought it theirs. It was hard to hate individuals, especially brave ones. It was easier hating a group. As whites — or as Texans — he could hate them. But these two had worked hard to set up a home and a farm. Now they considered it their land.

He realized sourly that night that his lust for killing Texans had faded under the bravery of that family. And he also felt the need to be with his family. The next morning, much to the others' surprise, he turned toward the *Llano*. He was still bothered knowing he would have to tell Tippett about White Buffalo. It saddened him to sickness. But telling Tippett could wait until spring, he decided.

BOOK 9

ZEKE TIPPETT, 1847-1849

34

Zeke Tippett was chopping wood in the small back courtyard of his adobe home in Taos when he heard the commotion. Though it was January and bitter cold, Tippett was sweating from the exertion. He thunked the ax into the chopping block and headed up the short, narrow alleyway between his house and the next.

He opened the wooden gate with its high — eight foot at the peak — arched top, and muttered, "Waugh!" He slammed the heavy oak gate shut and barred it. With the surrounding eight-foot-high wall, the house should be safe, he figured. He turned and ran inside.

"*Que?*" a worried Painted Wing asked. She had heard the commotion, and though she didn't know what it was, knew it meant trouble.

"I ain't sure. But it don't shine with this ol' chil'."

Enraged Indians and Mexicans surged through the streets. Tippett wondered where they were heading and what mayhem they aimed to commit.

Suddenly he spun and asked urgently, "*La niña?*"

"Upstairs." She jerked her head upward, indicating that their daughter was in one of the bedrooms there.

"*Bueno*. Now get the shutters closed and barred. *Pronto*."

As Painted Wing hurried through the house slamming the heavy wooden shutters closed and sliding oak bars across them, Tippett went into a small room off the sitting room at front. He returned in moments with his old Hawken rifle and a newer one. Two .36-caliber, six-shot pistols were jammed into the wide cloth sash that served as a belt. He dropped the two rifles on the scarred, unpainted wood table and returned to the small room.

When he got back again, Painted Wing had finished with the shutters and was talking quietly in Comanche with their last child — Leaves Behind, whom Tippett called Mary — who had just turned three.

Their other three children — White Buffalo, whom Tippett called Joshua; Born-In-The-Storm, whom Tippett called Cass, who would be ten years old this summer; and Light Calf, their first daughter, whom Tippett called Libby, who had turned five not long ago — lived in the village with Painted Wing's people.

Painted Wing sent the child running back upstairs as Tippett dropped the double-barreled shotgun, two full powder horns, and two small buckskin bags of lead balls on the table.

Quickly but methodically, he and Painted Wing loaded the weapons. The noise outside grew and stones banged off the house's thick adobe walls. Yells punctuated the cold air with increasing regularity.

Someone pounded on the heavy wood front door. Tippett grabbed the shotgun loaded with buckshot and headed to the door. "Get the hell away from here," he bellowed.

Gunshots cracked outside and the screams grew in intensity and frequency. The pounding at the door was replaced by a rhythmical thumping. Tippett figured the mob was using a battering ram.

"Dammit," Tippett muttered. Then he yelled, "Get away!" More banging answered him. Angry, he tore open a small gun port in the center of the door almost at eye level. He stuck the shotgun about an inch through the hole and fired both barrels. Several people screamed, powder smoke filled the room. But the thumping stopped. Tippett tossed the shotgun to Painted Wing and slammed the port closed.

Things quieted for a while and Tippett went upstairs. From an upper-floor window, Tippett watched as the mob flowed north past the town well. It looked like hundreds were congregating in front of Governor Charles Bent's house a block up and half a block west. Tippett peered through a telescope and spotted Bent's partly bald, stocky figure in the doorway of his house talking to the mob. A howl went up and then Tippett lost sight of the governor. But Tippett knew, as the mob swept inside Bent's house, that the governor was dead. Soon after, the rioting Indians and Mexicans intensified their rampage, killing and scalping any Anglo they could get their hands on.

Suddenly Painted Wing was at Tippett's elbow. "There're people at the back door," she said worriedly. "Callin' your name."

He hurried downstairs and listened at the back door. Then he heard, "Zeke. Zeke Tippett. Let us in, goddammit. Hurry."

Tippett ripped open the door and Cass Calder and George Bender shoved inside. Tippett slammed and barred the door behind them.

"Christ, these doin's don't shine with this ol' coon nonesoever," Bender said, his voice as nervous as always. It was hard to tell when he *was* scared, since he always sounded that way.

"What the hell's goin' on out there?" Tippett asked.

"Some ol' Injun told me the *Taoseños* and the Greasers ain't too happy the Americans took over," Calder said. "Got all worked up and started raisin' hell. Them savages're killin' and scalpin' all over."

"I expect Bent's gone under." Tippett explained.

"If I was among 'em, I'd go for Bent first," Calder said. "I'm damn sorry to hear it, though. The Bents've always been fair to me."

Tippett thought a minute. "Think I could get over to the store?" he asked. "I reckon I ought to see if Carter's all right and all."

"We went by there first," Calder said. "But it's locked up

tighter'n a bishop's daughter. That ol' coot ye got runnin' the place either got a heap of brains or a heap of scared."

Tippett nodded.

"What're we gonna do, Zeke?" Bender asked. He always looked like he was about to die of fright. But he was a good, steady hand.

"I don't know. If we had some of the old boys together, we could stand off this rabble and put an end to this shit right off. I wish Kit was around, instead of traipsin' off to Californy with that Frémont feller."

"There's usually a bunch of the boys over to Turley's place workin' for him," Calder added hopefully. "Maybe if'n one of us could get there, we might see if there's enough to put our own army together."

Tippett motioned the two into the other room and they sat. It might work, Tippett thought — if there really was anyone at the mill where Turley made Taos Lightning. Thirty or forty mountaineers could put a serious dent in the uprising. "Reckon it'd do," Tippett finally said. "But I ain't goin'. I got a family to think about."

"I'll go," Bender said, his sunken brown eyes flashing.

"Take the sorrel gelding in the stable," Tippett said with a nod. "Painted Wing, fetch some jerky. And a couple tins of powder and a couple of lead balls."

Though Turley's Mill was only twelve miles, it likely would take Bender a while to make it there, since he would have to ride at least a few miles east before turning northwest to miss the mobs and Taos Pueblo. He might make it in a few hours, but it might take a day or more.

"Ye got all ye need?" Tippett finally asked.

"Reckon so." Bender settled his slouch hat. Without another word, he headed out the back door and to the stable. Tippett went with him to open and close the gate at the back. Cass was just finishing up saddling a horse for Bender. Five minutes later Bender raced down the alley, heading for the canyon east of town. Before Tippett could slam the gate shut, he spotted two Mexican women and several children scurrying up the alley. They looked exhausted and their faces were creased with horror.

"Miz Bent." Tippett called urgently. "Miz Carson."

The first mentioned woman looked up, startled. Then relief splashed across her face. The other nodded wearily.

"Hurry," Tippett said. He slipped out and grabbed the two youngest children. He hurried them all through the gate. He set the children down, barred the gate, and herded the people into the house.

"Painted Wing," he shouted, "See that Miz Bent and her young'uns are fed and looked after. Miz Carson, too. *Pronto*."

"Thank you, *Señor*," Josefa Carson said gratefully. The other woman — Maria Bent, Josefa's sister — only nodded. She and her children followed Painted Wing and Josefa Carson down the hall to the kitchen.

"Miz Bent?" Calder asked, eyes wide.

"Maria Ignacia Jaramilla Bent," Tippett said. "Charles's wife."

"Jaramilla? She related to that rich old *hacendado*?"

"The old man's daughter. Kit's wife's her sister." After a moment, Tippett said, "We'd best find out about Charles." He wanted to hear it firsthand. They went into the kitchen, where the Jaramilla sisters and children were eating. They looked numb from shock and exhaustion. Their clothes were filthy.

"Can ye tell me what happened?" Tippett asked, taking a seat.

In Spanish and broken English, Mrs. Bent did, crying as she talked. "It was horrible," she said in a low voice. "Hundreds came...upset with *Americano* rule...they wanted...*Mexicano* rule back. Charles tried to speak to them, but they were...unmanageable."

Tippett patted her shoulder as Painted Wing hustled the children out. "Did they kill Charles?" Tippett asked. "I've got to know."

"Yes," she whispered. "I saw one of those heathens strike my husband in the head with a...with a..." She could not continue. She shuddered with fear at the thought of her mate's sickening death. The tears came unchecked, heavy, burning her cheeks.

"How'd ye get out?" Tippett asked when she had quieted a little.

"Josefa, my maid, and I dug a hole in the back of the house." She tried to grin but couldn't. "With a spoon!" She had always led a sheltered life, the daughter of one of the richest men in *Nueva Mexico*. She had always been pampered. Then she had married Charles Bent. Bent might have been a little uncouth, but he had amassed a considerable amount of money and then had been named the first governor of the vast territory when the Americans had taken it over a few months ago. To *Señora* Bent, this day was quite a great indignity, beyond the utter horror.

"We got through just as the savages burst into the house. As we scurried through the hole, I saw Charles..."

"It's all right," Tippett said uselessly, trying to console her. *How inadequate,* he thought. *I sound like an idiot telling her such foolishness*. He looked at Calder and was heartened by the huge man's presence. "Ye goin' to your father's?" he asked.

"No. Josefa's."

"That ain't gonna do ye much good with Kit gone."

"We will be safe there," Josefa Carson answered.

"Stay here," Tippett said firmly. "Me and Cass can look after ye."

The two Mexican women chattered between themselves a moment, before Josefa turned to Tippett, shaking her head. "We will go."

"That's foolish, dammit," he snapped. "I..." He stopped when Painted Wing rested a hand on his arm. He nodded. They needed to be in a place of their own. Being pure Mexicans, they would probably have no trouble in Carson's house, even if both of their husbands were Anglos.

"All right," Tippett sighed. "We'll help. Soon as ye're able."

Maria nodded thanks and Josefa quietly said, "*Gracias*."

Half an hour later, Mrs. Bent was ready to go. The noise in the street was still loud, but seemed to have lessened a bit. "I reckon I can let Cass take them all over to Kit's," Tippett said to Painted Wing.

"No," his wife said firmly. "You'll take 'em and make goddamn sure all's well." She had always had this foolish notion that Tippett was perfect, that if he was along everything would be all right.

"But I got to think about ye and Mary."

"You will go."

After fifteen years together, Tippett knew better than to argue when Painted Wing used that tone. Tippett led them out the gate, closed and locked it, and climbed the fence. They hurried through alleys and empty streets, skirting the plaza. Tippett carried the two small children, Calder the bigger ones. They reached the Carson home and a servant let them in.

"Ye sure ye'll be safe here?" Tippett asked suspiciously.

"*Si*," Josefa Carson said, embarrassed. She cleared her throat, then said, "We are grateful for your help, *Señor* Tippett."

Tippett nodded, uncertain. But he had Painted Wing and Leaves Behind to worry about. "Then we'll take our leave, Ma'am," he said.

Tippett and Calder walked toward the plaza, figuring to come up on Tippett's house from the front. The streets were almost empty.

"Goddamn it," Calder swore, pointing.

A small group of Taos Indians and Mexicans were coming toward them from the plaza. They spotted Tippett and Calder, and howled.

"I ain't aimin' to let these fractious shit balls take me, dammit," Calder exploded. He brought the Leman rifle up and fired. The .66-caliber rifle sounded like a cannon. Calder and Tippett could see a man lose a portion of his skull when the ball smashed into him. The rest of the small crowd scattered. Calder stood unafraid, laughing a few moments before resuming his walk.

Tippett and Calder turned north just before the plaza and strolled the short distance to Tippett's house. They took turns sleeping that night, one of them always looking out the second story windows as the insurgency continued.

Just after dark, a group filled the street. Tippett grinned grimly and fired the Hawken. One man tumbled over. From this distance, Tippett could not tell if the man was dead or just wounded. But the others looked around frantically, scared. Tippett reloaded and fired again. Another man went down, and this time Tippett was sure the man was dead. The small group fled in all directions as Tippett enjoyed a chuckle. He was not, for the most part, bloodthirsty, but after hearing what had happened to Charles Bent, he had no remorse for his actions.

About midnight, Calder came in rubbing the sleep from his eyes. He had a mug of steaming coffee in one huge hand and two rifles in the other. Three pistols were jammed into his belt. He looked tired but ready for action. "Anything happen, *amigo?*" he asked.

Tippett explained and Calder grinned. "Waugh! That's makin' 'em come. Maybe I'll get a crack at them bastards, too."

"If'n ye do, try'n hit somebody this time, eh?" Tippett joshed.

Once, when they were up along the Milk River, a small war party of Blackfeet attacked them. Calder missed his first two shots. Since then, Tippett and anyone else who knew would not let the big bear of a man forget it. Of course, if whoever was doing the chiding was not on the best of terms with Calder, he was risking his life with his words.

Less than fifteen minutes after Tippett left the room, Calder saw shadowy movements from down toward the plaza. "Ah," he said almost pleasurably. The thought of action always sent a thrill through his system. He lay his rifle on the window ledge and fired. Calder grabbed his second Leman — same size, same caliber — and fired.

For two days and nights Tippett and Calder stood their alternating guards. Occasionally, Tippett or Calder would fire off a shot or two as mobs surged past the house, killing a rebel. But the crowds began to dwindle and the two men began to wonder why.

On the fifth day, George Bender made it back to the house. With him were two mountain men Tippett and Calder had known back in the old days — John Albert and Charlie Autobees. All three were worn, weary, and hungry. Their eyes seemed a little glazed.

"What'n hell happened?" Calder asked as the three men tore into plates of spiced beans and slabs of roasted buffalo meat.

"We was at Turley's, mindin' our own business," Autobees said, sopping up grease from his plate with a hunk of bread. He stuffed it into his mouth and talked around it. "Then there was this howlin' goddamn mob outside half froze for hair. Christ, what a sight. Goddamn stinkin' Greasers and shit-eatin' Injins." He shook his head.

"Must've been five hundred of 'em," Albert said between bites.

"And only eight of us boys inside," Autobees said. "I don't mind tellin' y'all, I was nearabout set to piss my 'skins. But we fought 'em off fer a spell. Did a damn good job, too," he added grimly. "Would've kicked their asses fer sure, 'cept we ran out of powder and ball. We all decided to make a run for it. Reckon me'n John here're the only 'uns made it alive." Sadness crept over him, and he ate silently.

"I found what was left of the rest up at the mill," Bender said. "Come on these two north of it a ways."

"We was aimin to make it to Bent's up on the Arkansas," Albert muttered. "When Bill hears his brother's gone under at the hands of these goddamn Injins and their bean-eatin' friends, he'll be headin' down this way with some boys and make 'em all come, sure as hell."

"The Army's in Santa Fe," Calder said quietly. "That might help."

"I'll put my trust in the old boys, and Bent," Albert said.

"Me, too," Calder said. "But Santa Fe's a sight closer."

"Can ye boys ride some?" Tippett asked.

When the two nodded, he said, "Tell ye what. John, ye head for

Santa Fe. Tell Colonel Price what's gone on. Charlie, ye head to Bent's. Bill'll see to the rest."

The two nodded again and jammed more food into their mouths. There was no need to speak. It was what had to be done and they were the best ones to do it at the moment. When they had finished eating, each curled up in a different corner of the sitting room and slept like the dead. Before dawn, Tippett woke them. The two ate ravenously again. While they did, Tippett and Painted Wing made sure they had supplies — bacon, beans, jerky, pemmican, coffee, sugar, powder, and ball. Autobees and Albert nodded thanks. They set out, sneaking past the rebels and rode on, one south, the other northeast.

A tense five days later, the insurrectionists made a concerted effort to take Tippett's house. But the mob was in for a surprise. Tippett, Calder, and Bender — husbanding their powder and ball — held off the repeated attacks and killed several rebels.

The next morning, Colonel Sterling Price and his troops arrived from Santa Fe with a solemn John Albert as their guide. In the lead was Ceran St. Vrain and sixty-five men, mostly one-time mountain men. They were bloody and angry, but had driven off fifteen hundred or so Mexican soldiers on the way from Santa Fe.

The mob in front of Tippett's fled for the pueblo just north of Taos where they holed up. Price and his men, using cannon and howitzers, laid siege to the adobe pueblo.

Two days later, a dozen grim former mountain men, guided by Autobees, rode in. Each was more than half froze to raise hair to avenge Charles Bent, despite having fought their way through a group of the rebels to get into the town. But the Army held them in check and peace eventually prevailed. Price wanted to bring American justice, not vigilantism, to the area. The revolt ended the night of February 4, 1847 — except for hanging the leaders. Tippett was one of the men selected for the jury to see to that. Within a week, the former trappers — including Autobees, Albert, and Bender — had headed back to Bent's Fort.

Tippett and Calder caught up on some much-needed sleep. Then Tippett set about looking after his business. Calder rode out after a week. "Hell, ye're gonna try'n put me to work fixin' up that damned store, Zeke," he said with a grin. "I don't want no part of such doin's." And away he went, riding through a snowstorm.

Fixing and restocking the store took him through most of the summer. Tippett had wanted to head for *Comancheria* to see his children, as well as Gray Wolf. But it was too late in the year. But in the spring, he was ready to ride.

35

It was midmorning when Tippett spotted a solitary figure moving across the flat barrenness of the New Mexico Territory plains. Tippett stopped and stood in his stirrups for a better look. It was a Comanche, but it was strange to see a single Comanche riding this far west.

He rode two more miles before stopping to look again. They were less than half a mile apart now. Tippett pulled out his collapsible telescope, opened it, and looked through it. He grinned. Gray Wolf was riding the way a Comanche warrior should — proud and regal, certain of himself and his place here, and in life.

Tippett rode into a dip in the earth. When he re-emerged, Gray Wolf was gone. He figured the Indian was holed up in the copse of mesquite and *piñon* several hundred yards ahead on the bank of the Blackwater River. The river, often dry out here, should have some water in it since it had rained two days before.

Gray Wolf had hobbled his ponies, letting them graze on the lush new grass. He had gathered wood and was crouched in the shade of a stunted *piñon* building a fire.

"*Hola*, Gray Wolf," Tippett said riding in and dismounting.

Gray Wolf stood and turned to face him. Tippett was taken

aback by the sadness of the Comanche's face. "What's wrong, *amigo?*" he asked.

"After we've eaten," Gray Wolf said. The Indian seemed weary, worn down by life's troubles. It was disconcerting. Tippett nodded.

Gray Wolf went back to kindling the fire. While he did, Tippett unsaddled his horse, rubbed it down with some grass, hobbled it, and turned it out to graze and water. By the time he was finished, antelope meat was sizzling over the fire. Silently he filled his coffeepot with water from the small stream and poured in coffee beans. He set the pot on a flat rock in the fire.

They ate silently. Tippett was worried. He had never seen Gray Wolf like this and it made him edgy. He was afraid it involved one of his children living in Gray Wolf's village.

Tippett finished, but Gray Wolf was taking longer than necessary. Finally, Tippett said quietly, "Ye're gonna have to spill it sooner or later, Wolf. Might's well make it now."

Gray Wolf's eyes were misty when he looked at Tippett. He and the white man had had their disagreements. But they had always kept their friendship and respect. This was going to be the hardest thing he had ever done. He would have preferred facing a thousand angry Texans while he was naked and unarmed than to have to do this.

Despite the Comanche taboo against speaking the name of the dead, the warrior took a deep breath and then said in a short quick burst, "White Buffalo has gone to the land of the spirits."

"What?" Tippett blurted out. He knew what the Indian had said and he knew what it meant. He just did not want to accept it.

Gray Wolf said it again.

Tippett sat, staring across the stream toward the plain of greening grass and exploding wildflowers. His tongue worked at a small hole in one of his molars. A dull ache had started deep in his gut and radiated outward until it squeezed his heart. He had never been really close to his children. Not as close as he would have liked, or had planned. He was always traipsing off and there hadn't been enough time. Then they brought Josh to the village, and several years later, Cass. And, finally, two years ago, Libby. They would take Leaves Behind — Mary — next year, if Painted Wing had her way. Tippett thought now that he might have something to say about it this time.

It wasn't as if he had lost track of them when they were taken to the Comanche village, but he had even less time with them than before. He made sure he and Painted Wing got to the village at least once each summer, more if he could manage it. He even left Painted Wing there most of the summer when possible so she could remain close to her children. Still, Tippett felt a distance between him and his son the last time he had visited the village. But White Buffalo was his first-born, and a son to boot.

"How?" he finally asked in a whisper.

Gray Wolf told him in a flat monotone. When Gray Wolf was done, Tippett again sat silently listening to the cowbirds and jays, the wind rustling through the leaves, and the usually soothing babble of the stream. "Ye sure it was soldiers?"

"Yes." He paused. "There were some Rangers. Only a few."

Tippett nodded. "Ye know who was leadin' 'em?"

"No."

Tippett nodded dumbly. His mind was filled with sorrow at the loss of his son. "Is Libby all right?" he asked. When Gray Wolf looked blank, Tippett said, "Light Calf."

"She's well." He was nervous. Tippett was much too calm.

"And Born-In-The-Storm?"

Gray Wolf tried to smile. "He's well, too. He's learning fast. Almost as fast as his bro—" He stopped, face frozen.

Tippett nodded again. He stood, brushing dirt and grass from his buckskin pants. He could barely think or see. The last startled him, since he had always had good vision. But the world was blurry. It took some moments to realize that the tears in his eyes were causing the fuzziness. He blinked several times and the world began to clear.

"I got to get back to Taos," he mumbled. "Tell Painted Wing." Somehow, he managed to get his horse saddled. Without saying goodbye, he mounted and rode off. The pain in his heart went with him, a small dead spot in his chest. As he neared Taos, he worried about having to tell Painted Wing. When he reached home, he dawdled in unsaddling, currying, and feeding the horse. But he could not delay forever, so he walked into the house.

"Send them young 'uns off somewhere," Tippett ordered as he set down his rifles and saddlebags.

Painted Wing looked frightened, but she rushed the children — Mary and several neighbors — to the rooms upstairs. When she came back down, Tippett was sitting at the kitchen table with a steaming mug of coffee in front of him. She suspected that he had laced the coffee from a jug of Taos Lightning. She sat across from him, looking worriedly into his eyes. It was an uncommon thing for a Comanche woman to do, but this was an uncommon time. She took one of his big hands in one of her small, pudgy ones.

"White Buffalo's gone under," he said without flourish.

Painted Wing sat for some minutes staring, tears boiling over her lower eyelids and pouring down her cheeks. Her face had not become too creased yet, unlike most other Comanche women her age. Her life in Taos was far more comfortable than that of the women out on the *Llano*.

She leaped up and raced for the sideboard — and the butcher knife on it. It was the way of her people to mutilate themselves when death came among them. She would whack her hair short, maybe chop off a finger. She would gash herself until she was covered with blood.

Tippett knew this. What he didn't know was why the Comanches, and most other Indians, did it. But he was not about to let Painted Wing perform the rituals, no matter how important to her. He spun and took two long strides. He grabbed her, enveloping the pudgy woman in his long, strong arms. "No," he said softly.

She tried to fight him off but was not strong enough.

"I ain't gonna let ye do this, woman. I ain't livin' with a woman that's all carved up from her own doin's." Still she resisted, until Tippett growled, "Ye ain't in some goddamn Comanche camp now, Painted Wing. Now leave off this foolishness."

She seemed to almost come to her senses. Her body slumped against him. "Ye gonna be all right now?" he asked, worried.

"*Haa*-yes."

Reluctantly, he let her go. Painted Wing stumbled to her seat at the table as if she could not stand any longer. She plopped down with a heavy sigh, her face pinched with grief. Then she began to wail. It started as a low, eerie moan, building until it was an ululating, inhuman cry of anguish. She never seemed to take a breath, yet the high-pitched keening did not cease, or slow.

Tippett sat and listened for a while. It was not the first time he had heard a Comanche howl in grief. It had always set him on edge, though now he wanted to join her. But he couldn't. And after a while, he could not listen any longer. "Quiet down, woman," he said softly.

Still the haunting screech careened off the walls of the kitchen. Tippett's ears hurt as if his eardrums had been pierced.

"Stop it, woman," he said more loudly. Still no reaction. He lifted both hands and slammed the open palms down on the table, shoving up at the same time. "Shut up!" he roared. Painted Wing ceased as if throttled. She sat with mouth gaping, face twisted.

Tippett sat, filled with anger and sorrow. "I know how ye feel, Painted Wing," Tippett said softly. His throat hurt from the yell. "It feels like my heart's been ripped out. But that noise'll draw people. We don't need no one intrudin' on our grief."

The anguish that crossed her face chilled him. And he realized with a sudden flash of insight that Born-In-The-Storm and Light Calf were her only connections to her people anymore. Tippett had made her, through dint of trying to make life better and easier for her, almost an outcast with her own people. She no longer was really one of the *Nermernuh*; she had become too civilized. She lived in a white man's house in a white man's town and wore white women's clothing.

She had, because of all that, lost all her childhood friends. They were now women, like her, and if she was still living in her village, she would get together with them to work and sing and socialize. They would laugh and giggle and talk, and trade off the qualities — in bed and out — of their men. But she had none of that here. And most of the people of Taos wanted little to do with a Comanche woman, no matter how civilized she might appear.

So Painted Wing had no friends in town either. Her husband would go off for whatever reason and leave her in this cold, often unfriendly town. If not for her having always had children around her, she would have gone back to her people or at least forced Tippett to take her back there more often when he was to be away.

It was one reason she wanted her children to live as Comanches. As long as she had children there, she would always have a bond with her people no matter where she lived. And she knew she would always be able to go back, if anything should happen to Tippett. She loved her man, she would not deny that. Because she did, she had lived as he wanted to live. She was content with that. But still, she missed her people, customs, culture, and language. Now Tippett had made her stop one more of the old ways, and another link was broken for all time.

"I'll take ye back." Tippett figured she would like that.

She nodded, the mourning still reflected deep in her dark eyes.

"We'll leave come mornin'," he added lamely. He had made a mistake in stopping her in the release of her grief, and he did not know how to make it better again. He could tell her to continue with her wailing, but she would not. Not after he had yelled at her.

Painted Wing stood. "I'll get things ready," she whispered.

Tippett, feeling his gut wrench at the thought of how much hurt she must be feeling, polished off the whiskey-laced coffee.

Painted Wing was efficient. Despite her grief, she packed all that was needed and gave Tippett a list of things she wanted from the store. He left to get them, happy to be out of the house. He mourned his son, but he was not like people who let their grief make the world black for them for long periods. He would always have that small aching dead spot in his heart, but life had to go on and he intended to live his as best he could.

They left the next morning, Tippett on his horse, holding the rope to a pack mule. Painted Wing followed, holding the rope to another horse, which dragged a travois. Strapped into the travois, along with extra supplies as well as presents for Painted Wing's family, was the baby, Leaves Behind.

Tippett was a little worried, since Painted Wing seemed much calmer this morning. He hoped she was not ready to snap. But there was little he could do, but to push on.

In ten days, they were at the Comanche village. But Tippett could not bring himself to linger. "Ye have yourself a good visit, Painted Wing," he said lamely. "But ye damn well best not go carvin' yourself up or doin' any other such things while I'm gone. I come back and find ye've done some damnfool thing, and I'll leave ye here permanent."

Tippett rode back into the village a month later. He had spent the time roaming, letting his grief sift down until it was little more than a dull, ceaseless ache in his stomach.

Painted Wing was mostly over her grief and seemed happier. Tippett was pleased to see she had done no harm to herself. He thought it a good time to argue that they should bring their two older children home to raise them in white society. But Painted Wing insisted they remain in the Comanche village.

Tippett finally realized that she needed these links to the Comanches, and that it was a way she could prove to herself that her son's death was not for no reason. White Buffalo had died, she could convince herself, to keep the *Nermernuh* ways alive.

He thought that Born-In-The-Storm, at least, should return with them, though he was the older. "But Cass is the only male left in my line, Painted Wing," he argued. "A couple years, and he'll be ready for the war path. What happens if he goes under?"

"We'll have another son," she said, grinning for the first time in weeks. "I ain't too old." She had a lecherous look. "Unless you don't find me desirable no more."

"Ye're still passable," he said with a chuckle.

She hit him lightly and he lifted her and then eased her down onto the buffalo robe bed.

The next morning, they rode out, with only the youngest child, Leaves Behind. Tippett had decided last night that if allowing the two older children to stay with The People was what Painted Wing wanted — or needed — he would accept it. If things got to be looking bad for the Comanches, he could come back and get Cass and Libby.

36

The wailing in Gray Wolf's village was great and swelled to the heavens where even the Great Spirit could not help but hear its mournful woe. So many had died that they could not be buried. So many had died that the ages-old custom of killing many horses to accompany the warriors on their final journey was abandoned, for they would have had almost no horses left.

Riders went to the other villages to spread the word, or to seek comfort. But by doing so, they further spread the devastating disease.

Tippett rode into the midst of the howling grief of the Comanche village. It was obvious, as he dismounted in front of Gray Wolf, what had happened. He glanced around, fear icing his stomach. "Where's Painted Wing?" he demanded. "And my young 'uns?"

"Your woman," Gray Wolf said, his voice catching in his throat, "has gone to the Great Spirit. And the littlest one."

Tippett's eyes misted. "Shit," he muttered. Then, "The others?"

"Light Calf has the sickness. Born-In-The-Storm doesn't. He's been taken away by Hits-With-A-Fist."

Tippett nodded dully, trying to think. In all the times of danger, he had never been this befuddled. But this was an enemy he could not see to fight. The pain he felt was immense, sitting in his chest and stomach, trying to crush his heart and stop his breathing. He and Painted Wing had been together seventeen years. It was almost too much for him to contemplate that she was gone. "When did they die?" he asked, voice cracking.

"Yesterday. The child early, the woman last night."

"They been buried?"

"No. They..."

"Where are they?"

Gray Wolf jerked his head in the direction of Tippett's lodge.

"And Light Calf?"

"With Coyote Tail."

Tippett nodded glumly. He left his horse and two pack animals — the latter two carrying fresh buffalo meat — and walked to the medicine man's tipi. He entered without calling for entry and went to where his daughter Libby lay on a buffalo robe.

Coyote Tail danced around the girl and two Comanches, shaking a rattle. Tippett knelt at his daughter's side. She was pasty looking with an unhealthy sheen to her face. The firelight made her skin glow strangely orange. She was asleep and he did not disturb her. He left, glaring at Coyote Tail, and went to his own lodge. He hesitated only a moment before entering, stopping just inside to let his eyes adjust to the gloom. He was aware of the smell of death, mingled with the aroma of mesquite wood smoke, old grease, dirt, meat, and herbs.

He finally composed himself, holding his emotions on a short rein. He knelt beside Painted Wing, surprised at how tight he was holding himself. He wondered if perhaps he should be screaming his grief like his Comanche brothers.

Painted Wing looked at peace and Tippett brushed a stray hair from her forehead. He turned and walked to the other side of the lodge, to his daughter's body, and his reserve broke. He felt tears come, but he was not ashamed. In the span of only three years, he had lost his wife, his last child, and his first-born son. He had mourned for White Buffalo when he learned the boy had died, but the grief had not cut him nearly so deeply as this. And he did not know why. Perhaps, he thought, it was because as a male, and destined to become a warrior, it was almost expected that White Buffalo would die young.

But looking down at his youngest child, the fair-haired, light-skinned Mary, he let his emotions go. Though he had never mentioned it, Leaves Behind had been his favorite. But now she and Painted Wing were cold, and another of his children might follow soon.

Tippett went back to Painted Wing's body. He made his face blank, showing nothing. For more than an hour he squatted next to his wife's corpse, mind disjointed, thoughts of their life together bouncing around in his skull. He could see, as if it were only yesterday, her bold, lusty face when they had first met. He had been nineteen, tall and strong; she fifteen, and full of giggles and wanton ways.

She had been a strong, resolute woman, a fine helpmeet, Tippett thought. She had given birth to four children — White Buffalo, near the jutting, snow-covered San Juan Peaks; Cass during that hellacious storm at Bent's Fort; Libby and the last, Mary, both in the house in Taos — alone and seemingly without effort.

Painted Wing had still been amorous, despite the children and all her years with Tippett. Not long before they had left Taos, she had pulled Tippett toward the bed, demanding that he perform his husbandly duties.

"I ain't so young as I used to be, ye know," he argued.

Lust burned in her coal-black eyes and she had some rude things to say, most concerning his manhood. Until he grinned and said playfully, "I'll show ye whose manhood's dried up and gone, dammit."

She had remained hard-headed throughout their marriage, too, especially in insisting that the children be brought to the village so they could learn the old ways.

Tippett finally stood, stretching cramps out of his legs and back. He stepped outside, a little surprised to see the sun still shining brightly, and brutally hot. He found a harried Gray Wolf and said, "Please fetch some women to my lodge and have them fix Painted Wing up for a proper buryin'."

"No," Gray Wolf said sadly, but firmly, with a short, chopping motion of his hand. "None will touch her now, my friend," Gray Wolf said, softening a bit. "They won't touch anyone who's gone to the Great Spirit because of the sickness. Look around," he added, waving his arms in an arc. "We're ready to leave. The *Nermernuh* won't come here no more."

Tippett nodded, understanding, though a chill gripped him. He went back into his lodge. Normally it would have been torn down already, and Painted Wing's possessions taken by others. But the Comanches were afraid. Tippett searched through parfleches until he found the creamy elk-skin dress Painted Wing always wore on special occasions. With much sweating, grunting, and swearing, he stripped off Painted Wing's plain buckskin dress and worked the special one over her. He found vermilion and clumsily painted her cheeks and the part of her hair. Finally, he worked a pair of finely beaded moccasins onto her feet.

Sorrow caught him up again, but once more he forced it back. It was much easier physically to dress and paint his daughter, but far harder emotionally. With a heavy heart, he finally finished.

Numbly he went outside and took the buffalo meat from the packhorses and gave it to Gray Wolf. The Indian nodded and asked, "Are you taking care of them?" He nodded toward Tippett's lodge.

"Yes," Tippett grumbled.

"Good. You must do well by your woman," he added cryptically.

Tippett nodded. He quickly made two travois and hooked them to the pack animals. He placed Painted Wing on one and Leaves Behind on the other. He tossed several parfleches onto each travois before lashing the bodies and the luggage down. He got two ponies, stringing them on a rope, which he tied to the mules. Under the watchful eyes of the Comanches, he mounted his horse and rode southwestward. Two miles on, he stopped at the lip of an arroyo about five feet wide and four deep, running roughly north-south. He ground-staked the mules and eased the horse into the arroyo. He found what he wanted two hundred yards south.

The mules balked at being led down the steep, crumbly bank, but Tippett forced them, leading them to a group of small caves gouged in the west side of the arroyo. Muscles aching, Tippett got the bodies, one to a cave, into a sitting position — facing east, as was proper.

Feeling the sweat soaking through his muslin shirt, he got the parfleches and emptied the contents carefully into the caves with the bodies — a few cooking pots Painted Wing had favored, Leaves Behind's corn-husk doll, a knife, beads, awl, thread, and needles for Painted Wing, other toys, and a small, wood-backed mirror for Leaves Behind. He arranged the items so they would be near to hand. With heart leaden from sorrow, he brought up the ponies — Painted Wing's favorite and a gentle mare favored by the child. Quickly he slit the animals' throats. They squealed and fought before sinking down.

Tippett felt a grim satisfaction. The loss of Painted Wing and Mary was great, but they would be well taken care of in the afterlife. Tippett sank wearily onto his haunches across from the bodies. He said a prayer half-remembered from childhood and then tried to say some appropriate words. Few would come, and so he sat staring blankly, gnawed by his loss.

Raindrops snapped him back to reality. He did not know how long he had been there, but the rain was heavy, and the arroyo could become a raging torrent of water in minutes. He mounted his horse, gathered up the mules, and scrambled up the steep sides. He rode back to the village. But it was gone. Only a few empty lodges — including his own — stood, silent testimonials to the ravages of the disease. It was not hard to pick up the trail. Tippett followed it for some miles until he found the Comanches again.

A shaken, weary Gray Wolf greeted him.

"How long was I gone?" Tippett asked. He was bleary-eyed from exhaustion and shaking from hunger.

"A night." He led Tippett into his lodge, where Blue Eyes gave Tippett a bowl of stewed buffalo tongue.

"It is good what you have done," Gray Wolf said quietly.

Tippett nodded. He remembered something Gray Wolf had said. "Why'd ye want me to do special by Painted Wing?" he asked.

"She was carrying another of your children, my friend," Gray Wolf said very softly in Comanche. "She told Running Deer and Red Moon that she was going to tell you when you got back to Taos."

Tippett felt like someone had stabbed him in the heart. Tears rolled down his shallow, weary cheeks as he ate in silence, not tasting the food but needing its sustenance. It took a while to calm himself, but he finally did. Something nagged at him, tugging at the corners of his brain. But what? he wondered.

Suddenly his eyes widened. "Shit, where's Light Calf?" he asked frantically. In his grief, he had forgotten about her.

"Still with Coyote Tail." It was hopeless, his look said.

Tippett's shoulders slumped. He should do something, but his mind was clouded. His chin dropped onto his chest and the bowl slipped from his fingers. He began snoring softly.

"Dammit," Tippett mumbled, his eyes popping open. He staggered up. "Dammit all. Yes, it's possible."

Gray Wolf and the women looked at him suspiciously. Tippett ignored them. "Saddle one of your horses and get me a couple extras," Wolf. "Have one of your women fill my possibles sack with jerky and such." When the Comanche protested, Tippett snapped, "Jist do it."

Gray Wolf figured Tippett was touched. He leaped up and headed outside. Tippett hurried to the medicine man's lodge, plunged in, and knelt by his bundled daughter near the fire. Coyote Tail danced around her, intoning chants and sprinkling powders over the girl. Still fighting his sorrow, he called softly, "Libby?"

She opened her eyes. "Papa?" She spoke English, Comanche, and Spanish equally well, bouncing between them, using whichever suited the moment best. "I don't feel good."

"Don't ye fret, Libby honey. We're gonna get ye fixed up." He slung his Hawken, in a mountain-lion-skin case, across his back. Tenderly he lifted Libby, robes and all.

As he turned to leave, Coyote Tail stepped in front of him. "She will not leave," the medicine man said in Comanche.

"Get outta my way before I cut your heart out and feed it to ye."

The Indian stood fast, and Tippett roared, "Get out of my way!"

Coyote Tail moved. Gray Wolf was waiting with four horses. One was saddled and a possibles bag hung from the pommel. Tippett nodded and handed Light Calf to Gray Wolf. He jumped onto the pony and Gray Wolf handed the girl up. Tippett sat her in front of him on the saddle. Gray Wolf handed his friend the rope to the other horses.

Tippett kicked the horse into motion. By the time he passed beyond the ragged line of tipis, the horse was trotting. He kept the animal going on that pace until it could run no more. He stopped only as long as it took to make water, throw the saddle on another horse, and haul himself and Libby back up. He did that twice more, the only times he stopped. And he never slackened his pace.

Throughout the night and into the next day, he rode. He was on the last horse and weakening when he saw his objective.

37

Zeke Tippett galloped into Fort Graham, startling a number of soldiers, who watched in amazement as he brought the winded horse to a stop in front of the infirmary.

The doctor, having heard the commotion, stepped into the light and stood, eyes shaded by one hand, just outside the door of his hospital. "That you, Zeke?" Doctor John Drimmer asked. He had met the former mountain man several times when Drimmer served at Fort Scott in Kansas and liked him. Drimmer was tall, lean, and partly bald. He wore a black suit, white shirt, and steel-rimmed glasses and had a scholarly look about him.

"My gal's terrible sick, Doc. Ye got to help her."

"Bring her in, then. Quickly." The doctor stepped back inside, followed closely by Tippett. "How long's she been ill?" Drimmer asked, taking his first good look at the child.

"Few days. I was away on business..."

"I heard," Drimmer said

"...when I got back, I found Libby like this. My least one, Mary, went under, as did Painted Wing."

"Sorry, Zeke," Drimmer said in sympathy.

"Nothin' can be done for 'em," Tippett grumbled as he set Libby gently on a bed. "I'll grieve in my own way," he added, straightening. "But Libby here's almost all I got left. Ye gotta help her."

"I'll do what I can, Zeke. But you look exhausted. Go get some sleep. I'll wake you as soon's I know anything."

Tippett stood, undecided. He could feel the weariness clinging to him like a second skin. Then he nodded to the doc. Tippett walked wearily outside. The sun was bright and hot but he could feel a storm brewing. He led the horse across the dusty parade ground toward the livery stable. For a gold coin, the private on duty agreed to care for the horse. Tippett grabbed a pitchfork and tossed fresh hay into a pile, then sank gratefully onto it.

It seemed that he had just put his head down when he felt a shaking and heard someone calling, "Mister Tippett. Get up, sir. Doc wants to see you."

Tippett was on his feet, reaching for his pistol, before his eyes were open. Then awareness hit him. He rubbed his face to try to remove some of the gritty tiredness. Nodding thanks, he hurried across the compound through the heavy rain. He ignored the soldiers marching around the small, soggy parade ground. He burst into the infirmary. "She all right, Doc?" he asked nervously.

"She's had a bad time, Zeke, but I think she'll pull through. She's lucky she's half-white. Indians have no immunity to white diseases. Being half-white, she must've had some."

Relief flowed through Tippett like a flood. "Can I take her, Doc?"

"Where'll you take her, Zeke? She needs a lot of rest and care."

"Back to the village, I expect." He shrugged. He had been so intent on getting her help that he had not thought about what he would do if she lived. "The Comanches'll look after her."

"That's no kind of life for a girl as sick as Libby, Zeke. She needs fresh food, a bed, medical attention. She can't get those in an Indian village."

"If I take her to Taos?" Tippett asked hopefully. "I expect I might be able to hire someone to tend to her."

"Hire who? A Mexican? Or an Indian? I have nothing against those people, Zeke, you know that. But in such matters, they are most ignorant. They know nothing of cleanliness, proper medicines."

"Got any other ideas?"

"I've given it some thought in the short time since you brought her in." He paused, chewing his lower lip. "My sister and her husband are well off. They can no longer have children. They had two, but both died in infancy. Libby is about the age their oldest would have been. I think I can convince them to take Libby in."

Tippett looked at him in surprise. "Ye mean to tell me that two upstandin' folks back east somewhere are gonna be willin' to take in a half-breed Comanche girl?"

"Yes," Drimmer said, smiling. "And they live in San Antonio."

"Shit," Tippett muttered angrily. "Don't ye know what San Antonio means to the Comanches?"

"No. But it doesn't matter. She's only half-Comanche. And she's too young to know of the trouble between the Comanches and the whites."

"Christ, Doc, look at her," Tippett said, still angry. "She ain't gonna pass for white nowhere."

"That's true. But light enough to not look too Indian. With her hair fixed, a bath, and a pretty dress instead of those buckskin rags, she'll look like a Mexican girl."

"Oh, hell, that'll be shinin' doin's in San Antonio," Tippett said sarcastically. "Christ, war with Mexico ain't been over a year yet."

"She'll be treated well. I think she might even pass for half-white and half-Mexican."

Tippett thought for a few minutes, then said, "Reckon it wouldn't hurt none to send her there while she's mendin'."

"That's not what I meant." Seeing the question in Tippett's eyes, Drimmer added, "I meant for her to stay there permanently."

"No," Tippett said flatly. "I lost Painted Wing and Mary. And Josh only a few years ago. All I got left is Libby — and Cass, who's livin' in the village." He shook his head. He would not have Cass much longer. The boy would be a warrior soon and would grow away from his white father.

Drimmer looked out a window at the water running down the glass. The hospital and the commander's quarters were the only places with glass in the windows. "I think it'd be best for Libby."

"It don't seem right, Doc. I expect I'll have to think on it."

"I understand. But if it's all right, I'll send a message to my sister and see if she is amenable to the idea."

"I expect that won't hurt nothin'." He looked toward his daughter. In that crazy, blinding race to save Libby's life, Tippett had somehow transferred the favoritism he had had for Mary to Libby. He walked to the girl's bed and looked down. Libby was sleeping peacefully and looked like what she was — a six-year-old girl. She was too innocent for all these troubles. She needed — deserved — a mother. And, he thought ruefully, more of a father than he was.

With a wrenching numbness, Tippett walked to where Drimmer sat at his desk. "I got to go off a spell and think, Doc. Libby don't know about her Ma, so I'd be obliged if ye was to not say anything to her."

EIGHT DAYS LATER, ZEKE TIPPETT RODE BACK INTO FORT GRAHAM. Unlike the day he left, this one was warm with an abundance of sunshine. The humidity was up, making it a sticky, uncomfortable day. It did little to lighten Tippett's mood or to ease his worry.

Tippett dismounted in front of the infirmary, went inside, and asked without preliminary, "How's Libby, Doc?" He had been afraid something would happen to her while he was away, but he would not admit that, even to himself.

"Just fine," Drimmer said with a wide smile. "Not quite as perky as she could be, which is to be expected after a bout with cholera. But right as rain."

Tippett felt relieved. "Ye get word yet?" He gulped.

"Two days ago. Adelaide and William would be delighted to have Libby, Zeke. They're well off and will see that she's well cared for. She'd want for nothing and would get a proper education. You could ask for no more."

"I expect not." He sighed, the weight of what he had to say heavy on his shoulders. "But I just can't do it, Doc," he said, surprising Drimmer. He had more than half hoped Drimmer's relatives had said no. Then he would have been relieved of this onus.

"What'll you do?" Drimmer said in wonder.

"I'll take Libby to Taos with me, Doc. The store's doin' well and I've got some *pesos* banked. We'll make out." He rubbed his burgeoning beard. "I know I got a wanderin' nature. But, hell, I reckon even an ol' hoss like me can change was he of a mind to."

"I'd recommend against it, Zeke," Drimmer said insistently, recovering from his shock. "San Antonio has good schools, much better than any you could find in Taos. Adelaide and William would give Libby a good home." His eyes bored out from behind the steel-rimmed glasses.

"I know all that, Doc. But she's..." He hesitated. "Well." He paused again, trying to collect his thoughts. "It was Painted Wing's idea, ye know, to bring all the young 'uns to the village. Said she wanted 'em to learn the old ways. Well, Libby's my favorite now, and I want to do what I can for her. Sendin' her off with some folks we don't know just don't seem..." He stumbled to a stop, out of steam. He had run out of words.

"It's all right, Zeke," Drimmer said. He thought Tippett looked terribly sad and seemed to have aged just since walking in. The physician didn't agree with Tippett's decision, but he could understand. It was only natural, Drimmer guessed. He considered trying once more. Then Drimmer saw the look of quiet determination on Tippett's face and knew argument would be futile. He nodded sadly. "Adelaide will be disappointed, Zeke. But she'll understand." He stared out the window to the troops drilling on the parade ground.

He looked back at Tippett. "I'd recommend leaving Libby here a few more days, though. Just to make sure."

"I'm sorry to disappoint your kin, Doc," Tippett said without regret. "The time might come when I'll change my mind. Should that happen, I'll come see ye straight off."

"Fair enough." Drimmer paused. "Will you leave her?"

"A few days can't hurt." He cleared his throat and then asked, "It all right if'n I see Libby a bit?"

"Sure."

"Ye think it's safe to tell her about her Ma?"

"Some things don't get any easier with time, Zeke."

Tippett nodded and walked down the stretch of beds to the small, fragile figure in the last one in the corner. Libby's eyes brightened as she saw him. "Hello, Papa," she said weakly.

"Howdy, Libby," Tippett said, smiling wanly. "How're ye feelin'?"

"Not so bad."

"Well, that's good." He pulled up an old wood chair next to the bed and sat. "Ye miss me whilst I was gone?"

"Yes, but Doctor Drimmer was very good to me."

"*Bueno*." He took one of Libby's tiny hands in one of his big, work-hardened ones. "I got somethin' to tell ye, honey, that ain't gonna be easy for either of us." He paused, afraid that to continue would start tears and he'd be damned before he let that happen.

Libby looked up at him with wide, fear-filled eyes.

Tippett got himself under control. He sighed. "Your Mama's gone to the Great Spirit, honey," he whispered, the words painful.

The shock on his daughter's face was like a hammer blow to his heart. Then the girl cried and cried, great sobs racking her frail body. Tippett did not know what to do. He wanted to hold her but was afraid he would crush her fragile figure in his overwhelming grief.

"The cholera took her, honey," Tippett whispered, the pain of loss filling him to overflowing. His daughter's small brown face clouded before his eyes and he gulped. "Mary went under, too, taken by the sickness like so many of the others of the People."

"Why?" Libby asked, more frightened than she ever had been.

"I don't know, honey," Tippett said lamely. He wished he had a gift for words. He had never considered himself a smart man, but he felt useless at the moment in his inability to explain everything away for his suffering daughter, to make some sense of the madness that had engulfed them.

Still Libby cried. Tippett wanted to yell at her to stop, but he could not. Not when he felt like joining her. So, he sat silently and let her go on until she was finished. He gave Libby a worn bandanna. She wiped her eyes, then blew her nose several times.

"What's gonna happen to me?" Libby finally asked, sniffling, her lower lip trembling. "You gonna take me to live with Yellow Grass?"

"No," he said firmly.

"Why?" Libby asked, surprised and worried.

"A Comanche village ain't a fittin' place for a young lady," he growled. "I want ye to have a proper home and bringin' up." He grinned weakly. "So, I'm takin' ye home to Taos with me."

"Really? Can we go now?" She began to get up.

Tippett shoved her lightly, lovingly back down. "Doc Drimmer says ye got to stay here a couple more days to make sure ye're better."

"That'll be all right," Libby said in childish seriousness.

BOOK 10

GRAY WOLF, 1849-1855

38

The ravages of the epidemic solidified Gray Wolf's hatred of all whites. Walking Bear was unaffected by the illness, but Gray Wolf lost Running Deer, his second wife; two of his five children, four-year-old Cold Foot, and infant daughter Gray Blanket; and his grandmother, Cuts Through. The old civil chief Lame Bear also succumbed, as did one of Hits-With-A-Fist's children and several women and warriors.

But even at that, Gray Wolf knew that his and the other Kwahadi bands in the desolate Llano Estacado had suffered mildly compared with others. The Pehnahterkuhs and Nawkohnees west and north of them were decimated. All their civil chiefs died as did perhaps half their people. Small bands, even families, drifted forlornly.

So, it was left to the *Kwahadis* to defend the honor and sovereignty of the *Nermernuh*. And Gray Wolf was the one who took up the cudgel. He knew the deadly illness that had come among his people was somehow tied to the increasing waves of whites flocking through — and worse, into, in many cases — the Comanches' western homelands.

He talked often of it with Walking Bear. Gray Wolf's old friend, usually easygoing, also had turned resolute in his hatred for whites.

As the disease ravaged his camp, Walking Bear said to his friend, "It is bad medicine. We have done much to displease the spirits."

Gray Wolf grunted. "Many of the *Nermernuh* have not been living by the old ways, the proper ways."

Some warriors, led by Gray Wolf and Walking Bear, built a special lodge and sweated to purify themselves. Dancing and singing, they tried to make their medicine more powerful. But death still ran rampant in the camps. One day a person was hale; the next sickly, then dead. Gray Wolf took it upon himself to rid the camp of these evil spirits. He had always had strong medicine. Now he would try to find medicine strong enough to save his band — and maybe all the People.

Gray Wolf went off to his place for making his medicine. He usually enjoyed the quiet, and watching a soaring hawk; or a fat rattlesnake, abdomen round from just having swallowed a gopher. But he had more important business than admiring the scenery. For four days he fasted, seeking a vision that might help rid his village of this plague of bad spirits. After two days he no longer saw night's purple shadows or the sunrise. He was weak. Unfeelingly, he toppled.

He saw a large, powerful wolf. But the wolf, his symbol of power, was not stalking a victim as it usually was. Instead, it lay, tongue lolling out. The big, gray animal panted, his eyes glazed.

The wolf was alone, and dying. In his stupor, Gray Wolf shivered. A figure approached. The wolf strained to lift his head to see what he had heard. A riderless horse came and the wolf dropped his head onto weak paws. There was no danger; the horse would not disturb his death.

Onward the horse came. Its brilliant whiteness rose in the shimmering waves of heat, the glitter enough to hurt the eyes. The horse stopped at the wolf's side. He nuzzled the prostrate canine, snickering softly, as if trying to tell the wolf to rise.

The wolf strained but could not get to its feet. He had no strength left in his limbs. He was helpless, prey to anyone who came along. The white horse would not be able to protect him. To the west the wolf heard the soft padding of a mountain lion. Then two more. And still more. From the east and south and north. From every direction they came, yellow fangs dripping saliva, snouts curled up in menace.

The horse stood next to the wolf, neighing and pawing the ground. But the wolf knew the horse would flee soon. It did. The wolf watched as the horse galloped off, bushy tail and mane flapping in the wind. Suddenly the horse stopped and reared. He brought his hooves down in powerful blows that scattered the cougars in all directions. The horse charged frantically in a circle, rearing, then hammering down with big, iron-shod hooves. Lions roared and shrieked in impotent rage.

Then the mountain lions were gone, slinking off. Silence returned to linger over the wolf, and the horse, which had moved back to the wolf's side. Once again, the wolf tried to rise, but was unsuccessful.

The horse trotted off, and returned in moments with the body of a mountain lion clamped firmly in his teeth, the cat's tail dragging on the earth. The horse dropped the carcass in front of the wolf.

The sickly canine lifted his head and weakly tore off small chunks of the puma's flesh and swallowed them whole. He drank the blood. The gray wolf could feel his strength growing, bit by bit. For two more days he ate cougar flesh while the horse stood watch over him. On the third day, he stood. He wobbled, but he was standing. He heard a thundering rumble and the wolf spun slowly. The big white horse was racing across the land.

The wolf's attention was diverted by a jackrabbit bounding by. His feeble howl split the air, and then he was off, chasing the rabbit.

Gray Wolf awoke with a start. His shoulder hurt from where he had fallen on it. He was very weak, but he was alive, and his vision remained etched into his brain. He ate as much as his bone-empty stomach could handle and then slept.

He took two more days of gradually increasing his food at each meal before he felt he could go on. He pulled himself onto his pony. Gray Wolf was back in the village before nightfall. He ate, and then slept again. The next day he puzzled over his vision, trying to figure out its meaning. He regretted now more than ever old Lame Bear's passing. He would have liked to discuss the vision with the sage old leader. But there was no one to take Lame Bear's place, and so he was left to puzzle it out himself. After two days, he decided its meaning would become clear to him in due time.

However, he was pleased to hear that since the day after he had left, there had been only five new cases of the disease in the village. Gray Wolf might not understand his vision, but it was clear that its powerful medicine was already at work.

The next day, Zeke Tippett rode into the camp. Gray Wolf's hate flared. The rest of the village was no less enraged. Tippett was surrounded by an angry mob.

"This ain't no way to treat a friend who's brought ye a present, Wolf," Tippett said angrily. He pointed to the two pack mules behind him. Both held canvas-covered supplies. But the nearest had the carcass of a large mountain lion across the top, outside the covering.

The sight was like a splash of cold water in Gray Wolf's face. He started as if having just been woken from a deep sleep. Suddenly his vision was clear. With a few shouted words, he quieted the others.

"White Horse, my friend!" Gray Wolf shouted urgently. "Come, to the fire." He turned and spat instructions. He might not have any authority, but the respect he had earned would spur most to heed him.

When Tippett dismounted, Gray Wolf told a Mexican boy adopted into the tribe to take care of his friend's mount. But the packhorses were left. And, as he walked beside Tippett toward the fire in front of Gray Wolf's lodge, Gray Wolf led the packhorses.

The other warriors gathered in a semicircle at the fire, behind Tippett, facing Gray Wolf. They were anxious and angry. Death had stalked the *Nermernuh* too frequently of late, and they did not know why. Only that it had something to do with the *tahbay-boh*.

Gray Wolf motioned Tippett to sit. When the white man had done so, Gray Wolf, still holding the rope of the packhorses, said, "The *tahbay-boh* has brought bad spirits to the People."

The crowd growled, and Tippett's shoulders hunched involuntarily.

"But there's one here — a *tahbay-boh* — who's unlike the others. I know this from my vision. Few know what I have seen. Lame Bear, who could explain my vision is gone, and there's no one to take his place.

"I did not know what it meant. Until now. It was made clear when White Horse came." He described his vision in exacting detail. And then he explained its meaning, as Lame Bear might have done.

"I am that sickly old wolf, my brothers," Gray Wolf shouted. "And our friend and brother, He-Who-Is-The-White-Horse, is the white horse of my vision. That white horse saved the life of my spirit helper so the wolf could live, to fight enemies as of old."

The others sat in rapt attention, women and children ranked behind the warriors. Tippett did, too. He was not sure what his old friend was up to, but he knew his fate might hinge on what Gray Wolf was saying — and on how the other Comanches took it.

"In the past White Horse has saved me. Once from the bullets of the *tahbay-boh*. At other times with his wise counsel. But when he came here today, he brought the flesh of a mountain lion — as the white horse of my vision brought the flesh of a mountain lion to the sickly wolf. Now we all must eat the flesh of this puma. It will make us strong again, and frighten the bad spirits from our village and the *tahbay-boh* from our land.

"I have seen this. So, I say it is so. Let no one go against this power. That'd weaken our medicine, and the *Nermernuh* will suffer."

He sat, letting dignity settle on him like a cape, as startled talk buzzed through the assembled warriors. Walking Bear stood and strongly voiced his approval for what Gray Wolf had proposed, and his acceptance for Tippett's place among them. Runs-At-The-Enemy did the same, as did Hits-With-A-Fist and Buffalo Droppings.

Each warrior had his full say. None had anything bad to say about all that had transpired, though two questioned the accuracy of Gray Wolf's vision. They finally, however, accepted it as true, and threw their support to Gray Wolf.

When the warriors were finished, all eyes turned to Tippett. Uncomfortably he stood and said softly, "I ain't ever had such a vision myself, but if'n Gray Wolf says it's so, then it must be."

He sat and Gray Wolf stood again. He pulled the puma carcass from the horse and peeled its hide off. Then he sliced hunks of meat from the cougar and passed them around. When each person had a piece, Gray Wolf offered a few bits of the meat to the spirits. With a look of fierce hope, he sank his teeth into the raw flesh. The others followed suit. Not once did a look of distaste pass anyone's face.

39

Gray Wolf was proud as he rode out of his camp at the head of a dozen warriors. He was proud for several reasons. One, his medicine in the past several years had been mighty.

Since the white-man's sickness had left his camp almost five years ago, the *Kwahadi* Comanches had had an impressive string of victories over the *tahbay-boh*. Each summer, Gray Wolf had led his warriors on raids — against ranches and farms, even towns. He often attacked wagon trains — until travelers began to stay away from any land over which Gray Wolf's *Kwahadis* held sway. His forays into the fringe areas of Texas settlements had spread a fear that was almost palpable. Some settlers in outlying areas fled, not persuaded to stay any longer, not even by liberal homesteading offers. It bolstered the confidence of Gray Wolf's *Kwahadis*, as well as that of the remaining *Pehnahterkuhs, Yampahreekahs* and *Kotsotekas*. Though those bands had been decimated by the white man's diseases and warfare, they felt more secure in new camps above the Red River.

The Army could not defeat the Comanches, even if it could find them. Occasionally Rangers would catch up to the fast-moving war bands — and exacted a toll. Though Gray Wolf still hated all

Texans, he admitted a grudging respect for the tough, resolute Rangers.

But admiring thoughts of Rangers were not in his mind as the band of painted warriors rode out of camp under the glimmering, fat moon. Pride also occupied Gray Wolf's mind because his son, Black Arrow, was along on his first trail of war. That Born-In-The-Storm, son of his old friend, Zeke Tippett, was doing the same, increased his joy.

Gray Wolf had great plans for the two young men. He would shape them until they were brave, fierce, and totally ruthless. Both youths were accomplished horsemen, almost without peer. Black Arrow handled a twelve-foot-long lance with consummate skill; Born-In-The-Storm had no equal with gun or bow. They had shown much prowess in hunting. Now would come their real test. Gray Wolf had no doubt they would pass.

"Hear me, my sons," he had told the two youths before they left. "The *tahbay-boh* are like the timid deer that flee at the slightest sound. Already they fear the might of the *Nermernuh*. Soon our medicine will drive the *tahbay-boh* from our lands for all time."

The youths' eyes gleamed in the firelight and they could feel the pulsing drums in their blood. Even Born-In-The-Storm, who also carried the name Cass Tippett, felt this was right. He was not a *tahbay-boh*. Nor was his father. The *tahbay-boh* were the enemy.

The war party plunged deep into the heart of the settled Texas frontier. They rode arrogantly into the country that supported a scant few dozen struggling, but determined, towns. The Comanches were as quick as lightning, and more deadly. They would stab hard and then flee before the settlers could organize resistance or pursuit.

Black Arrow and Born-In-The-Storm acquitted themselves well, killing, scalping, stealing, plundering, and raping with wild and infectious abandon. Gray Wolf watched them with a cruel smile on his lips — an indulgent father proud of his high-spirited sons.

With growing arrogance, the Comanches headed toward San Antonio. It was perhaps a foolhardy thing to do since a string of military forts now protected the inhabited areas of Texas. But the *Nermernuh* did not care. Though Gray Wolf had enough sense not to attack San Antonio, he and his warriors considered everything else fair game. They harassed stagecoaches, towns, farms, and small Army patrols. With deadly speed, they swooped down on an unsuspecting settlement of whites who spoke a language even stranger than that of the Americans or Mexicans. But the German settlers of New Braunfels needed no language to express their fear when the Comanche horde swept over their town north of San Antonio. They battled as valiantly as they could, but they were hopelessly outnumbered, outfought, and outhated.

The Comanches besieged the settlement until it was aflame and its occupants dead or dying — except those the Comanches carted along for sport. Laughing at the flopping pieces of agonized flesh and bone that so recently had been human beings, the Comanches moved off fast.

"Where will we go now?" Walking Bear asked Gray Wolf several hours later. They had made a camp fifty miles away after a hard ride.

"To the great water," Gray Wolf said with almost a smile. "We were there many years ago, remember? Now we'll return — to show Black Arrow and Born-In-The-Storm what it's truly like to be a *Nermernuh* warrior. My name will burn on the tongues of the *tahbay-boh*."

"We'll take many things," Walking Bear agreed joyfully. This was life as a Comanche warrior should live it. He was no longer young and he thought it good that he still had some youthful zest in him.

"Like that last time," Gray Wolf said. "Such a time that was." It had been a glorious day for the Comanches when they had last raided the big town along the Gulf of Mexico. The Indians had been in wonder at the great ships with their billowing white sails. And the goods to be plundered! But equally gratifying had been the fear he had seen in those pale eyes, especially that one gleaming-white woman's. He had been unable to figure out her corsets and stays, and he had to satisfy himself with the fear he generated in those eyes — just before he brained her with a war club in his frustration.

"We'll make these *tahbay-boh* fear us and remember us like they have Buffalo Hump," Gray Wolf said arrogantly.

"Buffalo Hump had many honors," Walking Bear said, nodding. "You are much like him, old friend. Few can command so many warriors as you have done. None has medicine so strong."

Gray Wolf said nothing, but a sneer curled his upper lip and his broad, dark chest puffed out with pride. He finished eating and wiped his greasy hands on his filthy buckskin breechcloth. He looked toward the three women captives — all fair-haired, German-speaking young women, with plump breasts, deliciously heavy hips, and thick bottoms. Gray Wolf stood with a grin. He had long ago figured out the intricacies of white women's dress so that was no longer a problem. These three had been stripped before the Comanches had even ridden away from the burning settlement. There would be nothing to get in his way. And there would still be bright sparks of fear he would create.

He went to where the women were tied to stunted mesquites. All three had their hands bound behind their backs, and ropes were around their necks linking them to the tree. As he walked, Gray Wolf whipped off his breechcloth, showing himself to be rampantly ready.

The other warriors hooted and cheered, laughed, and made crude suggestions. Black Arrow, as arrogant as his father, leaped up and stripped off his blanket loincloth. He hurried after Gray Wolf, his manhood preceding him.

"There are three women, Born-In-The-Storm," Walking Bear said with a grin.

The half-breed smiled and hastily followed the example of Gray Wolf and Black Arrow who were parading their lances inches from the eyes of the three terrified women. In unison, the three warriors fell on the women. It became a contest to them to see who could hold out the longest, with Gray Wolf winning easily. Black Arrow spent first. Angry at himself, he shoved up and walked back to his fire, burning with embarrassment to the catcalls from the rest of the men.

But it was quickly forgotten as they ate more beef butchered from a stolen steer and drank black coffee, almost syrupy with sugar.

They rode for the coast the next morning but took time to attack a small settlement and two ranches. So, it was not until the following morning that they closed in on the town. But Littleton was far more populous than it had been years earlier, something Gray Wolf and Walking Bear had not foreseen. Raids in the area were now perfunctory.

Gray Wolf was angry at that. His hatred turned into a flaming rage that left a number of farms devastated — and the poor souls who had lived on them dying in agony. He led his men on an arc that curled up along the Trinity River and west across the Navasota and Brazos Rivers. They curved southwest toward the Colorado River, across it, and down along the Llano River. Their bloodlust had slackened little. But despite his unflagging hatred, even Gray Wolf knew he had to go home one day. Winter was only a month away and meat supplies had to be put up for their families. So, they turned toward the Llano Estacado.

Gray Wolf could not resist one more raid. The Comanches attacked a farm just after dawn. The residents had no chance, and soon the man, his wife, their three oldest boys, two youngest boys, and infant daughter were dead, mutilated and scalped. The Comanches ransacked the house, picking up guns, cloth and clothing they would take back to their women, coats and hats for themselves, and food. As some Comanches torched the house and barn, others stripped the family's one adult daughter. Looking for fun, warriors poked and jabbed at the teenager with their lances and knives.

She was ghastly white — from lack of sun and from fear. The men circled her in a continuous wave until they blurred before her sobbing eyes. They made crude noises and touched her in places she had touched only rarely herself. The fear built in her stomach until she vomited, splattering a few closer warriors. Some dribbled onto her heaving breasts. She shuddered with fear while the Comanches laughed.

One of those who had been sprayed with her vomit was angry at that. He grabbed the woman by her auburn hair. With a sharp yank, he wrenched her onto the ground. Suddenly he was atop her, and she screamed as he pierced her with his manhood.

She knew little of what happened next. It was too much of a blur as one warrior after another buried himself in her and pumped relentlessly until he was done. Another would eagerly take his place. Her mind screamed at her to endure, and survive. She closed her eyes and prayed any prayer she could think of, until this ordeal turned into a mere progression of grunting, foul-smelling men who covered her briefly. Suddenly it seemed over, since no one was on her. New fears surfaced. Perhaps if they were finished with her, they would kill her. Or worse, take her with them. She fought the panic that writhed in her insides like a big rattlesnake. Cautiously she opened her eyes. Oh, my God, she thought. One of 'em's smilin' at me.

Her insides roiled, but the one smiling said something in his own language to the others. One answered back, but a sharp look from the short, broad, dark Indian stopped the protest. Suddenly the men spun and were mounting their horses. Then they were gone.

"Why did you let her live and not bring her?" Buffalo Droppings asked in a snarl. "Are you no longer a man?"

They were riding hard, but Gray Wolf yanked at the grass rope tied around his pony's lower jaw as a rein. The horse stopped, snorting. Buffalo Droppings also stopped, as did the others.

"You haven't had enough of white women when you'll be with your wife soon?" Gray Wolf demanded, eyes burning with the fires of rage. "If you want that *tahbay-boh,* go get her. Bring her to your lodge as a wife." He knew full well Buffalo Droppings could not afford another wife. He could barely handle the one he had.

Buffalo Droppings did not know what to say.

"I left her so she can warn the other *tahbay-boh,*" Gray Wolf snarled. "Killing and scalping people will tell the *tahbay-boh* a story. But the story will be more potent if there is someone alive to describe how mighty the *Nermernuh* are. She will let all the *tahbay-boh* know the power of the *Nermernuh*!"

Buffalo Droppings was angry, but also ashamed at having questioned a war leader as great as Gray Wolf. He squirmed at his lack of sense. Gray Wolf knew how he felt. After staring at the younger man for some seconds, he turned his pony and raced off.

It was forgotten by the time they made camp that night, and the men were in a more jovial mood. With the thought of soon being with their families, they were all more at ease. And they were on the fringe of the Llano Estacado, and feeling safe.

"I will have a wife now," Black Arrow boasted to his friend Born-In-The-Storm as they sat over the fire. They had listened to the other men talking and each felt a yearning he had not experienced before. Both young men had enough horses and honors to make them suitable husbands, despite the fact that they were still quite young.

"And who will you pick?" Born-In-The-Storm asked with a grin.

Black Arrow smiled, too wary to speak. Born-In-The-Storm was his friend, but still, a man had to watch what he said.

"Must be White Flower," Born-In-The-Storm said with a laugh.

Black Arrow scowled, and Born-In-The-Storm knew he was right.

"I'm going to cast my blanket for Winter Moon," Born-In-The-Storm said firmly. He had had his eye on Winter Moon for some time, and wanted to make sure Black Arrow also was not considering her. He was relieved to know that his friend had set his sights on another.

40

"I think we got them red-skinned, murderin' sons a bitches now, Cap'n," Elmore Trent snarled. He walked his blowing horse next to that of Captain Horace Montgomery, Second Cavalry.

Trent wiped his running nose on the back of his hand and then smeared it on his wool trousers. He wore an off-white muslin shirt under a buckskin jacket fringed along the sleeves and yokes. A hat, front brim pinned up, knee-length black boots with the pants tucked in, and spurs with silver rowels completed the ensemble.

"They're camped along Beals Creek," Trent said. His normally high-pitched whiny voice was even squeakier since he was excited. "Eight, ten miles west." His words made soft plumes of mist in the chill September air.

"They the ones we've been trailing?"

"Does it matter?" Trent asked, his eyes burning like two small coals, reflecting the fires of hatred in his soul.

"I suppose not," Montgomery said, uncomfortable in the hot glow of Trent's eyes. He looked away. Montgomery was commander of Fort Spirit Mound, recently built along the Brazos near Clear Fork, a few days east of where they were. He had been getting reports of this marauding band of Comanches for weeks, but the Indians were always too far away. He heard of them through dispatches from others in the string of forts built in the past year or so along the jagged edge of the Texas frontier. The reports got closer and closer, until Montgomery finally received a dispatch from Fort Belknap warning that the Comanches were headed that way. Montgomery assembled his troops and at the last minute decided to lead the patrol himself.

Elmore Trent, one-time mountain man, was not the ranking scout at Fort Spirit Mound, but Montgomery thought him the best. Trent followed the Comanche trail for four days before arriving with his report.

"Can we catch up to them before dark?" Montgomery asked.

Trent shoved his hat back off his forehead a bit and leaned over sideways from his saddle to spit tobacco juice. When he straightened, he said, "Reckon so. But I don't advise it."

Montgomery was annoyed. The ferret-faced scout was diffident and it sometimes took him a coon's age to answer. Montgomery mostly accepted the traits. But he was in no humor for it at the moment. "Why?" he asked, grumbling.

"They'll kick our asses we catch 'em in daylight, Cap'n," Trent growled, as if speaking to an idiot. He often thought Montgomery a fool, though the captain did understand the one and only way to solve the Comanche problem. Trent had to give him that much. Not like those fools back in Washington who, never having been out here with all the death and destruction, issued pronouncements and orders on how to contain the troublesome Comanches. There was no containing the Comanches, Trent — and anyone else who had lived out here — knew. There was only one way to handle them — annihilation.

Montgomery was a little shocked, though he supposed he should not have been. Trent was nothing if not blunt. "Then what do you suggest, Mister Trent?" he asked quietly.

Trent leaned over and spit again. "Give your boys a rest." He waved his left hand in the general direction of the troops strung out behind them. "Till dark. Let 'em eat, and they can rest the horses."

"Would fires be permitted?" the captain asked.

"No. Those goddamn Comanches kin smell a white fire for twenty miles."

Montgomery figured Trent was exaggerating, as he — and most other former mountain men, he had learned — often did. But Montgomery knew there was some truth to it, so he issued orders quietly to his sergeant. The troops fell into the routine of making a cold camp.

Pickets were assigned, horses unsaddled and hobbled, pack mules unloaded, and the animals set out to graze on sparse, browned grass. Before long, the men not on guard duty were playing cards, yarning, or nibbling rations. Some napped, using their campaign hats to keep the blazing sun from their faces. They pulled out after dark. Six of the two dozen troopers were left behind with the pack animals. The others tied down whatever equipment they could to minimize noise. They rode into the star-lit night, afraid even to whisper.

Suddenly Trent, who was leading their way, stopped. He huddled with Liam Sweeney, the company's grizzled first sergeant. Sweeney was a big, hard-edged, no-nonsense man. Troops found out upon meeting him that he was no one to trifle with. Several had tried and had themselves knocked silly for their pains. Two had decided to desert after such treatment. Sweeney, a conscientious man, took this as a personal affront and went after them. He kept the deserters' ears in a bottle of alcohol on the small crate he used as a nightstand.

After his short, quiet conference with Trent, Sweeney directed the troopers into position.

"Are the Comanches always this lax, Mister Trent?" Montgomery asked in a whisper as he settled in behind the trunk of a stunted oak.

"Naw. But they're stupid bastards," Trent answered in the same low tones. "They figger they're close to home so they don't need to be watchful. Damn fools."

They fell silent and waited for the creeping dawn. The time seemed to drag as the soldiers nervously watched the dark figures, listening to the snores, and the shuffling of the horses. Gray eventually cracked the eastern rim of the world and before long had a soft pink edge to it. Trent raised his percussion Henry and eased back the hammer. Next to him, Montgomery gave a hand signal that his men should be ready. The signal whirled around the semicircle of soldiers.

Trent fired, and one Comanche never uttered a sound as he died in his sleep, his head shattered by a .54-caliber rifle ball. The other soldiers opened fire as the Comanches awoke before the first puffs of powder smoke had drifted into the trees. Gray Wolf was moving in an instant, running for the horses, roaring orders as he ran, heedless of the fusillade.

Black Arrow followed his father an instant later. Born-In-The-Storm grabbed his Colt Dragoon pistol even as he was whirling into a crouch on his blanket. He fired just below at a puff of smoke near a bush. He heard a yowl and was satisfied. He fired slowly and deliberately, trying to give Gray Wolf, Black Arrow, and Buffalo Droppings some cover as they tried to get to the horses.

Five soldiers, however, had been ordered before dawn to get as near to the herd as they could without spooking the animals. When the attack started, they swung onto their own heavy mounts. They shouted and yelled at the Comanche ponies. The animals milled.

A bloodthirsty Gray Wolf leaped onto the rump of an Army horse. There was a quick flash of steel, and then the soldier was flung off to the side, his neck spurting blood from the slashed throat. Gray Wolf rammed his heels into the horse's side and the animal shot forward, bearing down on another soldier.

Black Arrow, right behind his father, leaped at a mounted soldier who was broadside to him. He slammed into the Army man and both fell off. Black Arrow landed atop the soldier, and in an instant he had crushed the soldier's head with his war club. He jumped up, ready to leap on a horse. But a mounted trooper fired at him twice in quick succession at close range. Both balls caught Black Arrow, one high on the chest, the other just below and to the left of his nose. Black Arrow spun, dying, and fell atop the soldier he had just killed.

Buffalo Droppings jumped on a Comanche pony. He and Gray Wolf turned at least half the horses, while the three mounted soldiers pushed the rest of the herd onto the prairie away from the river.

"Git that son of a bitch," Trent screamed, pointing at Born-In-The-Storm, who still knelt on his blanket. Born-In-The-Storm had run out of bullets in his revolver, and was using his bow. Hits-With-A-Fist tossed him two other pistols, and the young half-breed stood his ground, firing calmly. Trent had fired at him three times and missed. "Goddamn it," he muttered to himself, angry. Others had an equal lack of success.

Still the half-breed knelt, unafraid. "Bastard's got some powerful medicine, the son of a bitch," Trent muttered as he reloaded. "Goddammit, we'll see jist how goddamn powerful his goddamn, buffalo-humpin' goddamn medicine is." He fired, and the heavy round ball knocked Born-In-The-Storm flat on his back with the impact. "That'll teach y'all to tempt me with such doin's, goddamn it."

Born-In-The-Storm struggled up. There was surprisingly little pain, he thought as he got into a kneeling position again, although it was awfully difficult to move. His limbs did not want to cooperate.

The Comanches fought desperately as Gray Wolf and Buffalo Droppings swung horses through the camp to give their friends some protection. And as soon as they had it, the Comanches flung themselves onto any animal they could grab and rode like hell.

As the wall of horseflesh moved in front of him, Born-In-The-Storm tried to stand. If I can do that, he thought, I can get on a pony and go. But his arms and legs would not help him and he sank back onto his heels. He felt no fear, just a strong sense of loss for the things he would never know. He chanted a death song. Pain was creeping into his chest making it difficult.

Then the horses were gone, and the dust began to settle as the Comanches fled. Soon there was only the sound of Born-In-The-Storm's fading death chant carrying mournfully on the breeze.

"Lookee, boys," Trent said, moving in the clearing. "They left one." He walked slowly toward Born-In-The-Storm, soldiers following. He stopped in front of Born-In-The-Storm, set the butt of his rifle in the dirt and leaned on the muzzle. "Sure is a noisy bastard, ain't he," Trent said malevolently. He listened for a few moments, then spit tobacco juice on the man's face. "Shit," he muttered. Then he said, "Here, boy, hold this." He straightened up and leaned his rifle toward the soldier on his left. When the soldier took the rifle, Trent pulled his knife. "Let's see how y'all like some of this shit, boy."

"What are you going to do, Mister Trent?" Montgomery asked, trying to sound officious. It came out nervous.

"Jist watch — if'n y'all got the stomach for it."

GRAY WOLF RAN THE ARMY HORSE AS FAR AS HE COULD AND THEN pulled into a stand of cottonwoods far west along the river. He was breathing hard, but the horse was really blowing, its sweat-flecked sides heaving in and out like giant bellows. He waited out the day, then rode back to the camp. He ignored the growling of his hungry stomach.

The soldiers were gone when he arrived at the old camp just after dawn. Before he rode into the site, he circled it, looking for the tracks. He grinned sneeringly. The fools had followed the ponies the Comanches cut loose.

He found Runs-At-The-Enemy first, near the perimeter of the camp. Then, Born-In-The-Storm, and lastly, Black Arrow. The bodies were scalped, and mutilated. He shook his head. The *tahbay-boh* did not believe he would meet the *Nermernuh* in the afterlife, and so had no reason for the ritual mutilating of the body as the Comanche did.

Gray Wolf howled in his grief, an animal-like keening that rose above the treetops, trying to find a home in the clouds.

Late in the afternoon, Gray Wolf did what he could for his father-in-law, son, and nephew, as he had thought of Born-In-The-Storm. There was little in the camp with which to send them on their way to the Spirit World, but Gray Wolf did what he could.

As he finally ate, he plotted his vengeance. But first would come winter, and then he would have to make medicine again.

This time, he vowed, his medicine would be unbreakable.

BOOK 11

GRAY WOLF, 1849-1855

41

Zeke Tippett walked into the Trailside Saloon in Cimarron, Kansas Territory. He was tired, filthy, bored, and lonely. He had been away from Taos for more than a year. Last summer, he had decided to bring Libby to the village for a visit. His itchy feet were getting the better of him and he needed to get away so he decided to ride along with his wagonloads of furs up to St. Louis.

He sent the wagons ahead, up the Santa Fe Trail, while he went eastward toward *Comancheria*. Libby was excited about seeing her old friends again, hardly remembering that only two years ago her mother and sister had died of the disease there.

Tippett had had some regrets at first about taking Libby to the village and leaving her there for perhaps a year — he figured that if he was going to be in St. Louis, he might as well make the most of it — but her excitement and joy soon quelled his concern. So, with several farewell kisses and hugs, Tippett had left Libby and rode hard northward, finally meeting up with the wagons midway between Upper Springs and Lower Springs. The rest of the trip was uneventful, except for a tornado and a brush with some Pawnees.

Tippett had enjoyed his time in St. Louis, comfortably settling into shabby rooms along the waterfront. He was within easy reach

— even when the cold and snow clamped an icy grip over the city — of several saloons, restaurants, and bawdyhouses.

Even that had paled by spring. Tippett was too drawn to open space to spend so much time in a city. So as soon as possible, he rode out. Two weeks later, out past Independence and Westport, he was in buffalo country. He rode slowly, alone and unafraid. He passed several wagon trains of freight going in each direction. Finally, he decided to stop in Cimarron, figuring to have a few drinks, perhaps a bath and a shave, and sleep in a real bed for a change. It was one of his few vanities — he had come to like sleeping in a soft, down-filled bed.

Tippett shouldered his way through knots of men in the saloon. The dozen tables were filled; other men stood talking, drinking, and arguing. The saloon — like most on the fringe of nowhere — was a rough place of sod, mud, and cracked wood. It had a dirt floor, no windows, and the bar was planks on barrels. It smelled of burned meat, urine, vomit, sweat, unclean people, and damp dirt. As filthy and unkempt as he was, Tippett did not stand out in such a place.

He bought a bottle of whiskey at the bar. Turning, he spotted a group of men leaving a table in a back corner. He bulled his way quickly through the crowd toward it. The only occupant left was a man snoring heavily in a drunken stupor. Tippett shoved the man to the floor and sat. From his possibles sack he pulled some jerky. He chewed a piece between sips of whiskey. Finally, he fired up his old clay pipe and sat back, a feeling close to serenity warming him.

He scratched at the growth on his neck and chin as he thought about getting back to Taos. And then heading out to pick up Libby. No, he decided, he would get Libby first, and visit with Gray Wolf a little, if his warrior friend was there. Then he and his daughter would go home to Taos. The thoughts were pleasant.

A plump, pleasant-looking half-breed shuffled up, clutching a thin cotton robe loosely around her. She sat. Tippett grinned and passed her the bottle without her asking. The woman nodded gratefully and sipped. As she leaned over to hand him back the bottle, the robe gaped in front, exposing billowing, coppery breasts. Tippett had not had a woman in several weeks now; this one would do. She took his hand and they went out back. Eight tents stood, the sounds of lovemaking coming from all but one. It was to that one that she took Tippett.

Inside, she shrugged and the robe fell, leaving her naked. She reached out a hand, and, with a grin, Tippett handed her the bottle. As she drank, Tippett shed his clothes.

The woman handed back the bottle, standing close to him, staring up. She was plainly attractive, but her eyes showed the ravages of too harsh a life and too much whiskey. She grinned lopsidedly and suddenly looked a little younger. She glanced down, noted his hardness, and then back up. She grinned again. "Looks like your weapon's primed, boy. Let's get it done. I ain't got all night."

"Ye don't? How's about a couple hours? If I was to pay for it?"

She grinned. "Cash first." When he handed her several silver coins, her eyes widened and she grinned again. She turned and put the coins in a small buckskin pouch under the cheap mattress. She turned back. "I reckon I can show you a real good time. mister. If you think you can get up for another go-'round without takin' all night for it, well..."

"I reckon I ain't all that old yet," Tippett commented.

The woman grinned once more and sank to her knees. It was not long before he gasped. Afterward, Tippett sank gratefully onto the nearby bed. The woman sat on the bed next to him and took the bottle.

An hour later, the woman was atop Tippett, pumping her pelvis harshly on him. She yelped, and Tippett groaned loudly.

Afterward, Tippett strolled back into the saloon. He had left the bottle of whiskey with the woman so he bought another. The crowd had thinned and the table in the back corner was unoccupied. He plopped down. The next table emptied and was immediately reoccupied. He puffed on his pipe, eyes closed. Suddenly his eyelids popped open, the tiredness sloughing off him. He glanced at the other table.

Lou Parkhurst, Sam Flinch, and Tim Marshall sat talking with a man Tippett did not know. Tippett listened to the three freighters who had almost killed Gray Wolf more than a decade ago. Tippett was glad he was screened by people drifting back and forth. That, the men's interest in their own talk, and Tippett's stubbled, dirty face and filthy clothes served to protect him from discovery.

"I heard Comanches dropped like flies," the unknown man said.

"Yeah," Flinch chuckled. "Even after the three years I still hear about the summer of '49 down in Texas and how the Indian problem was solved." He laughed and drank more.

"You ever thought of haulin' another load of such special *supplies*" — he accented the word — "down there?"

"More'n once," Marshall said nonchalantly.

"Hell," Flinch said with a harsh laugh, rubbing the vicious scar on his face, "I don't know as if them red-skinned sons a bitches'd let us anywhere near 'em now."

They laughed and then silently drank for a while. Then the unknown man asked, "Where'd y'all get them tainted blankets anyway?"

The others' faces darkened and they furtively searched the room to see if anyone was paying attention. Tippett ducked his head, resting it on the table, as if he were drunk. Then he heard, "It's none of your business, Hall." Flinch's voice was tight, angry. He furiously rubbed his disfigured jaw.

"Didn't mean nothin' by it," Morgan Hall said curtly. "I was just thinkin' we could get some more. There's got to be a few of them damned Injins that don't know where the sickness come from last time." His voice rose in intensity and fervor but not volume. His eyes were wild and he spilled whiskey as he jerked the bottle up.

"What's got you so worked up, Morgan?" Parkhurst asked.

"Goddamn Comanches killed my family. Butchered all of 'em.

They..." He choked to a stop and jolted down another mouthful of liquor.

"Maybe we can help you," Flinch said deliberately. He rubbed the ruined jaw under the giant beak of a nose. "But you'll..."

Their voices dropped to whispers, and Tippett sat back sipping whiskey, unable to hear them. His hooded eyes never left the other table. The pain of his past flooded over him and with it came a sharp dose of guilt. It all must be his fault, he figured. He had hurt these men, killed one of them to save Gray Wolf. By their seeking vengeance against him, the Comanches had suffered far more than he had.

Tippett's guilt and hate built throughout the evening as the other men talked, drank, and often laughed. But finally, they stood, weaving, and as a group, lurched joyfully out the door. Tippett rose, Hawken in hand, and followed them into the cool, humid night. The four were standing outside, still talking. Tippett slipped to the side of the door, away from the light spilling from the saloon's lanterns.

Hall said something low, and the others laughed crudely. Then Flinch muttered, "Shit." He headed down the dusty track that passed for a street, nearly getting run over by a horse.

Hall went the opposite way, around the corner of the saloon and toward the tent cribs behind it. Parkhurst and Marshall talked a few more minutes before staggering away. Tippett followed them. They entered the livery stable and kicked fresh straw into piles before slumping on them, wrapped in thin blankets. Tippett nodded grimly — they would be going nowhere the rest of the night.

Tippett returned to the saloon and went around back. Five tents produced sounds. Tippett stopped at each tent until he heard Hall's low voice, slurred by drink but unmistakable. Tippett slipped soundlessly into the tent. Hall lay on the bed, bare-chested but wearing pants and boots. The young prostitute was peeling off her thin wrap, baring her scrawny body. Tippett was a little surprised.

He thought they might have even been done, but as drunk as Hall was, he probably had trouble even striking a deal. Tippett clamped a hand over the woman's mouth. "Get out," he hissed.

"Who's there?" Hall asked, slurring his words, voice quivering in fear. He stood shakily as the naked woman hurried into the night.

"I hear ye like killin' Comanches," Tippett said harshly. He slid the bone-handled Bowie out.

"Who are you?" Hall asked, scared. "And what do you want?"

"The Comanches call me White Horse. Those that're still livin'," he added pointedly.

A chill rippled up Hall's back. "What do you want?"

"I don't take a shine to scum who like killin' Injuns but ain't got the balls to stand up and do it like a man."

"Get the hell out of here," Hall blustered. He relaxed a little. He figured this was a test concocted by the others to see how he would stand up. "I got no time for dealin' with shit like you."

"I'll be leavin' soon enough," Tippett said.

Hall was afraid again. Parkhurst had chosen well in this man, he thought. The look in Tippett's eyes was, Hall thought, quite real in its deadly earnestness.

"Soon's I finish my business."

"Piss on you," Hall snapped. "How dare..."

Tippett's knife plunged into Hall's chest, cutting off his words. Hall fell, shock glittering in his dying eyes. Tippett wiped his blade on Hall's pants and put the knife away. He left the tent like a wraith.

A few minutes later, Tippett was a shadow flickering across the inside of the livery stable. The deadly Bowie knife made two short arcs. Neither Marshall nor Parkhurst knew it when their lives ended.

He had been in the livery less than a minute before he was heading up the dirt path toward the hotel.

There was a grim satisfaction in it for Tippett. He had, through his fight with these freighters ten years ago, caused troubles for the Comanches. He could not make it right, but he could seek some manner of revenge. It was the Comanche way, and that was a comfort to him.

The Cimarron Hotel was two stories tall and made of adobe. Though it was a simple building and lacked most amenities, it still was about the best building in Cimarron. "What room's Sam Flinch in?" he asked the sleepy clerk.

"Number Twelve. Upstairs to the right," he answered, unconcerned.

Tippett moved without haste up the dusty stairs. He rapped on the door. There was a grumbling inside and then a shuffling of someone moving. "Wha... Who's there?" Flinch muttered as he yanked the door open.

Tippett smashed a fist into Flinch's face before the freighter got the door fully open. Flinch staggered back into the room, stunned. But the only sound he made was a soft grunt. He landed on his rump.

"Tippett!" he finally managed to gasp. He ran a hand across his misshapen face, smearing the blood from his huge broken nose. Surprise faded into a glittering hatred as Flinch stood. "I been lookin' fer you fer years, you Injin lovin' son of a whore," Flinch snarled. He grinned, his face hideous with the blood spread across the bottom half of it. "And now you come walkin' right in my goddamn door. Dumb bastard." He wiped his bloody hand on a pant leg. When his hand came back up, there was a wood-handled butcher knife in it.

With his heel, Tippett kicked the door shut behind him. He smiled with no humor and said, "Ye're gonna regret I've come, ye mule-pokin' sack of shit." Tippett eased out his Bowie.

"I'm just all a tremble," Finch said, feigning fear. "Shit, the rest of the boys are gonna laugh their asses off when I tell 'em about this."

"Ye can tell 'em in hell, boy. They're down there waitin' on ye,"

Tippet said nastily. He smiled at Flinch's shock. "I've saved ye for last." The voice was cold.

Flinch's shock was wearing off. "I'd hate to have had one of the other boys kill you. I want that pleasure myself. To pay you back for this." He stroked his misshapen jaw. Flinch grinned maliciously. "But I've done well enough in payin' back, I'd say," he added hoarsely.

Anger flashed hotly in Tippett's eyes. "I lost my woman and youngest chil' to the sickness," he said grimly.

"That so?" Flinch said indifferently. "Well, I reckon it's only right after what you and that buck did to me'n the others."

Tippett moved on Flinch, swinging the blade in a short arc curving in front of him. Flinch backed away as much as he could, but there was nowhere for him to really go in the small room.

Flinch remained confident though. He had always considered himself good with a knife and he was. But he found out he was no match for Tippett.

Tippett made two feints, a third, and then the knife sank to the hilt in Flinch's chest. Tippett watched with satisfaction as the light in Flinch's eyes faded. Flinch fell in a disjointed heap. Without qualms, Tippett lifted Flinch's scalp.

Tippett wiped the blade on Flinch's shirt and put the knife away. He left and strolled downstairs. The clerk, engrossed in an old newspaper, did not even hear Tippett glide by on silent moccasins.

42

Five days later, a disreputable-looking Zeke Tippett rode into Fort Spirit Mound. He stopped and tied his horse at the infirmary.

"Zeke!" Doctor John Drimmer said with obvious enjoyment. "What're you doing here?"

"Come to see ye, Doc," Tippet said, shaking Drimmer's hand.

Drimmer looked at him with raised eyebrows. "You ailing?"

"Nope, nothin' like that." Tippett paused, suddenly uncertain.

"Come on in," Drimmer said. They entered the infirmary and Tippett was surprised to see that all the beds were empty. Drimmer waved a hand toward of an ill-carved wood chair alongside the desk and Tippett sat gingerly in it, unsure it would stand his weight. It held. Drimmer sat behind his desk. He rummaged in a drawer and brought out a half-empty bottle of whiskey.

Tippett gratefully accepted the proffered bottle and drank a healthy portion. "Ain't bad," he commented.

"Doctors always get the best," Drimmer laughed. He took a smaller drink and set the bottle on the desk where both men could reach it. "

"And I appreciate it."

"How'd you know I was here?"

"Stopped at Fort Graham. Folks there said ye had been transferred here."

"Yessir, year and a half ago or so," Drimmer said with a shrug. "Now what's brought you here, Zeke?" he asked quietly.

Though it had been almost three years since Tippett had seen Drimmer, the doctor had changed little. "I've done a heap of thinkin' lately, Doc. It's nice as hell havin' Libby 'round, but," he shrugged in embarrassment, "it's hard on me to have her underfoot all the time. I ain't the kind to jist set around not doin' nothin'. I got to be on the move. I brought Libby to Gray Wolf's village for a visit last year since I had a hankerin' to travel. I was on my way back when..." he paused and sighed. He explained about the freighters.

"That got me to thinkin'," Tippett added with a soulless smile. "If'n them bastards did it once, they — or someone like 'em — will try it again. I don't want to risk my baby."

Drimmer said nothing and Tippett continued sadly, "Besides, I expect she's gonna be lookin' for a husband before too long. Such doin's don't shine with this chil'. I got to get her out of there."

"What're you planning, Zeke?" Drimmer asked. He thought he knew, but he wanted Tippett to be clear about it in his own mind.

Tippett looked tremendously pained. He did not want to do this, but he knew it was best for Libby. "Your kinfolk in San Antone still interested in takin' her in?" he asked, voice strangled by emotion.

"I'd say so. I could find out." His eyes questioned Tippett.

"I'd be obliged, Doc." Tippett gulped a huge swallow of whiskey.

"I'll send a message first thing in the morning."

Tippett nodded, too choked up to talk. He finished the whiskey and mumbled, "I'll be back in a week or so, Doc."

THE LAND WAS IN FULL BLOOM, FLOWERS PRESENTING A CARPET OF

dazzling colors, the few trees green. But Tippett paid little attention to it since he was immersed in his thoughts. He wondered how to break the news to Libby. It would not be easy. Still, he knew in his heart it would be best for her. He also wondered about seeing his son, Cass. Born-In-The-Storm would be twelve this summer, and as such, nearing the age to be starting on the warpath.

It was still strange to be heading for the village without Painted Wing. She had been dead three years, but her absence still hurt more than Tippett cared to admit. The Comanches married mostly for convenience and stayed married for the same reason. Tippett had married Painted Wing that way, but over their years together he had come to love her. He missed Josh, too. White Buffalo would have grown away from him by now anyway, but still, the young warrior had been his flesh and blood, and his firstborn.

Nearing the village, Tippett's sense of worry grew. As he rode into the camp with a phalanx of warriors, Libby looked up from her work outside the lodge of Blood Drips Down and Yellow Grass. She jumped up, shouting, "Papa!"

Tippett grinned and slipped off his horse. Spreading his arms, he braced himself for his daughter's friendly onslaught. When she landed in his embrace, he lifted her and swung her in a circle, hooting all the while. He did not care that the People were standing there grinning or laughing — or shocked. He did care, though, that he felt a tightness in Libby. He sensed that she was not as pleased with him as he would have liked.

"Somethin' wrong, honey?" he asked quietly as he set her down.

"No, Papa," Libby said, but Tippett did not believe her. She smiled suddenly. "It's good to see you, Papa."

"It's good to see ye, too, honey."

In the awkward silence, Tippett sensed Libby's reserve again.

"I've gotta go back to work now, Papa," Libby said, torn between sadness and joy. But she was not a baby anymore. She was almost nine and a half, and as such, serious about becoming a woman. There was much to learn, she knew, and she was responsible about it.

"All right, honey," Tippett said, a feeling of loss sweeping down over him again. He watched as Libby hurried back to her work.

"Come," Gray Wolf said, clapping a hand on Tippett's shoulder. "Red Moon will have food. We will eat and smoke. And talk."

"Born-In-The-Storm around?"

Gray Wolf nodded. "He will join us."

Red Moon and Blue Eyes unpacked Tippett's two mules and unsaddled his horse while the two men strolled into Gray Wolf's lodge. Born-In-The-Storm was waiting. Father and soon looked at each other for several uncomfortable minutes. Tippett thought Cass would be tall and he looked strong of shoulder and back.

"How're ye doin', son?" Tippett finally asked as he sat.

"Well, Pa." His voice was heavily accented.

"Been on the hunt yet?" Going on the hunt for a year or two was an important part of becoming a *Nermernuh* warrior. If a boy could do that successfully, then he could take the trail of war.

"No," Cass said, almost sullenly.

"He's asked to join the next hunt," Gray Wolf said in English.

"That true, boy?" Tippett asked, looking at his son. He accepted the bowl of stewed buffalo from Red Moon.

"Yes," Cass said, deadly serious.

Tippett nodded. His face was blank, but his insides were frozen. He knew now there was nothing he could do to stop Born-In-The-Storm from becoming a full Comanche. The boy had spent too many years in the *Nermernuh* culture and life. His resolve firmed to save Libby.

Still, he was not anxious to break the news to Libby, so for the rest of the evening Tippett and Gray Wolf talked of the events in their two worlds. Finally, Tippett went to sleep — alone, despite Gray Wolf's crude, laughing efforts to get him to accept a bedmate.

The next morning, Tippett reluctantly sought out his daughter. He found Libby working with Yellow Grass. The girl's eyes brightened as she saw him. But when she said, "Hello, Papa," it was with reserve.

"Mornin', Libby honey." He paused but there was no point in delaying. "Will Yellow Grass let ye off work a spell so's we can talk a bit?"

"I suppose," Libby said seriously. She turned and chatted a moment in rapid Comanche with the aging Yellow Grass.

They entered the lodge. Libby, ever the proper woman-in-training scooped stew into a bowl and handed it to her father. He smiled wanly. Libby sat and looked at Tippett half in fear, half in expectation.

Tippett set the bowl down, angry at his hesitancy.

Libby looked up at him with wide, fear-filled eyes, knowing something was wrong. Tippett shook off the self-doubt. "Libby, I ain't gonna leave ye here in the village no more," he said in a rush.

"Why, Papa?" The nine-year-old looked bland. She liked living with the People, but she liked Taos, too.

"It ain't a fittin' place for a young lady," he growled. "I want ye to have a proper home and a proper bringin' up."

"You're going to take me back to Taos to live with you again?"

"No." The word was flat.

Fear clutched at Libby's young heart.

"Ye remember Doc Drimmer?" When Libby nodded, Tippett said, "Well, he's got kinfolk in San Antonio. They've agreed to take ye in. They got money, and a big, fancy house. They'll take good care of ye."

"I don't want to go," Libby said firmly, small face determined.

"It's best for ye, Libby," he said lamely.

"I don't want to go," Libby insisted.

"Ye got to, Libby. That's all there is to it."

"Why?"

"Well," he drawled, then paused. He could not tell her he did not want her marrying a Comanche who more likely than not would treat her worse than a dog. Nor could he tell her she was all he really had left. He sighed, not wanting to say this, either, but figuring something near the truth was best. “The People’re gonna die out before long, Libby, what with all the settlers comin’. The *tahbay-boh* brought the cholera that took your Ma.” He almost choked on the bitter words.

“I don’t want to go,” she wailed.

“I’ll come see ye, Libby. Whenever I can. I go to San Antonio on business often enough.”

“I still don’t wanna go,” Libby said, though without whining this time. “I want to go home with you.”

“Ye can’t, honey. But maybe we can work it so’s ye can come see me of a time. Maybe not often, but sometimes.”

43

Tippett strode into his store in Taos. "Ho, Fred," he called out to his clerk. "How's things been whilst I was gone?" He knew what to expect for an answer and was always amused by it. He had just come from leaving Libby with Drimmer. He was not happy at remembering their tear-filled farewell and needed his clerk's comfortable, sour humor.

"Doing poorly, Mister Tippett. Poorly," Fred Carter said. His dour expression never changed and Tippett was sure the man wouldn't know fun if it bit him on the rump. But he was good at what he did, which was why Tippett not only kept him around, but trusted him.

"We losin' specie?" Tippett asked, not really worried.

"Heavens, no!" Carter spouted. He scratched the thinning hair at the crown of his head with the blunt end of his pencil.

"Then what'n hell's the problem?" Tippett felt like chuckling as Carter's face was even gloomier than usual.

"Several accounts are in arrears," Carter sniffed. "Quite in arrears."

"Whose?"

Carter consulted his sheaf of papers, though Tippett knew the clerk could tell him exactly who owed how much, down to the penny. "Well, the Alvarezes are three months' behind. And Mister Savoy has not paid us in some four months. Even Mister Carson is two months in arrears. There are others," he said in disgust, slapping the papers on the counter of the jumbled, well-stocked store.

"Kit's been busy fightin' Injuns, as ye well know. So, don't ye fret over his debt. I'll have a word with Luis and Joe. I expect once I've done so, they'll be in with some cash directly."

"You're too forgiving, Mister Tippett. Much too forgiving. You'll see your business ruined one day because of your giving nature."

Tippett laughed. "Hell, Fred, there's a heap more to life to worry about than some goddamn store." Sadness cut through him at the thought of Painted Wing, White Buffalo, and Leaves Behind. But he sloughed it off. They had gone to meet their Maker and he could do nothing about it. "Ye got any more good news?" he asked with a smile.

"Well, sir, I have had to hire an assistant." His voice faded.

"Ye did what?" Tippett asked in mock gruffness. "Without checkin' with me first? And when my business is gone beaver at any minute?"

Carter looked mortified, unable to see the humor twinkling in Tippett's eyes. "I am sorry, Mister Tippett," he said hastily, sounding — and looking — as if he had just swallowed a pound of lard. "I will let him go immediately! My apologies for having overstepped my bounds. I will see to it right away. Right away."

"Whoa, boy," Tippett said, unable to suppress a chuckle. "Why'd ye hire him?"

"I am hard-pressed to keep up with all the work, especially with you being gone so much," Carter said in slight reproof. He sometimes wished Tippett was around more often to make decisions. Then, again, Tippett's business sense was so bad, Carter felt better not having him around. "His name's Ben Winter. He is young. Not long out of college. But he knows his figures well. And he has a fine hand for script."

Tippett nodded. "That's fine," he said, amused at the relief in Carter's eyes. "If ye need him, that's fine." He turned to go. "Well, I'll leave ye to your work."

"Wait, Mister Tippett," Carter said, voice reaching new heights of excitement for him. When Tippett turned back he said, "There was a fellow come here yesterday looking for you. He did not offer a name. Just said he'd be back sooner or late. He is a big man, Mister Tippett. Huge. He wore a fringed buckskin coat. Had a big red beard and mustache. Quite a wild-looking creature."

Tippett laughed. "Cass!" he muttered. "It cain't be no one else. Ain't too many fellers big as he is. I ain't seen that scabrous ol' fart since the revolt. He say where he'd be?"

"No, sir," Carter said with some distaste at Tippett's crudities. "Just asked after you and left."

Tippett hurried out and up the dusty street, Hawken cradled in his left arm. Many folks greeted him and he returned them fondly. He stopped at each saloon, hotel, and boarding house he passed. He finally found Calder in El Gordo Castor, a small, crude, dark cantina that catered to the more rambunctious citizens, like former mountain men, scouts, freighters, and others who fit in nowhere else.

"Here now, ol' coon," Tippett bellowed when he spotted Calder. "This saloon ain't fit for the likes of ye, ye bear-baitin', buffalo-humpin', overgrown son of a bitch." As the big man turned, Tippett said, "Christ, it's good to see ye, *amigo*." His grin nearly lit up the dingy room.

Calder's smile was every bit as wide and gleaming as his friend's. "'Bout time ye showed up, ye fractious peckerwood," Calder roared. "Hell, I been settin' here on my ass waitin' for ye since the Shinin' Mountains weren't but a stack of pebbles."

They embraced mightily, then sat at the table Calder had taken over — and which everyone else had been giving a wide berth.

"Looks like ye've had yourself a hell of a start on me, amigo," Tippett said. "I'd best set to catchin' up."

As they drank potent Taos Lightning that was still easy to get here in the birthplace of that homemade brew despite the long-ago loss of Turley's Mill, Tippett asked, "What've ye been up to, ol' hoss?"

"Little of this, a little of that. Had me a saloon back in St. Louis for a spell. Sold that and opened another in St. Joe. But it warn't no fun, goddammit. Too many folks. And all of 'em righteous bastards part of one goddamn wagon train headin' to Oregon or Californy or another. Shit, warn't this ol' hoss's style."

Tippett grinned and slopped more whiskey into his tin mug. "I know how ye feel, amigo. Even though I got me the store, I get out ever' chance I get. I cain't stand bein' cooped up all the time."

"That's where my stick floats, too. I finally sold off that goddamn saloon and took to huntin' buffler for the wagon trains. I quit that after a spell since I couldn't stand none of them goddamn flatlanders, and took up leadin' Army patrols and surveyin' parties and such up along the Yallerstone and the Upper Missouri. But, hell, workin' with blue coats don't shine with this chil' neither."

"I still do some work for the Army. But the bastards ain't got the brains the good Lord give a rock. Christ, I've seen tree stumps with more brains." He swallowed whiskey.

Calder held up his tin mug in a salute. Tippett returned it, and they drank. Then Tippett said, "Ye got somethin' in mind for us?"

"I hear tell thar's a heap of gold to be found yet over in Californy. We set our minds to it, we could be there in no time a'tall." Calder grinned. "Maybe find us the mother lode."

Tippett didn't have to think about it. "Hell, why not? Ain't nothin' to keep me here no more. Why sure, let's go on and do it."

"Ye sure, Zeke?" Calder asked seriously. "I wasn't really thinkin' too well when I said that. But last I looked, ye was still packin' Painted Wing and had a passel of kids by her."

Tippett's face sagged and he drank deeply, finishing what was left in his mug. He poured more. "Got no family left, really, Cass," he said with infinite sadness. "My oldest boy was kilt in an ambush whilst he was ridin' with the Comanches. Painted Wing and my least daughter died of cholera in '49. Born-In-The-Storm — Cass — is livin' with the Comanche, and," he added sadly, "I brought Libby to Fort Spirit Mound to be taken down to San Antone just a bit ago." He explained about Light Calf.

"Probably best for her, Zeke," Calder said when Tippett finished. He paused, then said. "Seems ye've seen a heap of troubles, Zeke."

"Just a dose of bad medicine. It'll pass."

"Such doin's ain't ever easy to bear," Calder grumbled in heartfelt sympathy. "I'd left Shinin' Beads, Charger, and the babe we had in her village, I got me an Arapaho woman," he said with emotion. "She was a good woman — not like that goddamn pestiferous bitch Shinin' Beads — the finest. We had us a chil', too. Little girl. Shinin'est thing in the mountains, goddammit," Calder croaked. "I were out with the Army and left 'em at Fort Laramie. She was outside pickin' berries, with little Sally strapped to her back, when a couple goddamn soldiers thought it'd be fun to sport with my Belle. When she resisted, they took a knife to her. Christ, Zeke," he added, fighting with all his mighty power to keep back the tears, "they split her from crotch to throat like a goddamn sack of flour." His eyes were wild and red-rimmed and his breath came in jerky bursts.

"They left her and the baby there. Little Sally went under, too. Starved to death most likely." He stopped, chest heaving.

"Waugh!" Tippett growled. "I hope ye paid back in kind."

With an effort, Calder composed himself. He poured three-quarters of a mug of Taos Lightning down his gullet in one swallow. As he poured more from the fat earthen jug into the cup, he growled, "Well, the Army's missin' a couple boys now. And," he added with a devilish smile, "they're gonna be peckerless bastards in the Happy Huntin' Grounds, if they ever get there."

Sadness overcame Tippett again. The two men were silent as

they sat drinking, and thinking back on the disasters they had faced in their lives.

Finally, Calder said, "Well, shit, I reckon we've been glum long enough. Such thing's ain't easy for a man to live with, I'd be sayin', but it's over and done. What say we head for Californy?" Both brightened. Calder grinned and raised his glass. "Then here's to us, ol' coon. We'll find us some of that there gold and come back rich as kings."

Tippett grinned, too, and the two old friends toasted their new adventure.

When they had started on another jug of the harsh whiskey, Tippett asked, "Ye ever hear anything of the other boys?"

"I heard Elmore Trent's scoutin' for the Army. He got started doin' it for the Texas Rangers a while back. He's took a heapin' dislike to all Injins. Goes with the Army every time he figures there'll be a fight."

"I never did take a shine to that rat's ass. But I expect things'll be fine long's he keeps outta my way."

"That little shit ball needs stompin' on, and I am of the firmest opinion that I should've done it to him a long time ago." He sighed long and loud. "The rest of the boys've gone under. Damn. George was killed by a griz up on the Siskydee about three years ago. Jim was rubbed out about the same time by the Sioux as he was leadin' wagons to Oregon."

They drank a silent toast to their departed friends.

44

Tippett felt something different about the store as soon as he entered it. He tromped up to the counter where a young, handsome man waited. "Carter around?" Tippett asked.

"No, sir. He's..."

"Who're ye?"

"Name's Ben Winter. I run this store for Mister Zeke Tippett in the absence of Mister Carter." He said it proudly.

"You're a mite young fer such important doin's, ain't ye, boy?"

"I am well-qualified, sir," Winter said huffily. "Now, if you have business here, I'll be glad to help you. If not, I must ask you to move on." He tried to look fierce but did not quite accomplish it.

Tippett looked the straight-backed young man over. Winter was twenty years old. He was five-foot-nine and thin with a sharp, prominent chin and intelligent gray eyes. His white cotton shirt, black wool trousers, and short black boots were mussed. His dark hair was slicked back with grease and he was clean-shaven. He stared at Tippett evenly.

"Do ye know who I am, boy?" Tippett demanded. But there was a twinkle of humor in his eyes.

"Can't say as I do," Winter said stiffly.

"I'm Zeke Tippett," Tippett said simply. "Now where's Carter?"

Winter gulped, but did not take his eyes from Tippett. "I'm afraid to say, sir, that he has gone over the divide, just this winter past."

"Ye been runnin' the place by yourself?" Tippett asked.

"Yes, sir. But now you're back, I'll relinquish my duties."

"That what ye want, boy?"

"No, sir."

"Then it ain't necessary. The place looks to be doin' good."

"It is. Mister Carter taught me well, sir."

"Reckon he did. But by your looks, boy, I'd say he didn't impart none of his ill-humored disposition. We can be thankful for that."

Winter grinned. "It's been my experience, that a smile will fetch more business than a scowl." He paused. "You'll want to look at the books now?" Winter asked.

"I expect," Tippett said, not wanting to. "But it can wait."

"At your pleasure, sir," Winter said. Suddenly he whirled and charged at two Indian boys, each about eight years old. "Git!" Winter roared, chasing after them as the boys scooted outside into the dusty street. "Go on, git." He returned to the counter, facing Tippett.

"Ye got skunked, Mister Winter. They made off with some plunder."

"I know," Winter said evenly and Tippett understood. But Winter continued, "The Indians are not very well off, Mister Tippett. I would say you know that, though. I let some of the kids come in here and fetch up a piece of candy or an apple or two once in a while, and then chase 'em off. Like now. I tried giving them things straight off, but they wouldn't have none of it. It took me a spell, but I finally learned they prefer the game we play. Makes 'em feel they're getting away with something rather than taking a hand-out. I hope you don't mind. He looked crestfallen. "Mister Carter didn't approve, but I..."

Tippett nodded. He lacked almost all book learning. But he

more than made up for that with an uncanny knack of knowing a man's character. He had gotten a good feeling about Winter right off.

"You've done well," Tippett said kindly. He straightened from the counter, Hawken in hand. "Reckon I best cut the dry in my throat."

Winter grinned. "I understand, sir. You've been gone quite a spell, haven't you? What, a year? More?"

"Three." He smiled. "Three years of scrabblin' 'round in the dirt lookin' for the mother lode, and not a damn thing to show fer it 'cept some rheumatiz and a sore goddamn back. Well, carry on, Mister Winter. I'll be back one day to check them books."

It was four days before he did. Tippett had little use for bookkeeping and he made no bones about it. But he laboriously went over the scratched figures knowing Winter — and Carter before him — could have been robbing him blind. But he thought that unlikely.

Finally, he gave up. "I cain't set here no more with these goddamn numbers starin' me in the face, boy," he said to Winter. "I trusted Carter all these years, and ye been doin' well far's I can see since he went under. I expect I can put my trust in ye, too."

Winter nodded, glowing with pride.

"I expect I'll be ridin' out for a spell the next day or so. Want to go see my son over to the *Llano* and my daughter in San Antone." Tippett left. Two days later he was riding eastward. He gave no thought to allowing Winter to run the store by himself. Should Winter choose to steal from him there was little he could do about it, so he could see no point in worrying about the possibility. Besides, he trusted his instincts, which told him Winter was trustworthy.

The land was in full bloom, but Tippett hardly saw it. He was occupied, thinking about seeing Born-In-The-Storm. Being with the boy's namesake had gotten Tippett to thinking more and more about his son, Cass. It left him worried. Born-In-The-Storm would be seventeen this summer, and, as such, would have been on the warpath for at least a couple years. Tippett hoped Gray Wolf had looked after the youth.

Gray Wolf greeted him with sadness haunting his dark eyes. "I'm surprised to see ye, Wolf," Tippett said cautiously. "I thought you'd be out makin' things unpleasant for the *Tejanos*."

"Yes," Gray Wolf said distractedly.

"Where's my son?" Tippett asked, fear burrowing into his stomach.

"We must talk," Gray Wolf said, turning and heading for his lodge. Tippett left his horse and pack mule where they were and walked numbly after the Comanche, dread weighing heavily on him. They sat at the fire. There was no pipe, though food was served. "Tell it," Tippett spat out around a mouthful of stewed buffalo meat. He knew what was coming and wanted it over quickly. He had learned long ago that bad news went down easiest when swallowed fast.

Gray Wolf did, explaining swiftly but leaving out nothing. His voice remained flat, devoid of inflection throughout the narration, though his eyes watched Tippett carefully.

Tippett continued to eat the bland stew, outwardly showing no sign of the rage sweeping over him. To an observer it would seem as if he was being told the results of the latest hunt, rather than the violent death of his only remaining son.

Gray Wolf sputtered to a halt, and Tippett knew his old friend was nearly as heartbroken as he. Not only had he lost his own son, he also had been responsible for Born-In-The-Storm's death.

Tippett set down the empty bowl and sat unmoving. He was only vaguely aware that a heavy downpour had started outside, and then only because Red Moon and Blue Eyes bustled about lowering the sides of the tipi and adjusting the smoke flap at top.

After several hours, Tippett asked hoarsely, "You seek revenge yet?" The *Nermernuh* code called for a father not to rest until he took at least one scalp to avenge a slain son. Tippett had subscribed only halfheartedly to such a thing, but now it seemed sensible.

"No," Gray Wolf said bluntly. "It happened late last summer. There was no time to seek vengeance before the hunt. Then winter came, not the time for such things. We have just finished the spring hunt. Now that our families have meat, we can think about..."

Tippett sat in silence again. He was enraged. He wanted to criticize Gray Wolf, berate the Comanches for having put other considerations before seeking revenge for their sons. But he knew that what Gray Wolf had said was true, and that it was unreasonable for him to think anything could have been done sooner. So, he kept silent, letting the fires of anger flicker down to sparks. Such a feeling would keep the anger alive a long time instead of letting it die in a short burst of flame. Tippett filled and lit his pipe, each movement calculated as if his muscles were stiff and not working properly. He puffed a while, then asked, "You want guns, Wolf?"

The Comanche's eyes gleamed. "*Haa*."

"You come to Taos in fourteen suns. Come to my house at night." He explained how to find his house.

Gray Wolf nodded. Tippett knocked the ashes of his pipe out on a rock in the fire. He stood stiffly, feeling the weight of his hard life resting on his shoulders. Without another word, he stepped out into the downpour. He splashed through the mud and mounted his horse. He did not glance back as he rode out through the thunderstorm.

Two weeks later, Tippett heard a scratching at his back door. "That ye, Gray Wolf?" he asked warily.

"Yes," came the hurried whisper.

Tippett opened the door to let in Gray Wolf and Hits-With-A-Fist. Clouds obscured the moon and stars.

The Comanches sat on the floor. Tippett poured each coffee and put out a plate of dried buffalo meat and a dish of hard candies. The Comanches went for the candies and enjoyed the coffee. Tippett sat. He stared at Gray Wolf and said, "In exchange fer them guns, I want ye to do somethin' fer me. I want ye to go against the blue coats at Fort Spirit Mound. Ye know which one that is?"

"The one between the Colorado and the fork of the Bravos. Why that fort?" Gray Wolf asked.

"Those're the blue coats that kilt my boy — and yours."

"How do you know that? All blue coats look alike. And act alike."

Tippett reached across the table. With a forefinger, he tapped the insignia pinned to Gray Wolf's white-man style calico shirt. "Second Cavalry badge," Tippett said harshly. "They're the boys at Fort Spirit Mound. Ye told me ye picked it up after the fight."

Gray Wolf nodded. "Will you ride with us?" he asked.

"No. I cain't go to war directly with my own kind," he said, angry at himself for having such feelings. "Just one more thing," he added. "When you go against them soldiers, there's one I don't want to see harmed. He's a doctor, a medicine man, and he helped Light Calf when she was ailin'. Let him be."

"How will we know him?"

"He's a tall, skinny feller. Looks like he been scalped. Got near-about no hair on his head. And he wears spectacles — round glass things perched on his nose and held up by a stick behind each ear."

"He won't be harmed," Gray Wolf said.

Tippett nodded and went into another room. He returned with a new Sharps rifle. "Now, pay attention whilst I show ye how these work," he said.

45

Tippett sat on a ridge looking southward at Fort Spirit Mound and he shook his head in wonder. The fort, partially shrouded by early morning mist, was nearly as useless a thing as he had ever seen. The soldiers had spent so much time constructing it that they had had little time for chasing Indians. Now that it was done, they spent much of their time on worthless drills and on farming and in caring for their heavy, grain-fed horses. Only occasionally did they get out to fight Comanches, and Tippett was bitter when he thought how the soldiers should have passed up the opportunity to fight them just this once. Born-In-The-Storm would still be alive.

Nearly under the noses of the Army, Tippett could see the end of the Comanche war party moving through a grassy arroyo about a mile west of the fort.

He watched the Comanches. Despite their misfortunes of the past several years, they moved with confidence, almost arrogance. Gray Wolf's medicine was powerful, so the Comanches figured they had nothing to fear. Each warrior believed in it. If he did not, he would have stayed behind. Last year's fiasco seemed forgotten.

The fog burned off as the warriors crept up toward the fort near the stream the *tahbay-boh* called Dead Man's River. About half the fifty men continued up the crease in the land, nearing the fort. The rest headed toward the rise to the south, opposite the ridge on which Tippett sat, watching with interest.

Gray Wolf nodded. Hits-With-A-Fist and Buffalo Droppings rode boldly toward the open fort. There was no stockade fence; the Army was certain no Indians would be foolish enough to attack a fort, even if there were no walls.

The two Comanches stopped just out of range of the soldiers' rifles. They sat on their ponies, yelling imprecations, daring the soldiers to come out and fight. It took a couple of minutes, but the warriors' shouts finally attracted some attention from the soldiers. Though the soldiers knew no Comanche and the Comanches knew little English, the blue coats had a good idea of what was being said.

A big sergeant started issuing orders and the gaping soldiers moved. Some headed for the corral, others formed a skirmish line, and a few began to haul the small canyon forward.

All the while, Hits-With-A-Fist and Buffalo Droppings edged closer to the fort. Suddenly they whipped out rifles they had held concealed under their blankets and opened fire. One soldier went down instantly, a bullet piercing his brain. Another fell moments afterward. The men on the skirmish line fired as the ones at the cannon hurriedly shoved the weapon forward.

The blue coats' bullets hit no one, and the two Comanches whooped and made their ponies prance.

Twenty mounted soldiers suddenly burst out of the corral, onto the parade ground and then past the last of the fort's buildings, ready to kill these two impudent Comanches.

The warriors spun their ponies and raced off with the Cavalry in pursuit. As the blue coats passed the far edge of the southern ridge, Gray Wolf and his warriors charged out from behind it.

Behind the Cavalry, the rest of the Comanches shot out from the arroyo only yards from the fort, firing rifles. The soldiers in the fort, caught by surprise, frantically looked around, confused. The sergeant bellowed orders, but few men were following them. Several died immediately. The Comanches surged into the compound. Soldiers ran for the cover of buildings, some dying on the run. But a few made it to safety.

As the Comanches set fire to the wood buildings and tossed burning branches into the stone ones, a few of the solders, under the direction of the sergeant, began firing more methodically as they slowly retreated to a couple of buildings that had not been touched yet. Two Comanches went down. A few soldiers died at the hands of the Comanches when they fled the flames that licked at them inside the buildings.

The scene, even to Tippett high up on the ridge, was nightmarish — men screaming, horses squealing, gunfire, the hissing suck of flames. The compound was obscured by dust, and soon smoke.

With victory cries on their lips, and scalps stuffed into their belts, the Comanches raced triumphantly out of the fort, heading for the battle past the ridge.

Gray Wolf and his warriors had waited beyond the rise. When the soldiers who followed Hits-With-A-Fist and Buffalo Droppings rode into view, the Comanches swooped down on them like an eagle on a plump rabbit. The soldiers, outnumbered and outarmed, fought hard, seeking an opening in the dizzying circle of warriors, hoping to create a way back to the fort. They could not know that the fort was under siege. A few panicked soldiers ran off, fear getting the better of them. They were cut down quickly, their scalps ripped off, bodies mutilated.

Only the efforts of Sergeant Liam Sweeney — who had faced death more times than he could remember — saved the squad from annihilation.

"Aye, now, laddies," Sweeney bellowed in his thick brogue into the dust and screams. "Rally 'round me. Don't let yer old sergeant down."

He stood fearless in the center of a knot of kneeling men, oblivious to the arrows thudding into men and horses all around him or the bullets that kicked up divots of earth. He fired his Walker steadily. When that was empty, he pulled his spare one.

The sergeant's six-shooters, bought a few years back with his own funds, began taking their toll on the Comanches. Three were wounded and the others began to wonder about this tall, broad-shouldered man with the head of flashing red hair and matching beard. His medicine was powerful and the Indians began to avoid him.

Four soldiers were dead and eight wounded. The Comanches knew they had won and avenged their dead, especially when the warriors who had invaded the fort joined the attack on the patrol. There was no longer any point to sticking around. The cost was too high. Shouting, the Comanches broke off and raced away. They flaunted their trophies — scalps, army tunics, a few firearms, hats, a bugle — as they rode.

"Come on back here, ye yellow-assed sons a bitches," Sweeney roared. "Ye be worse than the damned Limeys, ye be. Me grandmother's got more balls'n ye laddies. Goddamn savages."

But the Indians were gone, and only a faint echo of their victorious voices floated back to the demoralized soldiers. Sweeney looked around at his troops, then roared, "What in hell do ye lads think ye're doin'? This is no time to be sittin' on yer duffs. Git yer arses movin', laddies. Unless ye'd all like to sit here and wait for those Comanches to come a courtin' us again."

The thought galvanized the men into action. Under Sweeney's orders, some rounded up horses, others looked after the wounded. Still others gathered the dead and slung them hurriedly over horses.

"Mathews, Steuben," Sweeney commanded. "Get up on yon ridge and see if ye can spot those laddies."

"Yes, sir," the two young men said in quiet, fear-filled voices. They moved off reluctantly as Sweeney continued to shout orders and the other men worked feverishly. They couldn't know that the Comanches were more than a mile away.

Tippett watched it all from his spot on the other rise. There was a grim smile on his lips. He watched as Sweeney finally got his men back to the fort. He waited several hours before riding down the north side of the ridge, away from the fort, and circling around to come in from the east.

Soldiers shored up buildings and put back the logs that hard formed the corral, many of which had been knocked down when the Comanches had driven off the horses that had remained; sergeants and corporals shouted orders; men dug graves or poured water brought from the river onto flames.

Odd, uncomfortable feelings pulsed through Tippett. He was glad to see that the killers of his son had been dealt with. But he was also saddened. They were white men, like him. Many were still boys, recruited in the slums of large Eastern cities, or foreigners fresh off the boats from Europe. They had little hatred for Indians mostly. Or at least that had been true. Such actions as today's would only foster or strengthen hatred on both sides. He spit and shrugged. He stopped in front of the remnants of the commander's office. No guard was posted since all the men were busy on repairs.

Tippett stepped through the doorway just in time to hear Doctor John Drimmer say, "...two more have died and another looks like he won't make it."

Captain Horace Montgomery and Drimmer turned as they became aware someone had entered. "How do, Zeke," Drimmer said. He was friendly, but Tippett could see tiredness in the man's eyes.

"Fine, Doc. Ye?"

"Passable."

"What're you doing here, Tippett?" Montgomery asked huffily. He had met Tippett some years ago and never cared for him. Tippett was too cozy with the Comanches for his liking.

"Saw the smoke, Cap'n. Thought I'd come for a looksee."

"Well, you've seen it." The implication to leave was clear.

"Who done it?" Tippett asked blandly.

"Comanches." Montgomery managed to settle himself some. "But we'll pay them back for this, Tippett. Our scouts will find the bastards who did this. And when he do, there'll be hell to pay. We got a new scout a while back. He had done some scoutin' and such for the Texas Rangers some years ago. I met him there. An old mountain man, like yourself. Elmore Trent's his name. You know him?"

Tippett's expression never changed, though it felt like someone had kicked him in the stomach. "I've heard the name, Cap'n," he said evenly, his voice not giving away any hint of his anger. "He any good?"

"The best. As vicious and mean-spirited as any goddamn Comanche. Even likes carving up dead bucks, like they do to whites."

Tippett felt his stomach lurch.

"The bastard's got a nose for Indians, Tippett." He managed a slight chuckle. "He can find 'em better'n our Tonkawas or Wichitas. I met him when my Dragoon troop was riding with some Rangers a few years ago. Trent found a war party the Rangers had been trying to catch for months. They asked us to join in the fighting. We kicked the shit out of 'em. Did the same to a war band last year."

Tippett spit out the wad of tobacco onto the floor, to Montgomery's disgust. "Ye know which band attacked ye today?" he asked, battling back his fury.

"You would know that better than me," Montgomery yelled.

"I would?"

"Yes, goddammit."

"You accusin' me of somethin'?" Tippett asked, straightening.

Montgomery's face was purple with fury. "I think you had something to do with this, Tippett," he roared.

"What makes ye think such a thing?" Tippett asked calmly.

"It was too well planned for an Indian's mind."

"You're a goddamn fool," Tippett said, allowing some testiness to emerge. "You've been out here fer years and ain't learned shit."

"Get out of my fort before I have you shot!" Montgomery bellowed.

"Shit," Tippett said lightheartedly, though he burned with hate.

Montgomery took some moments to get himself under control. Then he said, "I'll tell you something, Tippett. I don't really give a damn what band was responsible for this — they'll *all* pay. Any band I can find will pay in blood for what was done here today." He glared at Tippett, challenging him, wanting Tippett to admit he had helped plan this attack so he could have the former mountain man arrested and hanged.

Tippett was queasy. He realized to his horror that rather than ending all the bloodshed, all he had done was to increase it. And he knew the Comanches could not win. He battled his despair. "Such doin's might be more'n ye can handle," he said, bitterness surfacing.

"Get out of my fort, you Indian-loving son of a bitch."

"I'm headin' for San Antone, Doc," Tippett said. "Ye got any words fer your family?" Tippett hoped Montgomery would take the hint and send a couple of soldiers — or, better yet, Trent — after him. It would ease his mind to kill them personally. He also wondered where Trent was.

"Give them my regards, Zeke," Drimmer said, smiling.

"Get out of here!" Montgomery screamed, nearly shaking the walls.

46

Tippett had little trouble finding the spacious, adobe house not far from the old mission called the Alamo, near the east bank of the San Antonio River. He tied his horse to a post and climbed the two stairs. After a moment's hesitation, he knocked on the door.

A pretty, young Mexican answered the door. "*Habla Ingles?*" Tippett asked.

"*Si.*"

"Would ye tell *Señor* and *Señor*a Mitchelson I'd like to speak to 'em, *por favor?*" It was not a request.

She smiled and stood back to let him enter. When he did, she said, "Wait here." She disappeared but returned quickly with a man in an expensive wool suit.

"Can I help you?" the man asked.

"Ye Mister Mitchelson?"

"I am," the man said, no friendliness in his voice. He looked at Tippett with distaste. On his jaunt to California, Tippett had taken to wearing Levi Strauss denim pants. They wore almost as long as buckskin and were a lot more comfortable. And he wore knee-length Apache style moccasins, with his pants tucked in. His hat and clothes were soiled. Sweat stains discolored the old-style, off-white muslin shirt. "And you are?" Mitchelson asked.

Tippett held out his hand. "Zeke Tippett."

Mitchelson ignored the proffered hand, lighting a match under Tippett's already simmering anger. "What are you doing here?" Mitchelson asked. His face held a smile, but the tone was cold.

"I come to see Libby."

"I am afraid that will not be possible, Mister Tippett."

"Why ain't it?"

"I would think that since you haven't visited the child in the four years we have had her, that you have given up any parental prerogatives to her. I also think it'd be bad for the child. Despite her years here, she has much of the heathen in her yet. She is mending her ways under our kind and gentle ministrations, but for you to confront her now...she very well might revert to the savageness inherent to her mother's people."

"I ain't certain I take the meanin' of all you're sayin', mister," Tippett noted in a hard voice. "But my chil' ain't no savage, goddammit. Neither was her ma."

"Perhaps I misjudged things," Mitchelson said dryly. "It seems she has gotten most of her savage nature from you."

Tippett's face hardened. He stared into Mitchelson's eyes and did not much like what he saw there. "I come here to see my chil', hoss, and I ain't leavin' till I've done so."

"Impossi..." Mitchelson stopped when he found the muzzle of a Hawken under his chin, forcing his head up and back. His face was white as he looked across the vast abyss of two feet separating him from the man with the wild gleam in his eye and a rifle held under his chin. "You wouldn't do that, would you?" Mitchelson squeaked.

"That depends on ye," Tippett snarled.

Mitchelson's eyes rolled and he called to the Mexican girl who had opened the door. She had stood aside as the little drama unfolded. "Rosa, tell Libby she has a visitor. And be quick about it."

"*Si, Señor,*" Rosa said and hurried off.

Tippett never moved the rifle, while both he and Mitchelson could hear Rosa speaking quietly in a room off the hallway. Finally, Adelaide Mitchelson stepped into the foyer and stopped, mouth open in preparation of speaking. But no sounds came.

"Good day, ma'am," Tippett said pleasantly.

"You may put the gun down, Mister Tippett," she said firmly.

"When I see Libby, ma'am."

"Do so immediately. We are trying to teach her civilized ways. Her seeing this will not help."

"When I see her," Tippett insisted.

"You will see your daughter, Mister Tippett," Adelaide said without hesitation. "You have my word."

"You husband here seems to think I'll be a bad influence on her. Called me'n Libby's ma savages."

"Well, sir, I will apologize for my husband. I never met Libby's mother, but the girl is no savage. She has her heathen ways, of course, since she does not know otherwise. And you are wild, perhaps, and might be a little like the Indians, but I doubt you're a savage."

"Nice of ye to think so, ma'am," Tippett said wryly.

"You must understand, Mister Tippett, that we are concerned only with Libby's welfare. She has been treated roughly by the fates and we must teach her to be a proper, God-fearing young lady." She paused, then said, "And I doubt an occasional visit from her father will set her training back very much, do you, William?"

Her husband shook his head a trifle, a difficult maneuver under the circumstances. "I believe you're right, dear," he whispered. Suddenly the rifle was gone, and Mitchelson could breathe again.

Libby walked into the foyer. When she saw her father, she broke into an excited run, calling, "Papa!" Tippett reached out and scooped her up. He swung her around a few times, laughing. He set her down and stepped back. With a gentle smile that surprised the Mitchelsons, Tippett said, "I can't put my finger on it, chil', but there's something diff'rent about ye. I expect I'll puzzle it out soon."

It actually was quite obvious what the changes were. When Tippett had brought his daughter to Drimmer, she was only eleven. She would be fifteen within a month. She was taller than most Comanche women, but not nearly as tall as her father. She had gained his slimness rather than her mother's plumpness, although she had acquired Painted Wing's full curves. Her face had a delicate cast despite the hard cheekbones and angular jaw and chin. She would be considered pretty anywhere, particularly with her long, slightly curled, pitch-black hair and dark, bright eyes.

"Oh, Papa," Libby said happily.

"Maybe I'll have to move in here with the Mitchelsons soon," Tippett joshed. "Jist to keep all the young men away from you."

Libby looked embarrassed but happy, and Adelaide answered for her. "Several potential beaus have shown some interest in Miss Libby in the past few months. But we watch over her quite closely, sir."

"I'm sure ye do. I meant nothin' to give ye offense, ma'am." Tippett paused. "Ye folks mind if me'n Libby go fer a stroll? There're a few family matters I'd like to discuss with her."

"You're welcome to use our sitting room, Mister Tippett," Adelaide said. "You'll have privacy. But we have no objections to you and your daughter walking around town. However, dinner will be in an hour. We'd like her to be back then."

"Yes, ma'am."

"You are welcome to dine with us, Mister Tippett."

"I'm obliged. But I expect I'll be on the trail by then."

Tippett and Libby left and strolled about town, taking in the sights, sounds, and smells of the place. To Tippett, San Antonio was much like Taos. It was bigger, and Taos had more Indians, but there were many similarities — the dusty streets; earth-brown adobe buildings, some with painted doors or windows; the heavy use of Spanish; and the smell of corn and spiced food mingling with the sour odor of horses.

"What's do you need to talk to me about, Papa?" Libby finally asked.

Tippett stopped and Libby followed suit. Tippett sighed and said, "Cass went under last year. Killed by the Army whilst he was raidin' with Gray Wolf."

Libby was sad and felt an aching inside. But she was not as full of sorrow as Tippett expected. "I'm sorry to hear it," she said softly.

"That's all?" her father asked uncertainly.

"I'll miss him some, Papa. But I spent many years with the *Nermernuh* and I learned their ways well. If I was still with the People, he and I would've had little or no contact these last few years anyway. You know of our feelings in such matters."

"Yes, I do," he said sadly, thinking back on that day so long ago when Gray Wolf had stabbed Blue Star to death for accidentally touching him. Tippett still could not reconcile himself to such things, though he had become more accepting.

"But I'm sad for you, Papa," Libby said quietly. "I'm all you got left. Unless you've married again?"

"Waugh, an ol' coon like me's got no rights gittin' married. 'Sides, girl, who want this ol' chil' anyway?"

"Lots of women." Libby took her father's arm. They walked slowly. "We're the last of the family, Papa. And that makes me sad for you."

"Why?" he asked, surprised.

"You'll have only me to care for you in your older years."

"That'd be good enough fer this chil'."

She made a face at him and stuck out her tongue.

"I'll get along, Libby," he said quietly. His grief at having lost nearly his whole family was powerful. But he hoped time would ease that dull ache and he could get on with life. Perhaps he might even think of remarrying, if he could find someone willing to put up with his cantankerous ways. He was only forty-two. He might even consider starting another family. Then he realized he was being foolish.

"I'm sure you will, Papa, but I'd like to be closer to you. Sort of watch out for you some." She paused and licked her lips. "I'd like to come home, Papa," she finally said, staring at him in her desire.

"You are home, chil'."

"I mean back to Taos. Or..." she hesitated "...to the village."

"You're better off here, darlin'."

"I've learned what I can from these people. Had my schoolin' and such. I could do no better, or worse, now in Taos."

"But around here you'll find a proper husband. One with money and prospects. Such a thing ain't likely in Taos."

"Bah. You should see some of the callers I've had." She grimaced. "Ain't a one worth as much to me as one of your dirty old shirts."

He was a little shocked at her boldness, especially at so young an age. The Comanche women had taught her too much too early, he decided. When he thought about it, though, he realized she was only a year younger than Painted Wing was when he had married her. Still, this was his daughter, which made it all somehow different.

"The right feller'll come along," Tippett said as sternly as he could, which wasn't very.

"Humph," Libby grumbled, but she reached up and gave him a quick peck on the cheek to let him know she was not angry with him.

They wandered back to the fancy adobe house. "You'll come visit more often?" Libby asked, steadfast eyes demanding it.

"Yes, ma'am," Tippett mumbled. With a last smile, he turned and left.

BOOK 12

GRAY WOLF, 1855-56

47

Gray Wolf's glory soared after the fight against the soldiers of Fort Spirit Mound. Only one warrior had died and five wounded, one badly. But that was nothing compared with the fact that his men had defeated the blue coats so easily.

They did not slow their rush to distance themselves from the soldiers for almost twelve hours, though. They finally made camp, ate, and tended the wounded. In the morning, half a dozen warriors were assigned to take the dead and wounded back to their villages.

As those men rode away, a euphoric Gray Wolf faced his warriors. "Our power is strong!" he roared. "No one's greater than the *Nermernuh*. The *tahbay-boh* can't stand against us. We'll chase the *tahbay-boh* from our land. Who will ride with me against this weak enemy?"

The men were worked into a frenzy and all shouted that they would follow. How could any true *Nermernuh* warrior resist? They ran to their ponies and rode quickly out of the small camp, heading southward. As they rode, Walking Bear, who was beside Gray Wolf, asked, "Do you believe all the things you said?"

"You think I speak with the tongue of a *tahbay-boh*?" Gray

Wolf demanded. "Saying one thing here and something else there?" He was highly excited and, as usual, it clouded his thinking.

"We've been friends too long for you to say such a thing." Walking Bear sighed. "But you must know we can't beat the *tahbay-boh*. They are too many. And, except for the blue coats, they fight only when attacked, so they have more time for raising children."

"Yes, they're many, but they're weak and afraid. The *Nermernuh* are stronger."

"Buffalo shit," Walking Bear said. "They are so many. And more come every moon. White Horse has spoken of their villages in the East. You have even seen such places. I'd like to see the *tahbay-boh* villages in the East. To see if there is any end to the many people there. Or to see if, like White Horse says, they are as many as the blades of grass."

"Why do you ride with us if you're afraid? I have no place for warriors who are afraid of the blue coats," Gray Wolf said indignantly.

"I'm not afraid of them," Walking Bear said simply.

"Then why do you talk of such things?"

"Because they are true."

"I know," Gray Wolf said. His euphoria was fading, leaving him irritable.

"Then why don't you speak the truth to our warriors? You talk to them like they're children. You say we'll drive the *tahbay-boh* from our land, though you know this will never be. For each one we kill, ten take his place."

Gray Wolf looked at his friend and realized for the first time that Walking Bear was showing some signs of age. Wrinkles were etched heavily into his face, and he held himself a little more slackly in the saddle than he had not so long ago. His middle had thickened considerably and gray was splashed through his long, black hair.

Gray Wolf smiled softly. "To tell them that would fill them with despair. I am a *Nermernuh* warrior. I'll fight to the death for my people. Perhaps we can't drive the *tahbay-boh* from our land, but maybe we can keep them from the *Llano*. If we do that, maybe our village will be safe. Maybe not," he added with a deep sadness.

"But why do you lead?" Walking Bear asked in wonder. He was a simple man, not given to reflecting on the deeper meanings of life unless necessary. "Things'll become clear to them, whether this winter or in twenty winters. Then they'll know you've lied to them."

"This, too, I know." Gray Wolf's sadness and despair were reflected in his dark eyes. "But for now, they'll live in glory. Their families will be safe for a time and will look up to them as great warriors. There will be meat in our lodges. By the time they find out I've lied, there'll be nothing left."

He paused and looked across the rolling land cut through with arroyos and washes. Ridges humped up on the horizon and the grass was wilting under the searing power of the sun. Chunky bunches of white clouds drifted overhead, occasionally obscuring the glaring orange sun, bringing some relief. Buffalo grazed a little off to the west and antelope bounded by on springy legs a short distance east.

Many people would see this land as harsh and useless, but not Gray Wolf. And, apparently, not all white men, either. Gray Wolf could not understand why white men — who were so fond of scratching at the earth with their sticks — would want this land. Perhaps, he thought, it was just the taking it away from the People that motivated them.

"The end will come for the *Nermernuh*," Gray Wolf added morosely. "The long-knives won't stop fighting until the *Nermernuh* are no more." He grinned, finding a small measure of delight within himself. "But there will be many long-knives who won't be there to enjoy it."

"You see clearly, my friend."

Gray Wolf scratched absently at the lice crawling down from

his hair. "I also know I won't be here when the blue coats take our land."

"You've seen this?" Walking Bear looked sharply at his companion.

"No. I just know it. I'll go to the Great Spirit long before the People are no more. I don't want to be a burden when I've seen too many winters. I don't want to be like Two Fingers — a useless old man who can no longer make war; who has no juices left to stir his lance at the sight of a woman; too old and weak to hunt his own meat. Sorrow hangs heavy on men like them."

He brushed the sweat off his forehead with the sleeve of his calico shirt. "Or worse. By then, the People'll be living under the *tahbay-boh*. I don't want to be a man and live under the 'protection' of the blue coats. No, my friend, I'll die like a warrior."

Walking Bear nodded in acceptance. "I feel the same. I've already seen too many winters, I sometimes think." He chuckled. "And I seek the death of a warrior rather than the impotent death of old age."

Gray Wolf smiled a bit, knowing he still had his closest ally.

Several hours later they came to a farm in the near-barren, crazy quilt of land. Within minutes, the occupants of the house were dead or dying, and the house in flames. The Comanches laughed uproariously at the sight of a naked teenage girl who flopped about on the ground in the throes of an agony she could never have imagined. She moaned piteously, no longer having the strength to scream.

She had been caught right off and held by two warriors while the others destroyed her family. They had cut and ripped off her clothing. Then she had been violated — in vagina, mouth, and buttocks — by all but five of the thirty-eight warriors. Then one severed her Achilles' tendons so she could not stand. Another hacked off her breasts, howling in delight. He crowingly told of his plan to make tobacco pouches from each one. Still the girl lived, a whimpering bundle of raw nerves. With a contemptuous smile, one of the warriors strutted up, buck naked, and threw himself atop the girl. He viciously plunged root deep into her and thrust for a few seconds before spilling his seed inside her. She was too weak to even murmur a protest. The warrior stood, trumpeting his hollow victory. He urinated, some of it splashing the girl. But her mind had snapped and she did not notice.

The Comanches mounted their ponies and rode off, leaving the few whites alive to die of exposure, their wounds, or scavengers. They headed for the Rio Grande. It had been some years since they had raided Mexico, and Gray Wolf, for some reason, felt the urge to do so now. They ravaged northern Mexico, killing, always killing. Gray Wolf had forbidden the taking of prisoners. Within a week, they splashed back across the river and headed north, never ceasing their rampage. For some reason, though, Gray Wolf felt an uneasiness growing.

Walking Bear could see the look of concern on Gray Wolf's brutal, dark face. Finally, he asked, "What troubles you, Gray Wolf?"

"I don't know. Something makes me doubt my powers."

"You have strong medicine," Walking Bear insisted. "We've lost only one man. We've killed many *tahbay-boh*. And we have much glory." He grinned as he waved a hand at the warriors who were gaudy in serapes, cotton shirts, sombreros, and felt hats; a few even carried parasols. Almost a hundred stolen horses created a cloud of dust.

Two days later, realization struck Gray Wolf. "I know what's wrong, Walking Bear. There's no honor in killing these helpless men. They're not even blue coats, who at least fight sometimes. They're like old women, afraid to fight, or even to run. They just sit and wait for death. There's no chance to die a warrior's death against them. To die like a warrior, we must seek out the blue coats."

Gray Wolf also had it in his mind that if they could fight the Cavalry — and win — that perhaps they could drive the soldiers out of this country. And he reasoned that if the Army left, the white farmers would be afraid to stay because they would have no protection, so perhaps they would leave, too.

"The long-knives won't find us. They're always rushing about like birds that can't fly. Running here, running there. But we're always gone," Walking Bear boasted.

"We must let them find us, my friend."

Walking Bear looked at him blankly a moment and then grinned.

48

Winter was coming on fast, and Gray Wolf needed to hunt. He, Walking Bear, Buffalo Droppings, Hits-With-A-Fist, and a few others rode eastward. There were buffalo in the *Llano Estacado*, but Gray Wolf preferred the grassy plains east of the *Llano* along the Red River. The buffalo were plentiful there and the Comanches took tons of meat and hundreds of hides. The people would be well-fed and well-clothed this winter.

When the snows came and the temperature fell, the Comanches stuck close to their lodges. The men might go out on better days to hunt, but for the most part, they revived their home lives. Gray Wolf spent the winter in playing with his youngest children — three-year-old son Far Seeing and eighteen-month-old daughter Horse Hair. He also helped train his nephews in the arts of war and the hunt.

He spent considerable time, too, in casting balls for his rifle and pistols; and in making arrows, the latter taking much effort. He fashioned a new bow of Osage orange, backed with buffalo sinew, and reworked his old war club.

Still, there was much time for visiting other warriors, most often Walking Bear. The men would talk and smoke their pipes and trade stories. Often, they began a game of hand, hooting, shouting, or cursing as their fortunes turned.

Winter bored Gray Wolf for the most part. The other men enjoyed it, as it gave them relief from the rigors of the hunt, and from war. But Gray Wolf missed war. It was virtually all he lived for, and so the colder months dragged by.

But at last the days lengthened and warmed. Grass and flowers poked through diminishing patches of snow; rivers flowed more fully. Soon it was time for the hunt. Gray Wolf felt a sense of urgency for getting the hunt over with. He wanted to be on the war trail.

As soon as possible after the hunt, Gray Wolf rode out with Walking Bear, Hits-With-A-Fist, Buffalo Droppings, White Antelope, Eagle Wing, and Crooked Arm. Gray Wolf did not even delay long enough to send word to other bands that he was forming a war party. The small band spread its terror far and wide. But they saw far more long-knives roaming Texas than ever before. Still, the soldiers could not keep up with the fleet, sturdy Comanche ponies.

So successful was the small band that the men rode out again after the fall hunt. It was still warm in the *Llano*, but it was an unusual thing for the Comanches to do. They taunted the blue coats whenever possible. But they did it so easily that they soon became lax.

They made camp one day in a brush-choked spot along the Llano River. It was snowing, but not much. The men joked as they set up camp in the steely gray afternoon.

Suddenly gunshots erupted from behind the trees. Eagle Wing fell, wounded. “Run!” Gray Wolf bellowed. He plunged into the brush, Walking Bear rumbling beside him. Both fired their pistols as they plowed through the thicket, hearing their friends do the same.

Gray Wolf and Walking Bear burst out of the brush and stopped. Despite the cool air, they were sweating. “Look,” Walking Bear gasped, out of breath. He pointed.

Gray Wolf nodded. He ran for the Comanche pony that had bolted at the first sign of trouble. Its rope was tangled in a bramble bush. He freed the animal and leaped on. Kicking it, he raced toward Walking Bear. The two men's hands connected and Gray Wolf swung his friend up behind him. They thundered off. Twenty-five miles away, in the heart of the night, the horse faltered, stumbled, and finally fell. Both men leaped to safety. Gray Wolf slit the animal's throat and began butchering the pony.

Walking Bear gathered buffalo chips. Using flint, steel, and tinder, he soon had a small, hot, pungent fire burning.

The two warriors ate in silence, each immersed in his own bitter thoughts. Gray Wolf was enraged at himself. His arrogance had left Eagle Wing wounded, maybe dead, and the band without horses. His disregard of common sense would be his undoing one day, he knew.

Just before dawn, Hits-With-A-Fist, Buffalo Droppings, Crooked Arm, White Antelope, and Eagle Wing straggled into Gray Wolf's camp. The first two came together, Crooked Arm alone, and then Eagle Wing, helped by White Antelope. Each sat and ate, saying nothing. But Gray Wolf could feel their bitterness and disappointment.

The small group moved on the next morning, awkward and uncomfortable on foot. They took turns helping Eagle Wing who was not hurt all that badly, but he could put no weight on his left leg.

When he was not helping Eagle Wing, Gray Wolf walked apart from the others. His flagging spirits revived some when, about midday, they raided a farm and stole enough horses for them all. Granted, they were old farm horses, ungainly, plodding beasts. But they were horses.

Still, it was a highly dispirited group of warriors that rode into the village. His despair was worsened when he learned the blue coats were attacking Comanche camps through the colder months.

Gray Wolf's band was unmolested, but many others suffered under the Army's iron fist.

Hoping to restore his powers when the spring arrived, Gray Wolf rode off to his vision site. He focused his mind on bringing forth a vision. He fasted, sitting cross-legged before a small fire that soon burned out. Daylight faded into night, the cycle repeating itself for four days.

The vision came, wavering as if he was seeing something across the Staked Plains in the depths of a brutal, hot summer. Gray Wolf coaxed the vision forward, willing it to coalesce before his eyes.

It was much like his other visions: His spirit helper — or himself, however one looked at it — the great, gray wolf stalking a victim. There came a quick charge, like always, and then the dripping fangs were rending out chunks of flesh, tearing meat from bone. But something intruded: The slight figure of a young woman. Her skin was a soft, glinting copper color, her features finely chiseled. There was something haunting about the young woman, something familiar.

The young woman marched fearlessly toward the wolf, which glared at the slim figure balefully. But the woman was unafraid. Hail began to fall on the woman and the wolf — silver hail that glinted eerily in the strange light. It was accompanied by loud rushing noises. The hard, gleaming hail pounded on the two figures. The rushing noise grew until it boomed and cracked like thunder. The wolf howled and yelped as the hail pelted him, hurting him. The woman cried, her face etched in pain.

Finally, the wolf left the carcass of his kill — a human wearing blue cloth — walking off unsteadily as the hail continued to pound his furry flesh. The woman accompanied the wolf, which seemed no longer wary of the human. The woman also walked as if in pain.

The woman and the wolf ran as the hail crashed and thundered down on them all the harder. The two figures passed a body, another, and then one more sprawled on the barren land. Ravens and buzzards circled above. Still, the wolf and the woman walked, bleeding from the pounding of the hail. They were weak, but alive and moving.

Gray Wolf awoke suddenly, having fallen into the cold fire pit. He was covered with sweat, causing ashes to stick to his body. He shook from lack of food — and from his vision. He was still troubled when he rode into the village, and for many days he told no one of it.

Finally, he approached Walking Bear, his oldest and most trusted friend. With the passage of years, Walking Bear had learned many things, and though he was a simple man, Gray Wolf placed a lot of faith in Walking Bear's acquired wisdom. With hesitation, Gray Wolf told Walking Bear of his vision and asked the old war leader to explain it, if he could.

"My heart sees what the eyes can't," Walking Bear said solemnly, taking this new role into which he had been thrust seriously. "It's clear you are the wolf. And you will be helped by a woman."

"But who?"

Walking Bear shrugged his big shoulders. "The spirits don't show all. We must live by the wisdom of the spirits who will fulfill us."

Gray Wolf had no idea what Walking Bear meant with his cryptic statement. So he asked, "But what of the hail? And the bodies?"

"Hardship will come to you, my friend, and you'll lose some who are close to you. But the gray wolf will persevere, and live on. Perhaps accompanied by the woman helper."

Gray Wolf shook his head in consternation. It did not bode well for him, but yet it was believed he would live long under adverse circumstances. "Should I take up the trail of war again?" he asked.

"That's for you to say, my friend. I see in your vision many troubling things, but always the gray wolf lives on to fight."

Gray Wolf was still puzzled, and he thought considerably about it during the next several days.

Others in the band had heard of his dark, uncertain vision. They worried over it — and his ill-fated expedition the past winter. They decided it would not be wise to follow Gray Wolf this time. For them it seemed that their great war leader had lost his medicine.

Gray Wolf understood and said nothing. He decided to go alone. The only thing stopping him was worry for his family. Nagging at his mind was the sight of three decomposing bodies in his vision. He feared that his two wives and six children might be in danger.

But he had to go, and he left quietly one night under a full moon, taking six extra ponies. He did not know where he was going, so he rode aimlessly, hoping the spirits would give him direction. A week out, he found himself on a butte watching two wagons struggle along in a cloud of alkali dust. Two men, two women, and several children walked alongside the creaking wagons, pulled by gaunt oxen.

This scene held nothing from his vision, but Gray Wolf shrugged. He figured the spirits had drawn him here for some reason. Leaving his extra ponies behind, he charged down off the mesa, racing close to the wagons before letting go a war whoop.

The people were startled. The two men went for their guns, while the women and children scrambled for what safety the wagons afforded. Both men were so frightened and shocked that neither could aim properly. Though both fired quickly, the bullets from the old front-loaders were wide, hitting nothing but dust in the distance.

Gray Wolf cut down one of the two white men with his lance. As he did, he saw a woman leap from the back of the wagon and race away, terrified. Gray Wolf had been about to dispatch the other man, but he suddenly thought perhaps the fleeing woman was the one from his vision. He kicked his pony and the animal shot forward. In moments Gray Wolf caught the woman, whose bonnet, held by string at her neck, flapped on her shoulders. He pulled alongside her and grabbed her hair. He jerked her up across the pony in front of him. Without slowing, he headed to the mesa. Behind him he heard curses and shouts. Atop the mesa, he dumped the woman on the ground and turned to look down. The two wagons were moving, the man frantically cracking his whip over the oxen.

Gray Wolf dismounted and walked to the woman who scrabbled along the ground like a crab, fear puffing her face. Gray Wolf grabbed her hair and knelt close to her. He stared at the pale blur of a face.

"What're you gonna do?" she babbled, voice squeaking from fear.

Gray Wolf just continued to stare at her. Minutes dragged by, with the only sounds being the woman's raspy breathing, the rare snort from one of his horses, and the faint crack of the whip.

Gray Wolf finally decided this was not the woman of his vision. That woman was brave, fearless. This one looked as if she would die if he sneezed. Now his only problem was deciding what to do with her. He thought of ravishing her, but he did not really appreciate these women, with their ghostly skin under too many clothes. He could kill her, but he saw no reason for it, other than that she was a *tahbay-boh*.

"Get up," he said in English, shocking her.

When she did not react, Gray Wolf stood, pulling her by the hair. He tugged her toward his horses. Stopping at one, he said, "Get on."

"I can't," she whispered.

He bent slightly and cupped one hand. She stuck a foot in the cup. She pushed with the other foot, and he shoved with his hand. She straddled the horse, too scared to worry that there was no sidesaddle.

Gray Wolf mounted his pony. Leading the woman, he headed down the butte. The man with the wagons had been watching behind him fearfully. When he saw Gray Wolf coming again, he grabbed his rifle. He braced it on an edge of the rear wagon and waited for the Comanche to get within range. Suddenly the other woman shouted, "Ephraim! No!"

Gray Wolf stopped within a hundred yards of the wagon. "Get off," he ordered.

The woman did. Gray Wolf spun his horse and raced off, not sure why he had done such a thing.

49

Gray Wolf did not know what drove him, but he felt himself pulled southeastward. His visage was grim, for he was still troubled by his vision, worried about his family, and annoyed at having let the white woman go free. To alleviate some frustration, he attacked two isolated farms, killing all the people and running off their stock.

Even that did not comfort him, and he traveled on with a nagging sense that his medicine had turned bad.

He neared San Antonio and thought that perhaps the spirits had brought him here. He sat just outside the city, waiting for the sun to set. After examining all the information he had, he reasoned that the spirits had guided him here for a purpose. What better place to restore his power than to attack the big *tahbay-boh* city?

He slipped into the city under the cover of night. His nose and ears were assaulted by sounds and smells. Some were familiar — the sourness of horse urine and pungency of manure; snatches of laughter or snoring. But many — the spicy foods, perfumes, burning coal oil — were odd to him. He was not sure he liked them. He slid along buildings, down alleys, and up back streets. *Such bustle*! he thought. So much activity despite the darkness, so many people scurrying from one place to another. People laughed, talked and swore; guns were fired; church bells peeled; music tinkled from saloons; dogs howled or barked; people galloped by; even women strolled about.

Gray Wolf dismounted and left his pony a few feet back in the thin slot between two brown, stone buildings. He stood watching the *tahbay-boh* passing to and fro, looking like ants in their frantic need to be somewhere else. Someone neared him, and Gray Wolf melted into the alley's shadows. As the white man passed the entrance to the alley, Gray Wolf reached out and split the man's head with his tomahawk. The man had no time to utter a sound as he fell onto the dusty street.

Gray Wolf quickly dragged the body into the alley where he peeled off the scalp. With a sense of satisfaction, he backed his pony out of the alley. He moved on, a grim smile curling his cruel lips. He used the alleyways more now, relishing the stolid blackness they afforded. Only once more did he encounter anyone, and that person was soon dead. Gray Wolf tore off the scalp, but threw it aside disgustedly. There was hardly enough hair on it to make it worthwhile. But he grinned, thinking of the consternation such an act would breed.

He moved toward the river, which sparkled in the moonlight. It was quieter in the back streets and alleys, and Gray Wolf could more plainly make out individual voices. Once, he heard a familiar sound and he rode his horse up against a house wall and peeked past the fluttering curtain. With a grin, he silently watched as a fat, bald man wearing an ill-fitting suit made love — ever so briefly — to a horse-faced woman with stringy hair. Gray Wolf shook his head as he moved on — neither participant had removed any clothing. Such a thing struck the Comanche as quite humorous.

Not long after, he heard a voice he vaguely recognized. He stopped and cocked his head, listening. He turned grim. He could not place the voice, but he knew it. He heard it again, and he nodded, a cunning grin curling across his lower face.

Still mounted, he sidled up to the window from which the voice came. Cautiously he peered into the yellowish light. A young woman sat at a table. She was brushing her long, glossy, black hair and speaking to a pretty Mexican woman a few years older. The Mexican woman hurried about the room, doing things Gray Wolf could not fathom.

The young woman was looking into a large reflecting glass as she brushed her hair, and Gray Wolf could see her face. It was a dark face, but not as dark as the Mexican's. The young woman was pretty, Gray Wolf guessed, though thin for his tastes. Still, she was bosomy, and her hips indicated she held much potential for bearing children.

The Mexican said something Gray Wolf did not understand and both women giggled. Then the Mexican left, closing the door behind her.

Gray Wolf stood on the pony's back and slipped through the window. He was on the woman before she knew he was there, clamping a hand over her mouth. In Comanche he whispered, "It's Gray Wolf."

The woman's eyes, reflected in the mirror, had grown wide in terror at the first intimation of trouble. Now they blinked and she managed to move her head fractionally — enough so that she could see her attacker's face in the mirror. She nodded as best she could.

"Heed me, Light Calf. If you make a sound, you and everyone else in the stone lodge will die. Do you understand?"

She nodded, her heart calming from the fright it had undergone. She was no longer afraid. When Gray Wolf removed his hand, Libby turned to face him. In Comanche, she whispered, "What're you doing here, Gray Wolf?"

"I come to seek vengeance on the *tahbay-boh.*"

"You will be killed."

"No. The spirits gave me a vision. And they brought me to this white man's village." He paused. "They have drawn me to this stone lodge. You will come with me." The last was an order.

"Why should I do that?" she asked, surprised.

"Because you're *Nermernuh,*" he said. "And I say you will. Do you disobey the man who'd make you his?" The last surprised even him.

"I wouldn't mind going back to the People," she said almost dreamily. Then her face grew determined, and Gray Wolf was surprised. She was no wilting flower, he realized. "But you have two wives. I won't be the third." Her back was straight. It let him know she had more pride than to suffer such indignities.

"I'll take you whether you want to go or not," Gray Wolf snapped. He felt a need to exert authority, setting the standard for the future.

"You'd get more than you could handle." She stared levelly at him. She was only sixteen, but she was a strong, determined woman.

Gray Wolf was disconcerted by her forwardness. But he was growing angry. How dare she argue with him! "We will go. Now!"

"And what of my status?"

He relented. He would have his hands full trying to get both of them away from here under the best of circumstances. A struggling woman on his hands would worsen matters considerably. He would correct her ill manners later, at his leisure. "I will divorce Red Moon." She might be his first wife, but she was no longer young.

"You will divorce both," Libby insisted.

"One."

It had only been minutes since Gray Wolf had entered her room, but Libby had decided almost immediately that she would go with him. She missed her mother's people. Though she had lived with the Mitchelsons in San Antonio for almost six years, she had lived about that long in the Comanche village. She held fond memories of it. She was not sure she wanted to spend the rest of her life there, living like the People, but a visit would be nice. She would worry about the repercussions later.

At a month and a half after her sixteenth birthday, she knew her own mind. She had long ago determined to marry who she wanted, when she wanted, rather than have the Mitchelsons dictate such things. Her guardians had been applying pressure for her to marry the son of a town merchant — a man only a year younger than Gray Wolf. Such pressure colored her decision to leave with Gray Wolf.

As for the matter of Gray Wolf's wives, well, she had no intention of marrying the Comanche war leader anyway. She would go to the village as a guest. If he wanted to court her, he could do so. She also knew that if things in the village got bad, or if Gray Wolf gave her too much trouble, she could go to her father in Taos.

"I must dress," she said hastily. She pointed to her night dress.

"Be quick," he ordered.

Libby bit back the retort that bubbled up. Now was not the time to argue. She hurried to a bureau and yanked out some things. Without embarrassment, despite her six years living in the rigid white world, she yanked her shift over her head.

Gray Wolf could not take his eyes off the glistening brown skin that shimmered in the lantern light. A desire he had not felt in years swept him up, and he had to battle himself to keep from reaching out and taking her here and now.

But she had not dawdled. By the time the night clothes hit the floor, she had already scooped up a dress from the bed, having decided that drawers, corsets, and other such *tahbay-boh* torture devices were best left behind. She wriggled into the dress, which was two years old, and fitted too snugly over her full bosom and shapely hips. She already wore a pair of moccasins she had bought on the sly with her own money from a trader in town. They were one of her few illicit pleasures in San Antonio and she enjoyed wearing them in the evenings before bed. It was a link to her mother and the Comanches.

Gray Wolf slipped out the window and onto the horse. Light Calf was right behind him. She perched on the horse's rump, dress hiked halfway up her thighs. She put her hands around Gray Wolf's middle, and realized that despite his age, he was firm and strong.

She had a fleeting thought that maybe marrying Gray Wolf wouldn't be all that horrible. Gray Wolf moved out, forcing himself to keep from running the horse. They wove along the river, once again keeping to smaller side streets or alleys. Once out of the city, he ran the horse, heading west toward his extra ponies.

His anger was immense when he found that someone had stolen them. His pony was nearly used up from having been pushed hard with the double weight.

"We need horses," he said gruffly, fighting his rage.

"*Si*. There's a *rancheria* a mile or so from here. Northwest."

50

Gray Wolf walked the overworked horse. He did not consider walking alongside it, though he briefly pondered ordering Light Calf to do so. He realized angrily that Light Calf was not a woman to be ordered about so easily, and to mention such a thing would cause more trouble than the brief savings would warrant.

It did not take long for them to reach the ranch. It was small, with but a house, barn, and perhaps a dozen horses in a corral next to the barn. Gray Wolf stood near a mesquite tree and looked over the *rancheria*. It was evident the ranchers felt they had little to fear from Indians since they lived so close to San Antonio. The city and its environs had not been raided in more than a decade.

Gray Wolf left Libby with the pony. There was no need to give her orders. Despite her years in the white man's town, she knew what to do. With the silence of a shadow, Gray Wolf moved toward the corral. The horses were unaware of his presence until he was among them. Even then they were assured at the soothing voice, though the smell was odd to some of them and made those horses skittish. Gray Wolf grinned and shook his head, enjoying the little joke the spirits had played on him. Amidst the white men's horses were his own ponies.

He culled out his ponies, shooing them toward one side of the corral. For good measure — and to let these *tahbay-boh* know they had had a visitor — Gray Wolf cut out one of the ranch horses. Gray Wolf shoved down three fence railings. Then he leaped onto the back of a pony. With encouraging, soft words, he herded his other horses — and the stolen one — through the opening. He would not encourage it, of course, but he would be amused if the other horses escaped.

At the mesquite, Gray Wolf explained about the ponies and Light Calf chuckled. She took a pony, and within minutes they were racing across the sprawling hill country.

No one followed, but they ran the horses hard. They rode through the night and the next day before Gray Wolf stopped. He was tired but did not show it. He was angry, too, at the small indignities age was beginning to play on him — his behind was sore and his knees had lost some of their fluidity.

Libby was tired but cheerful. Gray Wolf had had the thought that by working Light Calf so hard she might be more bendable to his rule, but he realized now that such a thing was a foolish hope.

Under the canopy of willows and cottonwoods along the brushy, muddy banks of West Nueces River, they fell into deep sleep. Gray Wolf awoke first and shot a deer that had come down to the water to drink. The gunfire woke Libby, and she looked up, alarmed. When she realized they were not under attack, she drifted back to sleep.

Gray Wolf hauled the deer carcass up and started a fire. While the fire was growing, Gray Wolf deftly skinned the deer and butchered out several pieces that he set to cooking. Libby awoke, her head coming up as she sniffed, seeking out the wonderful aroma.

"You've been away from the People too long, Light Calf," Gray

Wolf said with a smile. He had decided he would try pleasantness — as much as possible — to win her over. She would take extra care in breaking since she had lived with the *tahbay-boh* so long. "You sleep like a bear in winter. That's not good."

She hung her head at having been chastised. But she didn't feel too badly about it. The statement was true; living with the *tahbay-boh* had robbed her of some of the ways of the People. "I'll do better," she said. "You will see." She meant it. She did not mean she was going to kowtow to him, but she knew her place, and how far she could push the bounds of her still-budding womanhood.

She walked away, and Gray Wolf figured she had personal needs to take care of. But she was gone too long for that, and Gray Wolf felt a worrisome twinge. He finally told himself that the *tahbay-boh* took so long at most everything else that they probably did the same with such things, too. Libby finally returned, holding up the bottom of her dress to form a basket. She squatted next to Gray Wolf. In the dress basket were blackberries, blueberries, pecans, and grapes.

Gray Wolf scooped up a large handful of berries, avoiding the nuts, and stuffed them all in his mouth. He chewed, juice dribbling down his chin. The fruits were tasty, and he enjoyed them. He was a meat eater, buffalo preferably. But he liked some fruits and vegetables when he could get them — corn and squash particularly, and grapes and chokecherries. Out in the *Llano*, such things were hard to come by, though the Comanche women used them and edible plants to spice up their diet when they could find them.

Gray Wolf grabbed large handfuls of the berries twice more, while Libby picked at the pecans. Finally, Gray Wolf reached for the last of the berries, and Libby, only semi-playfully, slapped his hand. He looked up at her sharply, surprise and anger coloring his face. But he said nothing as she popped the berries into her mouth. She wiped her hands on her dress and stood, asking Gray Wolf for a knife. He handed her one. "Stay," she said and headed for the fire.

She was confused. She was not of a temperament to be too deferential to any man. Certainly not as much as would be expected by a *Nermernuh* warrior — and one of the greatest of the Comanche war chiefs, to boot. Still, she knew she could not defy him too much. She was a woman, and as such, had certain responsibilities. Even in the white man's world it was so. Life was going to be a delicate balance for a while as she juggled Gray Wolf's demands with her own.

Light Calf speared a chunk of meat and carried it to Gray Wolf. He took the meat in his bare hands, and ripped off a piece with his teeth. Light Calf took a smaller hunk for herself. When they had eaten their fill, both wiped hands and faces on Libby's dress.

Gray Wolf looked at the sky. When they had awoke, it had been blue. But dark clouds had moved in. Thunder rumbled in the distance.

They pressed on, but slowly. Within an hour, they were riding through slanting sheets of rain and growling thunder. The storm varied in intensity for three days. Gray Wolf and Light Calf ate raw deer meat since starting fires was impossible. What wood they found was soaked, and the buffalo chips often used as fuel were useless.

They rode into the village a week later. Gray Wolf's face was arrogant, his head held high. Light Calf followed quietly, though not shyly. More than one person gasped when they recognized the woman in the light-blue calico dress.

Gray Wolf stopped when Walking Bear stepped in front of his horse. "I must talk to you, Gray Wolf," the older warrior said.

Gray Wolf nodded, showing no sign of the sudden lurch of his stomach. He slid off his pony and contemptuously tossed the reins at Libby. He followed Walking Bear into the lodge, trying to ignore the gasp behind him. He was sure it did not bode well, but he would not look. The two men sat. Light Calf stepped boldly into the tipi and also sat halfway between each man. No one voiced anything but the looks the two men cast at the woman said plenty and did so eloquently.

Walking Bear was disconcerted. A woman had done such a thing, and he was unsure how to deal with it. He had an urge to split her pretty head open, but he knew Gray Wolf — or, worse, White Horse — would kill him for it. Such a death would be ignoble. Silence dragged heavily in the air. Finally, Libby said brazenly, "Say what you must say, Walking Bear."

"It is not for your ears."

Light Calf knew he meant it was not meant for a woman's ears. But she did not care. "Gray Wolf has asked me to be his wife," she said almost defiantly, taking some pleasure in Walking Bear's shock. "I haven't consented," she added. "Still, if what you have to say concerns him, it concerns me as well."

"Such a woman will cause trouble, Gray Wolf," Walking Bear said to his friend, as if Light Calf was not there.

Gray Wolf shrugged. While Libby's forwardness was troubling, he was intrigued by it. He would, however, have to speak to her about it. It was one thing for her to be defiant in the confines of their lodge; doing so in front of others was another.

Walking Bear absently scratched his crotch, trying to think of how best to say what he had to say. He decided to just get it out as quickly as possible.

Gray Wolf waited, outwardly patient, but he squirmed inside. He had not been offered food, nor a pipe. He had not been allowed to go to his own lodge first, to freshen himself after the long days on the trail. Therefore, whatever Walking Bear had to tell him was bad. He wished Walking Bear would get on with it.

"We moved the camp east, looking for buffalo," Walking Bear said quietly. "Twelve suns ago, we stopped by a stream a little north of the Brazos. The men rode north a short way, having spotted buffalo. The women, children, and old ones stayed behind." He paused. "A band of long-knives attacked them."

Gray Wolf's stomach flopped again. He knew in his heart where this was going. He only had to wait to hear who had died.

"The woman and children scattered like buffalo hair in the wind. The hunters heard the gunfire, and yelling. We hurried there, and drove off the blue coats. But not before..." he paused "...your first wife and the quiet daughter, and..." He paused. "Your least one." They were..."

"Were they cared for properly?" Gray Wolf asked, concerned. After all, for them to get into the spirit world, they would have had to be buried in the correct way.

"Yes."

Gray Wolf nodded, thoughts awhirl. He and Red Moon had been together twenty-one winters, a long time. They had grown close during that time. Though Red Moon had lost her youthful beauty, having aged rapidly under the weight of her hard life, Gray Wolf had cared for her. She had given him several children, the last only three years ago.

He would miss his children, too. Arrow Feather was his youngest son, three years old this past winter, and as full of life as one could hope. His loud, inquisitive nature delighted his father. Water Carrier was seven years old, born of Red Moon. She was a quiet, serious child, whom Gray Wolf thought would make an excellent wife for a warrior one day. He would not, he knew, miss her as much as he would Arrow Feather, but her loss would be felt in his lodge and in the village. The death of any of the People was a hardship to all.

Libby sat with hands folded in her lap. She had lived with the People long enough to know this was a time to keep quiet. She had known Red Moon. She did not know Arrow Feather or Water Carrier but assumed they were Gray Wolf's children. Her heart went out to him.

Walking Bear glanced surreptitiously at the half-breed. Then he said to Gray Wolf, "Those three were the only ones killed."

Gray Wolf nodded, mind preoccupied. Then he looked up. "The

vision," he breathed. He nodded in understanding. "I must think on all this," he said. "I will return to my lodge."

Walking Bear nodded once. "And her?" he asked, indicating Libby.

"I can't bring her to my lodge now," Gray Wolf said distractedly. "Later will be the time for that."

If I agree, Libby thought, though she kept quiet.

"She will stay here," Walking Bear offered.

51

Gray Wolf was preoccupied for several days, and Libby was just as glad. It gave her an opportunity to observe him, and to reacclimate herself to village life. She was still uncertain whether she would become Gray Wolf's wife, and thought that watching his dealings with the People during a crisis might help her decide.

Almost after a week after he and Light Calf had arrived in the village, Gray Wolf called on Walking Bear. One of Walking Bear's wives handed a bowl of stewed buffalo to each man.

Neither man objected when Libby sat half an arc between them. Having had Light Calf living in his lodge for a week, Walking Bear was becoming somewhat used to the half-breed's odd behavior. In some ways he enjoyed it, though he would not feel the same if she was his woman. However, she was Gray Wolf's problem.

"I've come to take Light Calf into my lodge," Gray Wolf said after he and Walking Bear ate and had smoked a pipe.

Walking Bear shrugged. It was of little concern to him. But he thought Gray Wolf should take care of other matters first. "Are you aware of the others' feelings toward you?" Walking Bear asked.

"What're those feelings?" Gray Wolf asked suspiciously.

"There's much talk among our people, my friend. Some say your medicine has vanished like morning fog under the hot sun."

"Is this what you think?" Gray Wolf demanded, angry. He had always had a volatile temper, and with the events of the past month or so weighing on him, his anger was never very far beneath the surface.

"I didn't say that."

"I have much power!" Gray Wolf shouted, thinking that some of those who doubted him might be listening from outside. He would make sure they heard him. "I killed six *tahbay-boh* while I was away. I rode alone through all the *tahbay-boh* lands. Alone I rode into San Antonio and took Light Calf. No one saw."

"That does not mean you have your old powers." Walking Bear did not really believe that of his old friend, but others did, and he would play devil's advocate so Gray Wolf could convince them.

Gray Wolf was enraged, thinking his old friend had turned against him. "My medicine is strong!" he roared. "My power comes from my vision. You didn't know its meaning, couldn't see it clearly. You couldn't explain it," he added a little sarcastically. "But I see clearly now. I, Gray Wolf, the greatest warrior the *Nermernuh* has ever seen!" His chest expanded, barely able to contain his pride in himself.

"And what do you see?" Walking Bear asked, smiling confidently.

"The three bodies of my vision. They are the bodies of those of my family who died. The spirits said they'd die. I just didn't see it clearly. And," he added eagerly, "the hail in my vision — a hail of bullets from the blue coats' guns. It is all there." His eyes glittered.

"What of the woman in the vision?" Walking Bear asked. He smiled, letting Gray Wolf know he was on his friend's side.

Gray Wolf understood, despite his excitement. And he regretted his doubts about his friend. "Light Calf is that woman!" Gray Wolf crowed. "The spirits guided me to her, helped me take her from the *tahbay-boh* who kept her against her will..."

Libby almost managed to keep a straight face. Kept against her will, indeed!

"Light Calf is powerful medicine," Gray Wolf said.

Walking Bear grinned, but said solemnly, "You see clearly where others couldn't. Your medicine is still strong."

All three ate more stew, allowing time for anyone who had been listening to scurry off and tell others what they had heard. After a short time, Walking Bear said, "What'll you do about the woman?"

Libby sat straighter and looked at Gray Wolf.

"I'll take her to my lodge now. As my wife."

Both men looked at Light Calf, waiting for an objection. She sat, thinking. She was no longer confused or doubtful. Despite the time she had lived with the *tahbay-boh,* she was still half-Comanche by blood and one by training and inclination. She believed in visions and spirits. Now that she knew she was an important part of Gray Wolf's powerful vision, she could do no less than to become an important part of his life, too. Her only reservation was her status in the Gray Wolf lodge. Gray Wolf still had one wife — Blue Eyes — and Light Calf was not about to become second wife to anyone, leastways of a woman who had started as a Mexican captive.

Gray Wolf, who was studying Light Calf's face, saw the flickering emotions and confusion swirling in her light eyes. Suddenly he understood. "You'll hold a special place in my lodge," he said.

Light Calf smiled. In a gesture uncommon to most Comanche women, she looked into his eyes. "I will go with Gray Wolf," she said quietly.

Gray Wolf was glad. He had thought she would give him trouble. But he did not allow his happiness to show on his hard, dark face. He nodded once, curtly, and said, "Come." He stood and walked out, with Libby following meekly — for her, it was meek. She wondered if she had made a mistake.

Gray Wolf strode to his tipi, and Libby could tell by the way he carried himself that he was proud. She could not see his face, but she knew he would be wearing a look of arrogant assurance. She stepped into his lodge with a sense of dread. It was one thing to become the wife of a *Nermernuh* war chief; it was quite another for a virgin to face the marriage bed upon such short notice.

Gray Wolf shooed Blue Eyes and the children out of the lodge, much to Light Calf's relief. She had no desire to be deflowered in front of an audience. While she was old enough, and had learned enough from the Comanches before going to San Antonio, to know what was to go on, she really had little hope that Gray Wolf would be considerate of her. She was pleased to find out that he was making an effort.

His attentions continued as he led her to his bed of softly cured buffalo robes. He struggled with the button of her calico dress. He had considered that since his need for Light Calf was urgent, that he would just push her down, shove her dress up and sink home in her. But he knew she was unfamiliar with the marriage bed, and he did not want to rush her. She was special because of her importance to his vision. And the words of Light Calf's father came to him from over the years, telling him that to take his time would reap benefits for both him and the woman.

Still, the thoughts of a hurried buck and thrust were as strong as his frustration with the *tahbay-boh* dress. He even considered using his knife. Finally, Libby took his hard hands in her soft ones. "Wait," she whispered.

As Gray Wolf's hands fell to his sides, Libby undid the buttons holding the bodice of her garment. With a growing sense of fear — and anticipation — she shoved the dress down over her shoulders and pushed it past her firm, crimson-tipped breasts and kept it going. She had to wriggle her hips to get the ill-fitting dress over them. Once past her flaring pelvis, she let the soft piece of clothing fall to her feet. She stood naked but for moccasins.

Gray Wolf grunted, the only sign of the heat that flared through him at the sight of Light Calf's full, firm figure.

With a dry mouth, Libby stepped out of the folds of cloth and onto the buffalo robes. She was nervous but did not show it as she lay on the soft, musky-smelling furs.

Gray Wolf was far more considerate and gentler than Libby would have thought possible. She would have been shocked if she had known she had her father to thank for it. Gray Wolf stripped off his moccasins and breechcloth before kneeling next to Libby. He ran his callused hands over her flesh, stroking here, cupping there.

Libby's fear fled quickly, replaced by a comfortable warmth that grew in her midsection, making her thrash. Her buttocks wriggled down in the furs as the heat flooded her middle, encouraged by Gray Wolf's fingers. Suddenly a feeling unlike anything she had ever known burst from her loins and up to her head. She screamed softly, as her back arched, shoving herself hard against Gray Wolf's hand.

The warrior did not stop, though. Slowly, gently he stoked her inner fires again. Libby moaned, sweat glistening in the gully between her heaving breasts, and on her forehead and upper lip. Gray Wolf bowed his head and softly tongued one nipple, and then the other, back and forth, all the while rubbing her. Once again, she felt the rushing climax that made her shudder, and left her gasping. Still Gray Wolf continued his skillful working of her body. But this time, before she was at her peak, he suddenly removed his hand. Flush with ecstasy, Libby did not have time to think before Gray Wolf was kneeling between her legs. Carefully he eased himself into her.

Libby gasped, and her eyes expanded into wide circles of wonder, ecstasy, and a little pain as Gray Wolf pushed harder, entering her fully. He paused, allowing her body to adjust to his presence. Then Gray Wolf began to thrust slowly, each stroke making Libby gasp. She felt a bit of pain, but it was overwhelmed by pleasure. Gray Wolf picked up his pace. Suddenly Light Calf screamed as a feeling of almost blinding intensity shot through her body.

Her back bent high as she ground herself up against Gray Wolf with all her might. Moments later, Gray Wolf hissed and jerked with his release. Then he fell atop her. Both of them panted.

The tingling excitement stayed with Libby throughout the day, and she was happy to accept Gray Wolf's order that night to join him.

The next morning, Light Calf took her place as first wife in Gray Wolf's lodge. Blue Eyes was not pleased with the arrangement, but she stoically accepted it after Gray Wolf angrily turned down her request for her own lodge. She knew of Gray Wolf's vision, and she knew her place. Light Calf fell easily into the routine of work that formed the life of a *Nermernuh* woman. She butchered meat, cooked, made or repaired clothing, scraped and tanned hides, and gathered wild plants to augment their meat. And she accepted Gray Wolf when he wanted her.

Gray Wolf's patient lovemaking was not always evident. More than once it was a quick lay down, a painful, fast entry, and a few snorted thrusts before he was through and gone. Libby put up with these indignities, biting back her angry retorts. Still, she acknowledged some relief when Gray Wolf went on the warpath. But she was sad, too, since she was pregnant already.

While Gray Wolf was gone, Light Calf made a place for herself in the tribe's hierarchy. Because of Gray Wolf's position, and because of her place in his vision, she reached a higher plane among the women than any other. Indeed, she was on a level of her own, somewhere above the rest of the women, but still well below the status of the warriors. It made her workload a little lighter.

Gray Wolf was gone less than a month. He and the others returned in glory, and he was pleased at having gained retribution for the deaths of Red Moon, Arrow Feather, and Water Carrier.

Winter was spent in learning each others' likes and dislikes, skirmishing with each other, trying to balance Gray Wolf's rights and prerogatives as a great warrior with Light Calf's needs and demands to be considered more than mere chattel. Before spring, they settled on a shaky truce in which Light Calf was to be properly deferential in public. Inside their lodge, she would do her work but be allowed to her opinion and to make decisions on things that affected her.

BOOK 13

ZEKE TIPPETT, 1857-1862

52

Tippett stopped on the ridge and looked at Painted Rock three miles away. He felt an excitement he had not felt in some years. Certainly not in the year since he had last since Libby.

He had left San Antonio after visiting his daughter and wandered aimlessly, grieving over the deaths of most of his family and riddled with guilt for leaving Libby in San Antonio. He also burned with hatred for Elmore Trent. He felt lost, unsure of who or what he was, uncertain of where to go or what to do. He was not a man who turned to others in times of need. He never had been, and his sudden insecurity bothered and angered him. He thought he might need to talk things out with someone. There was only one man he could turn to.

Tippett turned north and east, and within a few weeks was poking his nose into every dive, saloon, and bawdyhouse in Westport, Missouri. He was drunk as a lord when Cass Calder found him, near stuporous, in a saloon appropriately named the Keg's Dregs.

"Come on, ol' hoss," Calder chuckled in his avalanche of a voice. He easily lifted Tippett and flung his old friend over his shoulder. He grabbed Tippett's rifle in the other hand and strolled out. No one paid them any mind. Such sights were not unusual in the Keg's Dregs.

Calder never pressed Tippett for information. He kept quiet until Tippett was ready to let it out. Tippett finally did as they huddled in Calder's shack on the outskirts of Westport. It was snowing heavily and the two men were sitting in creaking old rocking chairs near the fire. Each had a jug near to hand and there was salted buffalo meat on the fire. The wind moaned and groaned, whistling through the many cracks in Calder's cabin.

"How the hell can ye live in such a shithole?" Tippett had asked when he got his first good look at the cabin.

Calder had chuckled his grumbling laugh. "Hell, I lost everything but my balls and rifle in a faro game." He laughed. "I lost this place, too. But nobody wanted to lay claim to it." It took several minutes for the bubbling chuckles to fade. "Ain't got shit left for *pesos*." He shrugged. Not having money had never worried the big man.

Tippett told Calder his tale of woe. When Tippett had finished, Calder took a deep drink. He sat silent a while, rubbing a huge paw over the stubble on his chin. "We've both seen some mighty poor doin's, *amigo*."

"I expect." Tippett poured liquor down his throat.

"But ye cain't set here and let such doin's eat at ye." He paused. "Ye know what ye got to do, *amigo*," Calder said as quietly as he could manage with his voice.

Tippett had known it all along but had not wanted to admit it. Now he could not deny it in the face of Calder's stern visage and common sense. He almost smiled. This is why he had come here — to get sanction for what he must do. "I expect I do," Tippett said with a frozen grin. The wind keened as he reached for the jug again.

He left in March, as soon as he figured there would be grass for his animals. His hatred for Trent consumed him. He knew he would have no peace until he killed the man. He had tried to deny that for a year — far more, if he thought back to when he, Cass, Trent,

Bender, and Bledsoe had run out on the Rocky Mountain Fur Company.

First, he rode to Fort Spirit Mound. But the fort — falling down through non-use — had been abandoned, and the troops moved to Fort Painted Rock some miles south on Kickapoo Creek. Tippett rode there and stopped at Captain Montgomery's office. A soldier stood outside the small wood structure at attention, rifle smartly on his shoulder.

"You can't go in there, sir," the soldier said firmly.

"Get outta my way, before I knock ye on your ass."

"You kin try, sir," the soldier drawled, "but you ain't goin' in."

With a move the soldier saw only as a blur, Tippett whipped out his Bowie knife and held the pointed tip under the soldier's chin, at the juncture with the neck. The young man's eyes reflected fear as he felt the back of his head scrape the rough wood of the door. He gulped, his bobbling Adam's apple bouncing too close to the knife for comfort. "Like I said, sir," the soldier noted, "you can go in now."

Tippett moved the knife and the soldier stepped aside. Glaring at him once more, Tippett jerked the door open and stomped into Montgomery's office.

Montgomery swung around to face the door when he heard someone enter. "Tippett! What in hell are you doing here, you Indian-consortin' son of a bitch?" he roared.

"Lookin' for someone," Tippett replied easily after a quick glance around. They were the only ones in the room.

"Where'n hell's that private out there?"

"Still out there, doin' his duty."

"If he was doing his duty, you'd be flat on your ass in the compound. I'll see to him later. Now, get the hell out of this fort."

"Where's Trent?"

"Gone on to other duty."

"Where?"

"Last I heard, Fort Simpson. That was a while back. He might still be there. Maybe elsewhere. We don't write," Montgomery said.

"Why'd he leave?" Tippett asked, frustration welling up.

With viciousness Montgomery said, "Trent's done a good job for the Army, Tippett. Since the attack on Fort Spirit Mound, he has found several dozen villages of Comanches, all of which we put to the torch."

"Why ain't he still here, if ye're so fond of him?" Tippett snapped, biting back the growing tide of anger.

"We've done more than our share of dealing with the savages, Tippett," Montgomery said, digging the knife in a little deeper. "Other commanders, knowing the job Trent's done in bringing justice to the hostiles, sought his services. So, I allowed him to go to another post." He grinned maliciously.

"Ye're full of buffler droppin's."

"All right, Tippett," Montgomery said with a sigh. "Have it your way." Again the vicious smile. "Truthfully, we haven't seen much action around here of late. The Comanches here have been routed. Trent felt the need to move on to greener pastures." He paused. "What do you want with him anyway?" Montgomery asked, cocking an eyebrow at Tippett. "If I recall, you said you did not know him."

"I know him. And I'm lookin' to set things right," Tippett said in a voice that made Montgomery shudder. There was death in that voice. "I should've done it a long while back."

"Why?" Montgomery asked suspiciously.

"He's a blight," Tippett said no less viciously than Montgomery had spoken. "Had I put that baby-murderin' bastard under years ago, my boys'd still be alive."

"What?" Montgomery asked, surprised despite himself.

"My least son, Cass," Tippett said in cold tones. "was the half-breed in that band ye attacked on Beals Creek last year. Trent put him under, even if he didn't pull the trigger. I expect it was the same with my first son, Josh, too, in '46. Your men — and some Rangers — attacked a war party on Yellow House Creek. Ye was there."

"We were only protecting the citizens of Texas and the United States," Montgomery said with an almost religious fervor.

Grief and rage settled over Tippett like an iron shroud. "Hogwash," he muttered.

"If your sons hadn't been raiding with the damned Comanches — ravaging God-fearing whites from Mexico to the Red River — they'd still be alive. Trent went against them because they were hostiles."

"He's a back-stabbin', festerin' sore, and if ye had any goddamn brains, ye'd see that. But he's poisoned ye to his ways —attackin' innocent Indians."

"There's no such thing as innocent Indians, Tippett," Montgomery said defensively. "And I have no sympathy for you — or your sons. If they were on the warpath, they were hostiles." He had no regrets.

The Hawken rifle came off its resting place in the crook of Tippett's left arm until the muzzle was aimed at Montgomery's stomach. The captain froze, face blotchy with fear, as Tippett thumbed back the hammer. Montgomery was more afraid than he had ever been. He knew Tippett enough to know the former mountain man would kill him in an instant if it suited his purposes. So, Montgomery stood and waited, fear dripping with sweat off his chin, watching Tippett's stony face. He was close to killing Montgomery. Only the knowledge that by doing so he would bring the wrath of the United States Army down on him hard — preventing him from finding Trent — kept him in check.

Tippett relaxed and eased the rifle's hammer back down. "That'd be too easy. But ye mark what I'm sayin', dammit," Tippett growled. "Once I've seen to Trent, I'll be back for ye."

He swung around and was out the door before Montgomery could say or do anything. He rode out of the fort fast, lest Montgomery round up a patrol to come after him. He moved across the river and headed north, but no one came after him.

Tippett tracked Trent across the vast wastes of west Texas and parts of the Indian Nations, sickened at the trail of destruction Trent had left. It was no easier to look at those ravaged Indian villages than it was for Tippett to see the remains of a white ranch after the Comanches had swept over it. He stopped at Fort Mason and told the commanding officer he was a friend of Trent's from their trapping days in the Rockies. It gained him information, but not what he sought — Trent had moved on.

Tippett continued to follow Trent's blood-soaked trail. At other forts, Tippett used the same ploy. Some officers had used Trent's services, others had not. But Trent seemed to be always ahead of him.

In December, Tippett found the remains of a small Comanche camp on the Llano River. The blood, spent arrows, hoof marks, all told the tale, and Tippett was chilled. Gray Wolf had been among the Comanches here. Tippett could only hope that his old friend had gotten away safely.

The former mountain man followed the month-and-a-half-old trail north and found where another war band of Comanches had been attacked by Trent and Army troops.

Then the trail turned as cold as the north wind. Tippett considered going to Taos for the winter but decided against it. He felt he was close, even if the trail itself was cold. He stopped at Fort Belknap and went through his spiel with the commander. He held back his smile as the officer said Trent was stationed in Fort Massachusetts, up in Colorado Territory; had been reassigned — at his own request, as usual — only a month ago.

Tippett pushed northward into southeastern Colorado Territory, planning to head west into the San Juans, but winter was hard on the Great Plains, and he did not want to die in a blizzard before finding Trent. So, he holed up for the winter in the remains of Bent's Old Fort.

It was eerie being in the long-abandoned trading post on the Arkansas River. He had spent much time here and the memories were good. He could not believe Bill Bent had fired the fort in anger when he abandoned it, though there was no doubt that someone had burned it. His first weeks at the crumbling adobe fort were particularly strange since he was haunted by the ghosts of Painted Wing, White Buffalo, and Leaves Behind. Painted Wing's presence was strong, but an even stronger spirit sweeping over him was that of Born-In-The-Storm, who had been born right here. Tippett was tormented enough that he thought of leaving. But he managed to keep the demons and memories under control.

Winter finally released its frigid grip on the land, and Tippett headed west, into the Rockies. He made good time, since he had nothing to slow him — and because he was single-minded of purpose.

Major Arthur Wilkins greeted him after he had managed to threaten his way into the commanding officer's office. Tippett spun his tale.

"Yes, sir," Wilkins said evenly, "Mister Trent operates from here. Knows his business well." He seemed to grimace before looking reflectively at the ceiling, watching a scorpion dart across the logs. "Seems a lot of you old trappers make good scouts against the Indians."

"We lived with many tribes whilst we were mountaineers, Major," Tippett said sourly. "We know their ways and such."

"I see," Wilkins said, bringing his eyes down to look at Tippett. "And you've learned to fight like them, too?"

"Ye want to stay alive, ye adapt, Major," Tippett shrugged.

"Does that include the mutilating of bodies, Mister Tippett?" Wilkins asked. He seemed interested.

"I've taken scalps," Tippett said with neither pride nor regret. "Can't say I ever carved up the dead, though. Such doin's don't shine with this chil'."

"The Indians do it," Wilkins said wryly.

"They got reason. Whites don't. Most Army men don't learn Injun ways, so they think Injuns do things that seem unnecessarily cruel. They might think different, was they to know the reasons."

"Sounds like you're on good terms with the Indians."

"Comanches mostly. I've got Injun enemies, too. Some, like the Utes, are enemies 'cause I'm friendly with the Comanches. Others, like the Cheyennes, used to be enemies, but are friends now." Tippett paused to fill and light his pipe.

"Don't take me wrong, Major," he said, puffing. "Injuns ain't saints. They got their faults. They don't understand — don't *want* to understand — white ways. Trouble comes 'cause neither side tries to understand the other. All they see is that the others do things diff'rent, so it must be wrong." He shrugged again. There was no changing human nature.

Wilkins stared calmly at Tippett for some moments before saying, "Are you interested in scouting for the Army, Mister Tippett?"

"Nope. I've done some, but I got no interest in doin' so again."

"A pity," Wilkins commented softly. "Mister Trent is an excellent tracker and has no trouble finding hostiles." He paused a heartbeat. "And non-hostiles, too. He is a little too, er, shall we say enthusiastic, in attacking Indians bands for my liking."

"Ye'll not have to worry about such things much longer, Major," Tippett said in deathly cold tones.

Wilkins understood immediately. He nodded. He chewed his bottom lip, then said, "Trent's out on a patrol. He should be back in about a week. He went west, planning to loop to the south and then back here."

Tippett nodded and stood. He shook hands with Wilkins, saying, "Ye've been a big help, Major."

"I hope the assistance is mutual."

Tippett nodded and smiled grimly. Many things were evident, though they had not been voiced. Tippett turned and walked out.

Following the track of the small Army patrol as it wound up

into the mountains was not difficult, and two days later Tippett had the group in sight. But he did not see Trent. He tagged along for the rest of the afternoon. As the patrol made camp for the night, Trent rode in. Tippett grinned grimly. He hobbled the horse and let it graze on the new carpet of short, thick grass. Tippett had a cold camp that night, chewing on jerky and sipping water from his old wood canteen.

Tippett had planned to wait until morning and follow Trent, catching him away from the patrol, and dispatching him. But as he sat in the twilight, watching the fires flickering in the gloom, another plan presented itself. Tippett had begun to feel in recent years that he was losing many of the skills he had acquired in his mountain days. He decided this was the time to test whether that was true.

When the half-moon was almost directly overhead, Tippett roused from the doze he had allowed himself. He stood and breathed deeply of the cool, pine scented night air. He stretched, scratched, and belched. He sipped water and then moved off on foot, toward the Army camp. He flitted like a shadow from tree to bush, rock to tree. The sleepy sentry had no inkling anyone else was near as Tippett slipped by him. Tippett wound deeper into the camp, until he was in the midst of eight sleeping soldiers — and one loudly snoring scout.

Tippett stood looking down at Trent who was sleeping on his back, arms flopped wide, mouth agape. Tippett grinned forbiddingly. He pulled his Bowie knife and crouched. In one swift move, he clamped his left hand on Trent's throat, brought his left knee down atop Trent's right arm, and leaned his right knee on Trent's right leg.

Trent's eyes opened, and he was instantly alert. He could not yell since Tippett's hand cut off his wind, but he thrashed about, trying to free himself from Tippett's weight. The stars above began to wink out as his oxygen-starved brain faded and his struggles weakened.

Tippett, knowing Trent was nearly unconscious, eased off his throat a bit. In an enraged, hissing whisper, he said, "I jist wanted ye to know who it was put ye under, ye scrofulous bastard." He held up the Bowie so it glinted in the firelight. "Ye killed my two boys, and then carved one of 'em up; now it's your turn for such doin's."

Trent's eyes were wide with stark fear. He could not move his head, but his eyes followed as best they could, the shiny blade of the Bowie headed netherward. Suddenly Tippett's hand zipped from Trent's throat to cover his mouth. Trent tried with all his might to scream as the blade bit deep into his groin. But no sound came out.

His eyes reflected the searing agony he was experiencing as Tippett yanked the knife upward, through intestines, scraping over the pelvic bone, and into the belly cavity.

Trent bucked, and small snorts exploded through his nose, as he tried to escape the burning fire of the knife. He forgot trying to scream. He jerked, arching his back, one last time, as Tippett pulled the knife free and then jabbed it to the hilt into Trent's heart. Trent expired, his eyes still reflecting his fear and pain.

Breathing heavily, Tippett carved out Trent's privates. He did not like doing so, but he did it anyway. It was a payback for Trent's having done the same to Born-In-The-Storm. Tippett also wanted to make it look as if Indians had done it. It would make it easier for Wilkins to not send anyone after him, even if he had the desire to do so.

Tippett dropped the bloody pile on Trent's chest. Then, with a few deft strokes — and no remorse — he peeled off Trent's scalp.

53

Tippett walked into the Rocky Mountain Saloon in the town of Fort Garland. He was dirty and tired, but still excited. After killing Trent, he had headed toward his old stomping grounds of the three parks where he roamed for two months. He did not expect Wilkinson to send anyone after him for killing Trent, but if Wilkinson was forced to do so, Tippett wanted to make himself scarce for a little while.

Though he had enjoyed his time in the old, familiar haunts, he tired of it quickly. He wanted to see Libby and then get back to Taos. Such things were more important to him now. He was forty-four years old and had begun to feel like he had lost the past several years of his life. He figured he was too old to lose that much time. He even decided to renege on his vow to kill Montgomery. Slaying the soldier would mean more running, probably years and years of it — maybe even a lifetime. And at his age, revenge was not worth the lost time. So, he headed to Garland. It was near Fort Massachusetts, and he knew that by going there he would be taking a chance. But it would allow him to find out quickly if anyone was looking for him.

The saloon was a crowded, dingy place, much like any other

that catered to an Army crowd. Tippett moved to the bar, stopping next to two soldiers. He ordered a bottle of whiskey, poured a drink, downed it fast, and poured again. He turned to the soldiers and said pleasantly, "How do, boys."

They nodded but said nothing.

"I just got in. I was up north, scoutin' for Colonel Forbes." He figured the Army reference would make the two friendlier. "I heard a scout was killed by Injuns down here a while back. That true?"

"Yes, sir," the older of the two said. "A month ago, no, two. Injins snuck right into a patrol's camp and killed a scout named Trent." His eyes and voice showed his wonder. "Even whacked his dingus and balls off." His legs clenched involuntarily.

"They bother anyone else?" Tippett asked noncommittally.

"No, sir. That's the odd thing about it. Major Wilkinson — he's the commander at Fort Massachusetts — finally reasoned that the Utes knew Trent. He'd led patrols against them, so the Major figured they had a special hate for him."

"I expect so." Tippett said, relieved. He had been leaning on the bar and he straightened. "Thankee, boys. Hope ye two don't meet up with none of them Utes."

"They're mean bastards all right," the same soldier said. "Savages." He shuddered, thinking back on what had been done to Trent.

Tippett grinned slightly. He called the bartender over. "Give these boys a drink on me. He dropped a coin on the table and, carrying his bottle, left after accepting the soldiers' thanks.

Three weeks later, a disreputable-looking Tippett stalked into his store, calling, "Ben! Ben Winter. Where'n hell are ye, boy?"

Winter, his clothing disheveled, walked out of the back room. His face was a mixture of surprise and happiness. "Zeke!" he said. "Good to see you. You're all right? Where've you been? What've you been up to? You don't look well. You sure you're all right?" The questions tumbled out of Winter's mouth like water over a falls.

"Whoa, boy, slow down," Tippett said with a laugh. He felt

better now than he had for years. Perhaps, he thought briefly, he had cleaned the bad spirits from his heart with his acts of vengeance, despite their brutishness.

Watching the changes of expression that flickered across Winter's face, Tippett told the story, from start to finish. He did so quickly but left out none of the important details. The telling of it brought back a reminder of his grief, but he set it aside.

"I'm sorry to hear it, Zeke," Winter said in sympathy. "But a man like Trent needs to be dispatched in such a way."

"I expect." He paused. "My house still livable?"

"Of course," Winter said. "I hired a Mexican girl, Rosita, to care for my place. I have her go to yours once in a while to see that it was ready for when you returned." He laughed. "She thinks I'm *loco* for it, though. Everyone thinks you're dead."

"I don't feel dead," Tippett said with a laugh. "Though I expect I smell like it. Reckon I'll head home and see to gettin' cleaned up."

"You want to see the books?" Winter asked seriously.

"It can wait. Only reason I stopped here first was to see if it — and ye — was still around. There ain't no rush on the books. Unless ye got bad news?"

"Quite the contrary," Winter grinned.

"*Bueno*. Ye think Rosita could come to the house and open things up for me?"

"Of course. She'll draw you a bath, too, if you wish." His look indicated Tippett's wishes should have nothing to do with it. Tippett nodded and Winter said, "She also gives a hell of a shave."

"She do anything else for a man?" Tippett asked rudely, grinning.

Winter flushed, and that was enough of an answer for Tippett. "Ye object to sharin'?" Tippett asked with a grin and a wink.

Winter relaxed. "No, sir," he said truthfully. "I'll mention it."

"Jist tell her I'm interested. Ol' coon like me ain't quite a ruttin' buck no more, and if'n she don't take a shine to such an idea, I'll not bother her. I don't want ye orderin' her to do such a thing."

"Yes, sir. I'll fetch her right away."

"*Bueno*. Ye got someone to watch the store while ye're gone?"

"I hired a boy to help out. He has no education, but he shows a flair for numbers, so I expect I can train him for clerking one day."

"Sounds almost exactly what Carter said when he told me he hired ye." Tippett nodded. "I'll stop by a saloon first, and wet my dry gullet."

An hour later, he was luxuriating in a tin tub in a side room of his rambling adobe house. He lay back, relaxing in the warmth of the water and enjoying the almost-pleasurable scrape of the straight razor's blade across his flesh as the voluptuous Rosita shaved him. She was naked, as she had been since filling the tub. Her firm breasts swayed enticingly as she worked on Tippett.

One breast, its nipple thick and inviting, swung near Tippett's hand, and he reached out to cup it and then stroke it. Rosita murmured with pleasure. He left off that after a few moments, but his other hand slithered up one of her legs until it reached the apex. His fingers kept busy. Rosita shuddered with pleasure.

"Not now, *Señor*," she whispered.

He grinned and said, "My shave can wait." He manipulated her with his hand until she shook and shuddered with a climax. Her empty hand grabbed one of his shoulders to steady her. It took some minutes before she was calm enough to continue shaving him. As she did, she whispered, "*Bueno, Señor. Muy, muy bueno. Muchos gracias.*"

"*Da nada.*"

She finished the shave quickly and then slowly scrubbed him with soft soap. She spent much time working gently on his privates. While she did, Tippett toyed with Rosita again until she was moaning with delight. He grabbed her and pulled her into the tub with him. Hastily she worked onto him. Within moments both yelled in their ecstasy.

A long time afterward, Tippett and Rosita finally dressed. Rosita was dipping buckets into the tub, scooping up water, and taking it out back to dump it. "I'm goin' over to the store, Rosita," he said quietly. "I'll be back directly. Ye need anything, come on over."

"*Si, Señor*" She smiled. "Would you like me to stay? Tonight?"

"If it won't put Ben out none."

"On, no, *Señor* Ben is...shy, you might say." Her accent was light, but noticeable, and lent a lilting quality to her soft voice.

"Would ye like to stay here tonight?"

"*Si*!"

"*Bueno*."

At the store, Winter brought out the books. Tippett ignored them. "The hell with them things," he grumbled. "Jist tell me. How're we doin'?"

Winter looked near ready to burst as he welled up with pride. "Very, very well, Mister Tippett..."

"Zeke."

"Yes, sir. As he talked, he flitted around the room, arms waving and flapping. Tippett sat on the sole chair in the cramped office that was overflowing with papers. Tippett watched his clerk with amusement. "We've increased our profits tidily. And we've so much work I've had to hire several new employees — in addition to my assistant."

"Can we afford that?" Tippett was not put out, just curious.

"I wouldn't have done it otherwise." He stared at Tippett, his face bursting with excitement. This was to be his moment of glory. For months he had envisioned this in his dreams. "Hell, Mister...Zeke, we're doing so well, we've opened another store!"

For one of the few times in his life, Zeke Tippett was speechless. He sat, mouth agape.

"Opened one in Santa Fe last year," Winter said, grin threatening to reach around to the back of his head. "It's doing nearly as well as this one. And I'd say that in another year it'll be doing even better."

"Well, I'll be dipped in buffler shit and rolled across the prairie,"

Tippett breathed. "Ye've made 'em come now for certain, goddammit. Maybe I ought to go away a couple more years. Hell, ye'd own all of New Mexico Territory!" He laughed.

"We could try," Winter said with a chuckle. As usual, his light-hearted streak lurked not far below the surface.

"Shit," Tippett snorted good-naturedly. Then, after a moment's pause, "Damn, I'm proud of ye, boy. Couldn't be more proud was ye my own son." There was a flicker of sadness, but it fled right off.

If Winter's glow of pride in his accomplishment could have been harnessed, it would have powered every steamboat on the Mississippi forever, Tippett thought, glad he had put his faith in the young man.

"That's not all, Zeke," Winter said, looking a little worried. "I've — we've — branched out. I hope you don't mind."

"Branched out how?"

"Well, sir, I've started us a freighting company, hired a blacksmith and built a shop — he makes much of what we had been buying from St. Louis — bought into a sawmill, saloon, hotel, and restaurant. And," he gulped, "started several Indian trading posts."

"Where?"

"At a few of the pueblos here. And I have several traveling traders out among the Navajos, Zunis, and Hopis out west."

Tippett laughed. "Ye are somethin', boy." He stood. "I reckon my affairs are in good hands. Well, I expect I'll keep out of your way whilst I'm in town."

"You're leaving again?" Winter asked, surprised.

"Want to go see Gray Wolf and his people. Then mosey on over to San Antonio and see my Libby." He headed for the door, then stopped and turned back when Winter called.

"You sure you want to do that, Zeke?"

"'Course, why?"

"It's snowin' already."

Zeke looked out the front window. He had not remembered how late in the year it was. San Antonio would not have a problem with weather. Even Gray Wolf's village would be in a place where winter was mild, compared with what Tippett was used to. But getting there would be another story. The mountains east of Taos would be no picnic this time of year. He sighed. He wanted to see Libby more than he did Gray Wolf, but she would understand. Most likely, he thought ruefully, she did not even miss him. She probably had beaus lined up from the Mitchelsons' house to the Alamo. She would have parties and *bailles* and such. Besides, wintering here, in his own house, would be pleasant. He had a crude thought. With a wide grin, he asked, "Would ye have objections if'n I was to ask Rosita to spend the night, Ben?"

"You old coot," Winter said in humor. He laughed, then said, "None, Zeke. Enjoy." He winked. "She's something, ain't she?"

"Yes, sir," Tippett said emphatically. He winked. "But I expect I'll be settlin' in for the winter here, and Rosita might jist choose to spend her time with this ol' chil', what knows his way around a woman, instead of with some young buck like ye."

"There's a heap of other *señoritas* I ain't sampled yet," Winter said with another laugh.

Tippett grinned and headed out.

54

The village was a bustle of activity as men prepared for war and women tended hides and racks of drying meat. Under the tutelage of uncles and grandfathers, boys were busy at the games that would help them become warriors. The girls also had tutors who watched over them as they learned the things necessary in their life.

Tippett stopped in front of Gray Wolf's lodge. A woman just off to the side of the tipi laboriously scraped a pegged-down buffalo hide, swatting at flies as she worked. There was something vaguely familiar about her. She was not Blue Eyes, nor was she Red Moon. Tippett shrugged as he dismounted, figuring Gray Wolf had taken another woman — a captive most likely — as a wife.

The woman shifted, giving Tippett a glimpse of her profile. "Libby?" he asked, thinking he had lost his mind.

The woman looked up and yelled, "Papa!" She stood and they hugged.

"What'n hell are ye doin' here, daughter?" he asked, befuddled.

She looked at the ground. "I'm Gray Wolf's wife," she said simply.

"What is all this noise here...?" Gray Wolf grumbled as he came out of the cool dimness of his lodge. He smiled when he saw. "White Horse," he said with real pleasure. "Welcome, my brother."

"What'n hell's this nonsense about Libby bein' your wife?" Tippett demanded, trying to recover his senses.

The friendliness dropped from Gray Wolf's face. He had been challenged in the open over a woman. Such a thing was not to be taken lightly. "It's true," Gray Wolf said in Comanche.

"How'n hell'd ye get out of San Antone?" Tippett asked Libby. He was not so much angry as he was befuddled.

"Gray Wolf. He came to..."

"You will say no more," Gray Wolf snapped. "This isn't his concern." He pointed at Tippett.

"Like hell," Tippett said angrily. "She's my little girl, Wolf; she'll always be. Before she's your wife, she's my daughter."

"Go inside, woman," Gray Wolf ordered.

Tippett grabbed his daughter's arm. She tried to pull free, but her father's grip was too powerful. Nor had she tried very hard. "She ain't movin' a step till I figure out what's goin' on here."

"She is my wife," Gray Wolf insisted. "That's all you need to know. Now free her. She will leave so you and I may talk, as men. As brothers of the *Nermernuh*." Gray Wolf tried to sound conciliatory.

"Ye give either one of us another order, Wolf, and I'll knock ye on your ass right here in front of everybody, goddammit."

The two men stared at each other, their emotions plain for all to see. Finally, Tippett said calmly, "Ye mind waitin' inside, Libby?"

"I have work to do here," she commented.

"Ye mind if she works whilst we talk, Wolf?"

"No," Gray Wolf said flatly, plainly irritated.

Tippett let his daughter's arm go, and the young woman moved off, back to the hide. The two men went inside.

"You hungry?" Gray Wolf asked.

"No," Tippett said, sitting with his back to the tipi flap. He pulled out his pipe and filled it. Usually it helped soothe him; he hoped it would do so now. "Why'n hell do ye need another wife, Wolf?" he asked. Trying for levity, he added, "Red Moon and Blue Eyes cast ye over for some young buck with a bigger pecker'n yours?"

"Red Moon's dead," Gray Wolf said flatly. "Blue Eyes is still my wife." He saw the anger flicker in Tippett's eyes. "Light Calf is my first wife," he added.

Tippett nodded and plucked a burning stick from the fire to light his pipe. "I'm sorry about Red Moon. I didn't know. What happened?"

"Long-knives." It was all the explanation that needed to be given or heard, but Gray Wolf went through it all — from the raid on Fort Spirit Mound through his vision, his taking of Light Calf from San Antonio, and his subsequent raiding on the whites.

Tippett sat through the narrative in silence, nodding in sympathy or understanding. When Gray Wolf was done, he said, "I know how ye feel." He told his own story of the past three years.

Midway through his narrative, a baby cried inside the lodge, surprising Tippett. The sleeping infant had been so quiet, Tippett had not known it was there. Tippett glanced at the cradleboard hanging from a post. Libby came in and took the cradleboard down and tended to the child. "That your chil', Wolf?" he asked. "Yours and Libby's?"

"Yes," Gray Wolf said. "Our second son — Far-From-Stone-Village. Our first is much like his grandfather, and is called Light Horse."

"Well, I'll be damned," Tippett whispered. "I'm a grandpa. Let me see that chil', girl," he said, face beaming.

Libby smiled as she handed over the child. "We also call him Bill, after Mister Bent, who you used to talk about."

Tippett grinned in pleasure.

"Light Horse," Libby added, "also carries your *tahbay-boh* name."

Tippett did not know what to say. He was overwhelmed. He

glanced up at Libby who was smiling, and at Gray Wolf who looked like a cat that had just caught the world's fattest mouse. "Thank ye, both," he said quietly, pride welling up in his chest like a church chorus.

He played with the infant a while. It had been a long time since Tippett had held a child this small in his arms and he enjoyed it. He suddenly had yearnings to find another wife and start a new family. He sighed. Such thoughts were foolish. He handed Far-From-Stone-Village to his mother. "Well, where's Light Horse?" he demanded.

"With his uncles," Libby said. "I'll fetch him after a little." She left, carrying the cradleboard.

Tippett nodded absently and went back to his tale. But his mind was not completely on what he was saying. He did not like the idea of Libby being married to Gray Wolf — or any Comanche. But there was not much he could do about it, not when she had two children by the warrior. He could, he guessed, try to convince her to go to Taos with him — with the children. He put it aside. He would have to talk to his daughter first to see what her thoughts on the matter were.

Blue Eyes entered the lodge and began boiling buffalo meat. Soon after, Libby came into the lodge with Far-From-Stone-Village still in the cradleboard and holding the hand of a feisty two-year-old.

"This is my grandson — Light Horse?" Tippett asked. It still had not sunk in yet that the boy also was named Zeke.

"Yes, Papa," Libby said, joy and pride obvious in her voice.

"Well, come here, boy, and give your ol' grandpa a hug," Tippett said, holding his arms out wide.

The boy clutched at his mother's dress, looking frightened. "*Tahbay-boh,*" he whispered, as if referring to a demon. "*Tahbay-boh.*"

Tippett looked crestfallen, and Libby gasped in horror. "This's your doing, Wolf," she said heatedly. She knelt, resting the cradleboard against her knee, and faced her older son. "Not all the *tahbay-boh* are bad, Light Horse," she said quietly. She wasn't sure he would understand, but she added, "White Horse is my father, like Gray Wolf is your father. He is *tahbay-boh*, yes, but he is much like the *Nermernuh*. I'm half *tahbay-boh* because he's my father."

But the boy would not move. Libby looked angry and was about to order her son over to his grandfather. But Tippett grinned crookedly and said, "Let him be, daughter. He'll be all right after a spell. I expect he ain't ever seen a *tahbay-boh* before and jist needs to get used to it. He'll adjust and come to me in good time."

It bothered him only a little that the boy was frightened of him because of his pale skin. And Tippett was a little angry at Gray Wolf for having taught his son such a thing at so early an age. Then Tippett realized the boy probably was too young to understand that the *tahbay-boh* were evil, if Gray Wolf had taught him that. Most likely it was that the boy was frightened of the unknown. A strange man, his skin pale, whiskers stubbing his face, dressed in strange clothes, and suddenly trying to be friendly, would frighten any child.

Tippett and Gray Wolf began discussing war and the state of Texas, battles, the things of everyday life for two men such as these.

After they had eaten a proper evening meal, both men lit pipes and relaxed. Soon after, Light Horse tentatively wandered over to where Tippett sat. He reached out a tiny, dark hand and fearfully touched Tippett's cheek. Tippett sat looking at Gray Wolf, not paying the child any heed, letting the boy explore at his leisure.

Light Horse scrapped a finger across the stubble on Tippett's cheek and chin. He giggled and looked at his finger to see if it was hurt by the scratchy stuff.

"Was ye to come set in my lap, boy," Tippett said quietly, "ye could play with my mustache, if'n ye were of a mind to."

The boy's mouth rounded into an "O" and he backed off a step. But he was back soon, stroking Tippett's cheek, while the former mountain man talked quietly of inconsequential things with Gray

Wolf. Before he knew it, Light Horse had crawled into his lap and was lying there, tiny fingers fingering Tippett's shaggy mustache. Within thirty minutes, he was asleep in Tippett's arms.

Looking at the tyke, Tippett had a desire to take his two grandchildren to Taos with him someday — reversing the process he and Painted Wing had followed with their children — to teach them white ways. That, he decided, might be possible. But it was too premature to mention. He stood and gently lay Light Horse on his bed of robes.

"You'll sleep here, Papa?" Libby asked. It was more of an order.

"If Wolf don't mind."

"White Horse is always welcome in my lodge. And you may have Blue Eyes to keep you warm." It was a custom not practiced widely by the Comanches, but often enough. Usually it was one brother who "lent" a wife to another brother. Gray Wolf felt close enough to Tippett to consider him a brother, so the offer was made.

"Well, I don't know as if that's necessary, Wolf," he said. Any other time, he would have accepted. But he felt odd about it with his daughter in the lodge. Almost as odd was the thought of sharing the lodge with his daughter, who was now a wife — and a lusty one, too, if two children in little more than two years was any indication. She had, evidently, taken some white-man's ways.

"I ain't a child no more, Papa," Libby said quietly. "Such a thing won't bother me." She smiled.

"All right, Wolf," Tippett grinned, though reservations remained.

In the morning, his doubts had fled, though he had new qualms about staying in the village much longer — or at least in Gray Wolf's lodge. It was not easy for him to lay there and listen to the sounds of his daughter being made love to. Even if he was doing the same thing fifteen feet away.

Gray Wolf was gone, and Libby busy outside when Tippett stepped into the sunshine. It was boiling hot, and the day held the promise of worse. Libby looked up from her work, and smiled. "Hungry, Papa?"

"Yep."

"I'll fetch you something."

He nodded and headed behind the lodge to relieve himself. Afterwards he sat just outside the tipi and nodded thanks for the slabs of buffalo meat Libby handed him. "Set a spell, honey," he said, patting the dirt next to him. "I expect we ought to talk a bit."

She nodded and sat. Blue Eyes, who had been working with Libby, smiled at them. She stood and moved off, seeking fuel for the fires. Tippett looked his daughter in the eyes and asked, "Did ye come back to the People 'cause ye wanted to, or 'cause Wolf made ye?"

"It was my choice, Papa."

He shook his head and said, "I don't understand it, chil'. I give ye a place where there's folks with learnin', folks that give ye a good schoolin', nice things to wear, feed ye good. And ye run back here to the *Llano* with the first goddamn buck that comes along."

Libby laughed. "Does sound odd, don't it?"

"Surer than buffler leave droppings behind." His face was stern, but a smile tugged at the corners of his mouth.

"I know what you did for me was best, as you saw it, Papa. But I hated it there. At first, I hated you for bringin' me, but after a while, I realized you did it to make sure I'd be looked after proper. But you never thought to understand that I'm a *Nermernuh*. There ain't no amount of frilly dresses, book learnin', and fancy parties to take that out of me. I reckon the Comanche part won out."

"Ye sound mighty certain of yourself, honey," Tippett said slowly.

"What did you expect to happen there? Was I supposed to turn into some great, refined lady like the ones I heard about back East?"

"I expect I had somethin' like that in mind," he said wryly.

"That wasn't ever gonna be possible, Papa. Look at the color of my skin. But what's under the skin is even more important. Ma was a full-blooded Comanche. And you're more than half-wild. You can't set in a town more than a few days at a time. You're always out huntin', scoutin'. You've lived with the People long enough."

"Still don't mean ye couldn't've become a lady," he grumbled.

"Maybe if you'd have taken me there when I was Light Horse's age, it would've took. But not when I was so close to becomin' a woman. I got your blood, Papa. And Mama's. Blood tells. No schoolin' or frillies can change that. I'm *Nermernuh* and will be till I die."

"If that's the way ye feel, honey," Tippett said, trailing off. He was not happy, but he was not the sort to force her into something different. Every person had his or her own ways and that could not be changed. He could not change his daughter, so resigned himself to that.

"I do," she said firmly.

"Ye seem to have some strong opinions, honey. And an attitude not quite suited to a *Nermernuh* woman." He grinned at her.

She smiled back. "Gray Wolf and I have had more than two years to settle our differences that way, Papa."

"Didn't seem like it just after I rode in yesterday."

"That was my fault," Libby said, lowering her eyes. "I disobeyed him in front of others. I shouldn't've done that."

Tippett nodded, unhappy again. "Well, it ain't my way to get 'tween a man and his woman," he said, torn between sadness and anger. This was his baby here, his last surviving child, and it was not easy to give her up, especially to this hard life. "But if'n Wolf ever tries to lodgepole ye, get word to me."

She grinned. "It won't be necessary. I ain't scared of any man red or white. Anyone who tries to do me harm'll find he's got a hold of more than he can handle. You can stop worryin' about me."

Tippett smiled and shook his head. "That's like askin' the grass not to grow or the rivers not to run no more."

55

"How was your visit, Zeke?" Winter asked when Tippett walked into the store.

"It shined, Ben," Tippett said. He was so proud he looked near to bursting. "I'm a grandpa."

"The hell you say, Zeke," Winter said with a laugh.

"It's true." He explained about Libby and Gray Wolf.

"It doesn't bother you that your daughter is the wife of a Comanche war chief?" Winter asked.

"Some," Tippett admitted. "But she's a grown woman and knows her own mind. There ain't nothin' harder to deal with," he confided, "than a woman with a willful mind." He laughed.

Winter did, too. He hurried off to wait on a customer while Tippett left. He spent some days catching up with acquaintances. He stopped by the store now and again. Cold and snow had come on Taos and Tippett settled in for the winter, cozying up to Rosita. When spring came, Tippett headed to Santa Fe to check on the new store on a street just off the wide, tree-lined plaza.

He had been reluctant to go there since the last time he did the Army had needed his services. He was concerned the same thing would happen again. It did, and he spent the best part of the next year scouting against the Apaches again. He had wanted to go see his grandchildren once more, but saw no way of politely refusing the Army's request. He got back to Taos just after winter closed in again.

Several nights later, Winter rapped on his door. Surprised, Tippett let him in. "Sit, son," he said kindly. He held up the jug of Taos Lightning from which he had been sipping. "Ye dry?" he asked.

"Reckon I could do with a drop."

"Rosita!" Tippett called out. When the pretty young Mexican woman entered the room, Tippett said, "A glass for Mister Winter, *por favor*. And bring us some of them *tamales* ye were makin'."

"*Si*." She rushed off.

"I suspected this's where she's been lately," Winter laughed.

Tippett smiled. He had become very fond of Winter in the time he had known him. The young man was nearly as tall as Tippett, and, Tippett supposed, could be considered handsome. He was thin, with broad shoulders and big hands. He had a quick intellect and a good mind for figures. And he was tough enough to run the store with a firm but reasonable hand.

Rosita returned with a tin mug for each man and a platter of steaming, corn-husk-wrapped *tamales*. She set the platter down and then hefted the jug to fill each man's mug to brimming.

"*Gracias*," both men said.

She nodded and left.

"Ye don't mind I've kept her here a couple days?" Tippett asked.

"No, sir," Winter said. He grinned. "But my house is startin' to look like hell since she ain't been around to clean up."

Tippett laughed. "I'll send her over to see to it tomorrow." He hoisted his cup, holding it a bit in Winter's direction. When the clerk returned the gesture of salute, they both drank.

Winter's eyes watered, and he looked shocked as the Lightning sizzled down into his stomach.

Tippett laughed. He set his mug down and lit his pipe. Winter pulled out a thin Spanish cigar and lit it. Then Tippett asked, seriously, "Well, what brings ye here to *mi casa*, Ben?"

"There's talk going around that concerns me, Zeke."

"Talk about the store? Or me?"

"Neither." He grinned ruefully. "I've practiced what I was going to say, since it might sound foolish, and thought I had it figured out. Now that I'm here, though..." He stopped, blowing out smoke. Rolling the slim cigar in his fingers, he stared at the curl of gray smoke rising from its end.

"Best thing to do is jist start. What ye need to say'll come."

"I've heard talk of trouble brewing back in the States."

"What kind of trouble?" Tippett asked, sipping.

"Talk of war, Zeke. I've heard there is division over states' rights — mainly slavery. I've heard there's talk of Southern states seceding and forming their own nation. It's all very troubling."

"Goddamn troublemakin' governments," Tippett growled softly.

"I take it you're for neither side, Zeke?" Winter asked. He was smiling, but intent.

"Shit, no," Tippett snapped. "I been on my own since I was fifteen. Didn't need no goddamn governments then, and I don't need 'em now. Always tryin' to tell ye what to do and where to do it. Goddamn, we let 'em, the cow-humpin' bastards'll be tellin' us where and when to shit."

"You don't think the Union's right in this?"

"Hell, I don't know. I don't hold much truck with slavery. Never could understand such doin's. But it ain't none of my affair. I ain't ever owned slaves, and I ain't plannin' to treat black folks no diff'rent than any other kind of folks. Back in the mountain days, I got along with the Injuns and the Greasers, Germans, Britishers, even the goddamn Frogs. I got no reason to change my thinkin."

"What if war is declared?"

"God willin' and the creek don't rise, it'll stay back East."

"If it came here?"

"Ye are a pesky, word-twistin' son of a bitch, ain't ye, boy?"

Tippett swallowed some whiskey. "Was it to get out here, and I was forced to choose sides, I expect I'd have to throw in with the North. But I'd go a far piece to keep my goddamn nose out of it." He glared at Winter. "What's your thinkin' on all this?"

"I'm from Massachusetts, Zeke, so I'd have to admit my sympathies are with the anti-slavery forces. But since I've come out here, I find I am not moved by either side very much either. As you said, governments cause nothin' but trouble." He gingerly tilted the cup of fiery liquor to his lips and let a little pass by.

"Why'd ye bring all this up, Ben?" Tippett asked suspiciously. "Ye plannin' on leavin' my employ was I to stand with the South?"

"No, sir," Winter said seriously. "I just..." He stopped for another tentative sip. "How do you drink this donkey piss?" he asked rhetorically, to which Tippett grinned. "I'm just concerned is all. Listenin' to some folks, it sounds like war is certain."

"So?" Tippett shrugged. "Let them peckerwoods fight it out. It ain't our affair."

"It could be, Zeke," Winter said earnestly, leaning forward. "They start fightin' back East, we might not be able to get goods for the store. Or they might cost more."

"Hadn't thought of that," Tippett admitted unhappily. He reached out and grabbed a *tamale,* unwrapped it, bit off half and chewed slowly. When he swallowed, he said, "Them would be poor doin's, goddammit. Hell, all my life I've been a'runnin' from governments and their madness. Damn." He finished the tamale, then said, "What do ye suggest?"

"I think one of us ought to head to the States. At least to St. Louis. Maybe get a feel for things. See if war's likely, or if it's just some fools spoutin' nonsense."

He sipped, then said, "If there's a high chance of fighting starting, I reckon we'll need to see what it'll mean to our getting goods. Arrangements for transport and such." He shrugged.

It irritated Tippett a little that Winter was right. However, he was also glad the young man worked for him since such foresight was not among his own abilities. "Can leavin' be put off a while?" he asked.

"Reckon so. Why?"

"I'd hate like hell to get caught up on the Plains in a blizzard. There ain't a heap out there gonna help me from freezin' my balls off and I ain't so old that I want to lose 'em jist yet."

"Spring'd probably be early enough," Winter said reflectively. He paused, then asked, "So you'll go?"

"I expect. I'm used to the trail, I can't run the store like ye, and I know folks in St. Louis from back in the old days. Some of 'em's involved in politics. I expect they'll know somethin'."

They toasted each other and sat back to eat fresh *tamales* and drink Taos Lightning. But Winter still seemed troubled by it all, so Tippett eased his mind off such concerns with stories — liberally embellished — of his days in the mountains.

Snow and cold hit hard that winter and Tippett was glad he had postponed the trip east. It was not a journey he looked forward to. But the temperatures rose and the snow began to melt. Tippett left, and made good time arriving in Westport in late April. The situation was worse than he had thought. Two weeks before he arrived, Fort Sumter fell to Confederate siege. As soon as he heard the news, Tippett hurried to William Bent's farm on the outskirts of Westport.

"Well, ol' coon," Bent said as he let Tippett into his sprawling house. "I thought you'd gone under. Didn't you get my invitation to Mary's weddin' last year?"

"Nope." Tippett shrugged. "Who'd she marry?"

"An Ohio boy named Moore." He shook his head. "I was down in the new fort, takin' care of business like usual when I heard she was fixin' to marry him. I hauled ass up here fast as I could." He shrugged. "Wasn't as bad as I thought. Moore was down and out when Mary met him, keeping saloon. But he was a good enough sort. I lent him money to go into the mercantile business. They're doin' well. You?"

Tippett quickly brought his old friend up-to-date.

"What brings you here, Zeke?" Bent asked when Tippett finished.

"My clerk heard talk of war maybe startin' 'tween the states. Came to see if it was true. I expect I'm a little late." After Bent nodded, Tippett said, "I'm wonderin' if we'll have trouble gettin' goods. I don't expect it'll have much affect out west, but..."

"Like hell," the feisty Bent snarled. "This area's crawlin' with irregulars from both sides. They'll attack damn near anything they think helps the other side or to keep themselves supplied. The tribes are gettin' restless, too."

"What're ye gonna do about it?"

"I'm plannin' on takin' heavily guarded wagons. How about joinin' in? We'll put our wagons together, toss in some specie to hire men for protection. We'll make out."

After a moment's pause, Tippett said, "Ye ain't favorin' either side, are ye?"

Bent grinned. "You know goddamn well me'n Charles had slaves. We wound up freein' most of 'em, but I'd have to say my sympathies lie with the South. However," he added hastily, "I aim to stick by the government. I don't hold much truck with secession and such."

Tippett nodded sadly. "It's a poor thing this land's come to," he noted.

56

They had no trouble with the caravan that wound its way slowly to Bent's New Fort and then on to New Mexico Territory. It just took time — almost two months for the group of businessmen to get their supplies bought and wagons purchased and loaded. And it took two more months to make the plodding trip. Tippett thought of leaving the caravan at the fort and heading south to let Gray Wolf know of the war. But before they arrived at the fort, Bent asked Tippett to take leadership of the wagons from the fort to Santa Fe. He agreed.

Tippett dropped some of his wagons off at the store in Taos in early September, stopping only long enough to tell Winter, "Them foolish bastards back there went and did it, Ben. Goddamn fools actually went to war. Waugh! Such doin's just frost my ass."

He explained the rest and was on the trail for Santa Fe the next morning. He left his wagons with the others. Most of those were turned over to Ceran St. Vrain. Tippett hurried back to Taos where he caught up on business hoping to head to the *Llano Estacado.* But then he decided he'd better sit out the winter in Taos.

TIPPETT SKIRTED A BUTTE AND PUSHED HIS HORSE UP THE STEEP SIDES of a squat, long mesa. He crossed its length and stopped, looking out. He had a commanding view, and in the distance, he could see the tipis of a Comanche village near a small spring. Cottonwoods lined the stream, providing the only brightness in the desolate countryside.

"Come on, hoss," he said to his animal. "I reckon that's it." The horse made its way gingerly down the steep slope of rubble and loose dirt. The mule, towed behind, brayed out his irritation.

Tippett had left Taos about the first of March. Winter still lurked in the land, and he hoped he would not get caught in another blizzard. But he had felt compelled to get out of Taos after a winter of waiting. First, he wanted to tell Gray Wolf about the war, and, second, he was hoping to convince his son-in-law — Lord, he still had problems with thinking that! — to let Libby and her sons go back to Taos with Tippett for safety.

Rumors of the war possibly reaching into New Mexico Territory had grown during the winter, and by late February, it sounded as if the Confederate Army was either in the Territory or about to reach it. No one was sure.

Tippett discounted those rumors for the most part, knowing that the majority of the troops — both Confederate and Union — would be needed back East. Any fighting between those two armies out here was bound to be limited, and he figured that even if either — or both — side moved into the territory, it would have little effect on life in Taos.

He was more concerned about the rumors of fighting in Texas. With virtually all the Northern troops pulled out of the state, the Comanches would have free rein to rampage across it. Tippett figured Gray Wolf would find that out anyway, so he might as well be the one to tell him. He thought he would use the information to convince Gray Wolf of the wisdom of letting his family go to Taos, if only for the war's duration.

The village was still living its life of winter, though talk of the spring hunt had begun. Tippett greeted Gray Wolf, Libby, his grandsons, and others of the village, such as Walking Bear, and entered Gray Wolf's lodge. Walking Bear and several other warriors joined them. Light Calf and Blue Eyes served food all around.

Tippett thought it quite strange that his daughter was so subservient now, but when he looked at her, she winked and grinned at him. She was doing it, Tippett knew, to make Gray Wolf look good in front of the others. He also was surprised to not see any babies around. Apparently, he thought, Libby had learned to control her reproduction.

After the amenities, he asked, "Ye see many blue coats lately?"

"No," Gray Wolf answered proudly. "We have driven them away."

"Buffler shit. They ain't scared of ye."

"Then why have the gone?" Gray Wolf asked arrogantly.

"The *tahbay-boh* are fightin' amongst themselves back across the great river — the Mississippi. Some *tahbay-boh* bands have split off from the others. Sort of like ye takin' to war with the *Pehnahterkuhs*."

"The *Nermernuh* wouldn't do such a thing," Walking Bear said. He and the others were flabbergasted by such a thought.

Tippett shrugged. "Ye know the *tahbay-boh* ain't like the *Nermernuh*. So, they're fightin' each other, and the great chief of the *tahbay-boh* has called his long-knives back to help in the war."

"This is good," Gray Wolf said, his face brightening as the prospects such a thing presented became clear. "Now we can make war on the *tahbay-boh* without the long-knives to get in the way."

"Ye'll still have Rangers to contend with," Tippett warned.

"They're too few to be of concern," Gray Wolf said, dismissing the long-hated Texas Rangers

Tippett thought such feelings foolish, but he had to admit that the Rangers would be spread mighty thin across the Texas frontier.

Tippett listened as the Comanches boasted of what they would do to the white-eyes. One by one the warriors drifted off to spread the news.

Gray Wolf's eyes gleamed. Here was his chance. For so long he felt, deep down, that his cause was hopeless, that the People would never be able to drive the white-eyes out. But now it might be possible!

He looked like he was about to tell Walking Bear that they would skip the hunt, that they would make their medicine and leave on the war trail now, tonight, when the moon rose and when they had danced and gathered their power and...

He fought the rising tide of eagerness. He must have patience.

Walking Bear left. For the first time in many years, he felt young again.

Tippett looked at Gray Wolf who was tight with anticipation, and Tippett decided it would be a good time to broach the subject of taking Libby and her children to Taos.

"Ye given any thought to your family whilst ye'll be off raisin' hair on the *tahbay-boh*, Wolf?" Tippett asked.

"No," Gray Wolf answered, somewhat surprised at the question.

"Didn't expect ye had." Tippett picked a piece of meat out of the fire and chewed, knowing Gray Wolf was watching him, wondering. "But I'm concerned for my family." He nodded toward the back where Libby worked and Far-From-Stone-Village played. Libby watched the two men intently. "And I was wonderin' if'n ye mind much was I to take 'em to Taos with me whilst ye're off fightin'."

Gray Wolf's face and voice were stony. "How long will they stay?"

Tippett shrugged. He knew this could be sticky. "Through the summer. Maybe beyond. I expect the war ain't gonna last longer'n that."

Gray Wolf was unsure. "You will not take her back to San Antonio?"

"Shit, no," Tippett assured him honestly. "Not less'n she was to express such a desire to me. Which ain't likely."

"You'll bring them back when winter comes again," Gray Wolf said, no hint of doubt in his voice.

"If'n the war ain't worse, and I think they'll not be in danger out here," Tippett agreed.

Gray Wolf grunted, his head bobbing. "Light Calf may go," Gray Wolf said magnanimously. He grew stern again. "But the children will stay with their uncles."

"No," Tippett said flatly, glaring at Gray Wolf. "They're too goddamn young for much teaching of the People's ways. I'll bring 'em back with Libby."

"Then none will go," Gray Wolf asserted.

Before Tippett could say anything, Libby stood and moved to the fire. "We *will* go. All three of us," she said firmly in Comanche.

"Go back to your work, woman," Gray Wolf ordered harshly. He fingered a stick of firewood near his hand.

"No," Libby said calmly. "I'll go with Papa to Taos. And if you keep treating us in such a way, we won't come back."

Gray Wolf grabbed the piece of firewood and started to rise. He froze when he heard the thumbing back of a hammer. Carefully he turned his head to see Tippett sitting with a cocked Colt Walker pointed at him.

"Drop the wood and sit your ass down, Wolf," Tippett ordered.

Gray Wolf did and glared at Tippett, his face etched in rage.

"Don't get your balls in an uproar, Wolf," Tippett said, uncocking the pistol and putting it back in the holster.

"She has shamed me," Gray Wolf spit.

"Buffler shit. I know she's allowed to speak her mind here in your lodge."

"But we aren't alone," Gray Wolf hissed, uncertain now.

"Hell, I'm family. I ain't gonna spread the word that Gray Wolf's man enough to let his wife speak her mind once in a while."

Gray Wolf sat and stewed. But he finally forced himself to calm down. He knew that if he continued to insist upon having his way, Tippett would just take the woman and two boys and ride out.

There would be no way to stop him without killing him, and Gray Wolf did not want to do that. He also knew Light Calf would leave of her own will if Gray Wolf remained adamant. If he gave his permission, it would seem to the band that he was thoughtful, and magnanimous. “It shall be so,” he finally said.

That night, Libby and Blue Eyes put up a lodge for Tippett to use while he remained with the people. And Blue Eyes occupied the white man’s bed. She was not Rosita, but she would do.

Tippett stayed through the big hunt, in which he took a joyful role. He killed more buffalo than any of the People except Walking Bear. In a gesture to please his Comanche friends, Tippett held a Buffalo Tongue Feast for the band. And he gave away all the meat and hides, except for a small amount for the journey to Taos.

Just after the hunt, a new excitement swelled in the village. With the men preparing for war, Tippett felt it time to leave.

57

"Have you ever taken another wife since Mama died?" Libby asked as they rode. She had shown some of her independent thinking by boldly pulling up alongside her father and riding that way.

"Naw," he said, uncomfortable talking about it with his daughter. "Never had the time nor inclination, I expect," he answered lamely.

"It ain't right that a man should be without a woman."

"I never said I didn't *have* no woman," he chuckled, though he felt the flames of embarrassment singe his cheeks. "Ye know that." He still felt odd about having taken Blue Eyes while Libby was around.

Libby giggled. "Still, a man should have a wife."

"Hell, Libby," Tippett snapped irritably, "there ain't many women that'd put up with all my traipsin' about. And this chil's a might long in the tooth for such doin's. Most women, I expect, would want a young feller. Not some broke down ol' hoss like me."

"That's a load of hogwash, Papa," Libby insisted. "There's a lot of women be glad to have a man like you. You're a fine figure of a man. Or at least you'd be if you took better care of yourself."

"And what's wrong with the way I look?" he asked in high dudgeon.

"You're high smellin'. When's the last time you had a bath?"

"Jist before I left Taos, if ye'd like to know," Tippett said indignantly. But he looked down at himself. His flannel shirt and denim pants were coated with buffalo blood and grease. His shirt also was darkened by sweat stains, and he knew his pants were covered with mud and grass. He had not shaved in weeks. He shook his head, "I expect I am overdue for a rinsin'," he said, grinning. "But I don't expect ye're in any position to point out such faults, seein's how ye're a *Nermernuh* now, and the People never take baths."

"This is one *Nermernuh* who does, whenever I can." Libby said. She was indignant. "That's one thing I brought back from San Antonio. I know most white-eyes don't much take to bathing, either, but the Mitchelsons do. I think it had something to do with Doctor Drimmer."

"Reckon ye did learn a few things from them folks, didn't ye?"

"Yes," she admitted. "I don't even think about it sometimes, till after I've done something different and realize where it's come from."

"I cain't understand why ye left there, girl. I didn't want ye to grow up to be no unschooled ol' fool like your Pa."

"You stop it right now!" Libby snapped. "You might not've much schoolin', but there ain't many men can do all the things you can."

"Like what?" he grumbled.

"You know your numbers. You were a fine trapper, you're the best shot I ever seen. You're strong, brave — and a loving man."

Tippett grinned. "I expect this ol' chil' does have some fire left in him. Hell, ye never can say for certain, but ye jist might have yourself a little brother or sister one day."

Libby's face brightened, and she grinned. "You got to get married first, even if it's Comanche style."

"Don't go gettin' your hopes up," he said with a chuckle. "I jist said there *might* be a chance. I don't expect the chances are good."

They fell into silence. They had little to say on much of the ride. They were content just to be in each other's company. A smile, a touch, a few quiet words said more than long-winded conversation.

As they neared Taos, Libby's expectations bubbled out. She had not been there in ten years. She had left a child of ten, and returned a married woman with children of her own. Her face was bright with excitement, and her hands were tight on the reins. And then they were riding up the dusty main street toward the plaza, ignored by the slack-jawed people enjoying their *siesta*.

"Ye remember any of this, Libby?" Tippett asked.

"Some, Papa." She shrugged as faint memories tugged at her. Her eyes popped wide. "There's our house," she gasped, pointing, surprised.

"Yep," grinned. He pointed. "And there's the store."

"Looks bigger than I remember."

"We've built on it twice."

"Is that mean old Mister Carter still runnin' it?" Libby asked, wrinkling her nose.

Tippett laughed. "I expect he was mean. Had a good head for business, though. He passed on while I was in Californy. Before that, he hired a young man by the name of Ben Winter to help him. Winter took over when Carter died. Ben opened the place in Santa Fe I told ye about. Took us into other dealin's that are payin' off, too."

"I hope you rewarded him well, Papa."

"Well, no," he said, feeling foolish. "Never occurred to me."

"Really, Papa!"

They went around back of the house and into the small courtyard. Dismounting, they left the horses where they were for the time being.

It was said by many people that Zeke Tippett was one of the richest men in Taos, maybe one of the richest in all New Mexico Territory. But one could not tell it from his house. The adobe was crumbling and the courtyard was overgrown with weeds and strewn with refuse. The inside was little better.

"This place is a mess," Libby snorted as she entered.

"Don't ye go makin' light of my home, girl," Tippett said with a grin. "If'n ye remember, I've spent a heap more time in Comanche camps than ye have. And they ain't exactly the most carin' folks about their livin' quarters. This here's a palace compared to Gray Wolf's lodge."

"Maybe so," Libby said in distaste. It was true the Comanches were not the neatest people on Earth, but Libby had been looking forward to a real house that was tidy and well cared for. Her disappointment was heavy. "But I expected more from my Papa who's got so much money he can afford to have a big old house instead of a skin lodge. You could've hired someone to care for the place."

"I did. Me'n Ben used to share Rosita" — he felt a twinge in his groin, though he would never mention just what kind of sharing the two men had done with her — "but she run off. Ben hired some old hag, but I expect she don't show up often while I'm gone."

"That seems likely," Libby said dryly.

"Ye don't like the way it looks, ye can clean it all ye want."

"Maybe tomorrow. Right now, I've got you and my two boys to tend. I want to cook somethin' special. Can you take me to the store?"

Winter was startled when Tippett introduced his daughter and her two sons. "Your mother must have been a beautiful woman," he said truthfully, struck by Libby. "Since you certainly didn't get your beauty from your father," Winter added with a laugh. "Ugly old coot that he is."

She giggled, filled with pleasure. The sound was exciting to Winter.

Tippett tried to look hurt, but did not achieve it. Finally, he joined the laughter.

"When ye get what ye need, Libby, have one of Ben's helpers tote your packages for ye."

"Yessir," she mumbled, seemingly humble. Then she stuck out her tongue at him and said, "Old grouch." She giggled.

"Waugh! I've a good mind to lodgepole ye myself, and save Gray Wolf the trouble." Then he grinned. "I aim to go rid myself of this parchin' thirst. I'll be back to the house directly." He left for the nearest cantina.

"If I might make a suggestion, Miss Libby," Winter said.

"Yes?"

"I'd suggest you buy a dress and put it on here. Many townsfolk no longer cotton to Indians walking their streets." He shrugged. "A sign of 'progress,' I'm afraid."

Libby nodded, understanding. "Where would I change though?"

"Back room," Winter said. "I'll keep everybody away, and watch over your young 'uns for a few minutes."

Libby nodded again and quickly picked out a dress, a shiny one of dark blue satin. She went into the back room and changed, feeling an illicit thrill in the possibility that someone might see her — and in her decision to not wear undergarments despite the Anglo dress. Back in the main part of the store, she found Winter happily playing with Far From-Stone-Village and Light Horse.

She stood silently for a moment, watching Winter from behind, and she began to have doubts about having stayed in a Comanche village. She suddenly felt less than adequate, as if she was meant to do certain things and had forgotten them — or, worse, abandoned them. She shrugged, trying to shake the odd feeling off. It was only that Winter was handsome, interesting, close to her own age — and new to her. She moved forward. "Thank you, Mister Winter," she said, haunting thoughts pushed back into a pocket of her mind to be examined later.

"*Da nada*. Now, what else can I get you?"

It took two boys from the store several trips each to get everything back to the house. Tippett, who had been watching from a nearby saloon, strolled back to the store.

"I'm glad you're back, Zeke," Winter said. "I didn't want to say anything in front of Miss Libby, but I have news of the war."

Tippett's ears perked up.

Winter grinned. "Seems the rumors we heard last winter were true."

"The war's movin' into New Mexico? Shit!"

"Moved, Zeke. Moved." He laughed. "The whole thing moved in and out while you were gone. The Rebs come in just after you left. Took over Santa Fe and a few other places. They left most of the stores — includin' ours — alone. Two, three weeks ago, the Union marched in and took it back. Ain't seen much of neither side since."

58

Tippett and Winter went into the back room of the store, which served as an office for Winter. It was more cluttered than the store itself, with papers, cigar butts, food wrappings, and other assorted refuse on the floor or piled on the desk and the three chairs. Tippett cleared some junk off one of the chairs and plopped down, sighing. At Winter's startled glance, he chuckled and said, "Hell, don't look so worrisome. It's jist that my ol' bones creak of a time."

"How old are you, Zeke?"

"Near fifty, I reckon."

"Maybe you should spend a little more time in the store instead of riding all over God's creation."

"Shit, I'd go *loco*. Travelin's in my blood. It's a pull stronger'n any ye'll ever know. Stronger'n women, stronger'n whiskey. It's somethin' that gets in a man's blood and don't ever leave."

Winter laughed. "All right, all right. It was just an idea."

"Damnfool one, too." But Tippett laughed with his clerk. Finally, he said, with some reluctance, "Well, let me see them books, Ben."

Winters handed the thick ledgers over, and Tippett stared at the pages, not even seeing the numbers. In five minutes, he gave it up and threw them on the desk in front of Winter. He hadn't really come here for that anyway. "I cain't figure out a damn thing from them books, Ben. I don't know how ye can jist sit there and do that ever' day."

Winter shrugged. "We all have our callings. You're a man of the wilderness. I'm a man of books and letters."

"I expect." He chuckled. "But from all I can tell in them books, ye could be stealin' my balls right off'n me."

"I'm not," Winter said softly.

"Hell, I know that." He paused, then said, "I didn't really need to see them, Ben. I jist figured it'd look best if I at least set eyes on 'em. There's somethin' else I wanted to talk to ye about."

"What?" Winter asked, trying to keep his face bland. He was worried, though. "Something wrong here?"

"Hell, no. I don't know what I'd do without ye around here."

"The store in Santa Fe? Or the other businesses?" His worry grew.

"Goddammit, Ben, quit tryin' to put words in my mouth." He paused. Libby had been right. "I want to make ye a partner."

"Why?" Winter blurted out.

"For one thing, ye're always here, and I ain't. Ye've worked a heap harder'n I have to make this place shine. I expect ye ought to share in the profits, 'stead of jist takin' out a salary."

"This ain't necessary," Winter said, flustered.

"It is if'n I say it is. And I do, goddammit."

Winter looked embarrassed. "I'm afraid to say," he offered, "that I don't have any money to buy into a partnership, Zeke."

"I never said a goddamn word about no goddamn money, did I? That's 'cause ye don't need no goddamn money." He was in a huff. "We'll jist mosey on over to a lawyer's and see it's done all legal like."

In less than an hour, Winter returned to the store with the fresh ink on the legal papers not quite dry. He beamed with pride. Tippett left him with a friendly smile, a clap on the back, and headed for home where he explained with a broad grin as to what he had done.

"Papa, that's wonderful!" Libby exclaimed, hugging him happily.

Tippett and Libby settled into life at Taos. Tippett divided his time between the store and the house — mostly the latter. Under Libby's relentless nagging, he set about trying to fix the house and clean out the courtyard at back. Libby went about cleaning and decorating the inside of the house. She also would disappear a few hours a day. Tippett did not know where she went, nor did he ask after the first time when she had told him, "None of your business, Papa." She had laughed, kissed his furry cheek and then hurried out. She seldom took the children with her, entrusting them to the care of a half Mexican-half Taos Indian woman she had hired. Tippett suspected Libby was seeing a man. But he decided it was her business.

By early July, the house was in the shape Libby wanted. She stood, her right arm around her father's waist; Tippett's left draped over her shoulder. "Don't this place look better now?" she asked.

"I expect," he conceded. "But it was a heap of hard work, and I ain't so certain it was worth it. And, hell, ye buy any more furniture, and I'll be in the poor house."

"Oh, nonsense, Papa." She looked up at him and said firmly, "Now that the house is taken care of, it's time you did the same."

"No, ma'am."

"Don't you argue with me, Papa. There's a tub in the back room and I got plenty of hot water. And you're to cut this thing off," she gave his shaggy beard a tug. He had not shaved since last summer.

"I ain't doin' no such thing."

"You'll bathe and shave and put on clean clothes," she insisted.

He smiled. "Give me one reason why I'd commit such foolishness." He was not all that adverse to such things. He just wanted to get his daughter's goat, since he did not like being dictated to.

"We're having company tonight."

"What for?" Tippett asked, somewhat annoyed.

"It's Independence Day, Papa. Even though there's war back East, the people here want to celebrate. So, I invited company."

"Who?" Tippett asked, more irritated.

"You'll see. Now, are you going to do what I asked, or should I go get Ben so we can truss you up and do it for you?"

"Ye'd need Gray Wolf and all his warriors," he boasted. He looked down at her beautiful dark face and he could see traces of Painted Wing. It saddened and gladdened him. "Ye're a worse pesterer than your ma was, girl. And she was damned good at it."

"Get goin'," she ordered, pointing to the door behind which the tub waited. She seemed stern, but was flushed with good feelings, knowing she had just received the highest compliment she could hear from her father.

Meekly, Tippett entered the room. An hour later he walked out, chin and cheeks cleanly shaven. He retained the long, drooping mustache. He wore new Levi's and a soft, blue cotton shirt with puffy sleeves. The Levi's were tucked into knee-high, soft moccasins. The ever-present, horn-handled Bowie knife hung from his belt.

Libby walked up to him and placed her small, dark hands on his biceps. She looked up into his eyes and said, "I always knew you was a handsome man, Papa. You ought to keep better care of yourself."

"Bah," he growled, but he was proud. "I'm too old for such doin's."

"Bah, yourself. There's no reason you should cover yourself with dirt and grease, hidin' away from the world."

"Leave off naggin'," he said in mock sternness. "When's supper?"

"Soon's our company gets here. An hour, maybe less."

"Where're my grandsons?"

"Piñole took 'em for a walk." Libby had hired Piñole, the old half-Mexican, half-Taos Indian full time to watch the children.

Tippett grumbled but went into the sitting room where he slowly honed his knife until Libby called him. He stepped out of the room. Winter stood just inside the door, wearing a suit in which he looked terribly uncomfortable. Next to him was a woman about Libby's age.

"Papa, this is *Señora* Francisca de Vallejo Lugo."

Tippett shifted his weight from one foot to the other. "Please to meet ye, ma'am," he said. "Will your husband be joinin' us?"

"Her husband was killed by lightning a year ago, Papa."

"I'm sorry," Tippett said. "Then you've come with Mister Winter?"

"No, Papa," Libby said with a crooked smile. "Time to eat."

As they moved toward the table, Tippett took in Francisca's pretty, dark face and full, supple figure. Her skin was smooth and soft, her eyes liquid brown and framed by long, heavy lashes. Her lips were full and her hair hung long under her *mantilla*. The bodice of her black cotton dress fit tightly. She was an inch or so shorter than Libby and marginally heavier. Quite pleasing to the eye, Tippett noted.

They sat and began passing platters of food. Piñole sat with the two children at a small table a little ways from the main table. Tippett did not know what to say to Francisca, at least with all the others around. He was not much used to dealing with women who had some civilization. He was used to Painted Wing — a free and carefree Comanche woman — or those who plied their millennia-old trade in saloons and other sordid places.

After dinner, Piñole took the children off and the adults moved into the sitting room. Tippett lit his old clay pipe and puffed contentedly. But he excused himself as quickly as possible and headed for a saloon. He returned in better spirits and was relieved to see that the company had left. He sat and pulled off his moccasins. Libby handed him coffee and asked, "What did you think of Francisca, Papa?"

"Your friend seems nice, Libby."

"She's not exactly my friend, Papa," Libby said in exasperation as she sat. "I was hopin' you'd like her and maybe after a while think about marryin' her. Lord, you men are all alike."

Tippett burst out laughing. "Marry? Ye mean ye expect that purty young thing to come to want to marry an ol' hoss like me? Ye're *loco*, girl. What's she gonna see in this ol' chil'?"

"Plenty. And you're not all that old. Besides, you said you still had some fire left in you."

"That's true," he grinned, sipping coffee.

"Besides, you're a handsome man, well-known, and well-respected. You're doing well in business, have a fine house."

He looked at her, eyes twinkling. "So that's why ye had me bust my ass fixin' this place up? Seems a heap of work for nothin'."

"I doubt that. Despite your lack of manners, she said she liked you. I reckon I'll have her over to sup with us again tomorrow."

"Don't be foolish. She's barely as old as ye."

"Four years older. Besides, Gray Wolf's nearly as old as you. And she's been married before. She needs someone to look out for her."

"She know I got itchy feet?"

"I've told her. If things work out, she'd rather have you home. But she knows that if she marries you, she'll be taken well care of, even if you're gone."

"All right," Tippett sighed, finished his coffee. "Invite her." He looked fiercely at his daughter. "But I ain't promisin' nothin'."

Libby grinned at the mock severity. Tippett could find no good reason why he should not take Francisca — or some other woman — as his wife. She was young, attractive, and probably fertile. He could have another chance at fatherhood, at having someone to carry on his name. He only infrequently felt the weight of his forty-nine years. Still, something held him back, and he was not sure what it was.

If a marriage took place, it would be so cold-blooded, he thought. But his marriage to Painted Wing had been, too, though love had grown. There was no reason to believe it could not happen again. And, he thought, it would be nice to have the comforts of a wife again. He stood, and with a grunted, "Waugh!" he headed off to bed.

He was more comfortable the next evening when Francisca came to dinner. Tippett's tall tales and stories about life in Taos in the old days had the young woman smiling and chatting gaily.

Tippett began squiring Francisca around town, proudly strutting about with the beautiful, intelligent, and caring Francisca de Vallejo Lugo on his arm. And one fall day a year later, he blurted out, "Francisca, would ye consent to be the bride of this ol' chil'?"

"*Si*," she said happily, smiling up at him in the chilly sunlight.

BOOK 14

GRAY WOLF 1862-1874

59

While many of the Comanche bands signed truces with the Texans, as well as the Confederate Army, the *Kwahadis,* not yet pressed by advancing settlements, made no such agreements. Gray Wolf had ridden among the other bands, urging them to abandon the new ways of peace with the *tahbay-boh,* and go to war against their longtime enemies.

"Now is the time," he exhorted. "We should go to war with the *tahbay-boh* while the long-knives fight each other. We have power now!"

But his pleas fell on deaf ears, except among other *Kwahadi* bands who sent warriors to follow him. And even after they had begun their raiding, winning several victories, the others would not join. Rangers attacked several peaceful camps of Comanches simply because they contained Comanches, but yet the *Pehnahterkuhs* and *Kotsotekas* and *Yamparikas* refused to join with Gray Wolf and the *Kwahadis.*

"We have signed papers with the new great father," Gray Wolf was told time and again. "We have promised not to go to war."

"What you have done," Gray Wolf had growled at a *Yamparika* chief, "is give away our land. Land that is not yours to give away."

"The new great father — the *tahbay-boh* call him Davis — has offered us money so we can buy *tahbay-boh* goods. And he's promised to give us supplies so we can learn new ways."

"You have agreed not to be *Nermernuh*!" Gray Wolf screeched.

"The time of the *Nermernuh* is past," a chief named Burnt Shield said sadly. Burnt Shield was very old and had seen much in his life. He had not been a warrior for a long, long time. Instead, he sat in the lodge reserved for the old men where they swapped tales of days past. Since he could no longer have glory, he wanted to have some say in the People's affairs. This was the only way he could do it, he thought.

"It's *not* past!" Gray Wolf roared. He had never experienced such rage, even with the *Tejanos* after their traitorous slaughter in San Antonio more than twenty years ago. "This is the time for us to stand and fight. We can drive the *tahbay-boh* from our land!"

Gray Wolf's band of warriors included a young half-breed named Quanah, who, though a teenager, had already developed a reputation as a mighty warrior. The youth's mother, a white woman named Cynthia Ann Parker, had been taken back by soldiers and Rangers two years ago after a battle in which Quanah's father, Peta Nacona, was killed. Gray Wolf, an old friend of Peta Nacona, a highly respected war chief from another band of *Kwahadis*, decided to take Quanah under his care.

The band of warriors, fiercely holding allegiance to Gray Wolf, cut a wide swath through the Texas countryside, ranging over hundreds of miles. They asked no quarter, and gave none. Without the constraint of Light Calf and the children, he spent the summer on the rampage. He returned to the village for a short time in the fall to hunt enough meat for Blue Eyes and his other children. Then he was gone again, raiding south and east where it was warm all the time, and he did not have to worry about the cold and snow stemming his fury.

Finally, even the mighty Gray Wolf needed rest, so he returned to Blue Eyes and waited out the rest of the winter in the cool confines of his lodge in the *Llano Estacado*. But as soon as the weather warmed again, he called once more for warriors, trying futilely to encourage the eastern bands into joining him. But again, only *Kwahadis* rode out. They went north, and found that their allies — the Cheyennes, Kiowas, and Arapahos — thought like he did. Between their combined forces, they laid siege to the Santa Fe Trail and the north Texas frontier.

With his allies — who recognized his powerful medicine — Gray Wolf rode as far north as the white man's town of Denver, where they raided ranches, farms, and stagecoach relay stations.

Winter drove them southward, and while his northern allies went to their villages to endure the cold months, Gray Wolf led his *Kwahadis* in raids between the Brazos and the Rio Grande. He and his warriors — sometimes only a dozen, at other times close to a hundred — lay waste to whatever fell in their path. They slaughtered several dozen people, and stole thousands of cattle and horses. They kept the horses, but drove the cattle north before winter fully hit and gave them to their allies, who, in turn, sold them to Union soldiers.

His men weary, Gray Wolf at last agreed to ride for home. Once again, he spent a quiet winter in the desolation of the *Llano Estacado*, renewing his energy for the wars that faced him in the spring.

In the spring his other family returned to him. Zeke Tippett had been reluctant to leave Taos, but Libby insisted. She realized she was becoming far too fond of the warm, brown city — and some of its residents, one man in particular. So, she decided she had better get back to her husband. Tippett tried to argue her out of it, but she was adamant. So, with heavy heart, shortly after his first anniversary of his marriage to Francisca, Tippett, Libby, Light Horse, and Far-From-Stone-Village headed east toward *Comancheria*.

They took a wagon, with both boys in the back sitting on the jumbled pile of goods Libby wanted to bring to the People. Tippett had asked his wife to go with him, but she had refused.

"You'll be safe," he told her.

"I know," she said, touching his cheek. "But this is your other family. And you must be with them alone."

He nodded and left.

Gray Wolf restrained his joy, in public, at the return of his family. But inside his lodge, he almost fawned over Libby. And he was surprised at how much his sons had grown. Light Horse spoke passable English and Spanish, along with Comanche; and Far-From-Stone-Village had picked up more than a little of all three languages.

After the greetings were over, Libby went about distributing the goods she and her father had brought.

"How's your war goin', Wolf?" Tippett asked as the two sat in the Comanche's lodge.

"The *tahbay-boh* flee before us."

"I expect you're about half full of buffler shit," Tippett said with a laugh, angering Gray Wolf. The Comanche did not like Tippett making light of his crusade.

"Not all is true," Gray Wolf finally admitted. He shook his head in disgust. "Some *Nermernuh* to the east," he spit, "won't fight. They signed treaties with the soldier chiefs. They cower in their poor lodges, waiting for the *tahbay-boh* chiefs to give them things that never come."

"Ye gettin' no help at all?"

"Yes," he said, head bobbing in acceptance. "The Cheyennes and Kiowas fight with us."

Tippett said his goodbyes the next day and rode out on the wagon. He had a reason to get back to Taos now, and he knew that leaving Libby and his grandsons would get no easier with time.

Within weeks, Gray Wolf was preparing to go to war again. This time, he refused to waste his breath on trying to talk other bands into going. The *Kwahadis* would join the Cheyennes and Kiowas on the raid.

"Take me with you," Light Calf asked him one night before he left.

"No. You must stay here."

"But I could help you."

"A *Nermernuh* warrior needs no woman's help!" Gray Wolf hissed.

"Have you forgotten your vision? The one that brought you to me?"

"Your place is here," he insisted. "Where you'll raise our sons who'll become *Nermernuh* warriors to carry on the fight. That is how you must help!"

She obeyed, as a good Comanche wife should, and Gray Wolf rode out. But Libby was sick with worry, fear, and disgust at not having asserted herself this time.

Gray Wolf returned several months later. He was unscathed, as were his dozen warriors. They danced and shouted in victory. Gray Wolf boasted with the best, but he also made sure he praised Quanah. "You see," Gray Wolf said arrogantly. "No harm came to me."

Light Calf kept her silence, shamed at her worrying.

After the fall hunt, Gray Wolf and his warriors rode headed north. They thought there would be time for a few more raids with the Cheyennes and Kiowas.

Light Calf was sick as she watched her husband ride off. Fear gnawed at her again, but she said nothing. Less than a month later, as she lay asleep in her lodge, she had a powerful dream, one she could not get out of her mind when she awoke.

In the morning, she went to Coyote's lodge. Gray Wolf's mother, Burning Grass, had married Coyote a few years after Kills Twice had been killed by the treacherous Texans in San Antonio. Coyote and Burning Grass, neither of them young, lived well because of the Gray Wolf's largess. The wrinkled great-grandmother sat outside her tipi, her feeble fingers trying to work an awl through leather as she made a moccasin. "Sit, tell me what you've seen in your dreams."

"How did you know I wanted to talk to you about a dream?"

"It's barely past dawn, and you come to see me with lines of trouble on your face, daughter."

"You are wise, Grandmother." She paused. "I was an eagle, flying high, circling, always looking. And on the ground, I saw a gray wolf running very fast. Hard rain fell on him though there were no clouds."

Light Calf reached over and took the leather, needle, sinew, and awl from her old mother-in-law. She began working on it herself as she continued. "For many miles the wolf ran. His tongue hung out as he fought for breath. But still the hard rain fell. Finally, the wolf fell, stumbling, rolling over and over, as the hail fell on him.

"Then all was silent. The world lay still, as in death. Only the weak movements of his head showed that the wolf lived. I swooped closer to the wolf. I could see the blood on his coat." She paused, having to regain her own breath. Her eyes were blurry with tears.

"As I flew lower, circling closer, I could feel my wings grow. And I grew. Until with soft talons, I lifted the wolf and flew away."

"Gray Wolf faces danger. Maybe now. Maybe soon. These things aren't clear. But you will help Gray Wolf. You will carry him to safety."

"But how will I know where to go? What to do?"

"The spirits will make that clear."

Still worried and confused, Light Calf said, "Thank you, Grandmother. Your wisdom is great." But she did not believe it.

The dream returned that night and Libby awoke with her heart thumping in fright. But underlying it was a sudden understanding. Quickly she packed a few things. Then she ran toward the horse herd.

60

Minutes later, Light Calf raced out of the village, four extra horses pulled behind her. She had a satchel of jerky tied to her saddle. Dangling from her back was a small bow and a quiver of arrows. She wore a butcher knife, and a .36-caliber Colt revolver her father had given her, at her waist. Tied behind her saddle were two sleeping robes and a parfleche of pemmican. She realized, half an hour out, that she had no idea where she was going. She knew only that Gray Wolf planned to raid with the Cheyenne and Kiowa, so she rode north, eyes scanning the ground, the horizon, the ground again, looking for any sign that her man had passed by. She ate sparingly and slept little. Her back and buttocks began to ache from the many hours in the saddle, but she persisted.

After nearly a week, she was exhausted. She tied her horses to a wind-twisted mesquite tree that night and after a poor supper, fell into a deep sleep. She slept well past dawn, her worn body trying to reclaim some of its vigor. She awoke with difficulty, as if fighting through a smothering pile of buffalo hides. When fully awake, she heard noises. She strained her ears, trying to place and identify the sound.

"Guns," she muttered. Rifles, pistols, and — she realized with dread — cannon. With no more thought of food, despite her grumbling belly, she hurriedly saddled her horse and raced northward. But even as she thundered along, the sounds of the gunfire dwindled. Soon she encountered small knots of Comanche, Cheyenne, or Kiowa warriors racing away from the battle. Libby felt tears stinging her cheeks as they were whipped away by the wind. Angrily she brushed them aside and kept going, moaning repeatedly, "Too late. Too late."

She blinked, trying to clear her tear-blurred vision. She saw Gray Wolf ahead, his pony racing toward her. But there was something wrong with him. He weaved on the pony's back, and then tumbled.

Behind her husband, five long-knives were coming hard, one several score yards ahead of his companions. That one stopped near Gray Wolf, jamming his horse to a halt in a stirring cloud of dust. The figure walked toward Gray Wolf, pulling out his knife. Light Calf released the rope to the extra ponies and yanked the bow over her head. She snatched an arrow from the quiver. Kicking the horse to greater speed, she nocked the arrow. She saw the blue coat kneel next to Gray Wolf. With a plea to the Great Spirit for accuracy, she pulled back the bow string as far as she could and fired. She followed with another within a heartbeat.

At the same time, more than half a dozen warriors popped up out of a wash and headed off the other soldiers who turned back with the Indians hot on their heels.

Light Calf yipped in victory when she saw the soldier kneeling by Gray Wolf jump with the impact of the two arrows, spinning toward the side. She yanked on the reins and was off the pony before it had stopped. Bow in hand, she warily approached the man she had shot. She kicked the bushy-bearded man in the side, flipping him onto his back. She relaxed a little when she saw he was dead.

Libby turned quickly and knelt, tears springing into her eyes as she looked at Gray Wolf. She placed an ear to his chest and was relieved when she heard his heart.

She had nothing with which to make a travois, so she strained and struggled, finally managing to get Gray Wolf across his pony, which had returned to Gray Wolf, as it had been trained to do. She tied her husband on. She mounted her own pony and rode off beside Gray Wolf's horse, a hand on her man's back. As quickly as she could without jarring Gray Wolf too much, she rode to where she had spent the night.

Easing Gray Wolf off his pony, she dragged him onto a buffalo robe. Wiping sweat off her forehead with the back of her hand, she realized how hungry she was. She quickly chewed down some pemmican — which would fill her fast and remain in her stomach longer. Then she mounted again.

With a momentary twinge of worry that Gray Wolf might be discovered, she rode in search of their other horses and found them grazing nearby. She rounded them up and hurried to her camp. No one had been around and she breathed a sigh of relief. The Army must have followed the main band of Indians, she assumed. But she did not feel safe here and wanted to get Gray Wolf away as soon as she could.

Using a burning glass, she made a small fire of buffalo chips and scraps of branches. From a leather bag, she pulled roots, herbs, and a small, blackened pot. Deftly, despite her speed, she cooked up a poultice and then slathered it heavily on Gray Wolf's wounds. They were many, and Gray Wolf had lost a considerable amount of blood. She reasoned that Gray Wolf had been caught by a blast of grapeshot. Growing more worried, Light Calf bandaged Gray Wolf with strips cut from one of the two cotton dresses she had brought back from Taos.

Light Calf worked without allowing herself to think. If she allowed thoughts to intrude, she would break down with fright over Gray Wolf's condition. In her head, she figured Gray Wolf would not live; but in her heart, she could not accept that.

With Gray Wolf's tomahawk, she whacked off the two longest, straightest branches she could get off the mesquite. She tied one end of each pole together and attached it to one of the ponies. She finished up the rough travois by weaving a buffalo robe tightly around the wider section of the "V" formed by the long sticks. With another major effort, she managed to get Gray Wolf into the travois.

With a last look back toward where the battle had been, she mounted her pony. She could see nothing of the battle site, except a pall of powder smoke and dust. An occasional shot could still be heard, but they were far away. She rode off, holding the rope to Gray Wolf's pony. With relief, she noted that the other ponies followed.

Light Calf got along on catnaps as she stopped every several hours to freshen the poultice on Gray Wolf's wounds. She ate in the saddle, and stopped only long enough for the horses to eat a little, to relieve herself, and to see to Gray Wolf. Her husband moaned frequently during the slow journey, and it left her with mixed emotions. She was pained at causing him hurt; but she was also relieved, for if he was moaning, he was still alive.

Late on the morning of the fourth day after she had found Gray Wolf, Light Calf rode into their village. She saw other Comanches running to help her. It was the last thing she remembered as she tumbled, spent and exhausted, from her horse. She was not aware that Walking Bear caught her as she fell and carried her to her lodge.

Light Calf slept for sixteen hours, but still felt drained when she awoke. She paused only long enough to relieve herself before she sought out her husband. She found him in Coyote Tail's lodge.

"Go away," the old medicine man ordered. "You cannot come here. My powers are weakened when you are near."

"Buffler shit," Libby muttered, knowing Coyote Tail would not understand but thankful she had learned such a useful expression from her father. In Comanche she said, "I'll see Gray Wolf and then leave."

Ignoring further protests from the medicine man, Light Calf knelt at Gray Wolf's side. She was appalled at his condition. He sweated heavily in a delirium of fever. A slimy substance oozed from several of the holes in his chest. An arm and a leg were swollen, and seemed to be a funny color. The wounds carried a tainted odor. In fury she stood and turned on Coyote Tail. In Comanche, she hissed, "If Gray Wolf dies before I get back, I'll kill you."

"You weaken my medicine," Coyote Tail said in annoyance. "Go now."

She stalked to her own tipi. She paused only long enough to bolt down some jerky and a swallow of water, and then pack a few items. "I'll be back soon," she said to Blue Eyes.

She hurried to the herd and culled out several ponies. She saddled one and hung a satchel of food and another with a few personal items from the pommel. With a leap, she was in the saddle and charging out of the village. Again, she rode without sparing herself or the horses. She covered the three hundred-plus miles in four days.

In a copse a few miles from Taos, she stopped long enough to shuck her buckskin dress and don a cotton one after a quick bath in the cold stream. She shivered from the chill. Tossing the greasy, filthy buckskin dress into her sack, she pushed on, praying it would not snow. It was November, and snow was likely in this high country.

She entered town at a gallop and reined to a jarring stop in front of Tippett's house. She ran up the few steps. Without knocking, she tumbled inside. "Papa," she panted as Tippett grabbed her.

He plunked his daughter into a chair as Francisca hurried into the room. "What's wrong, Libby?" Tippett asked, worried.

She tried to speak, but could not because she was panting. With patience born of sitting in Comanche councils, Tippett waited her out. Francisca rushed out and then back with a tumbler of water.

Libby nodded thanks and gulped it down. In bursts, she began explaining. Still struggling, she drank more water, willing herself to calm down. At last she got herself under control, and said, "Gray Wolf's hurt bad, Papa. Took a load of grapeshot, I think. He's feverish and some of the wounds're high smellin'."

"He bein' tended?" Tippett asked, thinking hard.

"Old Coyote Tail's lookin' after him. But you know how he is."

"What do ye want me to do, darlin'?"

"Gray Wolf needs a doctor, Papa. A real doctor. And soon. It's been more'n a week since he was hurt."

Tippett did not want to say this, but he had to. "Listen to me, Libby honey. I expect he's already too far gone for a doctor to help him. If'n we could've got a doc there a day or two after he was hurt, maybe somethin' could've been done. But after all this time..."

Libby sat stunned, staring at her father for some moments. Then she wailed, "You just can't let him die, Papa. He's my husband. And you've been his friend for years."

"Shit," Tippett breathed. He doubted there would be anything he could do, but he had to try, as much for Libby as Wolf. "Francisca," he said urgently, "fill my possibles bag. I'll get Doc O'Mara."

Francisca Vallejo de Lugo Tippett had been married to him only a year and a half, but she was attuned to what kind of man he was. She nodded and rushed off.

"Libby, can ye keep goin' a while? I know you're near used up."

"I can make it."

"*Bueno*. Ye rest a spell. Have Francisca get ye somethin' to eat."

Tippett was back in twenty minutes with Doctor Thomas O'Mara. Moments later, a teenage Mexican boy popped in through the back door. "Your horses are ready, *Señor*" he said.

Tippett nodded. He handed the youth a coin. He kissed his wife. "I ain't sure how long I'll be gone, darlin'," he said. "Ye need anything, see Ben. I worry about ye." He patted the firm roundness of her pregnant belly. "Come on, Doc, Libby." He headed out back.

61

"I cannot go another inch without sleep, Mister Tippett," O'Mara said three days later. O'Mara was young, short, and plump with a crown of frizzy hair and pink cheeks covered with soft fuzz. He had taken over after Doctor Bomus had died half a dozen years ago.

"Keep ridin', Doc," Tippett said grimly. "Sleep in the saddle, if ye need to." It was bitter cold, but they had not had any snow.

"But I can't go on," O'Mara whined. "I am exhausted."

"Libby ain't had more'n a few hours sleep in a week. Ride."

O'Mara sighed. Never had he been so put upon as this. "Just where is this fellow anyway? You never said. And there's nothing out here." He waved his arm around, showing off the desolation. Now that they were out of the mountains, there was little scenery.

Tippett grinned just a little. "He's a Comanche, Doc."

O'Mara reined in and turned to face Tippett, who also stopped. "If you think I'm going to ride into a village full of savages to treat one of their number, Mister Tippett, you are sadly, sadly mistaken. Not after all the horrors those fiends have committed." He set his jaw. "I will go no farther."

Tippett's smile dropped and the Hawken leveled at the physician. "Then this'll be where ye're buried."

O'Mara's eyes widened. "You would not shoot me..."

Tippett thumbed back the hammer. "Time's short. Make your choice."

"Lower your weapon, Mister Tippett." When Tippett had uncocked the Hawken and set it across his saddle, O'Mara wiped perspiration brought by fear from his face. He clucked to his horse and moved forward. O'Mara gave Tippett no more trouble on the ride, and found that he could be somewhat refreshed by frequent naps in the saddle. But he was still gray with fatigue when the three people rode into the Comanche village the next day.

The physician was quite conscious of the hostile, dark glares that followed him. He gulped, trying hard not to show the fear that wriggled relentlessly into his bowels. His bladder twitched and his colon clenched with it. He had never been so close to Indians before — except the ragged, weary, ground-down residents of the Taos pueblo. Those people were not frightening, living in such poverty and dejection. But these Comanches were an entirely different proposition.

The Comanches were fierce-looking, arrogant, and prideful. They might be small of stature, but they stood arrow straight, and their piercing eyes made O'Mara decidedly uncomfortable. Thoughts of stories he had heard about these Indians — and the entertainments they preferred — made him shake with terror. Even as bone tired as he was, he felt alert, expecting to be seized at any moment.

Tippett, Libby, and O'Mara rode straight to Coyote Tail's tipi. Without announcing their presence, Tippett entered the lodge, followed by a petrified O'Mara, and then Libby.

Tippett pointed, and in the dimness of the lodge's interior O'Mara saw a still form. Over the alien smells of the Indian lodge, he noted the familiar odor of festering wounds. Worriedly ignoring Coyote Tail's malevolent stare, O'Mara knelt at Gray Wolf's side.

Coyote Tail moved toward the physician, but Tippett stepped in front of the medicine man, warning him, "Jist let him be, *amigo*."

The doctor sighed in relief and flipped the blanket off Gray Wolf. "Please hold some light over here so I can see," he ordered.

Libby grabbed a burning branch from the fire and knelt at her husband's side opposite O'Mara.

"Much better," O'Mara said. "Thank you, ma'am." For several minutes he mumbled to himself as he looked, probed, prodded, and touched. Finally, he stood, as if his knees gave him pain. "This man is in an awful way," he said softly. "I'm surprised he's alive."

"Can you do anything for him, Doctor?" Libby asked, her face etched in pain and tiredness.

"I doubt it, ma'am," O'Mara said sadly. "It's been too long." He sighed. "Those wounds are festered badly. He's got poison running all through him. The arm and leg are the worst. About all I can do is amputate them and hope he'll pull through."

"No," Libby said simply, though there was no doubt she meant it.

"It's the only way, ma'am." O'Mara's shoulders slumped wearily.

"No. Either fix him up whole or let him die," Libby said firmly, though her lower lip quivered. Her eyes were haunted with the painful decision, as well as exhaustion. "He'd as soon be dead as try'n live as a cripple. I..." she sucked in breath, "feel the same."

"But, ma'am..."

"No, Doctor," Libby said, regaining her resolve. "You know nothing of us. Without an arm and a leg, he'd be useless. Comanches who're maimed like that don't live long — often by choice. A warrior who can't make war, protect his family, or hunt is no good. He'd soon go off to die." Tears flowed down her cheeks, dripping off the corners of her chin.

"And you'd accept that?" O'Mara asked, not really surprised. He thought he could understand such thinking.

"It's the way of the People, Doctor," she said proudly. "I'd miss him, and hurt with the loss, but it's the way things're done here."

"You accept this, too, I suppose, Mister Tippett?"

Tippett talked over his shoulder, glaring at Coyote Tail. "Yep. If that was me layin' there, I'd want the same."

"Well," O'Mara said with a heavy sigh, "I don't know as it'll do any good. But I reckon I can try some things. And, if he dies then, well, we will have at least tried."

"A body can't ask no more'n that, Doc."

"So be it, then," O'Mara said. Some animation returned to his face, which had been gray with exhaustion. "Have you some water?"

Libby nodded and got a buffalo bladder used as a canteen.

O'Mara held out his hands, away from Gray Wolf. "Pour the water over my hands, please, ma'am." Libby did so slowly, as O'Mara scrubbed off what trail dust and such that he could. Then he nodded. The water stopped and he shook off the excess.

"Just keep that light on over here where I can see, ma'am," O'Mara said. He knelt at Gray Wolf's side again, pulling his bag toward him. He cut into the unconscious Comanche's chest. O'Mara stuck his fingers into the hole and probed.

He smiled when he touched the object he sought. He put a long, slim scissored instrument into the bloody hole. A moment later, he rocked onto his heels, holding up the piece of shot for all to see. He went through the procedure twice more in the chest, and then on the wounded arm and leg.

While the wounds drained out their foul-smelling pus, he wiped his hands on a cloth and then made up a poultice with powders taken from vials in his bag and mixed with water. He layered the concoction on each wound and then bandaged them. He stood, brushing sweat from his brow. It was hot and close in the lodge. Tiredness swept over him again. "That's about all I can do," he said wearily. "Now we must wait — and hope he's strong enough..."

"Ye need us to do anything, Doc?" Tippett asked, glancing back.

O'Mara pointed to Coyote Tail. "Just keep that heathen away from my patient." He sounded mighty possessive.

Tippett nodded. "Ye'n Libby go get some sleep. I'll watch Wolf."

O'Mara nodded. "Wake me if there is any change in him." Suddenly he froze, as a flash flood of fear washed over him.

"What's wrong, Doc?" Tippett asked, concerned.

"I... I..." How could he tell these two that he was so scared he thought he would urinate in his pants because he just remembered he was in a Comanche village? Where would he sleep? Would he be safe?

Libby grinned wanly. "He's scared, Papa," she said. "You'll stay in my lodge, Doctor. You'll be safe there. No one'll bother you."

O'Mara's relief was as great a flood as his fear had been. He nodded, and said in a squeaky voice, "Thank you, ma'am."

O'Mara meekly followed Libby out of the lodge. Tippett sat cross-legged next to Gray Wolf. "Either make yourself comfortable, Coyote Tail," he said, "or get the hell out."

With a face hard as stone, Coyote Tail sat, glaring.

Fourteen hours later, Coyote Tail was asleep, but Tippett was still alert as Libby and O'Mara entered the tipi. "Any change?" O'Mara asked. He was refreshed and his pudgy face freshly shaved.

"None that I can see."

O'Mara knelt over Gray Wolf while Libby held a torch for him. "His color's a little better," O'Mara said in some amazement. "At least I think it is. It's hard for me to tell on someone so dark of skin. No offense, ma'am," he added, glancing nervously at Libby.

"I understand, Doctor."

"He is breathing some easier," O'Mara said. He freshened the poultices and changed the bandages. He stood, amazed. "He seems improved, Mister Tippett. Go and get some sleep. You must be worn out."

"I expect I could do with some shut-eye, Doc. I ain't quite as spry as I used to be, ye know. Ye'll be all right here?"

"I believe so. Miss Libby has taken good care of me. She can get anything I might require, and I believe the two of us can keep that charlatan away from Gray Wolf. If he wakes up. Go on."

For more than two weeks they took turns sleeping and tending to Gray Wolf. O'Mara fluctuated between joyful hope and dull frustration. He worried and fretted. But he found that his services were in demand. People came to him with all sorts of complaints, though Gray Wolf still was not well. After all, Gray Wolf had been ill a long time and had been expected to die. The doctor had kept him alive — and whole — so far. That was enough for the others. O'Mara was well-liked by the village's children and he returned that affection. He was appalled at the living conditions here, and he was surprised the People were as healthy as they were. Most of his treatments were for things brought on by the hazards of a hard life.

Sixteen days after the three rode into the Comanche camp, Gray Wolf awoke, startling them. They were sitting at the fire. That all three were there at the same time was unusual these days. They spun almost as one and stared in disbelief. They rushed to Gray Wolf who was too weak to move. His eyes were open and he tried to speak.

"Not now, my friend," O'Mara said quietly, beginning to check Gray Wolf over. "Later you may speak. Rest."

Gray Wolf answered with a barely perceptible nod and closed his eyes, wondering who this strange *tahbay-boh* was.

Within a week, Gray Wolf sat with help and ate some broth with flakes of meat. The day after, O'Mara went to Tippett and said, "I've done all I can for Gray Wolf, Mister Tippett. The rest is up to him, but I don't think we have cause to worry. He is a remarkable specimen."

"Ye hintin' we should be on our way?" Tippett asked, grinning.

62

Under Light Calf's ministrations, Gray Wolf began recuperating. It was months before he recovered from the severity of the wounds, and was the next summer before he went on the warpath again. When he did, it was as a follower. He would have to prove himself all over again before the others would accept him as a war leader.

The first foray into Texas was with a band of *Kwahadis* led by Walking Bear. The older warrior was beginning to show the ravages of his fifty-five winters — there was gray in his hair, and wrinkles sat on his face like gullies rippling the *Llano Estacado*. Despite his advancing age, he was an able war leader, though unimaginative. Gray Wolf followed him with a fierce loyalty.

The riding, raiding, and plundering tired Gray Wolf more than he thought possible. Though he would never admit it, he was glad when the warriors turned their ponies toward home after almost a full summer of raiding. He rode into the village with head high and his back straight. But when he was in the peace and darkness of his lodge, he slumped against a willow backrest, releasing a huge sigh of relief.

"You all right?" Light Calf asked, concern creasing her brow.

"I'm tired. I've spent too many days on the war trail."

"Are you hungry?"

"No." He stood laboriously and headed for the robes. "I will eat after I sleep," he muttered. As he bent to lie down, he lost his balance and toppled. He mumbled incoherently and fell asleep. He awoke in a bitter, foul mood. He kicked and yelled and screeched, frightening Blue Eyes and angering Light Calf.

Gray Wolf sneered at Blue Eyes, who had aged some and was no longer quite so pleasing. He looked at Libby and growled, "Come to my robes. Then make me food."

"No," Light Calf said simply. "I'll make you food. I won't come to your robes." She was enraged. *How dare he ask such a thing in such a way*! she thought. Gray Wolf knew quite well that Light Calf was not in favor of performing in the marriage bed before an audience, though she was more than lusty enough when they were alone.

"Come to my robes, now," Gray Wolf roared.

"No," Light Calf replied again before walking out of the lodge, leaving Gray Wolf in the middle of his outburst.

Gray Wolf chased her. Grabbing her by the arm, he swung her around. "Come with me to the robes," he ordered angrily.

"I'll do no such thing," Light Calf said calmly. "Now let me go before I knock you down."

His anger multiplied and he threw back his arm to hit her. With a quick move, she stepped to the side and grabbed the hand. Using her not inconsiderable strength, she spun and jerked on the arm, then let it go. She walked off as the still-weak Gray Wolf hit the ground.

Gray Wolf's fury flamed as he stood, brushing off dirt and grass. He stared malevolently at Light Calf's departing back, as most of the people of the village laughed. Seething, Gray Wolf stalked back to his lodge, where he waited, silently and with his face carved in stone.

It was many hours before Light Calf returned. "Are you hungry?" she asked, as if nothing had happened.

Without a word, he stood and grabbed a hard, leather quirt. He advanced toward her. She pulled out her well-used butcher knife, wishing she wore her Colt revolver regularly — it would have been a more potent deterrent. They faced each other across the fire.

"Put that knife down, woman," Gray Wolf ordered.

"When you drop the quirt."

"I'll beat you until you beg for death," Gray Wolf spit, enraged. "It's my right."

"And why is it your right?" she asked sarcastically.

"I'm a *Nermernuh* warrior. You are less than one of my ponies."

"You didn't think such a thing when I killed that blue coat who was about to kill you and take your scalp, leaving you to wander in the emptiness. You didn't think such a thing when I worked to bring you here. And you didn't think it when I rode to Taos without sleep to get the *tahbay-boh* doctor who cured you."

"That time's passed," he said, unconcerned at her sacrifices. "There is no place for a disrespectful woman in my lodge."

"Then I'll leave," Libby said. "That is *my* right. It's been easy for you with me as your wife. You gave no horses to my father, you made no promises of meat to him, and you won't attend to his needs when he grows old and weary."

"That doesn't matter," Gray Wolf insisted. "You are disrespectful. You have made Gray Wolf look like a fool in front of his people."

"Then you shouldn't have acted like a fool. I won't be treated like one of your horses — worse. You know that."

"I want your body now, woman," Gray Wolf snapped, managing to keep the urgency out of his voice.

"And I'm willing to give it. But not when ordered, and not in front of her." Light Calf pointed to Blue Eyes. "You know that."

With a sneer, Gray Wolf tossed down the quirt. He walked

toward Blue Eyes. Libby, watching warily, slid the knife into the sheath.

As he walked, Gray Wolf shoved aside his breechcloth. He stroked himself several times. Stopping in front of Blue Eyes, he presented himself in front of her. Without expression, Blue Eyes encircled him with her lips. In moments, Gray Wolf pulled free. He stepped behind Blue Eyes and pushed her upper back. She bent forward, resting on her hands and knees. Gray Wolf threw her buckskin dress up and knelt behind her. With a sneer over Blue Eyes' back at Light Calf, who still stood, Gray Wolf roughly punched his hardness into Blue Eyes, who winced. She looked at Light Calf, her eyes liquid with humiliation, then cast her eyes down as Gray Wolf rammed into her repeatedly.

Light Calf stalked out of the lodge. She was gone only long enough to round up Far-From-Stone-Village, barely six, and Light Horse, seven-and-a-half. When she returned, Blue Eyes was sobbing quietly as she worked in back of the tipi.

Gray Wolf sat at the fire, as if waiting for food. When Light Calf entered, Gray Wolf said, "There you are. You will make food now."

"Buffler shit." She pulled out several hard-leather parfleches.

"What're you doing?" Gray Wolf asked, curious.

"Leaving," Light Calf said over her shoulder, not looking at him. "If I'm not wanted in the lodge of the great Gray Wolf, I'll find another lodge — here or elsewhere — where I will be welcome."

"No one else here will have you," Gray Wolf sneered. "They are afraid of Gray Wolf.

"Ah, and so that's why they laughed at the great Gray Wolf after his woman threw him on his ass."

Gray Wolf's eyes bulged. But he retained enough sense to know that Light Calf — despite her slim appearance and unlined face — could best him again, since he was yet weak. So, he said nothing.

It did not take long for Light Calf to finish packing her meager belongings in the hard leather boxes. She stood and said scornfully,

"I'm taking five of the great Gray Wolf's ponies. One for me, one for Light Horse, one for Far-From-Stone-Village, and two for my things."

"You will take none of my horses!" Gray Wolf thundered, standing and turning to face her.

"You may come to Taos for them in a moon," Light Calf said calmly.

He could not argue with her borrowing the horses. And, though he did not show it, he was heartsick at the thought of her leaving him. He had thought until now that she was just bluffing, trying to get him to apologize. But he could not — or would not — do that. And now it seemed that she was really going to leave him. He cursed himself silently. Light Calf was an excellent wife. But he was certain an apology — even if he could make one — would be too late now anyway.

He decided to let her have her way. He would ride to Taos in a month — to see his friend White Horse. And to pick up his horses. Perhaps he would also drag Light Calf home with him. Then all would be well, he told himself.

"You may take the horses," he agreed. "I'll come for them later."

Light Calf stalked out, followed by her sons, neither of whom knew what was going on, though they were certain it was not good. Still, both were *Nermernuh*, and they knew better than to cry or make a scene. Instead, they followed their mother and helped her as she saddled her pony and loaded two with parfleches. Less than an hour after her altercation with Gray Wolf in front of the village, Libby rode out, torn inside. Her rage at the treatment she received from Gray Wolf kept her fear and sadness in check. She did not see Gray Wolf and three other Comanche warriors who followed.

Gray Wolf, who loved Light Calf in his own way, felt her loss immediately. Once she had walked out of the lodge and seemed gone to him forever, he began to miss her — and to worry about her. She was armed with her bow, quiver, Colt, and an old percussion rifle her father had given her. She knew how to use them. But she was not a warrior, Gray Wolf told himself. There was no doubting her bravery, or her heart. But she had no skills honed from years of training.

Ten minutes after she had left, Gray Wolf rounded up Walking Bear, Buffalo Droppings, and Hits-With-A-Fist. They grabbed weapons and ponies and set out after Light Calf.

"We will drag them back?" Buffalo Droppings asked eagerly in his foolishness. Buffalo Droppings had had six wives in his life, none for very long. His ideas on women were dreadful, even for such a people as the Comanches, so none was willing to stay with him very long.

"No," Gray Wolf ordered. "They will not even know we are here."

"Then what're we doing?" Buffalo Droppings asked, peeved.

"Watching so that they are not attacked by Apaches or Utes — or *tahbay-boh*. When they're safe in the pale-faces' town, we'll leave."

Buffalo Droppings was not happy with such a thing, but he knew better than to argue with Gray Wolf and Walking Bear.

When they reached Taos, Gray Wolf said to the others, "Go now."

"And you?" Walking Bear asked.

"I'll stay. Light Calf told me to get my ponies one moon after she left. I'll wait here until then." He still hoped to bring her back to the *Llano*, but he would not admit that to the others.

"I'll stay with you," Walking Bear said. He suspected something of the sort, and decided to stay half because he wanted his friend to have someone to commiserate with; and to play a joke on his friend — making Gray Wolf uncomfortable that he would have an observer.

"Go," Gray Wolf growled.

"I will stay," Walking Bear insisted.

Buffalo Droppings and Hits-With-A-Fist needed no further

encouragement. They trotted off, leaving Walking Bear and Gray Wolf to argue.

But Gray Wolf could not argue with his friend. And he knew that no matter what he said, Walking Bear would not budge. Gray Wolf suspected Walking Bear wanted to hang around to see what would happen.

Two-and-a-half weeks later, leaving Walking Bear on the outskirts of the town, Gray Wolf slipped through Tippett's courtyard and up to the back door. Tippett greeted the Comanche and let him in, then offered him coffee.

"Your ponies are in the stable," Light Calf said.

"Come home," Gray Wolf asked, swallowing his pride.

"No."

Gray Wolf, angry again, gulped down his molasses-thickened coffee. He stormed out of the house, got his ponies, and rode off.

63

It was a long, bitter winter for Gray Wolf, relieved only by the taking of another wife — Yellow Bonnet. With the spring, though, he sought a vision that would bequeath him with great power once again.

The vision was disturbing. The woman reappeared. She and the gray wolf walked together, the woman's hand stroking the wolf's fur. Even when the wolf went off to hunt, an almost visible line connected them so they were never apart. Blue coats came in greater numbers than Gray Wolf had ever seen before. Yet all fell by the wayside, moving around the wolf and the woman as if the two were invisible.

Gray Wolf knew what the vision meant, but he told no one. He only told the others that he had seen a vision and it was powerful, making his medicine strong. He led the war party from his village this year, and would not accept subservience to the war leader of any other band. His son Buffalo Horn, an arrogant warrior of twenty one years, accompanied him. Gray Wolf had encouraged Quanah to join them, but the young warrior stayed to follow his band's war chiefs.

Life on the war trail was hard, since blue coats swarmed all over. Gray Wolf's band made a number of successful strikes. After each, they rode madly to put distance between themselves and possible pursuit. But this year they could not get away. It seemed that wherever they turned, they ran into a troop of long-knives or Texas Rangers.

After a month, something bothered Gray Wolf, but he was not sure what. He had an unsettling sensation that all was not well in the village. He spoke of it with Walking Bear.

Walking Bear stared at Gray Wolf a few moments before asking, "What was your vision?"

Gray Wolf told it quickly and without flourishes. Then Walking Bear said firmly, "We must go home, my friend."

Gray Wolf nodded. With the morning sun, he and his men rode hard for the *Llano Estacado*. They could see the coils of greasy smoke long before they arrived. But they learned that the Army troop that had attacked the village was small, and the warriors who had stayed behind — abetted by a war party of other *Kwahadis* — had managed to drive the blue coats off.

But not before several *Nermernuh* died. Yellow Bonnet had been killed, as had two of Walking Bear's grandchildren and one son; Buffalo Droppings' latest wife; White Star; and old Coyote Tail. Several lodges had been burned, and meat and other possessions destroyed.

Gray Wolf was enraged. The blue coats had never struck so deep in the *Llano*. Gray Wolf worried that all he held dear would no longer be safe. He painted his face again and called for warriors. Not many were willing to heed his call, and finally Walking Bear took Gray Wolf aside. "They are frightened," Walking Bear said.

"We are *Nermernuh*! We are frightened of nothing!"

"All men are afraid of what they don't know. We've always been safe here. Other bands — *Pehnahterkuhs* and *Yampahrikahs* — took the brunt of the *tahbay-boh* force. Now that the *tahbay-boh* have struck our homeland, many fear that all they've known will be taken."

"Then we must fight for what's ours." To Gray Wolf it was simple.

"The time is not right," Walking Bear said.

"Then I'll fight alone," Gray Wolf boasted.

"You'd be wiser to remember your vision," Walking Bear said. "It might be better against the *tahbay-boh* than your arrows and bullets."

"You think I should go to Taos and bring back Light Calf?" he asked, shuddering.

Walking Bear shrugged. He could only advise; Gray Wolf must decide.

"No," Gray Wolf said, mostly to himself.

Walking Bear shrugged again, and said softly, "The People matter more than pride, Gray Wolf."

Gray Wolf knew Walking Bear was right, but he found it hard to swallow. He stewed over it for three days before slipping out of the village in the dark. He rode hard, quirting a pony until it faltered, and then slipping onto another. Just after dawn on the third day, he crept across Tippett's courtyard and rapped lightly at the door.

Libby opened the door, saw who it was, and started to slam it shut.

"Wait!" Gray Wolf pleaded, slamming a palm against the wood. "Light Calf, wait! I have much to say to you."

Libby gazed at her Comanche husband. He was short, dark, and fierce looking. He was forty-six years old and beginning to show signs of his harsh existence. Gray mixed with his black hair, and wrinkles creased his face. Libby thought for a minute that he had aged several years in the one she had been away. She opened the door and stepped back to allow him to enter. She led him toward the sitting room, saying as she entered it, "Papa, look who's here."

"Wolf," Tippett nodded. He was pleased to see his old friend but was not sure it boded well. "Pull up a seat."

Gray Wolf sat in the middle of the floor, gazing up at Libby who stood looking down on him. "My words must be said to you, Light Calf," Gray Wolf said in Comanche. "Sit...please." It felt strange for him to say such a thing to his wife.

It was strange for Libby to hear it, and after a moment's surprise, she sat on the floor, facing him. Her simple, blue-cotton, white-woman's dress pooled out around her on the hardwood floor.

"Things have gone poorly for the People since you left," Gray Wolf said, gazing steadily at Libby.

Gray Wolf stopped to think of the right way to express himself. "Your presence is important to the *Nermernuh,*" he finally said. "Your medicine is strong for us." He faltered, embarrassed.

"I'm important to the *Nermernuh*?" Libby questioned haughtily. "Or is it that my medicine is strong for Gray Wolf? Is it that the great Gray Wolf's manhood is shriveled and small because Light Calf isn't sharing his robes?" she went on mercilessly, drawing a nervous chuckle from her father. Francisca, who did not understand the Comanche language, watched, wondering what was going on. It was evident by the expressions the participants wore that it was not good.

"I took another," Gray Wolf said. "She carried my child."

"Carried?" Libby asked, worried and suddenly concerned.

"They've gone to the Great Spirit." He did not seem sad, but Libby knew appearances could be deceiving. Gray Wolf explained.

"So, you think my returning will make the power of the People strong again?" Libby asked, nervously.

"Yes," Gray Wolf hissed, hating having to do this. He explained his vision in the barest terms.

Libby grinned, knowing she had the upper hand. "You want me to return?" When he nodded, she asked, as if twisting a dagger in a wound, "Do you also want me to be your wife once more?"

"Yes."

"I can't," she said simply, harshly. After the humiliation she had suffered at his hands, she wanted him to squirm.

His eyes popped wide in surprise, then narrowed in anger. "Why?"

"I'm the mother of your children. I won't be treated with the disrespect you've shown me."

He stared at her, torn between malevolence, anger, and worry. He tried to apologize, without making himself out to be wrong.

Libby sat silently, eyes on his face, not giving him any sign that she even heard what he was saying — or trying to say. He stumbled to a halt, and Light Calf then asked, "Were you wrong?"

"Yes."

"And you *want* me back?"

"Yes." It was said dully.

"You'll treat me with respect?" she asked, an edge to her voice.

"Yes," Gray Wolf said flatly.

"Then I'll come back with you," Libby said simply, surprising Tippett. The old mountain man had thought she would never go back. She had, in the past year, been making a pleasant life for herself in Taos. She had several suitors, including a shy Ben Winter. He guessed he did not know his daughter as well as he should.

Gray Wolf smiled, relieved. "It is good," he said. "But you must be punished for what you've done. Punished before the People."

"Why?"

"Because I am a warrior of the *Nermernuh*. And the People have seen me shamed in their midst."

"Are you so weak a warrior," Libby asked icily, "that you can't face them? Aren't the many honors you've earned enough for them? Or you?" She heated up. "You're the greatest warrior the People've ever seen. Your horses are so many they can't be counted. You've taken so many scalps our lodge poles would creak with their weight. Who among the People can say these things? None but Gray Wolf."

The warrior's chest swelled with pride. "You speak many truths for a woman." He thought for some moments, nodding his head. "I will not punish you," he said graciously. "But a woman should have more respect for her man — especially one so great as Gray Wolf."

"It's true," Light Calf said, nodding seriously. "I'll try to be more respectful. But," she added, surprising Gray Wolf a little, "a warrior as great as Gray Wolf should have more respect for his woman."

Without pause, he said, "A woman like Light Calf is to be cherished by the *Nermernuh*. And by me. You've done many good things for Gray Wolf and the People. I'll honor you."

It was Libby's turn to be shocked.

64

Despite Light Calf's return, no one would follow Gray Wolf again that summer. So Gray Wolf and Walking Bear went alone, just two old friends, warriors hoping to die by their code.

They returned after the fall hunt and had to hunt for their families. But they returned in glory, with a dozen scalps between them, as well as fifty horses and other plunder. They gave away the booty, calling those who had stayed behind cowards.

During the winter, Gray Wolf and Walking Bear discussed — as they had on the war trail — what Tippett had told Gray Wolf when he went to bring Light Calf back to her people: "Ye seen so many long-knives lately 'cause the blue coats and gray coats've made peace."

"When?" Gray Wolf had asked, surprised.

"We got word last winter." Gray Wolf looked concerned, and Tippett added, "And they'll be sendin' more blue coats soon."

Gray Wolf also spent much of the winter in renewing his matrimonial prerogatives — and responsibilities — with Light Calf. She, in turn, made it known that she would no longer tolerate Blue Eyes as another wife. She would allow the woman to live in the lodge and take care of the children and do more than her share of the work. But she would not accept Gray Wolf's taking Blue Eyes to the robes.

Gray Wolf agreed, though outside the lodge pretenses would be kept up. Blue Eyes was not consulted. Light Calf felt a little bad about treating Blue Eyes such, but she had spent enough time with the *tahbay-boh* now that such doings went against her grain.

In the spring, Light Calf and Blue Eyes were kept busy with the meat and hides Gray Wolf brought in. One morning soon after, Light Calf awoke lazily, feeling good about life. With a glow of warmth inside her, she patted her growing belly — and the new child within.

She realized Gray Wolf was not in their robes. She searched the village, but to no avail. She put it from her mind and bent to her work, trying not to worry. He returned four days later, drawn and haggard. He dismounted and walked with rubbery legs into the lodge. Light Calf jerked her head, and Blue Eyes rushed outside to care for Gray Wolf's horse. Light Calf fed her husband, spooning broth into his eager mouth. She knew he had gone to seek a vision and was exhausted.

After eating, Gray Wolf slept. In the morning he told Light Calf of his vision — and the power it would bring the *Nermernuh*. He took one more day to regain his strength, and then called for warriors.

He got a more favorable response than he had last summer, but not nearly as good as in the old days. Many warriors still worried that the long-knives would attack the village again. The war band — nearly thirty members strong, bolstered by men from other *Kwahadi* bands — headed out with a sense of renewed belief in their power. This would be the year they would finally drive the white men from their land. Gray Wolf's vision had told them the People would be impervious to *tahbay-boh* bullets. They could not be defeated.

Their raids were victorious, but the whites remained. Despite their relentlessness, their war parties in the next four years did not drive the whites away. Gray Wolf's medicine held for those four years, when suddenly it seemed to leave them.

Gray Wolf ranted and raved against the spirits, until he realized his son — Buffalo Horn, born of Red Moon twenty-five years ago — had violated one of the taboos of Gray Wolf's vision. Only Walking Bear's intervention prevented Gray Wolf from killing Buffalo Horn.

A few days later they were attacked by another Army patrol. They fought their way free and fled, shocked at their ill fates, heading hard for the *Llano*. But as they neared their northwestern homeland, Gray Wolf reined in his horse. "I will not flee," he said, anger surging in his veins. "Who'll face the long-knives with me?"

Nearly half the men agreed, and they turned southeast while the others headed for home. The warriors attacked a small wagon train and a straggling band of settlers who were away from their settlement, cutting wood in a river bottom. A few days later they swung down off a ridge toward a farmhouse. The Comanches could see the men running the few steps to their rifles. A withering fire raked the Comanche horde, but no one was harmed. The men in the field raced for the safety of the log house. Of the four, only one did not make it. He fell and rolled under the impact of half a dozen arrows and several bullets.

As the Comanches thundered through the freshly planted crops to circle the house, more gunfire erupted from inside. One Comanche fell, but he was up in an instant, blood on his left arm. The Comanches presented no real targets for the men in the house, but they had no targets either. Then the warriors heard firing from another direction. In consternation, they looked around. An Army patrol, firing rapidly, was racing down the slope of the ridge.

Almost as one, the Comanches swung off and raced west. But some of the warriors were not as agile or strong as they once had been, and two went down. Gray Wolf, looking back over his shoulder, saw Walking Bear slipping from his horse, a red stain spreading across his back.

Gray Wolf rammed his horse to a stop and turned. He raced back, firing his pistol. Buffalo Horn and Hits-With-A-Fist were right behind Gray Wolf. Buffalo Horn grabbed the reins to Walking Bear's horse.

Gray Wolf holstered his pistol as he stopped. He grabbed Walking Bear and lifted him onto the horse, then leaped onto his own pony. With Gray Wolf bracing Walking Bear on one side and Hits-With-A-Fist the other, they galloped away. Buffalo Horn covered them.

The Comanches widened the distance between themselves and the soldiers. A few miles away they stopped in the open. Gray Wolf posted guards to watch the horses and ensure they would not be attacked.

Gray Wolf knelt next to Walking Bear and cradled his head. He could see death in Walking Bear's eyes. "Soon we will be back in our village, and Sings A Lot will tend to you," Gray Wolf said.

"You lie," Walking Bear wheezed. "My eyes grow dim, but I still see more clearly than you. My time left on Mother Earth grows short."

"Do not say these things."

Walking Bear coughed and grimaced as pain coursed through his lungs. "I have seen too many winters," he gasped. He almost smiled. "Now I no longer fear the coming of more winters, as my teeth fall out and my legs grow too feeble to carry me. I have seen the old ones waste away. Now I won't have that shame."

He wheezed, and Gray Wolf thought Walking Bear had expired. But then Walking Bear's eyes opened and he said weakly, "I wish to die fighting, though. Not shot in the back while I flee the long-knives."

One of the guards yelled that the soldiers were coming.

"Help me stand," Walking Bear pleaded, fire in his eye. "Then leave me. I'll die well." His grin turned into a pain-racked grimace.

Gray Wolf helped him up and Walking Bear gasped. "Now I'll die as a warrior should." He choked and spit up blood. "Now, go."

Gray Wolf rallied his men and they grabbed their horses and roared off. Atop a short, almost flat ridge, Gray Wolf stopped and looked back. Walking Bear stood alone, firing his pistol. The other warriors drifted up alongside Gray Wolf.

As Gray Wolf watched, he could see Walking Bear take three more bullets, staggering back a step or two at each. But he brought down two soldiers. He fell when a fourth bullet punched into him.

The troops whooped, and several rushed forward, guns held haphazardly in one hand, knives held tightly in the other.

"No!" Gray Wolf screamed. The single word — in Comanche — lengthened and built on itself, developing and growing, until it seemed to take on a life all its own. By the time the last faint echoes of it had died away, Gray Wolf was halfway down the hill, quirting his pony as hard as he could. The other warriors hesitated only moments before charging after him, heedless of leaving the stolen horses unguarded. But Gray Wolf and the others would not let Walking Bear suffer the indignities these soldiers planned.

The Comanches were almost berserk in their fury as they charged the patrol. The soldiers who had rushed forward were slaughtered in moments; their companions fled with enraged Comanches at their heels. In minutes it was over, and the warriors gathered around Walking Bear's body. A few rounded up the stolen horses and Army horses.

Gray Wolf knelt over Walking Bear, whose chest and the ground around him were awash with blood. But his face was serene. Gray Wolf pulled his knife. His eyes hard, he hacked his long hair off raggedly at the shoulders. He let the locks fall beside his old friend.

Several days later, a sullen, bitter Gray Wolf rode into his village, bearing the body of his friend. While he knew it had been Walking Bear's wish — as it was his own — to die as he had, Gray Wolf was angry that it had happened while he was the leader of the war band. Once more he would have to prove himself. Less than a week later, he rode out — alone. Proudly and arrogantly he traversed the land. He carried no supplies other than his weapons and three extra horses. He rode unafraid into the deepest reaches of the settled Texas countryside, daring the *tahbay-boh* to attack him.

He was like a vengeful wraith, raiding a farmhouse here, a ranch there, a wagon train a hundred miles away. He stole horses until he could barely control them. With fresh scalps dangling from his lance and rifle, pushing more than fifty horses before him, he rode back into the village. Still, the maniacal Gray Wolf was not satisfied. A few days later, he rode off again, to be gone another month.

He entered his lodge and sat heavily, exhausted, but too proud to show it to any but his wife. "Food," he ordered.

"There's little," Light Calf said, annoyed. As a woman of the People, she knew his almost continuous warfare was accepted. But it would all be for naught, she feared.

"So?" he said, unconcerned. "I will take what there is."

"Will you seek meat now, before the winter comes?"

"I have no time for such things. I'm at war."

"And so, you'll leave your sons — and your unborn child — to die?" Light Calf demanded.

Gray Wolf shrugged.

"Leave the killing of the *tahbay-boh* to younger men," Light Calf said. She was almost ordering.

"Not to make war is not to live," Gray Wolf growled. "I have not yet seen fifty winters. I have many more ahead."

"The enemy are too many for you alone."

"They are not," Gray Wolf insisted angrily.

"They are. I have lived in *tahbay-boh* towns. I have seen their numbers. And their firepower. You can't match them." She paused. "And without meat, your children won't grow to take your place. And your unborn child will die with the mother, unable to raise more children to take the battle to the *tahbay-boh*. They won't live without meat to fill their bellies and warm robes to keep the winter's chill away."

Gray Wolf stared at her. Then nodded slowly. "You speak

wisely for a woman," he said. "I'll provide much meat for my growing sons. Far Seeing will join me on the hunt. But," he added with a grin, "there'll be much work for you, Light Calf."

"Blue Eyes will help. And I'm young. Not thirty winters yet."

"You're an old woman," Gray Wolf said, laughing. It was not true. Her face was unlined, and, except for the belly expanding to hold the growing child, she was trim, lithe, and not much different from when he had taken her from San Antonio more than ten years ago.

She laughed, too, and said teasingly, "You didn't think such a thing when you put this child in my belly."

"The winters have made you old and full of unkind remarks for your husband." Still laughing, he said, "I think it's time for me to find a younger wife."

"Oh, ho," Light Calf laughed, "the great warrior thinks he can take a younger wife when he isn't man enough to handle this old one?"

His eyes flickered with amusement and lust. "So? You think I can't handle an old woman like you? Maybe I'll show you. Maybe not."

Light Calf pulled her dress off. She dropped it and stood, proud of her pregnancy, her full breasts, her warm pubic region. "I don't think you can take care of a real woman," she teased. "Perhaps those girls will be overcome at your talk of your great deeds in battle."

"I've done many great deeds in other places," he boasted with a smile, voice hoarse with desire.

"You lie, old man," Light Calf said, smiling.

Gray Wolf stood and had his breechcloth off in a second. They tumbled on the robes, consumed by lust.

65

Gray Wolf impatiently sat out the winter, wanting to go to war, but also looking forward to seeing the birth of his latest child. His third son with Light Calf, Bloody Buffalo, joined fourteen-year-old Light Horse; Far-From-Stone-Village, thirteen; and four-year-old sister Little Owl, in June. While he had waited for the birth, Gray Wolf presided over a meeting with a group of visiting Kiowas and eastern Comanches. Those Indians had left the reservation agency and had come asking the *Kwahadis* to join them for war.

Gray Wolf agreed that he and his people would do so, and as soon as Bloody Buffalo was born, Gray Wolf rode out at the head of a large war party of *Kwahadis, Yampahrehkahs,* and Kiowas. The warriors cut a blood-stained path from Kansas to Mexico, from New Mexico's easternmost settlements to San Antonio. Only the need to hunt meat for the winter drove them back to their villages.

Gray Wolf and his warriors, flush with numerous victories without losing a man, took to the hunt joyfully. The women came along, and it was a festive occasion, reminiscent of the old days. The men had great success, and the women butchered out tons of meat.

They made a festival of it, gorging themselves on raw hearts and livers and long, slinky tubes of buffalo intestines.

Winter was mild, and Gray Wolf decided to make some raids southeast, where the cold never came. In the spring, he again joined Kiowas, Cheyennes, and other *Nermernuh* in making war on the white-eyes.

Their successes gave the Comanches confidence, and Gray Wolf urged that his band make their camp for the fall hunt farther north so that he might talk more easily with those wavering in their determination to fight. A spot near the opening of Blanco Canyon, on what the *tahbay-boh* called McClellan Creek, was chosen.

Once the hunt was over, Gray Wolf went to the other bands in the area. "The long-knives are many," he admitted to them. "More and more come into our land. They bring wagons, they kill our buffalo. But they are no match for us. We will kill them all!"

Few warriors felt powerful enough to argue with the great Gray Wolf, who often was seen these days in the company of the medicine man Isatai. The handsome Isatai said little while Gray Wolf spoke, but his presence was always noted. The Comanches kept a jaundiced eye on Isatai, not quite sure about the young medicine man. But since Gray Wolf seemed to put much faith in the mystic, the others accepted him, though they could not be called followers. Still, Isatai reportedly had overwhelming powers, and with the hard edge of despair slicing at the last bands of *Nermernuh* out in the *Llano*, they wanted to keep all options open.

Late in September, a large force of soldiers swept down on the *Kwahadi* camp in Blanco Canyon. In the swirling cloud of dust and powder smoke, Gray Wolf rallied his warriors. They fought desperately, covering the escape of their women and children. Through fierceness and reckless bravery, they drove off the blue coats. Then the warriors rode out to meet their families, feeling haunted and hunted.

"Was it bad, Gray Wolf?" Light Calf asked.

"No one died," Gray Wolf said stonily. "But many warriors were captured. And thousands of horses were taken."

"What will you do?"

"First, get the horses back. Then try to free the warriors."

Light Calf nodded and said, "I'll take the children to the *Llano*."

"Isatai will lead. I'll need the warriors with me."

Some of the woman, children, and old men left, led by Isatai. Others remained behind, wanting to be close to their captured men. They, and some warriors, decided to winter near Fort Griffin. Gray Wolf, angry at them, said nothing as he led his warriors toward the Army encampment.

The blue coats had captured so many horses they had trouble watching them all. It was easy for Gray Wolf and his war-hardened warriors — and some not so hardened, like Light Horse — to take most of the horses back. But they had no luck in freeing the captives.

Soon after, Quanah suggested that the People offer to exchange captives they had for their warriors, and Gray Wolf agreed. But the soldier chief, whom Gray Wolf learned was called Colonel Ranald MacKenzie, rejected the idea.

Angry, Gray Wolf headed east, wanting to see Fort Sill where the tame *Nermernuh* were kept. Outside the gates, he and a few warriors challenged the blue coats to come out and fight. But they would not. Sneering, but with the sickly sourness of disgust riding in his belly, Gray Wolf and his men left. They made it safely back to their new haunts in the desolate western reaches of the *Llano Estacado*, between the Red and Canadian Rivers.

They did some raiding that winter, as Gray Wolf hoped to take his people's minds off their recent defeat. It worked, and they were in higher spirits as spring approached. After the hunt, Gray Wolf sought a vision. It was a powerful one, though not so strong as in the past. Still, it gave the *Kwahadis* hope, and they traveled northeast. For the first time, they would join their allies in the Kiowas' annual Sun Dance. This Gray Wolf had seen in his vision.

The *Kwahadis* found the gathering of Kiowas on Sweetwater Creek. They took little part in the Dance, but watched and listened avidly. After the dance, the Kiowas talked of war. Word of the talk reached the agency, and the new agent, J.M. Haworth, did not like what he had heard. The Kiowas were saying that they, aided by the fierce bands of *Kwahadis,* would raid mercilessly unless the two great Kiowa war chiefs, Satanta and Big Tree, captured the year before, were freed.

Gray Wolf liked such talk and looked forward to making war on the *tahbay-boh* again. He turned wary that the Kiowas would remain peaceful after the governor of Texas did release the two Kiowas. But the Kiowas decided war was desirable anyway, and Gray Wolf brought his *Kwahadi* bands along, as did Quanah, who had gained quite some renown even at his young age. He was, Gray Wolf thought, much like a youthful Gray Wolf, with the same fires burning in him. Light Horse was a full-fledged warrior, and also went. And fourteen-year-old Far-From-Stone-Village was along as a member of a war party for the first time.

The force attacked two wagon trains on the Santa Fe Trail, taking plunder and a dozen scalps. But Gray Wolf was unhappy with so many warriors together. They moved too slowly to suit him, and the plunder would be spread too thin. So, he rode off — with most of the *Kwahadis* and the best wishes of the Kiowas.

An Army patrol was the first to feel Gray Wolf's fury. The Comanches caught the soldiers on a dusty flat. The Indians followed the soldiers, keeping just out of rifle range. The blue coats raced their horses trying to get away from the superior force of Indians. But the Comanches, with extra ponies, kept following. Soon the military horses began to falter, and several men lagged behind. Some Indians charged, hanging over the sides of their horses for protection.

Light Horse and Far-From-Stone-Village were among those who charged, while Gray Wolf watched proudly. His sons might have *tahbay-boh* blood, he thought, but they showed none of the white side now.

Far-From-Stone-Village felt his heart pounding with the excitement as he swung his Winchester repeater under his horse's throat. He fired, snapped the rifle down with a flick of the wrist, and then back up, ready to fire again. He suppressed the urge to whoop as he saw his bullet tear a chunk of a soldier's neck out. Gouts of blood spurted as the trooper grabbed his gushing throat and fell.

He was past three straggling soldiers who had stopped and dismounted. One was dead, struck down by Far-From-Stone-Village's bullet. Another was wounded, though not seriously. He and the third soldier killed their horses and hunkered down behind the beasts.

Light Horse leaped over the warm barricade. As he did, he reached out with his lance, counting coup on one soldier. Such a thing wasn't done much anymore as the Comanches were forced to fight for their very existence. But Gray Wolf had made sure his sons learned the proper ways, even if they were used infrequently.

Just after Light Horse counted coup, Hits-With-A-Fist followed, firing his rifle. One soldier, half-sitting up to defend himself, had his face blown away by Hits-With-A-Fist's shot.

Two other warriors stopped their ponies and tumbled off, finishing the third soldier with their knives and tomahawks. They all whooped, facing the rest of the fleeing soldiers.

"Come," Gray Wolf ordered, not entirely sternly, as he and the remaining warriors rode up. "The other blue coats must die!"

It did not take long before the six other troopers were dead, mutilated and scalped, their rifles and pistols in Comanche hands. Then the *Kwahadis* were heading south once more.

They raided seven farms, two ranches, a weary band of Texas Rangers, an Army supply train, two wagon trains of settlers, and a small settlement east on the Brazos.

Then the Army, which had patrols swarming all over from

dozens of forts, began catching up with the Comanche war band. After several skirmishes, the Comanches swung northwest toward their homeland. Still, the troops seemed to be everywhere, and Gray Wolf used all his skill and experience to get away from them. Finally, the Comanches left the soldiers behind and returned to the village.

Light Horse had gained much glory. But Far-From-Stone-Village had been even more devastating, reminding other warriors of a young Gray Wolf. He was merciless, thriving on shedding blood.

Within a day of returning, plans for the hunt were made. But buffalo were hard to find — live buffalo, that is. The Comanches found rotting carcasses by the thousands, left by the hide hunters.

During the winter, the men mostly brooded, their spirit sagging from the almost unbroken line of troubles that had beset the People.

66

By spring, the *Kwahadis* of Gray Wolf's band were in a more willing frame of mind to heed the words of Isatai. After the defeat at Blanco Canyon, despair settled over the Comanches. Such depression made the People pliable and ready to believe in a messiah.

The young medicine man sought a vision. In it, Isatai went far above the clouds, rising above all that was on Mother Earth. And there, he spoke directly with the Great Spirit. The Great Spirit told Isatai that the *Nermernuh* would be victorious, either killing all the *tahbay-boh*, or driving them out of their land forever. Then the buffalo would return in numbers too great to count even if the People did nothing else. Isatai told the Comanches they would live as in the old days. Life would be good. Meat would be plentiful, the women fruitful, the children strong, and the men again lords of their land.

The *Kwahadis* believed because they wanted to. Such things as Isatai said had long been in Gray Wolf's dreams, and the aging war chief was determined to see that they came true.

Isatai called for the *Nermernuh* to have their own Sun Dance. Gray Wolf helped spread word to other bands of *Kwahadis* and then other groups of Comanches. The *Nermernuh* would believe Gray Wolf because of his reputation. If he said these things were true, they must be.

The *Nermernuh* outside Gray Wolf's small band of *Kwahadis* were reluctant to believe in Isatai, but eventually the strength of faith in what Isatai proposed — rather than the source — won out. Especially when Isatai belched up a wagonload of cartridges.

Since Gray Wolf wanted to see the life Isatai envisioned, he did all he could to see that it would come to fruition — including riding to Taos with Light Calf and some of their children. He bought a wagonload of cartridges and brought it to the village at night. It mysteriously appeared in a flash of smoke when Isatai belched.

Such power made believers of even the most skeptical warrior, especially when Gray Wolf said he believed in Isatai's vision.

In May the *Nermernuh* — *Kwahadis* led by Gray Wolf and Quanah; *Yampareekahs*; *Kotsotekas* — and Kiowas and Southern Cheyennes gathered at a spot on the Red River not far from the agency that was supposed to rule over the Comanches' lives. It was almost as if Isatai and Gray Wolf were daring the troopers to find them and stop the Sun Dance.

The Sun Dance was a success, the warriors felt, building up their might and power. Riding out as the moon bobbed high in the night sky, the Comanches — bolstered by scores of Kiowa and Cheyenne warriors — headed southwest. Gray Wolf had been chosen paramount war chief for this expedition, and rode arrogantly, his creased, bronze face distorted with the hate that ate at his insides.

Though he was not totally taken in by the magic and medicine of Isatai, Gray Wolf still felt invincible. There were hundreds of Comanche, Kiowa, and Cheyenne warriors — led by the finest warriors those tribes had produced: Gray Wolf himself, Quanah, Lone Wolf, and Stone Shield. No one would be able to best them.

Light Horse and Far-From-Stone-Village were among the warriors. The former, sixteen, was father of a six-month-old girl,

Red Lodge. The latter was not married but had decided he would take a wife soon.

After several days, as dawn was cracking over the countryside, spreading weak shadows, the mass of warriors sat on a ridge looking down on an old adobe trading post a quarter of a mile away.

"There," Isatai said, pointing, "We will start our destruction of the *tahbay-boh*." The medicine man sat proudly on his horse, chest puffed out with arrogance. He was naked, except for moccasins, and his body covered in yellow paint. "Go, my brothers," he said. "The Great Spirit will guide you as you destroy the *tahbay-boh*!"

Gray Wolf looked at the place. He remembered when the Bent brothers — those great friends of the Cheyennes, and friends of White Horse Zeke Tippett — had built Adobe Walls. It had been abandoned for years, though the hated buffalo hunters sometimes used it. Such seemed to be the case now, and Gray Wolf thought it only proper that the *Nermernuh* begin the war to return life to normalcy by attacking buffalo hunters.

As the sun brightened the dull brown of Adobe Walls into a warm gold, Gray Wolf led the first charge. But the whites were expecting the warriors, which surprised the Indians. Heavy fire erupted from within the thick mud walls. Several warriors fell. They were scooped up and carried back up the hill.

Gray Wolf knew the men in the old post were buffalo hunters, and as such, deadly shots. But he could not quit trying to rid the country of the enemy now with the possibility of success so close.

He rode down again and again and again. At times he would take a short break — to gain his breath or to change ponies — and let other warriors charge into the hail of gunfire. By midafternoon, Gray Wolf knew the fight was futile. But still he continued throwing himself down the hill with savage fury. Just before noon, Light Horse was blasted off his horse.

Gray Wolf let out a wail of grief and raced toward his son. Light Horse stood up, weaving, blood soaking his chest. He weakly sang a death song. Gray Wolf thundered up, extending his left hand. Light

Horse grabbed it, wincing as pain burned through him, and let Gray Wolf pull him onto the pony. Gray Wolf quirted the horse, galloping up the hill. Gray Wolf stopped and let Light Horse slide off who stumbled and fell, his legs too weak to hold him up. Gray Wolf jumped down and knelt by his son, hardening his heart to this latest misfortune.

Light Horse tried to smile but could not. Gray Wolf held an animal skin of water to his son's lips and let the young man have his fill. Far-From-Stone-Village joined them.

Light Horse's eyes were glazed. Gray Wolf knew his son was in pain and was proud he made no sound of weakness. "Goodbye, brother," Light Horse said, groping feebly for Far-From-Stone-Village. "Goodbye, Father. I..." His head fell sideways, and he died.

With grim countenance, Gray Wolf carried Light Horse's body away from the jumble of men and horses. He set the body down. Without a word, he walked back toward his pony. He climbed on and rode to Isatai. "Join the battle, Isatai," he said sharply.

The medicine man said nothing, only shook his head.

"Your power brought us here, Coyote Shit," Gray Wolf said harshly to Isatai. "We're here because you brought us here."

Isatai sat stony faced, staring down the hill.

"Your war paint is the proper color for such a coward," Gray Wolf sneered. Other warriors chuckled grimly; some added taunts, accusing Isatai of having no balls, of being a false prophet. The jeers built, but still Isatai refused to fight. Soon all the warriors were taunting Isatai or watching to see what he would do.

Suddenly Isatai fell from his horse. A few moments later, the stunned Indians heard the report of a rifle from down in the adobe building. The warriors needed to see no more, and fled.

Gray Wolf rode toward the *Llano Estacado* with Light Horse's body. He did not go to the village. In a site he deemed good, he made the proper ceremonials and buried his son. With Far-From-Stone-Village at his side, Gray Wolf rode off to war once again.

The two warriors rode north, starting a wide loop, striking

where they could, slipping past ubiquitous Army patrols. They ended at the village, where Gray Wolf comforted Light Calf. They took in Red Lodge when Light Horse's wife got carried away in her grief, nearly killing herself and the child. Light Calf did not hack at herself. Instead, she sat for two days, wailing a high-pitched howl of pain.

But life had to go on. Gray Wolf knew it, and Light Calf knew it even better than he. The band moved off for the hunt, ranging far north of their usual hunting grounds to find buffalo. They did, but the travel was hard on the suffering band.

As Gray Wolf's *Kwahadi* band made its way back toward the *Llano,* they were approached one night by a *Pehnahterkuh* who had been living on the reservation for some time. Gray Wolf sneered when he greeted the man. Then he asked, "What do you want here?"

"The long-knife chief sends word that *Nermernuh* who wish to live in peace with the *tahbay-boh* should go to land east of Cache Creek."

"Why would I do that?" Gray Wolf asked, wanting to laugh at such audaciousness, but unable to find much humor in it.

"You'll be branded an enemy of the blue coats."

Gray Wolf laughed without humor. "I *am* an enemy of the long-knives," he growled. "I don't need a soldier chief to tell me that."

"The blue coats will come for you," warned the warrior, whose name Gray Wolf did not even deign to mention, if he even remembered.

"Let them," Gray Wolf sneered. "I won't become a tame *Nermernuh* like you — one who's given his balls to the *tahbay-boh.*" He spit at the man. "You should have the name White-Man-Humps-Him." There were several chuckles of derision from other warriors. "Is that what the blue coats do with you? Do they bend you over a meat rack and ram their pizzles up your ass? Go, before I have the women whip you."

The man skulked out, his face burning in shame.

Soon after, a warrior named Broken Bow visited Gray Wolf. "Has a tame *Nermernuh* come to you to plead that you bend over and offer your ass to the *tahbay-boh?*" Broken Bow asked.

"Yes," Gray Wolf said, grinning savagely. "I threw him out."

Broken Bow nodded. "He — and others like him — have gone to all the camps of the People for the same thing."

"And?" Gray Wolf questioned.

"No *Nermernuh* will accept such a thing," Broken Bow said. "None that are free. And few Kiowas will listen to someone without balls."

"It is good."

"Many of the bands plan to gather for the winter. We will meet in Palo Duro Canyon to plan our next battle against the *tahbay-boh.*"

"I'll bring my people," Gray Wolf said again.

"And the false one? Will you bring Isatai?"

"No one in my band has seen Coyote Shit since..." There was no need to continue. All would know.

Within a week, Gray Wolf's band made its way down the narrow, treacherous path into red-walled Palo Duro Canyon. Light Calf talked with old friends after her lodge was set up. Above, winter was coming, with a cold wind sweeping across the barren prairies. But here it was comfortable. The People had plenty of meat, and in the canyon there was wood, grass, good water, and camaraderie, all that one could hope for.

Gray Wolf awoke one chilly morning in late September before Light Calf. He was behind his lodge, rubbing sleep from his eyes with one hand, holding his draining dingus with the other. The pains of a long and hard life afflicted him — creaking knees, old wounds that ached when rain threatened, stiff muscles. He sighed.

He heard something, and the urine almost stopped as his other hand dropped. He stood still, waiting to hear it again. He finished relieving himself and stuffed himself into his breechcloth. He had pulled his blanket around him, and was turning when he heard it again.

Dim light filtered down into the canyon from above the rim, refracting off the mist rising from the stream. Gray Wolf craned his neck, searching. The camp was calm, with only a few men moving about. Most of the People had not even awakened.

Suddenly a burst of gunfire rattled through the camp, coming from where the trail from above ended. Then came another burst. Soldiers poured off the cliff-wall trail and into the camp, firing.

"Light Calf!" Gray Wolf bellowed. He tossed off his blanket and ran for the horse herd.

BOOK 15

ZEKE TIPPETT, 1874-1878

67

Zeke Tippett rode into the Comanche camp in a howling snowstorm and was shocked to see the condition of the camp. The people were drawn and haggard, the lodges threadbare and pocked with holes.

He stopped at Gray Wolf's lodge and called for entrance. A weak, haunted voice bid him enter, and the white man stepped inside. Tippett was just over sixty-one, but he was still vigorous. He hunted frequently and was quite often found showing his two sons — Kit, eleven, and Jim, seven — the ways of the wilderness. He spent less time with his daughter, Frannie, nine, but doted on her when he could.

He spent a little more time in the store than he used to, but not too much. He often rode between the stores in Taos and Santa Fe, occasionally driving the wagons. He did a little surveying and some scouting for wagon trains. Despite his age, he was still straight and tall, his back unbent. His hair had grayed completely, but he still had a full head of it. And, though his face was wrinkled with age and his life out of doors, the eyes had not dimmed.

He gave himself a few moments to adjust to the poor light inside the lodge. "Papa?" he heard, and he stared into Libby's shrunken eyes in the dim light cast by the orange embers of the fire. It never ceased to amaze Tippett that Libby still called him Papa, despite being just past thirty years old. But that amazement was subordinate to the shock at her appearance. Libby was a shell of her former self. And Gray Wolf looked up at him with haunted, faded eyes.

"Goddamn!" Tippett breathed. "Libby, ye all right?"

"I'm all right, Papa."

"Where's the young 'uns?"

"Some ain't so young any more, Papa," Libby said, shuffling to him. She was haggard but there was still life in her eyes. She had lost weight but remained strong. "Light Horse was killed at Adobe Walls. We have his daughter, Red Lodge, with us. She's only eight months old."

"I'm a great-grandpa?" Tippett asked, surprised.

"Yes, Papa," Libby said, smiling wanly. "Bloody Buffalo and Little Owl are with us. So's Far-From-Stone-Village, though he's also a warrior. Blue Eyes died in Palo Duro Canyon."

"Let me see the young 'uns," Tippett ordered.

Far-From-Stone-Village stepped up, sneering. He looked healthy. Tippett nodded. "Fetch some firewood, boy," he said.

"That's woman's work," Far-From-Stone-Village said haughtily. Then he saw the look on Tippett's face, and he hurried outside. He was back in minutes with wood, which he put on the fire. The flames rose until there was light, warmth, and almost cheer in the lodge.

Tippett checked Bloody Buffalo, Little Owl, and Red Lodge. "Humph," he snapped. The children were in poor shape, but not near death — yet. Tippett turned angry eyes on Gray Wolf. "Why ain't ye got no meat here, dammit?"

"No more buffalo," Gray Wolf said, eyes full of pain. "The *tahbay-boh* killed them all. Only bones and rotting meat are left. We're forced to eat nuts and roots, small animals. But we must live to fight again." A bit of the old fire stirred in his eyes.

"Why don't ye head to Fort Sill? Ye'd get rations there."

"The blue coats will kill us all."

"Like hell they will." He paused, and sighed. "Well, shit, it looks like ye ain't gonna make it through this moon, let alone the winter. I got a wagonload of supplies outside. It'll tide ye and the others here over for a spell." He had heard what was going on in *Comancheria*. It was why he had braved the winter to get here.

Gray Wolf nodded and stood. He had mixed emotions. The food would keep them all alive, but he hated taking anything from anyone, even an old friend. On legs shaky with hunger, he and Stone Village followed Tippett into the maelstrom.

Tippett roared into the biting wind, and slowly the People straggled out of their lodges, hope flickering in their faces. Sickened at heart, Tippett passed out the food, blankets, and other supplies. As soon as that was done, he said, "I'll be back in a few weeks, Libby. I'll bring a couple wagons of supplies this time."

At the last moment, he decided to take Bloody Buffalo. The youth objected, but his father finally ordered it and he went reluctantly.

It took a month, but Tippett made it back to the village. He had left the store in charge of a new clerk Ben Winter had hired and trusted. Winter had insisted on coming along, driving the second wagon; Bloody Buffalo drove a third.

Tippett figured the People would make it now. But for how long, he did not know. After distributing the supplies, he sat in Gray Wolf's lodge. Tippett, Gray Wolf and, after a little while, Libby, talked. Far-From-Stone-Village and Winter — who had entered the village nervously — sat at the fire with the others, but said nothing.

"How'd ye get in such a way, Wolf?" Tippett asked. "This have anything to do with the fight up in Palo Duro?"

"Yes. We had made meat. We gathered in Palo Duro to talk of bringing the fight to the *tahbay-boh*. But the long-knives attacked.

Most of us escaped, but the blue coats got almost all our horses. We heard they shot them."

He shuddered, thinking back the three months since it happened. "They got our lodges, meat, blankets, everything. We fled with a few horses and what we could grab in the first minutes."

Gray Wolf sighed deeply, as if living was painful. Libby served food. It was unusual for a Comanche woman to feed the children first, but neither adult male said anything. Then Libby sat at the fire.

Between chewing pieces of salted beef or noisily sucking up broth, Gray Wolf continued. "When we got back to the *Llano*, we had little. We went hunting with the few horses we had. But we found few buffalo. Winter came harder than we expected. So..." He shrugged.

"It's gonna get worse, Wolf," Tippett said. "The blue coats don't take no more mind of winter. They keep up the fightin' all year now. They've built a passel of forts, pressin' in on the *Llano*."

"I know." With a full belly, Gray Wolf's outlook had improved minutely, and with it returned some of his old arrogance.

Tippett sighed, knowing there would be resistance to what he was about to say. "Let me take Libby and the kids to Taos with me."

But it was Libby who answered. "No," she snapped, eyes flashing.

"Goddammit, Libby, don't go gettin' knobheaded on me now."

"Our place is here, Papa," she said, a little contritely. "Besides, the people of Taos would never accept us."

"They did the last couple times ye were there."

"They accepted me because I'm a woman, Papa," Libby pressed, angry. "And the last time we was there, the young 'uns was little more than babies. Now Far-From-Stone-Village is a warrior. He won't be accepted. The people in Taos might accept the younger ones now when they're little. But not when they're grown. I went through enough name calling and such when you took me to San Antonio all those years ago. I ain't gonna see my children suffer that pain and humiliation. I am *Nermernuh,* and so are my children. Better they starve to death with the People than endure a life of shame for being *Nermernuh.*" She hung her head, angry and sad. "I've buried family here, Papa. Kids, friends, even Mama."

Tippett knew everything she said was true. When he had first come to the Comanches, half-breeds were more easily accepted in some frontier towns. But things had changed greatly over the years. Libby's children were, by blood and inclination, more Comanche than white. Still, they were his family, and he loved them.

"I could take 'em from ye," Tippett said. "I could take ye along, too, ye know, girl. Ye ain't so big, and I ain't so old I couldn't throw ye across my horse and ride on out of here."

"There'd be death among the People, then," Gray Wolf said.

Tippett nodded, trying to think of something he could say.

"I think you should heed your father," Ben Winter said softly.

Libby smiled at him, and the clerk's heart squirmed. But he felt sick when she said, "My mind's made up. I'm too much of a *Nermernuh* to see my husband die while I'm off safe in a city somewhere."

"That your last word?" Tippett asked, feeling useless.

"Yes, Papa."

Tippett nodded, unable to speak because of the sickness that twisted his guts.

Libby went outside. A few minutes later, Tippett looked at Winter who seemed mighty nervous. Tippett nodded at him and said, "Ye'll be safe, Ben. Go on and take care of your business."

Relieved, Winter hurried outside. He really had to urinate, but he also wanted to talk with Libby. He went behind the lodge, hoping Libby would take longer than he was. He had just buttoned his pants and turned when he saw her. She came to him.

Her dark eyes stared luminously up at him, and he suddenly felt tongue-tied. He saw only the beautiful, vivacious woman he had met a dozen years ago, not this drawn, but still attractive, Comanche woman.

"I..." Winter started.

"If you're gonna tell me to go back to Taos, save your breath, Mister Winter."

"Mister Winter?" The pain at the snub reached into his entrails.

"I'm a married woman, Mister...Ben. A grandmother."

"I love you, Libby," Winter said forlornly. "If you came back to Taos, I'd ask you to marry me."

"My place is here, at my husband's side," Libby said, staring at him. He was aware that the pain, reflected in her eyes, was as deep as his. "No matter how I feel."

Winter nodded. Libby gripped him lightly on each side of the head. Then she kissed him hard, her tongue probing deep into his mouth. She finally released him. She was weeping as she whispered, "Some things were never meant to be, Ben, no matter how much we might wish them different." She turned and stumbled away.

Winter stood watching her for a moment, then realized how cold it was. Sadly, but with a bland face, he hurried inside. He did not look at Libby when he re-entered the lodge. He looked calm and at peace. Still, it was difficult for him to be here, with Libby so near, and the next morning, he said, "I think we ought to be gettin' back, Zeke."

Tippett acceded, feeling the weight of his years.

68

Tippett spent the rest of the winter wrestling with his conscience at having left Libby and the children in the *Llano*. Having Francisca harping on it did not help. Francisca liked Libby — after all, she was the one who had brought Francisca and Tippett together. So, Francisca worried for Libby, and the children, young and old.

Winter hated himself for not forcing Libby to return with him and Tippett. So, he, too, added his voice to the cacophony Tippett heard.

But mainly it was his conscience that disturbed Tippett. The end for the Comanches was coming faster than anyone had foreseen. Tippett knew the Comanches could not continue their way of life indefinitely. Diehards such as Gray Wolf would only make it worse.

In less than a decade, the Comanches had gone from being the lords of all the southern plains to scattered remnants barely subsisting on what crumbs the world offered. Even as recently as three or four years ago they still had some hand in their fate. Now, though, they were broken.

Tippett had not wanted to admit it, but he had acquiesced to

Libby's pleas to stay behind largely because he saw hopelessness in her eyes. She knew there was little time left for the People, and she wanted to live out the rest of her life as best she could with her husband. Tippett understood that.

But as spring spread over the high country, the oaks and walnuts bringing forth new foliage, Tippett had no more doubts. He had heard reports that the Comanches were finished; that even the last of the great Comanche war chiefs were preparing to surrender. He would go to the *Llano Estacado* as soon as he could and rescue Libby, her children, her grandchild, and any other young ones he could coax along.

Once his mind was made up, he moved fast. He and Winter — who insisted on coming along — loaded two wagons with supplies. But with such a harsh winter, they could not leave until almost May.

"You bring that girl and those *niños* home, Zeke," Francisca ordered as Tippett climbed onto the hard seat of the bigger wagon.

"They ain't all babies no more, Francisca," he said wanly. Francisca glared, and he nodded. "I'll bring 'em home, darlin'." The wagons — each with a saddle horse tied behind — creaked away.

But Tippett could not find the village. He found the spot along the Brazos where they had wintered, but all that remained were the flotsam and jetsam of a subsistence life. He searched and searched, frantic inside, but not showing it.

Winter did show it, asking frequently, "Where could they've gone?"

"I don't know, son," Tippett would answer and forge ahead. He checked all the spots Gray Wolf's band liked to use for wintering, summering, or hunting. But the People were nowhere to be found. With mixed feelings of fear and worry and hope, Tippett turned toward the Indian Nations — and the agency at Fort Sill. He clanked onto the reservation and stopped in front of the agency building. A few moments later, he was speaking with the agent, J.W. Haworth.

"There are so many Comanches here," Haworth said after

Tippett asked about Libby. "I can't know them all." He was very sympathetic.

"Mind if I look for 'em?" Tippett asked coldly. Any fool would know a warrior of Gray Wolf's reputation.

"I'm not certain, Mister Tippett," Haworth said. "We can't just have people, even relatives, wandering around loose here."

"I ain't gonna ask ye but one more time, *amigo*," Tippett said.

Haworth looked into the cold blue eyes and shuddered. Tippett might be past sixty, but he was still strong, determined. He showed few signs of his age. "Look around all you wish, sir," Haworth croaked.

Tippett nodded. "I brung two wagons of goods. Mind if I pass 'em out?"

"No, sir," Haworth answered, sweating.

"Thankee. I'll leave the wagons here whilst I look around. I expect they'll be safe." It was not a question. Tippett walked out, an impressed Ben Winter in his wake.

It took several hours of roaming on horseback through huddled knots of destitute, heartbroken Comanches spread out in brushy camps, but Tippett and Winter finally found Gray Wolf and his family. Sorrow and resignation were etched in Gray Wolf's and Libby's faces. All their children — and some not theirs — were there, bedraggled and near starvation. The family sat outside their lodge — a ragged tipi full of holes. They had almost no possessions. Only three scrawny horses were nearby. Their clothing was rags.

"Where's Stone Village?" Tippett asked after he had exchanged greetings with his apathetic daughter and a sullen Gray Wolf. He took a seat. Winter sat next to him, looking mopishly, his feelings evident, at Libby who kept her eyes cast down.

"He's a warrior," Gray Wolf said, without interest. "He's out fighting the *tahbay-boh*. He and his new wife are roaming the *Llano*."

Tippett nodded. "If'n ye can get word to him, tell him he needs anything, to come to the store in Taos — or to the house."

Gray Wolf shrugged, unconcerned any longer.

Tippett turned to Libby. "Look at me, daughter," he said. When she turned lusterless eyes on him, Tippett said firmly, "I'm takin' ye and all the children ye can gather with me back to Taos."

Libby shook her head. "It's too late for us, Papa," she said, voice quivering. "I want only to stay with Gray Wolf until the Great Spirit calls us." She shrugged, devoid of hope.

"I ain't askin' ye, girl."

"They all stay," Gray Wolf said, a momentary flicker of the old flame crackling in his eyes.

"Buffler shit, Wolf," Tippett said frostily. "Ye cain't provide for your family no more, so I'm gonna do it. They're my kin, too."

The two men stared at each other, wills locked. Gray Wolf would be glad to have Libby and his children and grandchild go live with Tippett. But he was still too much of a warrior to sit and have anyone — even an old friend — dictate to him. If only White Horse had come and told him in privacy, then Gray Wolf could have made it look like he had suggested it. Now he would lose more pride.

Tippett had an inkling of what Gray Wolf was thinking. But he didn't give a damn any more. His first concern was for his family. He also was angry at himself for letting Libby and the others get into this fix. He should have insisted they come with him during the winter, maybe even several years ago when he saw that things were beginning to go bad for the Comanches. But he had not, and now she was a dispirited woman sitting here waiting to die.

Gray Wolf broke first. He knew he had no more power, no more medicine. He was a dried-up old man, emasculated by the blue coats, forced to live worse than any dog in a Comanche village in the old days. He nodded once, knowing he had no way to prevent the inevitable.

"I won't go, Papa," Libby said when she saw it.

"Yes, ye will, girl," Tippett said firmly, but gently. His hard, insistent look stopped her from objecting. She sat silent, staring at him, but he thought he saw a faint flicker of hope leap into her eyes.

Winter thought he saw it, too, and his heart pounded with anticipation. With her in Taos, he could court her, taking her mind away from Gray Wolf. He loved her deeply, still, though this last year or so had aged her somewhat; it did not matter to him.

"Gather up all your young 'uns, and any others ye want. Have 'em ready. I got two wagons of food, Wolf. Ye can pass out the supplies."

Gray Wolf did not seem interested.

"I'm gonna go get the wagons and tell Haworth I'm takin' ye out of here. Shouldn't take long." He was grim.

"He won't let us go, Papa."

"He will if he plans to see the sun set tonight," Tippett said savagely. "Soon's we get back with the wagons, we'll unload the stuff for Gray Wolf to handle. Then we'll leave out." He and Winter headed back toward the agency building. Tippett found his wagons surrounded by soldiers. He was not certain whether they were there to keep him or the Comanches away from the wagons. He and Winter entered Haworth's office. Haworth sat at his desk, looking nervous. Lieutenant Amos Cook stood next to the desk, on Haworth's left, amused. Near the hearth was Major Horace Montgomery, who was arrogant.

"Amos," Tippett nodded at Cook, who returned the greeting. Cook was one of the few military men Tippett could bear. He had met the officer when he had served with Kit Carson during the Civil War.

"We don't look kindly on folks threatening our agent," Montgomery snapped. It was evident Montgomery thought little of the Indian agent.

"I didn't threaten him," Tippett said evenly.

"That ain't what Haworth said."

"He ain't the first man ever lied," Tippett shrugged.

"Be that as it may, Tippett, I'll have to investigate. In the meantime, I've confiscated your wagons. A well-known Indian-lover like you most likely has brought in all kinds of contraband."

"I always knew ye was a coward, Montgomery," Tippett sneered. "I didn't realize jist how much of a chicken-shit little fart ye were."

Montgomery's face was livid. Cook hid a grin behind a hand.

Tippett grinned malevolently. "What I got in them wagons is food, blankets, and such. Was ye to ask nice, I might even let ye take a look. But even if I was runnin' guns to the Comanches, I couldn't be carryin' too many. And for ye to be so goddamn, buffler-shit scared of the possibility of a few spiritless Comanches with guns shows jist what kind of man ye are. More like a *berdache*."

Montgomery sputtered before saying in an angry hiss, "You're under arrest, Tippett." Montgomery shouted for his troopers outside.

Tippett hoped Cook would not be too eager to follow the order. As the door opened, Tippett lashed out with the butt of his Sharps, smashing the first soldier through the door in the mouth. Tippett reached out, grabbed the man, and yanked him inward. The man fell, moaning.

There was another soldier behind the first, and Tippett kicked him in the crotch. The man puffed up as he sucked in air, and grew red with pain. Tippett grabbed him by the hair and jerked him into the office, too. Seeing other soldiers heading his way, Tippett slammed the door and flattened against it. He swung the Sharps up to cover Montgomery, who was trying to pull a Colt from the flap holster.

Winter had produced a .36-caliber Navy pistol and was covering Montgomery and Cook, however. Montgomery froze with his hand on the pistol. Cook stood, grinning, arms folded across his chest. Tippett nodded and spun back, sliding the bar across the door. He faced Montgomery, glancing at the two soldiers groaning on the floor.

A pounding began at the door. "Call 'em off, Major," Tippett said.

"No, sir," Montgomery said, thrusting out his chin.

"I'm plumb tired of your bullshit, Montgomery," Tippett said. "Call 'em off or I'll shatter a knee, ye peckerless bastard."

"You don't, I will," Cook said sharply. He hated Montgomery, and all Montgomery stood for. He had made it clear early on that he would take no guff from Montgomery. Montgomery had tried to threaten the younger officer, warning him that he would have Cook cashiered.

But Cook knew about the Comanche raid on Fort Spirit Mound. And so, he told the commander, "You do so, Major. I'm sure General Sherman — and Washington — would like you to explain just how it was you lost half your command at Fort Spirit Mound."

Montgomery had glared at Cook then, as he did now, knowing he was powerless. He gulped and did as he was told.

The pounding on the door stopped, though Tippett was aware at least a few soldiers were staring in through the window. "Tell 'em to go about some other business," Tippett ordered.

With a grimace of hate, Montgomery did so.

"That's better," Tippett said, relaxing. He wiped sweat from his forehead. "Ben, watch them two blue coats. Either tries anything, plug the little shit."

Winter nodded. He was less nervous now than he had been when he was with Libby. He had shot men before on several occasions, all times when someone had tried to rob the store. He never liked it, but he was not reluctant about it, either.

"Amos, I expect I can trust ye, but still I'll have to ask ye to set your pistol on the desk and step away from it."

Cook smiled, knowing he was in no danger from Tippett. He did as he was told.

"Mister Haworth, I'm takin' my daughter out of here, as well as her kids and any others she rounds up," Tippett said. "I'm also gonna give Gray Wolf's band the supplies I brought." He saw the flash of scheming leap into Montgomery's eyes, and he sneered at

Montgomery. "If'n I hear something bad ever happens to Gray Wolf, I'll blame ye, Major. And pay back in spades."

Montgomery was so angry he was speechless.

Tippett spit on the floor. "And to make sure we get out of here safe, ye three'll escort us to Gray Wolf's camp and off the agency."

"I'll have your ass shot for this, Tippett," Montgomery snapped. "Or hanged. But be sure, you'll pay for this humiliation. You'll never leave this post alive," Montgomery smirked. "And I'll make sure Gray Wolf and his whore suffer unmentionable troubles."

Tippett took two steps, letting the Sharps swing down in his left hand. His right smashed Montgomery in the face. Montgomery stumbled back, hitting the wall, which kept him upright. He rubbed his jaw with his left hand, while his right headed for the pistol again.

Tippett grinned grimly. He waited until Montgomery had the pistol halfway out. Then he set his Sharps down out of the way, and leaped on Montgomery. The old mountain man surprised everyone — except himself — with his speed and strength, as he pummeled Montgomery until he was a bloody mass on the floor.

Breathing heavily, Tippett stood and pulled his knife. "I ain't raised but one other white scalp," he rasped. "Elmore Trent's. Ye remember him, Major?" He didn't wait for an answer. He grabbed Montgomery's thinning sandy hair with his left hand. He brought the knife forward.

"Zeke, no!" Winter and Cook shouted at the same time. Winter was certain he could not shoot his friend, but he had to try to prevent this. And while Winter's attention was diverted to Tippett, Cook had quietly grabbed his pistol from the desk.

Tippett turned to glare from one to the other, his eyes filled with an animal rage. Then he grinned and straightened. "I'd suggest ye resign your commission, Major. Or ask for reassignment back East somewhere." He slid the knife away.

As he reached for the Sharps, he heard a shot. He crouched and whirled, snatching out one of the new .44-caliber Remington Frontier pistols he carried. He grinned again when he saw that Winter had put a shot in the floor between the legs of the trooper with the smashed face. He had been going for his gun, but Winter's warning was sufficient. Cook also had his pistol trained on the soldier.

Tippett straightened, and said, "All right, let's go."

"Shouldn't we do something about the Major?" Winter asked.

"Why?"

"Do you expect these soldiers to act kindly to you after you just kicked the shit out of their commanding officer?" Winter asked.

Cook laughed. "It'd be more likely they'll give Zeke a medal for it," he said. Montgomery, only half-conscious, moaned. "Ain't too many of those boys out there got any love for this vexatious tub of shit." He thought for a moment, then added, "And, seein's how he's incapacitated, I reckon I'm in command of the post till he recovers."

Tippett returned Cook's grin. "That'd make life a heap easier, I expect," he said. "But we'll take him along just in case."

"How about them?" Winter asked, waving his pistol at the soldiers.

"You boys harbor any ill feelings toward these two?" Cook asked.

They shook their heads, all nervous like.

"Didn't think so. You two will report to the infirmary."

"Yes, sir," they chorused.

69

Tippett kept a close watch behind him for the first two days, but as expected, no one followed them. All had gone off as planned.

The soldiers outside the agency office looked on impassively as Tippett, Winter, Cook, Montgomery, and Haworth came out. Tippett climbed onto a wagon and hauled Montgomery up after him. Most of the troopers grinned when they saw Montgomery's face.

Winter and Haworth rode on the smaller wagon, while Tippett propped Montgomery between himself and Cook. They clattered to Gray Wolf's camp near Cache Creek, where Tippett, Winter, and Cook and an unenthusiastic Haworth unloaded the goods.

Gray Wolf tried to hold down the flutter of excitement the supplies brought him. He hated taking anything from the white-eyes, but he would starve or die of exposure without them. And he began to hope he could take up the fight again, join Far-From-Stone-Village.

Tippett left the smaller wagon and piled Libby, Bloody Buffalo, Little Owl, and Red Lodge into the larger wagon. Libby was showing small signs of life — and pregnancy — cheering Tippett.

Montgomery was helped into the back of the wagon. The battered commander shrunk up in horror at the closeness he was forced into with the Comanches. Haworth, grinning slightly, climbed into the back, and Cook joined Tippett and Winter on the wagon seat.

Their stops at the agency office and then the fort a short distance away, were brief — just long enough to drop off the agent and two officers. "Don't be a stranger, Zeke," Cook said.

"I expect I can drop by occasional, if Montgomery ain't around."

"I think we'll be seeing less of the major," Cook predicted.

Tippett did not think they would be followed. He trusted Cook. The lieutenant was not prone, as were many officers, to judging Indians too harshly. He knew the Indians — at least in recent years — were doing little more than trying to survive.

They traveled slowly across the dusty, grass-covered high plains. Tippett went by instinct and knowledge, avoiding popular trails. Despite his assurances to Libby, he knew his daughter and the children would have a hard time assimilating into white society, even in a melting pot like Taos. So, he wanted to avoid trouble until he could get to Taos where they would at least have some chance of fitting in. Once acclimated, they could better suffer the shameless comments of fools.

Francisca welcomed them into the house with affection. The new children mingled well with Francisca's own, fitting in easily. Libby adapted well and generally was accepted by the people of Taos.

Still, there were newcomers to the town, people who had not been there long, and who were not so accepting of Indians, Mexicans, blacks, or half-breeds. Libby steered clear of them when possible, and defended herself against them when necessary. She, and Tippett and Francisca, taught the young ones how to cope with such attitudes.

The day after their quiet arrival in Taos, Ben Winter knocked at Tippett's front door. He was duded up in a suit of checked wool, a bleached white shirt, a string tie that pinched his neck under the starched collar, and brightly polished boots. He smelled of lime water and carried a bouquet of wildflowers.

Ramona, the Tippetts' maid, looked at him in surprise. She was even more so when he said politely, "I've come calling for Miss Libby."

"A moment, *Señor* Winter," she said warily. She called for Francisca, who hurried out.

Francisca managed not to laugh when she saw Winter, or when she heard his explanation. "Well, come in, *Señor*," she said elegantly. She took him to the sitting room and indicated a plush chair. He sat, and Francisca said, "I will see if Miss Libby is receiving visitors."

Libby entered some minutes later. She was still drawn and weary but looked better than she had the day Winter and Tippett had found her on the reservation. The fact that she was far removed from the dispirited life of recent years was bringing her around. To Winter, she was still the most beautiful and desirable woman he had ever met.

He had eyes, of course, and could see the crinkles at the corners of Libby's mouth and eyes. He could see that she had thickened a little around the bottom, and more so at the middle with the growing pregnancy. He knew she was a mother four times over, and would be for a fifth soon; and even that she was a grandmother. But she was still attractive and much younger looking than many other women. And more, she had something inside that reached out and clutched Winter with an unrelenting grip. He had acknowledged years ago that he loved her, and would wait for her as long as there was any possibility. Now he saw the chance, and he wanted to ensure that nothing would go wrong.

He had waited nervously for her to appear, and when she did, he stood, holding the flowers out awkwardly.

She took them, sniffed their aroma, and smiled wanly. "Thank you, Mister Winter," she said quietly.

"Again, Mister Winter?" The fear of rejection bloomed strongly.

"Sorry, Ben." She sat on the brocade sofa and patted the space next to her. "Sit." He did so, nervously. She clutched the flowers and looked at him with sad eyes. "I appreciate your attentions, Ben," she said seriously. "But I'm afraid I can't..." She began to weep lightly.

"I know this is awful soon," Winter said quietly. "We only got here yesterday. But I've loved you for such a long time...I wanted to make sure you knew right off I was still interested." He plucked anxiously at his lower lip. "I'd like you to be my wife, Miss Libby."

He held up his hand to stop any objections she might make. "I don't want an answer to that right now..." He paused, then said, "Well, yes, I do. But I ain't going to pester you for one. All I want to know for now is if you're interested in me. If you ain't, I'll take my broken heart and leave you be. If you are, I'll ask to come callin' regular and hope that'll stop any other man from coming 'round." He sat on the edge of the sofa, facing Libby, holding his breath.

Libby stared into Winter's eyes, wondering how any woman could be so lucky as to have two such divergent men as Ben Winter and the Comanche warrior Gray Wolf want — and, yes, love — her. She was in her mid-thirties, but inside she felt young again. "Why do you want me?" she asked. "I'm almost past the time for bearing children. We might not have any of our own. And I'm carrying another man's child."

"None of that matters, Libby," Winter said, shrugging. His eyes burned with sincerity. "Your children — yours and Gray Wolf's — will be mine — ours." He smiled wanly. "And the one you're gonna have will be ours, too. I don't mind. And if the good Lord should bless us with a child of our own, we'll I won't love Bloody Buffalo or Little Owl — or even Red Lodge — any less."

Tears streaked down Libby's face. Awkwardly, Winter put his arms around her and tried to comfort her. He stroked her hair, and the smooth cotton of her dress along the back; even that slight contact exciting to him. He was befuddled. He had no idea if this meant she was interested in him and happy, or if she wanted to tell him to go away but didn't want to hurt him. So, he waited, trying to soothe her.

Finally, Libby's sobs stopped and she pulled away. He offered her his handkerchief. She turned away briefly to dab at her eyes and blow her nose. She looked back at him, and smiled. Once again, she felt sixteen in her heart. "I'd like for you to come courtin', Ben."

His heart reached heights he had never thought possible. "I'll be by all the time. As much as you want," Winter said happily.

Her brightness dimmed. "There's still Gray Wolf," she murmured.

"You'll never be able to go back to him, you know," Winter whispered. He was sad about it because Libby was sad about it. "And," he added in hesitation, "you was never married legal-like."

Libby smiled wanly. "Maybe so. But it was a marriage still. Gray Wolf and I had a lot of years together. That counts for something."

"I didn't mean to say it didn't, Libby," Winter answered honestly. "All I meant by it is that since you can't go back, there'll be no legal impediments to us marryin'."

"I loved him, you know. He had many faults, but I think he loved me, as much as any Comanche warrior can love a woman."

"And that," Winter said understandingly, "is why I don't expect an answer on you becoming my wife now. I know you cared for him. If you hadn't, you would've left him years ago. You had enough chances. I don't want to push you, Libby. I just want to be allowed to love you."

Libby brightened. "And for that, you have my willing permission."

He wanted to whoop and shout, and might have even done so. But suddenly her lips were on his, her tongue in his mouth. He threw his arms around her and held her, gladly, passionately accepting the kiss.

When finally it ended, he sat back breathlessly. He had had many experiences with women, including some who knew well what they were doing. But he had never been kissed quite like that. He realized that much of its power came from the deep feelings they had for each other.

He grinned hugely, the world open and inviting before him. "You sure don't kiss like no grandma, ma'am," he breathed fervently.

"There's other things I don't do like a grandma," she said boldly.

"And you're going to make me wait to find that out, ain't you?" he said with a laugh.

"Yes, sir." She grinned lewdly.

He stood, reluctant to leave, but knowing that to stay would benefit neither. "I'd best get back to work, or my boss'll fire me."

She giggled, feeling little-girlish.

Winter walked out with a sprightly step. He might be forty, but he felt like a teenage boy. He called that night, and every one thereafter. Four months later, a girl they named Molly was born. A month after that, Winter and Libby married. They and their varied children moved into a big house a few blocks north of the plaza.

And, as a surprise to everyone, a year and a half later, Libby, at the age of almost thirty-nine, gave birth to a healthy *tahbay-boh* child, who was called Libby after her mother.

70

One day in November 1878, a rider came from Fort Sill with a message for Tippett. He opened the paper while the soldier stood by. He still needed no glasses, something that pleased him immensely. "It's from Amos Cook," he read. "He says Montgomery left shortly after I got Libby. Took his retirement. Cook's commander of the fort — and the agency. He says he needs my help."

Francisca did not need to ask if he would go. After all their years of marriage, Francisca knew her husband quite well.

Two weeks later, Tippett tied his horse outside Cook's office at Fort Sill. He walked up and stopped in front of a soldier at the door. "Name's Zeke Tippett, son. Tell Lieutenant Cook I'm here."

"*Cap'n* Cook, sir," the soldier said smartly, rifle at parade arms. "I'll tell him." He opened the door and called inside. "Cap'n Cook, sir. A Mister Tippett to see you."

"Send him in."

The trooper shouldered his rifle and stepped aside.

"Thankee, son." Tippett strolled in. He grinned at Cook. "So now it's Cap'n, eh, Amos? Hell, the Army'll promote anybody these days."

"That's the Gospel truth, Zeke," Cook laughed. Cook stood and came around his desk to shake Tippett's hand. Cook indicated a young man standing to the side. "My aide, Lieutenant Conroy."

"Sir," Conroy said politely but with reserve. He had heard much about the former mountain man and had expected a decrepit old man. What he saw was a man of sixty-five, tall and unbent. Tippett appeared strong, which Conroy confirmed when he shook Tippett's callused paw. There were plenty of age lines on Tippett's face, it was true, and his hair and mustache were white as new snow, but Conroy, a strapping man of thirty would think twice before tangling with him.

Tippett nodded at Conroy, shook his hand, and then sat.

"The lieutenant and I don't always see eye-to-eye," Cook said, sitting behind his desk. "But he's a good man. And he ain't adverse to a little difference of opinion with his commanding officer."

Sitting in the chair, Tippett brought Cook up-to-date on his extended family. Cook, in turn, told Tippett of how Montgomery had sent out his resignation papers by special courier the morning after Tippett had taken his family away. It took several months — during which Montgomery did little — for the papers to clear, but finally they did. "And then I got stuck commanding this godforsaken post," Cook added, with another chuckle.

Tippett nodded and took the cigar Cook proffered him. He lit it, and said, "Now that all the social nonsense is out of the way, what do ye want with me, Amos? Your message said it was urgent."

Cook blew out a smoke ring. Then he said, "Zeke, I need you as a scout."

"I'm too old for such doin's, Amos."

"Old, hell," Cook laughed.

"What do ye need a scout for anyway? All the Injuns've been rounded up and put in cages."

"As is right," Conroy interjected.

Cook glanced at him and grinned but said nothing.

"Eh?" Tippett said, cocking an eyebrow at the young lieutenant.

"All Injuns are murderous savages, Mister Tippett. I've seen what the Comanches do to white women — and white men."

"This, I expect, is one of the areas in which ye and him disagree, eh, Amos?" When Cook nodded, Tippett said, "Lieutenant, what ye've said is true enough. Cain't deny that. But I've seen soldiers at work on Injuns. Ain't much diff'rence."

"That's only retribution for what they've done, sir. They've been butchering settlers for years."

"Ain't nobody I know of asked them goddamn settlers here in the first place," Tippett said, puffing on his cigar. He found that these days it was harder to raise his ire with such talk.

"The land was put here for God-fearing folk to use. It was of no use to anyone while those savages were on it. They sure don't use it."

"How long ye been out here, Lieutenant?"

"Since shortly after the war, sir," Conroy said stiffly, as if embarrassed it had not been longer.

"Then ye been out here long enough to've learned something about Comanches and other Injins. And ye know that what ye jist said is a pile of buffler shit. The Comanches were usin' this land."

"But..."

"That's enough for now, Lieutenant," Cook said in friendly tones. "We need Zeke's help, and don't want to drive him off, do we?"

Conroy grinned lopsidedly. "No, sir." He looked at Tippett. "Actually, sir, while I think the Comanches — and the other Injuns — are a bunch of murderin' savages who could do with a good dose of military civilizin', I do sort of admire them." He shrugged, knowing that made no sense. But he thought Tippett would understand.

"All right, Amos, what do ye need me to scout for?" He was not inclined to take on the job, whatever it was, but he would at least give Cook the benefit of listening to him.

"I can tell you're just waiting to turn me down, Zeke, so I'll not delay in telling you. One of our Comanches is missing."

"So? What's one goddamn Comanche out of all these? Ye sure as hell can't be worried about one ol' Comanche runnin' around, can ye?"

"I am when it's Gray Wolf."

Tippett stopped with the cigar halfway to his mouth. He sat up straighter. "Tell me about it."

Cook made a motion with his hand. Conroy nodded and got a bottle of whiskey and three glasses from a cabinet along one wall. He set the glasses down and filled them. Each man took one. Tippett downed his in one fluid motion and then refilled the glass. The others drank more slowly as Cook talked.

"Gray Wolf was peaceable enough when he first come in. Once you took his wife and the kids off his hands, he started slipping off the reservation on occasion. We think he was joining his son..."

"Stone Village," Tippett interjected.

"Yes, that's the one. Anyway, there were some raids, mostly down in Texas. But we had trouble running the renegades down. Finally, a scout from Fort Belknap ran down Stone Village and killed him, his wife, and several others in their party."

"Damn good thing, too," Conroy said softly.

Cook said nothing; he just watched Tippett's face harden. The old mountain man watched the curl of smoke from his cigar for a moment before turning stony eyes on Conroy. "Stone Village was my grandson, Lieutenant," he said flintily.

Conroy blanched. "I'm sorry," he said. "However, if he hadn't been a renegade, he'd still be alive."

"If ye can call this livin'," Tippett said, chucking a thumb toward the window and the agency not far away.

"These Indians are alive, Mister Tippett," Conroy insisted.

Tippett shook his head at the obstinacy of some people. He had seen it too often in whites and in Indians and in Mexicans. It seemed to him that people were the same the world over when it came to being stubborn and seeing wrong in the things all other people did.

"For a Comanche, Lieutenant, there ain't but two things in life — the hunt and war. It's all a Comanche warrior lives for. Ye take them things away, and a Comanche male has no purpose. Especially war. For a Comanche, war's the only way to gain honors, to gain respect. Ye should understand that, Lieutenant, bein' a soldier and all."

"I do," Conroy said quietly.

"Well, ye've taken both away from the Comanches. That's why all them warriors're settin' out there lookin' like no sun's gonna rise tomorrow. It ain't gettin' beat that's demoralized 'em. It's bein' penned up. If'n there was any buffler left, they'd still be out fightin'. To them, dyin' like warriors is the only way to go under." He paused. "What ye've done is take away their manhood. Like ye cut their balls off and handed 'em to 'em on a plate."

Conroy winced and gulped.

"After he learned that Stone Village died," Cook said, "and we suspect Gray Wolf was with his son at the time and managed to escape — Gray Wolf seemed to have lost everything. He would just sit day and night in front of his lodge. Somebody'd come along now and again and make sure he ate. But that was about it." Cook sighed. "You know how the agency started passing out the beef rations, Zeke?"

Tippett shook his head and stabbed out the remnants of the cigar.

"The beeves are rounded up in a pen; then they're released, one at a time. The warriors use whatever old bows, lances, and shit they got, riding poor agency ponies, and run the beeves like they did buffalo." He shook his head. "It was supposed to make them feel better, kind of give them a taste of the old life. But, damn, it's a pitiful thing to watch."

"Shit," Tippett breathed in annoyance.

"Gray Wolf wouldn't even take part in that. He just sat. Didn't go out on the hunts we allowed. Trouble is, while the Comanches were supposed to be hunting, they were raiding. The government finally decided to have one great last buffalo hunt at the end of the summer. We were to escort all the Comanches who wanted to go.

"Fifteen hundred Comanches went, including women and kids. Beforehand, they had their dances and everything. It was to be a joyous occasion. Gray Wolf agreed to come. In fact, he seemed to have a new lease on life."

"Ye find any buffler?" Tippett asked, knowing the answer.

"Not a goddamn, single one, Zeke," Cook said, angry and sad at the same time. "We found heaps of rotting carcasses. Christ. We rode on from one old hunting ground to the next, from creek to creek. Comanche scouts spread out for miles. But nothing. Damn!" He sat back to calm himself. "When we headed back this way, every one of those Comanches had the look of death in his eyes."

All three were quiet. Even Conroy felt the burn of shame. Whipping the Comanches fair and square in war was one thing; this was another entirely.

"What's all this got to do with Gray Wolf?" Tippett finally asked in a hoarse voice, suspecting the answer.

"We took roll call before we left and after we got back. One man was missing after that roll call here."

"Gray Wolf?"

"Yep. He was an important enough man among the Comanches that we tried to keep an extra good watch on him. Mainly we wanted to be sure he wouldn't cause any trouble. He might've seemed disinterested in life, but some of the Comanches still looked on him with great favor."

"Ye sure he didn't jist go under?" Tippett pulled out his plug of tobacco and sliced off a piece with the Bowie knife.

"We're sure." Cook leaned forward, resting his elbows on the desk. "The bastard just up and disappeared."

Tippett laughed low in his throat after spitting into a spittoon. "I'll be a son of a bitch," he breathed. "Any horses missing?"

"Hell if I know," Cook shrugged. "We had so many he could've taken a couple dozen and we'd never know."

"And now ye want me to find him for ye?"

"Yep." Cook sat back, his chair creaking loudly in the otherwise silent room. The faint sounds of troops drilling drifted in through the one open window.

"Why?"

Cook toyed with a scrap of paper on the desk. "We can't have a warrior like Gray Wolf running around," he finally said. "There's too many who'd follow him come hell or high water. There's only a couple like him left. Quanah's another."

That made sense to Tippett from a military standpoint. "What're ye gonna do with him when — if — I was to bring him in? Kill him?"

"Not if he comes in peaceably," Cook said. "There are some others that'd like to hang him," he added, glancing sharply at Conroy. "If only to help keep the others in place. Make an example of him."

"Why me?" Tippett asked, steepling his fingers before his face.

"Zeke, you're close to the Comanches. You're family to Gray Wolf. You probably know where he'll go, what he'll do, where he can hide."

"Like I said, Amos, I'm too goddamn old for something like this."

"Not only would some like to hang Gray Wolf," Cook said. "But there's others'd be just as happy to kill him where he's found. A lot of soldiers involved in mopping up after the Comanches down in Texas would think taking the great Gray Wolf's scalp'd be quite an honor."

"So?" Tippett didn't like the direction in which this was heading.

"There's a scout riding out of Fort Belknap now that's supposed to be one of the best. From what I hear, he wants Gray Wolf's hair, and the commander down there is plannin' to let the bastard loose with several troops of the Sixth Cavalry. You want Gray Wolf to live, you better find him, Zeke. If Eldon Trent finds him first, he's a goner."

"Who?" Tippett burst out, straightening up in the chair.

"Eldon Trent. You know him?"

"He any relation to an Elmore Trent?"

"Word I get, that was his old man's name. You know the father?"

"Used to." He did not explain further. He chewed his lower lip a moment. "I'll need some supplies."

"Whatever you need." He paused, then said, "Lieutenant Conroy will lead the patrol that will go with you."

"Will Gray Wolf be safe in his custody?"

"Lieutenant?" Cook said, looking at his aide.

"My personal feelings don't matter," Conroy said. "But I got to admit that if we catch him, I'll be hoping he tries to escape."

71

Within an hour, Tippett was leading Lieutenant Conroy and six Cavalry troopers away from the agency on Cache Creek, heading southwest onto the rolling, open plains. Snowflakes sifted down.

"You think you know where he is, Zeke?" Conroy asked as they rode.

"The *Llano,* I expect. That's his home." Tippett looked wistful. "Most folks think the *Llano Estacado* is hell here on earth. But the Comanches think it's beautiful." Conroy could tell from Tippett's tone that he felt the same. "I expect Gray Wolf's goin' home to die."

"Perhaps we should hurry, Mister Tippett," Conroy said. "There are settlers moving into the region now, and there could be trouble."

"There's no tellin' exactly where he is, Lieutenant," Tippett said, shifting his weight in the saddle. His behind was sore. "The *Llano* is bigger'n many states. Lot of country to cover, once we get there. And there's no certainty he ain't left it for parts unknown. That's jist the best place to start. It's gonna take time, Lieutenant."

Conroy was not happy with it, and he cast a suspicious glance at Tippett.

The old mountain man turned a hard gaze on him. "Ye think I'm gonna lead ye on a wild goose chase, that it, Lieutenant?" He could see by the officer's face that he was right. "I'll tell ye this, sonny, I will try my damnedest to find Gray Wolf. I want to bring him back to the agency alive and in one piece before the Army or that scum Trent finds him. And before he causes any trouble. Just because I like him and he's family in a way, don't mean I condone everything he's done. But ifn he's in the *Llano,* I'll find him. Ye have my word, Lieutenant."

It took only a moment for Conroy to nod. "Cap'n Cook says he trusts you, so I will, too. But if..."

"There ain't no 'but if,' boy. If I don't find him it won't be from not tryin'. And if ye don't believe me at that time and think to go against me, I will kill ye."

"I might have something to say about that."

"Ye might. But it won't change the fact that ye'll be dead. I've faced a lot tougher men than ye and your boys here."

Conroy stared at him for some seconds as they rode. Then he nodded again. "Damn, if I don't believe you, Mr. Tippett."

AS THEY NEARED THE *LLANO,* TIPPETT RODE OUT NEARLY A FULL day ahead of the troopers, swinging in a large arc, eyes scanning the ground. He felt better than he had for years, despite his mission. To him, the Comanches had some good views — such as the one that man was meant to live riding a spirited horse across the vast openness. It was no good for a man to be cooped up in a city, with no air to breathe, no fresh smell of trees, flowers, grass, and buffalo. But the feeling did not last. It was too lonely out here, with nothing to break the mind-numbing monotony. And he was aware of his age. His bones felt each jolt of the horse. And the temperatures set old wounds to aching.

The ride, through all its majestic loneliness, made him think on the old days. He wondered about Cass Calder. He had not seen his huge friend in many years, and hoped he was well. As he crossed Goat Canyon, he remembered Painted Wing. Despite the years, her death still saddened him. There had been so much death around him, and still he lived on.

He did not understand it. He was not a special man, had no extra power with the Almighty. Yet despite the many deaths around him, he had been blessed with more than his share of good. He had Libby and his children and grandchildren; he had found luck a second time in marrying Francisca. He had good friends like Ben Winter and even Amos Cook. The good thoughts cast off the melancholy. He was never much of one for low thoughts. He accepted the travails of life, enjoyed the good things, and left the sad in their own special place.

He pressed on, beginning to see faint signs of Gray Wolf's passage — a soddy with the bleaching bones of its four inhabitants; a butchered steer with the broken arrow shaft sticking out from between two ribs; the bones of a horse that had been ridden to death; a small covered wagon and the rotting corpses of its owners.

The trail turned sharply west, easing out of the *Llano*. The land began to rise, heading into the mountains. Tippett wearily made a small camp.

He was sitting there the next morning, oiling his Sharps Big Fifty when he saw a rider. He made no haste, however, to hurry with what he was doing. He also carried two .44-caliber Remingtons and next to him lay a new Winchester .44/40. Tippett was still working on the buffalo gun when the rider approached his camp.

"Mind if I have some coffee?" the rider asked, dismounting.

"Help yourself," Tippett said, looking over the newcomer. The man was in his mid-thirties, lean and hard looking. He wore faded blue denim pants, pointed boots, and a red cotton shirt under a fringed buckskin coat. Two Colts encircled his waist, and Tippett saw another, smaller-caliber, Colt in a shoulder holster under the jacket. He was unshaven and Tippett could not tell what color the man's eyes were since they were shaded by the broad-brimmed hat.

The man squatted and poured a cup of coffee. He blew on it and then took a sip. "Damn, that's strong," he snorted, looking at Tippett. "There ain't no more buff'lo in these parts, Mister."

"Yep."

"Then what're you carryin' that big buff'lo killer for?"

"It's got its uses."

"What's an old fart like you doin' out here anyway?" He waved the cup at the boulders, lightning-split trees and slabs of stone.

"Huntin'." Tippett worked on the rifle but also watched the man.

"Huntin' what?" the man laughed.

"Same thing ye are, sonny." Tippett slammed a shell into the Sharps as the man looked at him in surprise.

The man set the cup down and shifted so one of his Colts was within reach. "What's that supposed to mean?"

"Ye Eldon Trent?"

"Yep," he answered, suspicious. His hand inched toward a Colt.

"This ol' chil' don't take a shine to no pissant shit-eater like ye come trompin' out of the *Llano* hopin' to raise hair on a Comanche. Like killin' old Gray Wolf's gonna give ye some balls."

"Who the hell are you?" Trent asked, wonder and rage fighting within him. His hand rested on the revolver butt now.

"Name's Zeke Tippett. And I'm the meanest son of a bitch on either side of the Shinin' Mountains." He swung the Sharps around so it was aimed at Trent's heart. "And ye're gonna be one dead chil' ye pull that Colt."

Trent froze. He was frightened, but puzzled, too. The name had a familiar ring to it. "Do I know you, old man?" he asked.

"Not directly. But your Pa might've mentioned me." He grinned maliciously when Trent's head came up, revealing his eyes. There was recognition — and hate — in them. "I see that he has. Ye know, boy, ye look a lot like your ol' man. Always reminded me of a scabrous gopher."

Trent seethed. Tippett spit and then said, "Now ease them pistols out slow, one at a time, and toss 'em gently over this away."

Trent considered trying something. But the muzzle of the Sharps never wavered, and he thought better of it. One by one he eased out the two Colts and tossed them gently in Tippett's general direction.

"The one in the shoulder rig, too. And the knife."

Trent was disgusted, but he tossed them out, too.

"Stand and shuck your jacket."

Trent rose and dropped the jacket. He turned in a slow circle when told to do so. Tippett saw no other weapons.

"Finish your Arbuckle's, boy." When Trent squatted again, scowling at him, Tippett said, "I expect ye're about half froze to put me under. Well, ye're gonna get your chance. Soon's ye finish."

Trent tossed the coffee out. "Get it over with, old man."

Tippett set the rifle down and picked up Trent's knife. He played idly with it, looking at Trent. "Your father was a peckerless oaf, boy," Tippett said almost dreamily. "It's why I put him under. Ye can avoid the same by gettin' on your horse and ridin' east."

"Kiss my ass, old man," Trent snarled. "First, I'm gonna carve you up, then I'm gonna go git that baby-murderin' bastard Gray Wolf and cut his balls off fer trophies."

"It's the only way ye'll ever have any." Tippett flicked the knife. It stuck into the ground, quivering, an inch from Trent's crotch. Tippett rose and pulled his Bowie. "Time to *fandango*, boy."

Trent grabbed the knife and stood. He grinned. "Shit, I'm gonna love carvin' you up, old fart."

Tippett smiled, but it was without humor or compassion. He stepped forward, and Trent backed up, until they were both beyond the fire and in a little, rock-strewn clearing. Sun streamed down, lending little heat to the coldness of the day. They eyed each other warily, crouched, waiting. Suddenly Trent lunged. When Tippett moved, it was far slower than in the old days, but faster than Trent expected. He swung his left arm out, blocking the thrust of Trent's knife. At the same time, he took a step forward with his left leg and swung his right leg up, bent at the knee.

The thigh slammed into Trent's stomach, knocking his breath out. Tippett stepped out of the way and Trent fell to hands and knees, wheezing as he tried to get air into his lungs. Tippett waited and watched. Finally, Trent stood, stomach and chest pumping hard. "Ye still got a chance to walk away with your life, boy," Tippett said.

"Piss on you, old man." Trent stalked forward again, much more wary. He decided to let Tippett make the first move, then counteract.

But Tippett was having none of that. He simply waited, alert, as Trent moved back and forth in front of him, waving the knife. "Ye want me, boy, ye'll have to come and get me," he said with a sneer.

Trent moved in fast, slashing the blade in front of him. Tippett faded back and back, waiting for an opening. Trent's foot hit a stone and his ankle rolled. The last thing he saw was a brief glint of sunlight on Tippett's blade as it flashed in on his throat.

Tippett cleaned off his knife and then tossed Trent's body across his horse. He stuffed Trent's weapons into the man's saddlebags. Soon after he finished, Conroy and his patrol rode into the camp. "That Trent?" he asked, pointing to the body.

"Yep."

"Major Burke over at Fort Belknap'll keel over when he finds out about this."

"I don't give a buffler's pecker what he thinks."

"Me either," Conroy grinned. "You have a track on Gray Wolf?"

"He's up in the mountains. He's afoot and can't be too far ahead."

"Let's go get him, then."

"Company, Lieutenant," one of the troopers said.

Another Cavalry troop rode in. "Where's...?" the lieutenant

leading led the patrol started. He stopped when he saw Trent's body. "What happened here?" he asked.

"He had an accident," Tippett said.

"What kind of accident?" It seemed that the sneer was permanently etched on the man's face.

"A fatal one," Tippett said with a straight face. Several of Conroy's men chuckled.

"We are after renegade Comanches," the new lieutenant said. "Since we've lost our scout, Mister, you'll take his place."

"Eat shit," Tippett said, almost amused. "I work for whom I please. And ye, ye buffler pecker, don't please me a bit." More chuckles from Conroy's men.

"I order you...!"

"You don't order shit, Lieutenant," Conroy snapped. "I'm ranking officer here." His tone left no room for debate. The new officer could not argue anyway, since he was a second lieutenant, while Conroy was a first lieutenant. "You and your men will take the body of your scout back to Fort Belknap. We're also pursuing renegade hostiles and we'll deal with them. Since we're the troops based at the agency with jurisdiction over these Indians, you have no business here."

"Major Burke will hear of this! What's your name?"

"Lieutenant Mark Conroy. Now haul ass, Lieutenant! Before it's draped over a horse like your scout's."

The lieutenant jerked his horse's reins around. "Get Trent," he bellowed as he raced off. One of his men grabbed the reins to Trent's horse and the troops raced off, under the taunts of Conroy's men.

72

Tippett sat across from Gray Wolf, the big Sharps resting across his lap. Two old warriors, two old friends.

"Christ, Wolf, shut up that goddamn singin', would ye."

The mournful sounds of Gray Wolf's death chant slowed and then stopped, the last few notes drifting into the day's cold air. He stared at Tippett with weary eyes.

"We been through some shit together, ain't we, Wolf?"

"Yes." The Comanche smiled a little, remembering the old days. "We have seen many winters, *amigo*. We are no longer young, whose blood carried us to great deeds. We miss our teeth, and our bones creak when we use them. And," he added, grinning, "our pizzles no longer harden at the mere sight of a young woman's breasts."

Tippett grew sad. "Hell, them days wasn't all good."

Gray Wolf nodded. "It's true, my brother. We've lost wives, children. But for me and my people..." He trailed off. "How is Light Calf?" he asked suddenly. "And the children?"

"Libby's married to Ben Winter," Tippett said, embarrassed.

Gray Wolf nodded. He understood that Libby would not be expected to live celibate. "He's a good man," Gray Wolf said.

"They've got a child," Tippett said. "And they're raisin' all of yours and Libby's — includin' the one Libby was carryin'."

Gray Wolf's interest waned. Quietly, he said, "I won't go back, White Horse. Kill me or let me go."

"I don't want to do the first, and I don't expect I can do the second, Wolf. I got to take ye back."

"To what?" Gray Wolf asked, pain of the loss of everything he had ever known coloring his eyes. "There's nothing for me at the agency, where the *tahbay-boh* says I must live. We aren't even *Nermernuh* anymore. We don't follow the old ways. The blue coats have made geldings of our men and whores of our women. There's no honor sitting on our asses with our hands out waiting for the scraps the *tahbay-boh* give us. I want to die like Walking Bear did."

"I know ye do, Wolf. But I jist can't let ye ride on out of here. I got many honors among my own people," Tippett said proudly. "I jist cain't go back there and tell 'em I couldn't find ye."

"Then kill me," Gray Wolf said almost as if in agony. "Or I'll kill you." He lifted the pistol and leveled it at Tippett's chest.

"It ain't right that we should try'n harm each other," Tippett said, swinging the Sharps up. "And gettin' a hole punched in your chest ain't gonna be much of a warrior's death." His tone was flat.

Gray Wolf grinned slightly and shifted the pistol away. He looked through a break in the rocks. He could see the flat valley that spread out a few miles away. "Long-knives come," he said flatly. He looked back at Tippett. "I won't go back. I'll live free, or die here."

"Ye got to go back, Wolf," Tippett said, not allowing any of his exasperation to show. "Or they'll hunt ye for the rest of your days."

"Let them come. Better that than the agency."

The two sat thinking back the almost fifty years since they had met; old warriors who once rode these lands proud and unmolested. Now it seemed the *Llano* teemed with people. There was hardly a place any more for men like Zeke Tippett and Gray Wolf. Age and civilization had passed them by. But such old warriors did not know how to fade away; they had to fight on no matter how hopeless the outcome seemed.

"Ye know, Wolf," Tippett said suddenly, "there might be something we can do about all this here."

"Speak," Gray Wolf said skeptically. "My patience grows short. The long-knives'll be here soon. They'll kill me, if you don't."

"I expect I'll jist have to kill ye, ol' friend." He laughed when he saw Gray Wolf's eyes narrow in anger — and anticipation. "Actually, what I aim to do is fire this here Sharps. Them blue coats'll hear it. I'll haul my ass down the mountain and tell them boys I shot ye dead whilst ye was runnin'." He gloated.

"The long-knives might be damn fools," Gray Wolf said, grinning, "but they're not that stupid. They'll ask to see the body."

"There's crevices all over the goddamn place. Includin' one right over yonder." Tippett pointed with the Sharps. "I'll jist tell 'em ye fell in one. They'll never know."

"You'd do this for me?" Gray Wolf asked, not really surprised.

"Yep." Tippett spit out the overworked glob of tobacco. "But ye got to promise me some things." He paused. "I know ye want to go under as a warrior, fightin' to the end, Wolf. But ye do that, and it'll come back on me. Ye got to promise me ye'll stay here in the mountains and not go raidin'. Ye need food or horses, steal 'em without butcherin' folks in the doin'."

"I can't do that, White Horse. I'm free, and I'll die free."

"Then I ain't..." He stopped. Suddenly he grinned and said, "Then promise me ye'll head for Mexico — and stay there. I don't care what ye do there. But don't go on a killin' spree along the way."

Gray Wolf's eyes brightened. "It has been many winters since I fought *Mexicanos*. They don't have as many soldiers as the *Americanos*. But there're many horses to be taken. Women, too." The thought grew pleasing. He smiled. "I will do what you ask, White Horse."

"Ye got any weapons other'n that pistol? Food or anything?"

Gray Wolf shook his head.

"Christ, ye're one bone poor ol' chil', ain't ye," Tippett chuckled. He went to his horse, feeling the years on his shoulders. He rummaged in his saddlebags and pulled out a box of .44-caliber cartridges and two butcher knives. He tossed them to Gray Wolf. "That should keep ye goin' to Mexico. Jist get there. I hear ye're hangin' around this country, and I'll hunt your ass down and put ye under."

Gray Wolf nodded, unconcerned by the possibility.

"Don't fool with me, Wolf," Tippett said. "Ye force me to do that, I'll raise your hair, too, so ye can't go the Spirit Land."

Gray Wolf finished loading his pistol. One knife went into the empty sheath; the other and the extra cartridges were placed in a pouch dangling at his waist. "I will do as you say," he said somberly. He had given his word and would keep it. Of course, Tippett was older, and Gray Wolf thought he might outlive his old friend. But his face betrayed none of his emotions. He stood and the two stared into each other's eyes. They clasped hand to forearm and held tightly.

Gray Wolf turned and trotted down a slim trail that wound through the rocks to the south, the years dropping off with each step. Tippett fired the Sharps into the air. The boom bounced off the face of the mountains and came back at him.

Sadly, Tippett watched Gray Wolf's departing back. With the trotting Comanche went Tippett's own old way of life. Then he grinned. He had just done a good thing. With a sudden lightness, he rode out.

A LOOK AT SHERIFF'S BLOOD (ROCKY MOUNTAIN LAWMEN BOOK 1)

Jonas Culpepper is the no-nonsense sheriff of San Juan County in Colorado, patrolling the vast empty lands with his 200-pound mastiff, Bear. His dedication has won him the respect of everyone on the right side of the law. But he is a fierce and relentless foe of those who cross him or those he has sworn to protect. So when the Durango-Silverton train is robbed by Mack Ellsworth and his gang of villains, it is Culpepper's duty to run them down and bring them to justice. But his job is made all the more dangerous when his enemies include men on both sides of the law. And when Culpepper's wife is kidnapped, hell comes to San Juan County in the form of one enraged lawman.

AVAILABLE NOW ON AMAZON.

ABOUT THE AUTHOR

John Legg has had more than 50 Westerns published, including a number of series novels, and one book of Western nonfiction. He has also done a number of articles on Western history for national magazines. He has been a newspaper copy editor for more than 30 years. He has an MSJ from the Medill School of Journalism at Northwestern University.

Find more great titles by John Legg, here.

29601577R00331

Printed in Great Britain
by Amazon